ONE MAN'S TRASH

The Heretic Doms Club, Book 1

by Marie Sexton

Copyright

Copyright 2017, Marie Sexton

Cover art by Garrett Leigh of Black Jazz Design
Edited by Linda Ingmanson
Formatting by Kelly Smith

http://mariesexton.net

All Rights are reserved. No part of this book may be used or reproduced in any manner without written permission, except in the case of brief quotations embodied in critical articles and reviews. The unauthorized reproduction or distribution of this copyrighted work is illegal. No part of this book may be scanned, uploaded or distributed via the Internet or any other means, electronic or print, without the author's permission.

This book is a work of fiction. The names, characters, places and incidents are products of the writer's imagination or have been used fictionally and are not to be construed as real. Any resemblance to persons, living or dead, actual events, locale or organizations is entirely coincidental.

Published by Marie Sexton, 2017

EBook ISBN: 978-0-9988501-3-9
Paperback ISBN: 978-0-9988501-2-2

It is the mark of an educated mind to be able to entertain a thought without accepting it.
—Aristotle

Out of suffering have emerged the strongest souls; the most massive characters are seared with scars.
—Khalil Gibran

Chapter 1

Warren's scars ached.

It made no sense. How could scars earned in a war almost fifteen years earlier suddenly start hurting again just because he was low on sleep?

Logical or not, driving home from work at seven o'clock on a Saturday morning, they throbbed in time with his heartbeat. One across the bridge of his nose, one along the right side of his jaw, another intersecting his left eyebrow, each one telling him he needed at least eight uninterrupted hours of dreamtime.

As if he didn't know that already.

Working all night was nothing new. The way he made his living often called for odd hours. Warren kept his left hand on the steering wheel and used the fingers of his right hand to rub each scar in turn, trying to quiet them down. All it really did was make him think about the horrible morning in Afghanistan when he'd earned those scars.

His phone rang as he communed with his past, and he groaned. Probably another client calling him away from the nice soft bed he had waiting at home, but a glance at his phone told him the caller was one of the few people he called "friend."

"Good morning, Phil."

"Oh, is yours good? Because so far, mine sucks. I could kind of use your help." Phil was a pharmacist at a local Denver

5

Phil pushed his hair out of his eyes and cracked a bare hint of a smile. "I did, until some doctor with an ego the size of a house came down to the pharmacy to tear me a new asshole."

"And you didn't bend over and take it like a good boy?"

This time, Phil really did smile. He always reminded Warren a bit of Alex P. Keaton from *Family Ties* when he did that. "Do I ever?"

Warren shook his head, letting the obvious double entendre pass. Instead, he pointed to the ruined car. "You think that's who did this? Some doctor with his nose out of joint?"

"No. They may be arrogant assholes, but no doctor I know would sink to something so juvenile. This seems like real rage, not just a bruised ego, know what I mean?"

"I guess so." Warren eyed the car. "So, what exactly do you need me to do?"

"I called for a tow." His gaze moved over Warren's shoulder. "Ah. Speak of the devil."

Warren hung back while Phil dealt with the tow truck driver. Once he'd signed the last bit of paperwork, Phil turned to Warren.

"Give me a ride home?"

"Of course." They climbed into Warren's 4Runner. It was old and beaten, the paint faded and flaking, but it got him from point A to point B. Warren started the engine. "So why didn't you call Gray?"

Gray was a mutual friend, and a cop. He would've been the logical choice, but Phil shook his head. "You know how Gray is. When it comes to his job, he always toes the line. He'd want me to file a report and press charges. All that bureaucratic bullshit. And the guy who I think did this? I don't want him arrested."

Warren raised his eyebrows in surprise. "You want me to rough him up?" It wouldn't be the first time he'd been paid for that service, but he would never have expected it from Phil.

"Of course not. Frankly, he'd probably like it if you did."

"Okay." Warren was a bit relieved that wasn't where this was headed. He turned south, angling toward Phil's neighborhood. "So what's this guy's deal?"

"He's a mess. That's the thing. He's just a kid, and he's as fucked up as they come. He doesn't need Gray harassing him. He just needs to be straightened out."

"Who is he?"

Phil sighed. It took him a moment to answer. "He went by the name TJ, although I don't think that's really his name."

"What makes you say that?"

"He never answered to it right away. Like he kept forgetting that's what he'd told me to call him."

"You still haven't told me who he is exactly, or how you know him."

"He lived with me for about three weeks. He's...well, he's a hustler, basically."

Warren turned to look at Phil in surprise, then had to remind himself to keep his eyes on the road. "You had a whore living with you for three weeks?"

"See, this is the other reason I didn't call Gray. Because he gets all judgy about shit like this, and I thought I could count on you to be a bit more diplomatic."

Warren found himself chuckling. "Okay. So, you had a rent boy temporarily residing at your domicile. Does it sound better that way?"

"It does, actually." He laughed. "Look, I know it sounds crazy—"

"Not 'crazy.' Just not like you. You usually kick them out two minutes after the festivities end."

"I know. I don't really even know how it happened. We met at a party. I took him home for the night. Left for work the next morning, and when I got home, he was still there. Seemed odd, but I wasn't going to complain about getting to go another round with him. And after that, he just sort of stayed." Phil shrugged and pushed his hair out of his eyes. "He basically traded sex for room and board. And it was good for a while. The kid's hot like you wouldn't believe, and he's dynamite in the sack. So it worked, you know? Things were good, right up until they weren't."

Warren nodded. "Funny how it works that way." He could think of a dozen instances in his own life that fit the same bill. But he wasn't in the mood for a repeat performance of "All the Shit That's Gone Wrong in My Life." He focused instead on the other part of what Phil had said.

Dynamite in the sack.

The thought of taking home anybody who might earn that type of comment from Phil was enough to trigger a warm glow of arousal in Warren's groin. And goddamned Phil had always been like a bloodhound when it came to sniffing out arousal. He grinned over at Warren.

"You're wound up tight, aren't you?"

"I am not."

"Yes, you are. Don't think I can't tell. When was the last time you got laid?"

"A fucking lifetime ago, if you must know." Or at least that was how it felt, although it'd probably only been a few months. But there was more to his edginess than that. "I've been working security. That's where I was all last night."

"Security?" Phil blinked over at him. "Where?"

"Not *where*. More like *who*. It's personal security for some girls, you get what I'm saying?"

Phil's innocent little white-collar eyes went wide. "You're pimping?"

"Do I look like a pimp?"

"Hm." Phil propped his chin on his fist and pretended to study him. "Kind of. You just need a velvet top hat."

"Fuck off." But it gave him a laugh at least. "These girls work freelance. They're mostly college students or single moms, just trying to make ends meet. They like to have some muscle along in case things get ugly." And they liked Warren as their escort because he looked scary, but the only payment he asked for was a few crisp green bills. He never requested or expected service from the girls he protected. "I spend the whole night standing outside motel room doors, listening to people fuck." He squirmed a bit in his seat, thinking about it. He generally preferred men to women, but sex was sex. It was hard to be that close—close enough to smell it and hear it—and not end up aroused.

"Wow. I was right. You really are wound tight."

"Thanks for the reminder, Captain Obvious."

Phil smiled. "Any time." But then his smile devolved into confusion. "Wait. How does dressing like a cop help you guard hookers? Don't you just scare off their clientele?"

"If they were walking the street, yeah, but they don't. They work out of a motel. They set the appointments up ahead of time by email or text, and they tell the johns not to mind the Rent-A-Cop by the front door."

"Okay. But why dress like a cop at all?"

"A couple of reasons. First, before the customers go in, I tell them the rules, and I let 'em know what exactly will happen if they break 'em. Something about having a big guy in uniform lay down the law, they tend to listen a bit more. Even knowing I'm not really a cop, there's this little voice in their heads telling them this is serious, you know? Second, the area these gals work isn't exactly prime-time real estate. It's a shady, fucked-up neighborhood in a shady, fucked-up world. Whatever vice you're looking for, somebody down there's selling it." Drugs. Guns. Stolen MacBooks and iPhones. He'd once had somebody offer to sell him an eight-year-old boy. Warren didn't call the police often, but he had that night. "When I first started this gig, I'd go in street clothes, but I'd be lucky to go fifteen minutes without somebody propositioning me in one way or another." He shrugged, turning the corner into Phil's upscale neighborhood, which backed up against a lake on one side and a golf course on the other. It felt a million miles removed from where he'd spent last night. "When I'm dressed like this, they see a guy who looks like a cop guarding a motel room, and they decide it might be best to take their business elsewhere."

"Wow." Phil shook his head. "You've put a surprising amount of thought into this, haven't you? Ever thought about directing that attention to detail toward something a little more legitimate? Something a bit more on the legal side of the law?"

"No." He didn't have to look at Phil to know Phil was grinning at him.

"When was the last time you talked to your uncle Bill?"

"When was the last time somebody told you to shut the hell up?"

"You told me to fuck off a few minutes ago. Does that count?"

"Apparently not, 'cause you're still talking."

Warren pulled up in front of Phil's house. It was nicer than Warren's, by a long shot. Then again, Phil came from money, and he made decent money too. Phil spent a minute scrolling through his phone, and a second later, Warren's phone dinged a couple of times.

"I sent you a picture of TJ, and the address he had me leave him at back when we parted ways."

Warren checked the picture. He was a damned good-looking kid, maybe about twenty-two, with delicate bone structure that was almost feminine. "You think he's upset about your breakup, or what?"

"I don't know. I can't imagine why. It was pretty casual to begin with, and it ended weeks ago. It's not like we ever had anything deep, but I can't think of anybody else." He shrugged. "I could be way off base. See what you think. If you tell me it wasn't him, I'll believe you."

"And if it is? You never said what you wanted me to do to him."

"I don't know exactly. Use your best judgment. Just make sure he's persuaded to stay away."

"You got it." He watched as Phil unbuckled his seat belt and climbed out of his car. Phil was a good-looking guy too, all white bread with the crusts cut off, neat and tidy and fit. He reminded Warren of a wound-up spring, and there was an aristocratic edge there that was tempting. He was the type who always had to be in control, and Warren suddenly wanted to break that control in the best possible way.

Phil was halfway up his front walk when Warren rolled down the passenger-side window. "Hey, Phil?"

Phil turned. "What?"

"How about you let me come in for a bit? I could tie you down, spend a few hours making you forget about those arrogant doctors."

Phil laughed, as Warren had known he would. "There you go again, always trying to put me on the wrong side of the rope."

Warren debated going home and changing. Then again, the not-quite-cop getup might be good for what he had to do next. He did, however, stop for coffee on the way.

It was just after eight when he pulled up in front of the address Phil had given him. It was a duplex—two identical dwellings attached by a central carport. One front window had a Confederate flag as a curtain, and the other a rainbow flag. It was a safe bet which door Warren had to bang on.

It took a fair bit of knocking before somebody came to the door, although it wasn't TJ. This man was in his late twenties, with a shock of black hair falling across his forehead. He opened the main door but left the storm door closed between them.

"Can I help you?" he asked through the screen, still rubbing sleep from his eyes.

Warren flashed his badge. Like the uniform, it was completely fake, but most people didn't bother to check it. "What's your name, sir?"

"Harry Truman."

Warren blinked at him. "Are you serious?"

Harry rolled his eyes. Warren suspected he'd heard that question a thousand times before. The jokes probably got old. "It's a family name. Blame my granddad."

"I'm looking for TJ."

His eyebrows came together in what seemed to be genuine confusion. "Who?"

Warren pulled up TJ's picture on his phone and held it up. This time, Harry's face showed obvious recognition, along with a flush of what Warren thought might have been shame. "Oh. He told me his name was Tom." He crossed his arms, looking suddenly defensive. "Did he report me? Is that what this is about? Are you here to arrest me?"

Curiouser and curiouser. "I suppose that depends on what you have to say."

Harry moved closer to the screen, glancing behind Warren as if to see if he had backup with him. "Look, I didn't mean to hit him, okay? I know that sounds pathetic. It's probably what all abusive men say. I'm sure you don't believe me, but, I swear to you, I've never done anything like that before." He shook his head adamantly. "Never. It was awful."

"I suppose he was asking for it."

"Yes! Wait. Did he tell you that?"

Warren's stomach turned. What exactly had Phil gotten him into?

"So is he here?"

"No. That was two days ago. I asked him to leave." To Warren's surprise, the man seemed about to cry. He brushed angrily at his eyes. "I've never hit anyone before. I don't want to be in a relationship like that, you know? I don't think I can be with somebody who pushes me to do something like that."

Warren debated. He wasn't sure whether he believed this guy or not. Then again, it didn't matter. His purpose here was finding TJ, or Tom, or whatever the kid's name was. Handling domestic disputes several days after the fact was definitely not his domain. "Do you know where he might be?"

Harry chewed his lip for a minute. Finally, his cheeks blazed red. When he spoke, his voice was so low, Warren had to lean his forehead against the screen to hear him. "There's this place downtown. It's kind of a sex place, you know? They have booths and—"

"You mean Leroy's?"

The relief on Harry's face was almost comical. "You know it?" Then he eyed Warren's uniform. "I guess maybe not the same way I know it."

"I'm not here to harass you about where you go to get your rocks off. I just need to find TJ."

"Well, sometimes he works the back, you know? That's where he was the last time I saw him."

"The glory hole?"

Harry's head jerked in a nod. "Yeah."

Wow. This was definitely turning into an interesting morning. "Okay. Thanks for your time." He turned to go, but was caught short by the Confederate flag in the neighboring window. "That guy ever give you a hard time?"

"Who, Frank? Not since he learned I vote Republican. I play poker with him every Friday night." He laughed. "I usually win too."

Warren didn't necessarily understand, but he didn't need to. His friendship with Phil, Charlie, and Gray had taught him to appreciate the outliers. Whatever had gone on between TJ and Harry, Warren found himself smiling. "I like a guy who can think outside the box."

Leroy's didn't open until ten, and if anybody had told Warren he'd spend his Saturday morning waiting for that dive to unlock its door, he would have told them to go to hell. But he'd made Phil a promise and he had every intention of following through.

He debated going home for a shower, but the temptation to fall into bed after that would be too much to resist. Instead, he stopped at a greasy spoon for breakfast. He polished off a plate of eggs and hash browns, and chased it with another cup of coffee. He sat there rubbing his aching scars, and thought about what Phil had said.

Yeah, he was wound up tight. A roll in the sack would do him a world of good, but it was hard to balance what he liked against what was safe.

Or against just how *un*safe he wanted to be.
Weekend traffic had increased dramatically by the time he left the diner, and parking downtown was always a bitch. It was just after eleven when he finally pushed through the front door of Leroy's.
The front section was old-school: racks of magazines; a wall full of assorted battery-operated sex toys, each one in plastic packaging that'd practically require a blow-torch to open; shelves of lotions and lubricants; and a few blow-up gag gifts in the corner. Leroy himself sat behind the counter.
"Warren. Jesus, man. I haven't seen you in a hundred years." Leroy was pushing fifty, bald on top, with long gray fringe pulled back in a sad ponytail. He eyed Warren's uniform. "Why are you dressed like a cop?"
"I'm not." Warren leaned against the counter. "You got a kid working in back?"
Leroy squinted at Warren and tucked his *New Yorker* magazine under his arm. "Am I in some kind of trouble here?"
"No trouble. I'm just trying to round this kid up. I hear he might work the back for you sometimes. His name's TJ?"
Larry shook his head. "I don't know any TJ."
"Tom?"
"No."
Warren sighed. He pulled out his phone and showed Leroy the picture. "This is the kid I'm looking for."
"Ah. Yeah. He goes by BJ here. Not exactly subtle, but it works."
"Is he here now?"
"You sure I'm not in trouble?"
"I'm not a cop. You know that." In fact, Warren had done a few odd jobs for Leroy over the years. "Like I said, I just need to have a few words with him."
"Yeah, he's back there. He brings in a good crowd too. Do me a favor and don't scare away my customers."
Warren didn't make any promises.
The back hall was dark, and God, did it smell like sex. The floor seemed to suck at Warren's shoes. He did his best not to

15

think about what exactly had soaked into the carpet. Closed doors lined each side, with an open one punctuating the end. Four men stood in line, ranging in age from early twenties to late fifties. As Warren got closer, he heard the moans of whoever was currently being serviced. Those waiting had arrayed themselves across the hallway just outside the door, all of them straining to watch the show.

"Out of the way, gentlemen." Warren pushed between them, cutting short protests of "Hey, wait your turn!" by holding up his badge. That got rid of three of the four.

So much for not ruining Leroy's business.

The bathroom had only two stalls, with the glory hole in the wall between them, but the two participants had foregone the idea of anonymity. One knelt on the dirty floor while a man in a perfectly clean pinstriped suit took his pleasure. It was a sexy sight, no two ways about it. The guy being serviced might not have been anything special, but the kid on the floor was giving it all he was worth. If his enthusiasm was fake, he was one of the best damned actors Warren had ever seen. He certainly put most of the men in porn to shame. He looked like he was in heaven, there on a dirty bathroom floor, sucking the cock of a man at least twice his age.

Warren figured the least he could do was let the guy finish. He crossed his arms and stood back to watch. Unfortunately for the man in the suit, he opened his eyes halfway through his orgasm, saw what he assumed was a cop, and just about jumped out of his skin.

"Jesus!"

He pushed past Warren and the one waiting customer to run down the hall, still zipping up his pants.

And finally, Warren found himself facing TJ. The kid didn't even get off his knees. He just looked up at Warren through long eyelashes that accentuated his delicate, china doll features. A faint bruise colored his left eye. He didn't bother wiping the cum off his chin as he smiled up at Warren. "Impatient, aren't you? I promise, I'm worth the wait."

ONE MAN'S TRASH

For half a second, Warren debated taking the kid up on the offer, but this really wasn't the time or the place. He took TJ's arm and pulled him to his feet. "I need to talk to you."

"I'm not doing anything wrong."

"Yeah, sure." Warren turned him toward the wall and fished the kid's wallet out of his back pocket. The name on the driver's license wasn't TJ or Tom or BJ. "Taylor Gavriel Reynolds." Twenty-four years old, listed as five-seven, one hundred thirty pounds, brown hair, brown eyes. Warren might have called the hair dark blond, but otherwise, the description pretty much matched the kid in front of him. Warren slid the wallet back into place. "You're coming with me."

Warren dragged him out of the stall, past the last customer who called after them, "So, I don't get my turn?" and past Leroy, who hid his scowl behind his magazine.

"We're consenting adults," Taylor said as they went through the front door. "It's not illegal."

"Either they're paying you and you cut Leroy a portion, or they pay him and he cuts you a portion. Either way, yeah, it's illegal." Whether or not it should have been wasn't up to him.

He opened the passenger door of the 4Runner and placed TJ, or Taylor—whatever his name was—inside, then went around to climb into the driver's seat.

"You can't arrest me."

"Why not?"

"Because you're not a cop. Your uniform's fake."

Score one for the kid who gave blow jobs. "I just want to talk."

"That's what they all say, three seconds before they undo their pants."

"You know a guy named Phil Manderson?"

Taylor opened the glove compartment and came up with a napkin. He used it to wipe his chin. "I know a lot of guys."

"I'm not asking about 'a lot of guys.' I'm asking about Phil. He said you lived with him for a few weeks."

Taylor sat back in the seat, his eyes flicking from side to side as he searched his memory. "Phil? Is he a big guy?"

17

"No. He's a pharmacist."

"Oh yeah!" Taylor's face broke into a broad smile. He was damnably cute. "The kinky pharmacist. I remember him. He was one of the nice ones. That was one of those deals I sort of kicked myself for ruining."

"Ruined how? What did you do?"

"I don't know. I don't remember." He couldn't meet Warren's eyes as he said it, though. "I always piss them off eventually." He shrugged, looking down at his napkin. "I'm kind of high maintenance."

"Where were you last night?"

"At a club. Tracks. You know it?"

"Yeah, I know it."

Taylor's smile turned flirtatious. "I thought you would."

"Tracks closes at two. Where were you after that?"

"I went home with some guy." Another shrug. "I don't know his name. He had an apartment in LoDo. He was quick. Finished in about three minutes flat, then passed out cold. I stayed at his place until around seven, when he woke up and started panicking about his girlfriend coming home. He gave me cab money, though, so I left. Found some coffee and breakfast. Then went to wait at Leroy's." He leaned closer, resting his elbow on the console between the seats. "So you're a friend of Phil's, huh?"

"Maybe."

"You into the kinky stuff too?"

Warren thought about his and Phil's shared past. They'd never been lovers, but they had plenty in common when it came to what got them off. "Maybe."

Taylor leaned back in the seat, spreading his legs, letting the fabric of his jeans stretch tight across his groin. He ran his fingers over the bulge there, and grinned when Warren couldn't keep from watching. "Interesting."

That was one word for what was going through Warren's head. The kid was distracting as hell, but he didn't strike Warren as the vindictive type.

And like providence, Warren's phone rang. He wasn't surprised to see it was Phil calling. "What's up?"

"Hey." Phil sounded as tired as he had in the hospital parking lot. "Listen. I'm an idiot. I sent you on a wild-goose chase."

"You don't think it was him?" Warren didn't bother using a name.

"I just got a call from the hospital. It turns out there's an administrator there who's in the middle of a nasty divorce. Want to guess what she drives?"

"You're kidding."

"Apparently her soon-to-be-ex called to gloat about ruining her brand-new Cabriolet, but of course, her car wasn't ruined. So she put two and two together and now I know I sent you after TJ for no reason at all. I'm sorry."

"It's fine."

"Did you find him?"

Warren eyed the boy in his passenger seat. "I did."

"You didn't do anything mean to him, did you?"

"Not really."

"Good. Tell him I'm sorry for thinking he did it."

"Don't worry. We never really got that far."

"Good." Phil sighed. "Jesus. Fuck my life. I'm going back to bed."

"Good idea. I can be there in thirty minutes to tuck you in."

Phil laughed. "You're not my type, and I'm not yours. Besides, I'll be dreaming by then anyway. In the meantime?"

"Yeah?"

"Go get laid."

"I'll see what I can do." Warren slid the phone into his back pocket, his eyes still on Taylor. "Looks like I dragged you out of the office for nothing."

"It was a nice way to add a bit of excitement to my morning." He leaned close again. "Where to now?"

"Me? I'm going home. You can go back to Leroy's, if that's what you want."

Taylor grinned. "How about if I go home with you instead?"

Unbelievable. The kid had some balls, that was for sure. "Let me guess—room and board in exchange for sex?"

"Not just sex." Taylor moved quickly and easily across the console between them to straddle Warren's lap in the tight confines of the car. It was a move he'd obviously perfected. He put his lips against Warren's neck, sliding one hand down to cup Warren's groin. "Anything you want to do to me, I can take it. You can fuck me, hit me, tie me up. Whatever gets you off. Phil told you I'm good, right?"

"Yeah, he told me." Warren concentrated on keeping his erection in check. "Sounds great, until I wake up one morning and you've stolen my TV and cleaned out my accounts."

Taylor sat back against the steering wheel, his eyes wide. "I don't steal from my hosts. Ask Phil. Ask Harry Truman. You talked to Harry, right? You must have if you found your way from Phil to Leroy's." He grinned and leaned close again, stopping short of kissing Warren. "See? I even come with references." He laughed. "Never thought I'd say that in this line of work."

It was tempting, not least of all because Phil was right—Warren was wound up tight, and this kid obviously knew how to do what he did with no strings attached. And Phil had said he was dynamite in bed.

The lithe fingers working their way inside his fly were damned persuasive too.

"When was the last time you got tested?"

Taylor sat back again to meet his eyes. "When I started seeing Harry. He insisted. And I haven't been with anybody but him since then."

"You expect me to believe that?"

Taylor laughed. "I haven't let anybody fuck me since him. How about that? Blowing guys isn't the same." His grin turned wicked. "Oh. I get it. You want to go bareback. Jesus, that's awesome, baby." His pupils dilated and his breathing sped up. He wrapped his hand around Warren's cock and pushed close enough for Warren to confirm he wasn't the only one in the car with an erection. "Just thinking about it makes me hot."

Crazy as it seemed, the kid was genuinely aroused, and for better or worse, that was pretty fucking persuasive too.

"Let's do it," Taylor half whispered, half moaned in Warren's ear, his hand stroking inside Warren's pants. "You can have me bareback as often as you want. You can have me right now, right here in this car, if you want."

"No." Warren took his arms and gently pushed him away.

"No, meaning not at all, or no meaning 'not here'?"

"Not here." They were too visible and way too cramped. "Let's go home first."

Taylor's lips spread into a broad smile, and he slid back into the passenger seat. "I had a feeling you'd see things my way."

"I don't allow drugs in my house. If I catch you using, the whole deal's off and you'll be out the door."

"Not my thing, baby. I'm clean."

Warren believed him, not because he trusted Taylor, but because Phil was even less tolerant of drugs than Warren. If drugs had been the problem, he was pretty sure Phil would have mentioned it.

Taylor hooked a thumb over his shoulder toward Leroy's. "Give me a minute to grab my things?"

"Where are they?"

"Leroy has a room in the back he rents out in twenty-minute increments. He's been letting me sleep there since Harry kicked me out."

It made sense to let the kid get his stuff. Of course, he might just use it as a chance to run away. If he wanted to leave, Warren wasn't going to stop him. Still, he was strangely reluctant to let Taylor out of the vehicle.

"I'll get it for you."

Warren climbed from the car, pulling his shirt down to cover the bulge of his waning erection. Leroy directed him to a back room that held nothing more than a rollaway cot with a bare mattress, where Warren found a giant duffel bag. He flung it over his shoulder and headed for the door.

"That kid makes me good money," Leroy said as Warren went past. "Tell him he's welcome back here after you kick him out."

"What makes you think I will?"

"Everybody does."

The drive home was tense, not least of all because Warren couldn't stop thinking about what would happen once they got there.

"This is your place?" Taylor asked as they pulled into the driveway.

"It is." After four tours in Afghanistan, he'd come to Denver to work for his uncle, but going from combat to the quiet life of an electrician had nearly driven him mad. He quit the job and spent a year sleeping on the streets, trying to make all the violence and bloodshed and death he'd seen overseas somehow fit into the same world as the carefree neighborhoods of Denver, where people actually had to ask whether or not the war was still happening. He'd nearly convinced himself to re-enlist when his dad died, leaving Warren the house in Casper, Wyoming, where he'd grown up. Warren had vowed never to live there again, but the money he made on the sale had been enough to let him buy a tiny little home of his own.

And then he'd met Stuart, and everything had been good for a while.

Right up until it wasn't.

Warren never used the front door. He waited for Taylor to grab his duffel, then led him up the sidewalk to the back of the house. He noticed Taylor eyeing the dead rosebush next to the patio. It wouldn't have been in bloom in February anyway, but it was clearly long past dead. Warren often thought he should dig the thing up just so he didn't have to be reminded of his past failures every time he entered or exited his house, but he'd never gotten around to it.

"I take it you're not much of a gardener," Taylor said.

Warren didn't bother answering.

The back door led to a mudroom, where Taylor dropped his bag. He followed Warren into the kitchen. For Warren, just walking through the door triggered his need to sleep. His weariness hit him head-on, and he practically swayed on his feet.

"You okay?" Taylor asked.

"I haven't slept in more than twenty-four hours."

Taylor moved close and looked up at Warren through his long eyelashes. He cupped Warren's groin in his hand. "Tell me what I can do to help."

Even as exhausted as he was, Warren sure as hell wasn't going to say no now. After all, this was the main reason he'd brought Taylor home with him. It'd been way too long since he'd had anything that qualified as sex with another person. Just the thought of it and the feel of Taylor's hand between his legs was enough to make his pulse race and his weariness recede a bit.

He unbuttoned Taylor's pants, and Taylor grinned at him. "Impatient, aren't you?"

Warren pushed the jeans down over the boy's hips. "I don't want them in the way when I'm ready."

"You're not ready now?"

"Not yet." He brushed his thumb over Taylor's full bottom lip. "You said at Leroy's that a blow job from you was worth the wait."

Taylor's grin only grew more wicked. "Want me to prove it?"

"I do indeed."

"Anything you want, baby."

It didn't take Warren long to decide it hadn't been an idle boast. Anything the kid lacked in technique, he more than made up for in enthusiasm. He really seemed to enjoy what he was doing, and when Warren grabbed a handful of his hair in order to change the speed, Taylor relented with a gratified moan and let Warren thrust as deep and as fast as he needed to. Warren's aggressiveness only seemed to arouse Taylor more. His soft whimpers made Warren feel wild in a way he hadn't in ages.

He would have liked to stand there having his way with Taylor's mouth all day, but it'd been far too long, and the urge to come was too great. On the verge of his climax, Warren pulled Taylor to his feet and bent him over the kitchen table. His desperation made him aggressive, and he slammed the boy down hard, holding both his wrists tight in one hand. He drove into Taylor with a ruthlessness he rarely allowed himself. He had only Taylor's saliva as lubricant, making his entrance rough and a bit abrasive, and the result was sheer bliss.

The moment Warren penetrated him, Taylor let out a strangled cry, his body trembling as his orgasm hit him. It was unexpected—even Taylor seemed surprised—and that made it gratifying as hell. It took only three hard thrusts for Warren to come, and God, it was worth it. It was the best orgasm he'd had in ages, largely thanks to Taylor's unexpected response. The kid might have been little more than a whore, but he seemed to genuinely get off on his work.

Nothing could have turned Warren on more.

Only a second after finishing, Warren's lack of sleep crashed over him like a tidal wave. It was a miracle he'd managed to stay on his feet this long. And here he had poor Taylor pinned to his kitchen table like he was about to be handcuffed. He let go of the boy's wrists as he pulled out, although Taylor didn't move from his place on the table. Warren couldn't help but admire the sight. Taylor was gorgeous, especially like this, still breathless form his orgasm, his bare ass presented to Warren like some kind of gift.

The kid might be gone by the time he woke up, but at that moment, Warren sort of hoped he'd stick around.

"I'm exhausted. I hope you don't take it personally if I hit the sack."

Taylor shook his head. "I don't mind."

"Good. Help yourself to whatever's in the fridge. Your room's down the hall, last door on the right. Don't let the bed scare you."

"What?"

"And one more thing?"

"Yeah?"

"Don't wake me unless the world's ending."

And with that, Warren stumbled down the hall, into his own bedroom. He closed the door behind him and fell face-first into bed.

Chapter 2

Taylor lay there for a moment after his new host had gone, wondering at his own physical response to the sex. Sure, he'd been turned on—he always got worked up giving blow jobs—but he rarely let himself climax so easily. He'd learned over the years to ride his arousal for hours and sometimes even days at a time. He loved dragging it out for as long as he could. His sudden orgasm when the big fake cop pushed into him had come as a surprise.

Not necessarily an unwelcome one, though. He had a feeling this particular host was going to be one of the more enjoyable ones.

The door at the end of the hall closed, and still Taylor lay there, catching his breath, letting the pleasant shivers that came after an orgasm that good subside. Eventually, the discomfort of the table overcame his post-climax euphoria. He stood up on quivering legs, pulling his pants back into place as he looked around his new lodgings.

The neighborhood was old and barely hanging on to its lower-middle-class roots, but the inside of the small, ranch-style house was clean and ruthlessly tidy. The furniture all looked to be only a few years old, and in good condition. The walls were completely bare. It felt more like a hotel room than a home.

Taylor used a paper towel to clean up the mess he'd made on and under the table, then started his inspection.

ONE MAN'S TRASH

The mudroom they'd come through had a door to a single-car garage, housing a dented, nondescript white sedan. The mudroom itself contained a washer and dryer. Luckily, Taylor hadn't taken his duffel any farther than that. Most of his stuff had been dirty when Harry had kicked him out. He might not last long with the fake cop, but he could at least get a couple of loads of laundry in.

Once he had his first load running, he checked the table by the front door. He'd discovered over the years that he could learn a lot about his hosts by going through their mail. He didn't find much this time—just two unopened bills, both addressed to Warren B. Groves.

At least now he knew his host's name.

Warren was a big man—at least six-foot-three and built like an ox. The scars on his face weren't large, but they couldn't be ignored. He was the kind of man who could be dangerous. The knowledge sent a shivery thrill through Taylor, part fear, part excitement. Yes, Warren might hurt him. Then again, Taylor had learned over the years that just about any man could be dangerous, when you pushed him hard enough. And Taylor had a way of pushing.

He left the mail on the table, unopened.

The only thing of interest in the living room was a bookshelf, which held a few knickknacks and an array of books. A couple of shelves held fiction—political intrigue and courtroom drama, based on the titles and covers, but Taylor didn't really know books. Another shelf held psychology textbooks. Taylor frowned, running his fingers over the spines, each with a University of Wyoming bookstore sticker. Growing up with a psychologist as a father had taught him to loathe the profession. He hoped that wasn't what Warren was. The last shelf was a mixed bag: true crime, plus several books on personal defense and private investigation techniques.

Taylor frowned again, weighing those against the fake cop costume. Some kind of security guard, maybe? But if so, why was there no name tag or company logo on the uniform shirt?

He'd figure it out eventually.

27

He crept down the hall and stood outside Warren's bedroom, his ear pressed to the door. The guy was a snorer, and Taylor smiled. Thank goodness he'd have his own room to sleep in. And the fact that Warren was sound asleep meant Taylor had time to *really* snoop around.

The house held three bedrooms—the one Warren slept in, the one that would be Taylor's, and a tiny one midway down the hall. The latter was set up as an office, with an old-school metal desk like the kind his middle-school English teacher had used. A giant iMac took up most of the desktop. Taylor checked the computer but found it password protected. He didn't know enough about Warren yet to hazard a guess at the password, so he left the computer alone. A metal file cabinet in the corner was also locked.

Warren B. Groves was paranoid. Interesting.

The only thing of interest in the desk drawers was a handful of photos. A few appeared to be from Warren's childhood—a couple of a young boy Taylor presumed to be Warren with an old woman, and another of the same child with what Taylor assumed was his mother. Those were of little interest to Taylor, but he found three that were more recent. One showed a much younger Warren dressed as a soldier, standing next to two other men in fatigues, all of them cradling scary-looking guns. What looked to Taylor like a heavily armored Jeep could be seen behind them. Taylor had no idea where they were, other than someplace distinctly "not America."

The second photo showed a smiling Warren nose-to-nose with another man, as if they'd been caught just before a kiss. It had been taken in the backyard of Warren's house, while the roses by the back patio were in full bloom. So there'd once been a partner who mattered enough to keep the photo, and that partner must have been the gardener, given the current state of the roses.

The third picture showed Warren, Phil, and two other men, in what appeared to be somebody's living room. Phil was the only one not wearing black leather. Warren was scowling at the camera, while the man next to him laughed. The big, heavily tattooed man on the end had a riding crop in his hand. Some kind of BDSM group. It wasn't surprising, given what Taylor knew about Phil.

He looked at the three photos again and noticed something else: one of the soldiers in the first photo was also the laughing man in the third photo. Warren's war buddy was also one of his BDSM friends. Taylor wondered if they'd known each other before the war or met over there and decided to come home to the same city. Had they been lovers?

Taylor made sure the photos were in the same order he'd found them and put them back in the drawer. The only thing in the closet was a gun safe, which was also locked. No clothes. No boxes of memorabilia or paperwork. Absolutely nothing personal. The lack of belongings told Taylor that Warren wasn't the type to get attached to things.

That was a good sign.

There were cabinets built into the opposite wall of the hallway, but they held only the usual assortment of towels, sheets, and blankets, plus a couple of dusty board games.

A quick survey of the garage didn't reveal much, besides the white car. The only thing of interest was a box in the corner. Taylor dug through it, and found several dark-colored windbreakers and hoodies, a few stocking caps, and several pairs of leather gloves. Odd that they were in the garage, but maybe Warren used them when he changed the oil?

Whatever they were for, they didn't tell Taylor anything interesting.

The only place left to search was Taylor's own room. It held a queen-sized four-poster bed with a cheap bedspread. Two bedside tables flanked it. A dresser sat against the opposite wall. The bit of dust on the furniture showed the room didn't see much use. A small door in the corner led to a tiny bathroom, which included a claw-foot tub outfitted with a shower attachment. Taylor smiled again. He'd even have his own bathroom. He mentally vowed to make this setup last as long as he could, assuming Warren wasn't abusive or something.

Then again, "abusive" had never scared Taylor, and his vows to let good things last never amounted to much. His demons always got in the way.

A few bottles still resided in the medicine cabinet, but they were only the usual assortment of over-the-counter painkillers and cold meds, most of them expired. The cabinet under the sink held cleaning supplies and a toilet brush. A glance into the toilet showed that it hadn't been used or cleaned in a while. Taylor had noticed over the years that otherwise tidy people often forgot to check the toilets in their guest baths. He didn't mind a bit of housework, though. It only took him a minute to fix it.

He found a few clothes in the dresser drawers, all way too small to fit Warren. Presumably the absent partner's, but one never knew. The bedside table drawers were empty except for one forgotten, nearly empty bottle of lube.

The thick, square posts at each corner of the bed seemed bigger than they needed to be. Upon closer examination, Taylor found heavy steel loops bolted through them, arrayed at a variety of heights. When he realized their purpose, his heart skipped a beat.

"Don't let the bed scare you."

It was designed for tying somebody down.

And that led him the closet.

Here, he found Warren's BDSM gear. A quick inventory revealed several different types of whips and flogs, a few dildos of various size, a harness, a pair of chaps, several male chastity devices, and what looked like a fold-up wooden table, the exact use of which he could only guess at.

He'd known to expect this. Still, seeing it sent that same delicious thrill through him—part fear, part arousal—as he imagined Warren using any of this on him.

Yes, he had a feeling this arrangement could end up being quite memorable.

But the world wasn't ending, so he followed orders and let Warren sleep.

He spent the rest of the afternoon finishing laundry and watching TV, although he kept the volume low so as not to wake his new host. Warren finally emerged from his bedroom just after six p.m., wearing nothing but a pair of boxers and a T-shirt. He leaned against the living room doorway and studied Taylor.

"Still here, huh?"

"Did you expect me to leave?"

Warren almost smiled. He was a good-looking guy, with close-cropped black hair and dark, piercing eyes. A smile would have made him gorgeous, but Taylor suspected it didn't happen often. "I wasn't sure what to expect, to be honest."

"I thought we had an arrangement."

"Guess so." Warren absentmindedly rubbed the small scar on the right side of his jaw as he stared out the front window, seeming uncomfortable. Most guys were, the first few days. It took time to get used to having a whore in the house.

"You never told me your name," Taylor said. Of course, he knew it already, but it was better to play dumb than to let Warren know he'd been snooping.

"It's Warren. What about you? You want to give me a fake name, like you did with Harry and Phil?"

Taylor squirmed a bit at that question. It was true he hated using his real name. There was no telling when his parents would hire another private investigator to track him down. But Warren had already seen his ID. "Call me whatever you want. It doesn't matter."

Warren didn't even blink at that. "You hungry?"

"Starving, actually. You said I could help myself to whatever was in the fridge, but it's pretty much empty."

"Yeah. Sorry about that. I don't really cook. You like pizza?"

"What do I look like, a freak? Of course I like pizza."

"What do you want on it?"

"Anything." Taylor gave him his best smile. "I'm easy."

31

Warren actually blushed a bit at that.

The pizza arrived with Canadian bacon, pineapple, and olives. Taylor never would have pegged Warren as the "pineapple on pizza" type, but whatever. They ate in silence, relying on the TV to keep things from being too uncomfortable.

It wasn't until they were finished that Warren said, "I have to work at nine."

"Until when?"

He shrugged without meeting Taylor's eyes. "Depends. Sometimes I'm home by two or three. Sometimes not until morning."

"What do you do?"

"Different things."

Taylor found that oddly elusive. "What does that mean exactly?"

Warren's jaw worked as he debated. "You might say I'm a freelance contractor."

"Funny. That's what I tell people when they ask what I do for a living too." He smiled to take the edge off the words. Some guys were easily offended. He didn't think Warren seemed like the type, but he knew to play it safe these first few days. "So, what are you doing tonight specifically? Can you tell me that?"

Warren debated a bit more, then relented. "On the weekends, I work personal security for a couple of girls." He picked at a cuticle. "Escorts, I guess you could say."

"You mean hookers." This time, Taylor's smile was completely genuine. So Warren wasn't a hypocrite. He wasn't the type who preached "family values" while hiding a male whore in his back bedroom. The fact that he made his living at least in part by protecting sex workers was in his favor as far as Taylor was concerned. "So, what exactly do you do, as their security?"

"I mostly stand outside a paper-thin motel door all night in case there's a problem."

"Listening?"

"Only as much as I need to."

They fell silent for a moment, the TV adding a bit of background noise. But after a few minutes, Warren's gaze slid his way, his cheeks slowly turning red, a quiet question in his eye.

Taylor resisted the urge to laugh. Who'd have guessed the big BDSM daddy would be one of the shy ones? Taylor got down on his knees between Warren's legs and ran his hands up the man's thick thighs.

"Don't be bashful, baby. I won't know what you want or when you want it if you don't tell me." He caressed the heavy bulge in Warren's shorts and looked up at him through his lashes. "Or you can just take what you want, whenever you want it. That's what I promised, and I meant it. Like I said, I'm easy."

Warren made a low growl, deep in his throat, as his cock grew hard under Taylor's caresses. "I don't want to be an asshole."

"Don't worry." Taylor kept his hand moving. "You'll never want it too often or too rough for me, I promise. I'm always ready." And it was true. Taylor had always been a highly sexual person, and there was something about having just a bit of force used against him that made him wild. He was convinced being slammed over the table earlier was half of why he'd come so fast. Now, feeling the heat of Warren's erection through his shorts and seeing the lust in his dark eyes was all it took to make Taylor hard again.

God, he loved his job.

He pushed Warren back on the couch and shoved his shirt up, out of the way. Warren was a big guy but not overly hairy. A faint, thin trail led down from his navel to the elastic of his boxers, and Taylor followed it with his tongue. He left the boxers in place but wrapped his mouth around the head of Warren's cock, letting the heat of his mouth soak through the thin fabric.

Warren sucked air through his teeth, pushing his groin toward Taylor with a moan. He'd told Taylor earlier that he'd been up for more than twenty-four hours. That meant it'd probably been about that long since he'd showered too, and Taylor could tell. Warren didn't smell dirty or sour like some men, but his musk was heavy and seductively ripe, undercut by the lingering smell of their sex, from when Warren had fucked him over the table. It was hot and erotic in that base, dirty way Taylor always craved.

Taylor moaned, working his lips around the head of Warren's cock. He slid his hand through the opening in the fly and wrapped his fingers around the base of Warren's erection. The scent, and the memory of Warren's aggression in the kitchen, and the strangely seductive thrill of sucking him through his boxers, sent a sensuous, warm glow of arousal down Taylor's spine, deep into his groin. He panted, moaning and stroking, wondering if he could make Warren come like this. He liked that idea. Then again, their quick tryst on the kitchen table had been little more than a teaser. Maybe he'd straddle Warren's lap and let the man truly fuck him this time.

But the very next minute, Warren grabbed Taylor's arm and pulled him away.

"Something wrong, baby?" Taylor asked, his voice throaty from his own arousal.

Warren's jaw clenched, but he didn't say anything. Instead, he took Taylor's arm and pulled him down the hallway, through Warren's bedroom, into the master bath. He turned on the shower and stripped naked, his thick cock poking straight out in front of him like a battering ram, then dragged Taylor fully clothed into the tub.

Taylor knew how to play this game.

He picked up the soap, smiling. "Don't worry. I know exactly what you want."

He spent a long, long time just washing and stroking and caressing until Warren was breathless and panting, his back against the tile wall. Finally, Warren took a handful of Taylor's hair and shoved him to his knees.

The man sure loved his blow jobs. He held Taylor's hair in one hand, the other hand tight on the back of his head.

Sometimes he held Taylor still and fucked his mouth ruthlessly. Sometimes he relaxed and let Taylor take the lead. He made very little noise. He rarely opened his eyes. But the more turned on Taylor got—the more he whimpered and moaned as his own arousal took over—the more Warren responded. And holy hell, it was hot. No matter how many cocks Taylor sucked, he never got tired of it. Warren had that perfect mix of tenderness and force that always made Taylor weak and desperate. He easily lost himself to the feel of hard, wet flesh sliding between his lips and the sounds of their shared lust. His erection strained against his wet jeans, and he squirmed as he tended to Warren, desperate to gain just a bit of friction against his cock. He could have unbuttoned his jeans and used his hand, but he was afraid he'd finish too quickly again. He didn't want to come. He just wanted to ride this glorious wave as long as he could.

It took a hell of a lot longer than it had that morning for Warren to finish, and by the time he did, Taylor was shockingly near his own climax again. Just a few simple strokes would have brought him to an orgasm, but he chose to deny himself the release. Instead, he stayed on his knees for a moment, breathing deep, happily drowning in the depths of his arousal.

Jesus. It'd been years since anybody had pushed him to the edge so easily.

Warren cleared his throat. "Uh… you want me to—"

"No." And he didn't. Not yet. Taylor took a few more deep, calming breaths before looking through his lashes up Warren's wet, naked body. "But whenever you get home, however late it is, don't be afraid to wake me."

Chapter 3

Warren left the house with his head spinning. Two thoughts kept circling each other in his mind.

One: Taylor was sexy as hell. Something about him seriously turned Warren's crank. He was already thinking about the next time he could feel the kid's mouth around his cock.

Two: Letting him move in was one of the stupidest things Warren had ever done. "References" or no, Warren was being a moron.

He debated it for most of the drive. Finally, just before arriving at his destination, he took advantage of a red light to dial Phil's number.

"Warren." Phil's voice echoed through the car's hands-free system. "Did you get laid?"

Warren clenched his jaw. He should have known that question was coming. He countered with a question of his own. "Did Taylor ever steal from you?"

"Who?"

Damn. He'd already forgotten about the fake names. "TJ."

"No. Why? Oh, Jesus. Wait. Did you take him home with you?"

Warren didn't answer, but he was glad the people in neighboring cars couldn't hear their conversation.

Phil laughed. "Damn. When I said to get laid, I didn't mean with him. Then again, why not? He's hot, right? He's certainly always willing. At least now I feel like a bit less of an ass for letting him move in with me when I did."

"You never answered my question."

"What? Oh. No, he didn't steal anything. Like I said, things were good, up until they weren't. And frankly, you might have better luck with him than I did."

Warren turned into the parking lot of the motel his clients favored and pulled into a parking place. The girls were waiting for him, and he held up a finger telling them it'd be a minute. "What makes you say that?"

"I always had the feeling he just needed somebody to really take him in hand, you know? Like, lay down the law. Establish some real discipline."

"Well, isn't that your thing? Taking control? Why would it work better for me than you?"

Phil sighed. "What he needs is different from what I like to do. I don't know how to explain it exactly, except to say the kid has a wild streak. And yeah, he was a good lay, but I didn't really care enough in the long run to help him fight whatever demons he's running from, especially since the last thing he seemed to want was help of any kind. Know what I'm saying?"

Warren considered. Sugar and Candy—and no, those probably weren't their real names, but Warren didn't need to any more than what they told him—looked impatient, tapping their toes on the sidewalk. "No," he confessed. "I'm not sure I do."

Phil sighed again. "Well, you will by the end. We can talk about it then."

Warren ended the call and climbed out of the car. He took a minute to make sure he had everything he needed—the fake badge in his pocket, a blackjack tucked into his belt, and a nine millimeter Smith & Wesson hidden at the small of his back. The gun was licensed, and his concealed carry permit was up-to-date. He'd never used it, but four tours in Afghanistan had taught him it was better to have a gun and not need it than the other way around.

"Sorry for the delay," he told the girls.

Women, he corrected himself.

He had a hard time thinking of them as anything but kids, to be honest, but they were legal, as far as he knew. He guessed them each to be early twenties. Warren was thirty-eight, and all he could think when he looked at Candy and Sugar was that his youth had never felt so distant.

"Anything I need to know?" he asked.

Candy, who was over six feet tall in her heels, shook her head, her long black hair swinging like a curtain behind her. She chewed her lip, her gaze sliding sideways to her friend. Warren turned to Sugar, waiting. Sugar was petite and blonde, although he suspected the latter was fake. Her makeup was thick tonight, and in the fading light, Warren thought he saw a bit of a bruise next to her left eye.

That reminded him of Taylor, and he had to force himself to stay focused.

"Trouble?" he asked her.

"My ex? Robby?" Everything sounded like a question. "He's been around a lot? He doesn't like me working, you know?"

Warren nodded. "Was it Robby who gave you that shiner?"

She put her fingertips over it, long purple nails brushing her eyelashes. "Does it show too much? I don't want the johns getting ideas."

Warren shook his head. "You'll be fine. Keep the lights low." He was less worried about her customers than the ex. "What's he look like?"

She scrolled through her phone and finally held up a picture. Robby looked to be in his late twenties, with a goatee and a cocky grin. In the picture, he wore a flannel shirt with the sleeves ripped off and a ball cap that said, "I love pussy."

Classy, he wasn't.

"Send that picture to me, okay?"

She nodded and bent her head to do it.

"You think he'll come here looking for you?"

"He's not supposed to, but that doesn't mean he won't."

"You have a restraining order against him?"

"Not really." She chewed her lip nervously. "It's complicated?"

"Okay. Well, if I see him, I'll send him on his way."

They both looked relieved at that.

And then, it was time for work.

He had an arrangement with Candy and Sugar that was mutually beneficial. They always rented adjacent rooms so he could cover them both at once. Then each girl paid him two-thirds his normal rate, which meant they got a discount and he made extra.

The girls had a lot of regulars on Saturday nights. Warren was on a first-name basis with half of them. There were schoolteachers, insurance brokers, and dentists, most of them over forty, at least half of them married. Warren kept his eyes on the time, making sure no customer overstayed their welcome. But mostly, he stood outside the doors and listened.

The girls made a lot of noise. There were two reasons for that. First, most of the johns seemed to like it that way. Second, it was a signal to Warren that everything was okay. If things were quiet for too long, he'd knock. If everything was okay, they'd answer. If he got no answer, or if it was only the john who answered, Warren went in. He had keys to both rooms and a solid right kick that would do the trick in a pinch. In all the years he'd been working security like this, he'd only had to go in a handful of times.

Still, in each of those times, the situation had been ugly. He'd caught men beating girls, strangling girls, and attempting to force access to orifices they didn't have permission to use. Even though most of the johns were just normal guys, Warren had always looked down on them.

Now, with a rent boy living in his guest room, he was suddenly one of them.

That made him think about Taylor. Combined with the sounds coming from behind the two doors he guarded, it was enough to make him edgy again.

At least this time, he'd have a way to handle it, other than jerking off.

Luck was with him. He'd been out until dawn the night before, but this time, the girls closed up shop at three, and Warren climbed gratefully into his car and drove home.

He halfway hoped Taylor would be waiting up for him, just so he wouldn't feel like such an ass asking for sex again, but the house was dark and silent when he let himself in. He went quietly down the hall. Taylor's door was partially closed, with a note taped to it at Warren's height. Warren leaned close in the darkness to read it.

Penciled across the paper in large print was a single word: ANYTIME.

Warren's heart pounded a bit louder as he pushed the door open. Taylor was sound asleep, curled into a ball, completely hidden by the blankets. Warren crept inside, still unsure if he'd wake the boy or not. He moved the blanket just enough to see Taylor's face. A bit of moonlight fell through the curtain, across the bed, and Taylor's long lashes cast deep shadows under his eyes.

He was beautiful, but sleeping like he was, he looked like nothing more than a kid. Warren knew from checking his license he was well past legal.

Still.

Awfully young.

Warren turned to leave, but the old floorboards creaked under his heel. Taylor woke with a start. "Wha— Oh."

"I didn't mean to disturb you."

"I don't mind. I said anytime, and I meant it." He stretched, grinning up at Warren. "How was work?"

Warren chuckled at the strange normalcy of the question, given the circumstances. "Invigorating, as always."

"Oh yeah?" Taylor pushed the covers down, revealing a slim, completely nude body. "I can invigorate you more, if you like."

Warren laughed, but he didn't need a second invitation. He stripped quickly, debating exactly what he wanted to do.

He'd been thinking all night about having the kid on his knees again, but now, looking down at his slender, fit body, Warren had other ideas.

"How do you feel about having your hands tied?"

Taylor moaned and reached down to wrap his fingers around his cock. "Like I said, whatever you want."

"You shouldn't trust so easily."

"You want to discuss my poor life choices, or you want to chain me up and fuck me?"

It was a fair question, and not one Warren needed to debate.

He hadn't gone through the stuff in the closet in a while, but he knew right where to find the leather wrist cuffs. He attached them to the rings on the columns at the head of the bed. The thought of what he was about to do made him hard and anxious. He turned to Taylor, trying to decide if it was only arousal in his eyes, or if it was fear. "You can say no."

Taylor shook his head, his breathing already coming harder. "I never say no."

Warren stood, yanking the covers away to leave Taylor totally exposed. The boy's cock lay hard against his flat belly. He spread his legs, and something on his thighs caught Warren's attention. Warren leaned closer, running his fingers over the light ridges.

They were scars.

"Who did this to you?"

"I did it to myself," Taylor said without embarrassment. "Before I learned I could get the same kind of release other ways."

Warren had only completed two years in college majoring in psychology, but they'd talked plenty about cutting. Still, it was something Warren didn't entirely understand. "What other ways?"

"Giving head. Being fucked." There was laughter in his voice. "Letting men I don't know tie me up so they can talk all damned night."

Warren chuckled. "I haven't tied you up yet."

"So what are you waiting for?"

Good question. Warren smacked the boy's thigh playfully. "Turn over."

Taylor did as he was told, and Warren took each wrist in turn and secured them in the cuffs. Then he stood there for a minute, marveling at how fucking hot the boy was, his slim body a dark stripe against the white sheets. Taylor squirmed, moaning as he rubbed his cock against the bed. Warren shook his head, wondering what exactly he'd done to deserve such a prize.

He knelt between the boy's legs and gripped Taylor's perfectly shaped ass cheeks in his hands, kneading the soft flesh. He was gratified by the moan it elicited. He spread the boy wide, running his thumb roughly up the boy's crack. He'd always loved what pigment did to the genitals of both men and women. Women who were pale and pink sometimes had dark labia. Men who were light-skinned often had cocks, perinea, and rims a shade or two darker than the rest of them. Warren was glad to see Taylor hadn't gone for the bleaching fad. He put his thumb over that dark place and moved it in light circles, testing Taylor's response.

Taylor gasped and strained against his bonds, angling his hips up, offering himself to Warren.

This time, Warren wasn't in a hurry.

He lay on his stomach and buried his face between Taylor's cheeks, stretching him wide with his hands while using his tongue to tease Taylor's rim. Some men didn't like analingus, but Warren loved it. He spent a long time teasing Taylor, circling his entrance before diving in deep. Taylor went wild, bucking his hips and panting, begging between his breathless moans. Warren kept it up, sometimes turning to lightly sink his teeth into Taylor's cheeks, sucking and nibbling hard enough to raise bruises without breaking the flesh, and each time, Taylor responded with a deep, throaty groan.

He hadn't been lying. He could take a bit of pain.

Warren slid one hand underneath Taylor's hips to wrap his fingers around his cock, then slowly slid two fingers of the other hand past the boy's rim.

Taylor's groans dropped in timbre, and Warren fucked him with one hand while the boy humped his hips up and down, driving his cock through the fingers of the other hand. Taylor gasped and moaned, and Warren thought he might be close to climaxing, but when he gently brushed his fingers over Taylor's prostate, he simply went rigid, as if holding his breath.

That meant he had an amazing amount of self-control when it came to his orgasms. Warren liked that.

He went back to what he'd been doing, using both hands together, occasionally brushing Taylor's prostate just to see how far he could push the kid. Taylor never came. He cried and begged and humped harder, but he didn't orgasm. Warren found his enthusiastic restraint hotter than hell. He alternated his fingers and his tongue on top while jerking Taylor off with his other hand until Taylor was ragged and breathless, his face pressed into the bed, whispering, "Please, please, please," into the sheets.

"Please, what?" Warren asked.

Taylor didn't answer. He was too far gone. He'd ceased bucking his hips, although he held them up at an angle, giving the hand around his cock plenty of room to work. "Please," he said again. "Oh God, please."

Warren decided that was good enough for him. He let Taylor go and moved quickly on top of him.

"Oh, yesssss," Taylor whispered as Warren pushed the head of his cock inside. Taylor strained against his bonds, pushing his hips up to accept Warren's cock, and that was all it took to break Warren's self-control. He'd meant to go slow, but instead, he pushed in deep and hard. The only lubricant between them was what was left from his mouth. It was enough, but only barely. It made their coupling rough in the way Warren loved best, but he didn't want to hurt the kid.

He tucked his head against Taylor's neck, willing himself not to thrust. He forced the words through clenched teeth. "Do you need more lube?"

"Stop talking and fuck me already!"

Warren didn't need to be told twice. He groaned his gratefulness and began to thrust, his movements fast and hard. The bed pounded against the wall, their naked flesh slapped together, the smell of their sex strong and musky in the small room. Even with his hands bound, Warren knew exactly what Phil meant when he said Taylor was dynamite in bed. He was wild as hell, bucking and loud, one minute talking dirty, the next minute begging shamelessly. Warren was glad he lived in a house and not an apartment with shared walls. Between the bed hitting the wall and Taylor's cries, they made one hell of a racket.

He stopped once to add some lube, despite Taylor's protests, and the renewed ease of their thrusting only made them wilder until at last Warren knew he couldn't keep his orgasm at bay another minute. He reached underneath Taylor to grip his cock. Taylor's hips bucked one more time, and he came hard, his cries turning from pleasure to surprise, and Warren let go at last, pushing in deep one last time to empty himself into Taylor's wonderfully tight little ass.

He collapsed, exhausted in the best possible way. He couldn't remember the last time he'd had three orgasms in a twenty-four-hour period, let alone ones that weren't self-induced.

He kissed Taylor's shoulder, easing his weight up so he didn't squish the poor kid. "You okay?" he asked quietly.

Taylor nodded, his breath shaky. "I don't usually come that easy."

"Oh, honey. If that was 'easy' for you, we're going to get along famously."

Warren was still mostly hard, and Taylor squirmed, pushing his hips back, allowing Warren to slide in a bit deeper. "I love the way you fuck me. I'm ready for you to do it again right now, if you want."

"You're crediting me with way more stamina than I actually have."

"Tomorrow," Taylor said, falling limp against the sheets. "Tell me you'll fuck me again tomorrow."

Warren laughed and reached to undo the leather wrist cuffs. "Yeah, I think this little arrangement is going to work out just fine."

Warren slept until eleven on Sunday and woke feeling better than he had in ages. He debated taking Taylor into the shower with him again, but decided to let the kid have a break. Besides, Warren was nearly fifteen years older than Taylor, and he wasn't sure he had it in him to go another round again so soon anyway.

Definite proof he was getting old.

He showered alone, then took Taylor to the grocery store so they could stock up on food for the week. Taylor hadn't been wrong about the depleted state of his kitchen.

"What do you like?" Warren asked as they entered the grocery store.

Taylor almost batted his eyelashes at Warren. "What do *you* like?"

Warren shook his head, halfway amused. The complicity could be fun, but if the kid was going to live with him, even for a few days, he'd need to eat. "I survive on a whole lot of TV dinners. That sound good to you?"

Taylor almost winced. "Not really."

"That's what I thought. So tell me what you like."

Taylor picked up a tomato and turned it over in his hands. He seemed oddly hesitant to say whatever it was he needed to say. "I can cook." He seemed to say it more to the tomato than to Warren. "I'll make the meals, if you want me to."

"Why would I argue with that?"

Taylor shrugged and set the tomato aside. "I mean, I'm not a super chef or anything. I can't promise anything gourmet. But I know my way around the kitchen, and doing what I do, I usually have the time."

So he was dynamite in bed, *and* he cooked?

At that moment, Warren wasn't sure he'd ever let him leave.

In the end, Warren happily pushed the cart around the store while Taylor dropped in hamburger, chicken breasts, eggs, pasta, and a stupid amount of produce. He also asked for a box of old-fashioned popsicles, as if Warren might say yes to everything else but no to a two-dollar box of frozen, brightly colored sugar water. The week's worth of groceries cost a bit more than usual, but Warren had a feeling it'd be worth it. He caught himself stealing glances at Taylor as they drove home from the store. A kid this cute, that good in bed, and willing to cook on top of it all, and yet he apparently had a history of getting kicked out by his "hosts"?

Warren found the mystery of it all intriguing as hell.

Normally, Warren didn't get much work from Sunday morning until Wednesday night. Sugar and Candy both worked weekends only. He had a different girl on Wednesdays who went to guys' homes, and another on Thursday who mostly worked out of cars. But protecting escorts was only one part of what paid Warren's bills. After putting groceries away, he left Taylor watching TV, happily sucking a popsicle—and damned if *that* didn't inspire an erotic thought or two—and went into his office to check his email.

Most weeks, his obscure listings in a few select places didn't get much notice, and Warren took only a small fraction of the jobs people offered. This week was no different. Four different people looking for help offing their spouse. Warren quickly replied that wasn't his gig. One person wanted a getaway driver for a "heist." Warren chuckled at that, shaking his head. Probably a bunch of ridiculous kids thinking they were going to play *Ocean's Eleven* in Denver. No doubt they pictured vaults of money just waiting to be taken when in reality, they'd be damned lucky to get thirty dollars and change from a 7-Eleven. He told them no too.

But the last email caught his attention.
My friend and I are being blackmailed. We can't go to the police. We can pay $2000. Can you help us?

"Good question," Warren mumbled to himself. "Only one way to find out."

An hour later, he had a meeting arranged.

As big as Warren was, and scarred to boot, it wasn't easy to blend in, but Warren did his best. He donned jeans, a gray hoodie, and a Broncos baseball cap.

Taylor looked up from the TV as Warren came in. "Going somewhere?"

"I have a meeting."

Taylor batted his eyelashes at him. "I thought you said you were all mine until Wednesday."

Warren chuckled, not fooled for a minute by the kid's flattery. No matter how good the sex between them had been so far, Taylor probably didn't care all that much whether or not Warren was around. "Something's come up. I won't be long."

That got him a smile. "Okay."

He'd set the meeting for a local McDonald's. There were security cameras on the drive-through, over the registers, and aimed at the children's play area, but the rest of the dining room was uncovered, and the clientele at McDonald's was diverse enough that Warren and his potential clients wouldn't be noteworthy.

Except the two women who showed up would have been noteworthy just about anywhere. Both were slender and gorgeous. One was black, the other white. Even dressed as they were in jeans, with their winter coats hiding their top halves, they were striking. They carried themselves with a bit more grace than the average Big Mac aficionado.

"Are you Bruce?" one of them asked.

"That's me." It was his middle name, technically, but the one he always used for jobs like this. "And you are?"

"Grace," the black one said, shaking his hand.

"And I'm Avery."

"Thanks for coming." He gestured toward the front of the store. "You ladies hungry? Lunch is on me."

A small wrinkle appeared between Grace's perfectly arched eyebrows. "It's four in the afternoon."

Warren shrugged. "Call it an afternoon snack, then."

Avery shook her head, her long blonde hair swinging behind her, and both girls sank into the little plastic seats across from him. For a second, there was only awkward silence. Warren was about to ask them for details when Avery suddenly spoke.

"Do you know who we are?"

Warren sat back in his seat, eying them. "Should I?"

They both put hands to their chests, exchanging a glance that told Warren they were relieved.

"Sometimes people recognize us," Grace said.

"The thing is," Avery took up the tale, "we work for— Well, let's just say we work for a well-known sports franchise here in Denver, and our contract includes a…" She waved her hand in circles as she searched for the word she wanted, eventually turning to Grace for help.

"A morality clause," Grace said. "Which somebody is using against us."

"Who is this 'somebody'?" Warren asked.

"His name's Ted Spencer," Avery told him. "He's a reporter on one of the Denver news stations. He mostly covers sports." She brushed her hair off her forehead and leaned a bit closer. "A couple of months ago, he told me he'd do a story on me. And I was stupid. I mean, I can't believe how dumb I was. I fell for it, and, well—"

"You ended up in bed with him?"

Her furious blush was her only answer.

"Hey, it happens to the best of us," Warren told her. "Don't beat yourself up." Although he knew she'd continue doing it anyway. "So let me guess—he has pictures?"

"Worse," Avery said. "Video."

"And he's been blackmailing you? For how much?"

"A thousand dollars a week."

Warren whistled. "Wow. You have that much?"

"I've used most of my savings. I could pay him a bit longer, but not much. And then I found out he'd done the same thing to Grace."

Grace nodded, but where Avery was embarrassed, Grace was clearly angry. "He gave me the same bullshit about doing a story on me. He took me out for dinner, and ordered a bottle of wine, and then…" She shook her head. "I think he might have used something, but I don't know for sure."

"'Something,' as in a date rape drug?"

She shrugged, dejected. "I don't know. Maybe? It just seemed like I shouldn't have been that loaded after two glasses of wine. I don't even know how I ended up in that hotel room with him. But then two days later, he sent me an email."

"Same amount?"

She nodded. "A thousand dollars a week."

"And you don't want to go to the cops?"

Both girls adamantly shook their heads, but it was Avery who answered. "A sex tape? No way. We'd lose our jobs. Doesn't seem fair, but that's how it is. Neither of us can afford to be fired."

"How much have you paid him so far?"

"I've paid him seven times," Avery said.

"Plus three from me," Grace said.

"Ten thousand dollars total." And chances were, these weren't the only two girls Ted Spencer was pulling this particular game with. Warren leaned closer to the women, glancing around to make sure nobody was paying attention.

They weren't.

"I think I can help you, but not for two thousand. My rate is five. But—" He held up a finger to stop their dismayed protests. "*But*, you only pay me if I can get back the ten you've already paid him."

Avery put her hand over her mouth. "Can you do that?"

"Plus get him to stop?" Grace asked.

Warren smiled at them, although he knew the smile combined with his scars could be disarming. "I'll certainly do my best."

Chapter 4

Warren spent the rest of the evening and most of Monday learning everything he could about Ted Spencer.

Grace and Avery had told him Ted was a reporter on a local Denver news station—a fact that was easily confirmed. He was active on social media, which was enormously helpful to Warren. Warren used a couple of his fake accounts to follow Ted on Twitter and Instagram, and sent him a friend request on Facebook.

Ted accepted immediately, no questions asked.

He was thirty-four and engaged to a gorgeous brunette. It looked like the engagement had been going on for at least two years already. Stringing his fiancée along, or was there more to it than that? It was clear from his social media posts Ted thought of himself as something of a celebrity. He posted at least three selfies a day, and talked constantly about bumping into "fans." He also liked going out for drinks after work.

Warren developed a plan. He needed to act soon, before Ted demanded another payment from Avery and Grace.

"How would you feel about helping me out with something?" he asked Taylor on Tuesday over dinner. Taylor had fixed spaghetti, garlic bread, and salad. The sauce was out of a jar, the bread out of a box, and the salad out of a bag, but it was still one of the best dinners Warren had eaten in ages.

The mind-blowing sex certainly wasn't the only benefit to keeping Taylor around.

Taylor wiped his mouth with his napkin and sat back in his chair. They were in the kitchen, the window over the sink offering a spectacular view of the dead rose bush in Warren's backyard. He really needed to get rid of that stupid thing.

"Helping out how?" Taylor asked.

Warren hadn't quite thought through how to describe what he wanted done. "You'd be working with one of my clients, Candy."

"Are you trying to pimp me out?"

Was he? Yes and no. "Look, you can say no."

But once he'd spelled it all out, Taylor only smiled. "Sounds easy enough."

A couple hundred dollars slipped into the palm of a young intern at Ted's station ensured Ted would be at his favorite bar after work on Thursday. From there, Candy and Taylor took over. The biggest risk was that Ted might not take the bait, but whatever Candy and Taylor did worked perfectly. Ted left with them two hours later. Warren sat in his car, watching as they took Ted into the motel room Candy always used.

The camera was already set up, live-streaming to Warren's phone. He watched it all unfold from the front seat of his car, torn between arousal and amusement as Ted fell blindly into their trap. Taylor and Candy worked well together, stringing Ted out and leading him along until he was begging for all kinds of things.

It was perfect. In theory, catching Ted with a woman would have been enough, but in reality, this was better. Ted struck Warren as the type who took great pride in his conquests. Getting caught with a woman might have been inconvenient, but it wouldn't have threatened his entire world. He might even have turned it into something to brag about.

Getting caught on his knees, pleading for a chance to suck off a male prostitute?

That was blackmail gold for a guy like Ted. Fair or not, Warren knew Ted would be far more likely to pay up with Taylor in the picture.

An hour and a half later, Candy and Taylor slipped out the door. Warren handed Candy the five hundred dollars he'd promised her. She offered Taylor a ride home, but Taylor opted to wait for Warren. He settled into the passenger seat of the 4Runner and gave Warren a grin. "That was kind of fun, to be honest."

Warren shook his head. "You're insatiable."

"So what now? Take me home and tie me down for a while?"

Warren laughed. "That's a possibility. But first, I need to go have a little talk with our buddy Ted."

"Good luck."

Warren had parked as far from the room as he could while still having a clear view of the door. He felt Taylor's eyes on his back all the way across the asphalt. Finally, Warren leaned his big frame against the door, ready to shove his way inside. He knocked three times. "Room service."

Ted was actually stupid enough to open the door. "I didn't order any—"

One hard push was all it took to enter the room. Ted fell back a few steps, holding his hands up as if to protect himself. Warren closed the door behind him, shaking his head. "You really think a dump like this has room service?"

Ted had his work shirt on and buttoned, but other than that, he wore only boxers and black dress socks. His mouth opened and closed a few times, but nothing came out. Finally, he managed to stammer, "Wh-Who are you?"

Warren flexed his shoulders and grinned, letting Ted get a good look at his scars. "My name isn't really relevant."

"What do you want?"

"I want to talk about how you're going to get me ten thousand dollars, Ted."

Ted gulped. His cheeks began to turn red. He glanced toward the bedside table, where his phone sat. "I'm calling the cops."

Warren let him get so far as to pick the phone up before speaking.

"Good idea. Let's call the cops down here and tell them how you've been blackmailing two cheerleaders to the tune of a thousand dollars a week. Each." It hadn't taken much googling to figure out exactly which Denver organization the two women worked for. "I bet the cops would love an excuse to look into your finances. I wonder how many other victims they'll find, once it hits the news."

Ted winced. He set the phone very slowly back on the bedside table, as if it might accidentally call the police all on its own if he mishandled it. He ran his hands through his already messy hair. "I should have known this was a setup."

"You should have. But you didn't." Warren held up his phone and waggled it for Ted to see. "You wouldn't believe how well you can see everything on this little screen. That part where you snorted coke off Candy's stomach? She had you right in front of the camera." He pointed to the little blinking light, just barely hidden behind the TV. "Somebody as familiar with blackmail as you, I thought you'd be more careful, but you were just in too big of a hurry to get the pants off that underage male whore."

Ted gulped again. "He's underage?"

Warren shrugged. "Could be. Who's to say he isn't? Either way, I'd say the video of your evening here would be enough to make your poor, dearly departed mother roll over in her grave."

"My mother's still alive."

"Well, that's even better, isn't it? Mother's Day's just around the corner."

Ted sank slowly onto the bed. "Oh my God."

"Yes, you did say that a lot on this little video. Twenty-two times, by my count."

"Tell me what you want."

"Like I said, I want the ten thousand dollars Avery and Grace paid you, and I want it by tomorrow night."

Ted held his arms out, his eyes wide. "How am I supposed to come up with ten thousand dollars that fast?"

"Not my problem, Ted. Maybe you could call up some of your other victims and ask them how they come up with the money they pay you. I'm sure they have all kinds of advice."

Ted put his face in his hands. "Oh my God."

"Twenty-three."

"You can't do this to me," Ted groaned. "You can't!"

"I can, it seems. But unlike you, I won't be coming back week after week. You have one chance to make this all go away."

It took Ted a couple of long seconds, but he finally said, "I'm listening."

"I want the money by five o'clock tomorrow night. Take it to a place down on Colfax called Leroy's. You give it to Leroy, and tell him BJ's friend will be by to pick it up. If that doesn't happen?" Warren waggled the phone again. "I have a long list of places to send this video, starting with your mom and fiancée and ending with every other news station in Denver. I'm sure they'd love a chance to dish some dirt on the competition. You understand how this is going to work, Ted?"

Ted didn't take his face out of his hands, but he nodded. "Yes, I get it."

"If you ever contact Avery or Grace again, this home movie of mine goes viral. And if the videos you already have of Grace or Avery appear anywhere—and I mean anywhere from Pornhub to Tumblr—I'll know, and my video makes the evening broadcast. Are we clear?"

"Clear," Ted groaned. "Jesus Christ, I know how it works."

"Glad to hear it," Warren said. "I hate dealing with amateurs."

He whistled to himself as he walked back to his car, where Taylor waited.

"That went well," he said, as he settled into the driver's seat. He closed the door and glanced over at Taylor. "Who brought the coke?"

"Candy. I didn't do any."

"Good." He was glad. He wouldn't have kicked Taylor out for that—not when he'd been doing Warren a favor—but he was still glad it didn't have to be an issue. He pulled out his wallet and held five hundred-dollar bills over to Taylor. "Your cut."

Taylor eyed it but didn't move to take it. "I don't want it."

"Look, I'm not trying to insult you, but fair's fair. Candy got paid, and you should too. You did more than your share."

Taylor gripped his hands between his knees and stared resolutely at the dash, his cheeks slowly turning red.

Warren put his wallet away, slipped the money into his own breast pocket, and started the car. "Let's go home."

Taylor was oddly quiet the whole way, and Warren debated what to do to fix things. He hadn't meant to insult Taylor. He'd just figured it was only fair to give Taylor a cut. Hell, if he was being honest with himself, Taylor probably deserved more. He'd done the dirty work, so to speak. All Warren had done was flex his muscles and make a few threats.

It wasn't until they were home that Taylor came to him. Warren was on the couch, debating whether he had time for a nap before heading out for the night. Thursday nights, he protected a woman who went by the name of Taffy. She worked the streets more than any of his other clients. Warren would spend most of the night hiding in the shadows, watching as she serviced johns in their cars.

Taylor slipped quietly from his place on the other end of the couch and climbed into Warren's lap, straddling his thighs. He put his hands on Warren's shoulders.

Warren waited, unsure if this was Taylor initiating sex—although he was usually much bolder in his propositions—or if this was something else.

What Taylor said was, "Tell me why you do it."

Warren wrinkled his brow, confused. "Do what?"

"All the stuff you do. Guarding whores and helping people who don't want to call the cops."

"It's a job. That's all."

Taylor shook his head. "I don't think so."

Warren put his hand against Taylor's cheek. Taylor's driver's license listed his eye color as brown, but they were more like gold, almost the color of a lion's fur. Warren was struck by how young and delicate they made Taylor look. "Tell me why you don't want the money."

Taylor didn't even blink. "You first."

Warren dropped his hand and let his head fall back on the couch. "Why? It doesn't matter."

"I think it does to me."

"Fine." He hadn't even quite realized it himself for a long time. It had been Phil, Gray, and Charlie who had finally helped him understand. Still, he found it easier to stare at the hollow of Taylor's throat as he talked, rather than into those strangely beautiful eyes. "Technically, my dad was an electrician. But that was a cover more than anything."

"So what was he really?"

"A dealer. And a mean, abusive asshole." His mother had taken the brunt of the abuse until Warren became a teenager. After that, it was almost as if they took turns. "You know, it wasn't like the movies where it was constant. He'd be totally normal for months at a time, but then something would set him off." Warren shook his head. "There was one time when I was about twelve, I honestly thought he was going to kill my mother. I went to call the cops, but my mother yelled for me not to. As he's beating her, and she's bleeding all over the floor, she's yelling, 'Not the cops, Warren!'"

"Because of all the drugs in the house?"

Warren nodded. "Yes. No matter what he did to her, she didn't want him going to jail."

Taylor touched Warren's cheek. "See? The reason does matter."

Not from where Warren sat, but it wasn't worth arguing about. "Your turn."

Taylor sighed, but to Warren's surprise, his lips curved into the barest hint of a smile. "I went to that room because you and I have an agreement. Whatever you want in exchange for room and board. So I didn't earn that money."

It'd only been a week, but hearing their "agreement" spelled out so matter-of-factly made Warren cringe. He shook his head. "No. We agreed on sex—with *me*—in exchange for room and board. Nothing about that includes what you did tonight."

"I didn't mind."

"That isn't the point. And I think there's more to it than that."

Taylor bit his lip, his head tilted to the side. "Okay." He moved his fingers gently over Warren's face, touching each scar in turn, as if making sure they were real. "I don't want you to get mad, though, all right? I feel like we have a good thing going here. I don't want to mess it up by telling you the truth."

That certainly piqued Warren's curiosity. "I'll do my best."

Taylor sighed and rested his hands on Warren's chest. "I have money."

Warren blinked at him, trying to decide how those three words fit into the conversation. "You have money? What do you mean? Like, money you've stolen?"

"No. It's mine."

"A lot of money? Are you telling me you're secretly rich or something?"

Taylor laughed. "No, nothing like that. It's a trust fund, but—"

"*What?*"

"No, wait." He held up one hand. "Everybody gets the wrong idea when they hear that term, but it's not like you think. I mean, it's money, yeah. But it's not like I'm filthy rich. It was supposed to be for college, but when it became glaringly obvious I'd never get that far, my dad put it into an account for me."

"How much money are we talking about here?"

"About eighteen grand."

"Wow." Taylor was right. It was far less than Warren had assumed upon hearing the words "trust fund." It wasn't enough to live on indefinitely. Still, it wasn't pocket change. "So, what does that have to do with the five hundred dollars?"

And why, if he had almost twenty grand in the bank, was he trading sex for room and board?

"The thing is, I hate using it. My dad still has access to it. He knows every time I touch it. He's used it before to find me. I feel like every dollar I spend is a big white flag telling him what a failure his son is. So I only use it if I really have to. Like, if I have no place else to stay and it's too cold to sleep outside. That kind of thing."

Warren nodded, although he was still reeling, trying to figure out how this fit in with whatever Taylor was trying to tell him. "So why would that make me mad?"

"Some guys feel like I cheated them, once they realize I'm not penniless. But I never lied about it."

Warren pursed his lips, considering. It was odd, choosing to work as a hustler rather than using what had been given to him, but in the end, it didn't change a thing. They had an arrangement. Plus, Taylor was right when he said they had a good thing going. Sure, they'd known each other less than a week, and yes, Warren woke up every day wondering if that would be the day Taylor disappeared from his life forever. But knowing he had money stashed away somewhere didn't change how he felt.

He liked having the kid around, and not just because the sex was damned good.

Although that sure didn't hurt either.

"Some guys start wanting rent," Taylor said. "Or they want me to pay my part of the groceries. I guess in some ways that's fair, but I won't use that money. Not unless I really have to."

"It's fine," Warren said. "We're fine. You don't need to explain. As far as I'm concerned, we're in exactly the same place we were before." He slipped his fingers into his pocket and pulled out the five hundred-dollar bills. "But you earned this, fair and square. This isn't about your dad or whatever battles you're fighting with him. And it isn't about us, and whether or not you're earning your keep. It's about you doing your part to help me bring home five thousand dollars. I think a ten percent cut is—well, frankly, it's probably fucking cheap, if we're being honest. You could ask for fifty, but—"

"No." Taylor smiled, shaking his head. He gnawed his lip again, considering. "Ten percent, huh?"

"That's what the math says."

"It doesn't sound so bad when you say it that way."

"Candy didn't balk about taking hers, I'll tell you that. As far as I'm concerned, you both more than earned it."

Taylor's grin grew. He slowly took the five hundred dollars out of Warren's hand. "Okay. I think you've talked me into it."

"Good."

Taylor leaned forward, his eyes taking on a seductive glint that was already familiar to Warren. He stopped short of kissing Warren, though—he always did. His hand drifted down Warren's chest to caress his groin.

"All that work with Candy and Ted, but I never did come."

"I noticed."

"Want to tie me down and see if you can do better?"

Warren laughed. "I thought you'd never ask."

Chapter 5

Taylor spent most of Friday alone. He'd had only a couple of hours with Warren the night before, then Warren had been out the door to protect Taffy for the night. Taylor heard him come home around four in the morning, but Warren hadn't come to Taylor's room like he sometimes did. He'd gone straight to bed and slept until noon. He was gone again less than three hours after waking, and being Friday, Taylor knew he likely wouldn't be home for at least another twelve hours.

Taylor settled in for a long evening.

He would have liked to go out for dinner. Not anything fancy, necessarily, but he didn't feel like cooking when Warren wouldn't be home to eat with him. If only Warren had given him permission to drive the other car, but he hadn't, and Taylor wouldn't risk upsetting him over something like that. Warren's house wasn't within easy walking distance of anything interesting, and Taylor abhorred the city bus. Better to just make the best of his day alone.

It was just after five when the doorbell rang.

Taylor loved when people came to the door. After years of sitting around other men's homes, waiting for them to return, he'd learned to take his entertainment where he could. A door-to-door salesman was always good for a few minutes of distraction before admitting it wasn't his house, and no, he didn't know when the owner would be back. Sometimes he told them he'd only broken in for the afternoon, just to see whether or not they believed him. He loved Mormon missionaries too—those poor, sexually repressed young men walking or bicycling from house to house, trying to spread the word of God. Taylor enjoyed seeing how blatantly he could flirt with them before they went running for the hills. He'd once explained to a pair of them in graphic detail how to Eiffel Tower somebody. He'd worried one was about to have a coronary on the doorstep, but he thought the other had been intrigued. He was quite sure he could have talked him into trying it, if it hadn't been for his more prudent companion.

Anytime the doorbell rang, Taylor wondered what could happen. Over the years, he'd talked a Schwann's driver out of frozen treats, signed a dozen political petitions with false names, and had nearly made a woman passing out pamphlets for the Jehovah's Witnesses faint dead away on the front porch.

But when Taylor opened the door this time, he found an older version of Warren standing on the step. The likeness was uncanny. The man, whose name tag said "Bill," was just as big as Warren, although without the scars or the consummate glower. The white van parked at the curb pronounced him an employee of Harper and Sons Electricians.

"Oh." The man fell back a step, clearly caught off guard. "Uh, is Warren home?"

"No. Are you his dad?"

The man scowled, looking so much like Warren that Taylor almost laughed. "Hell no. I'm his uncle. On his *mother's* side."

That latter seemed to be important, given the emphasis. "Oh. Uncle Bill. He mentioned you once, I think." Not really, but whatever.

Bill glanced past Taylor, into the house. "I just finished up a job around the block. Thought I'd stop by, since I'm in the neighborhood."

"I'm sorry you missed him. Do you want to come in?"

Bill laughed. "Well, I could sure use a pit stop, to tell the truth."

"Sure." Taylor stood aside to let him in. "Help yourself."

Taylor waited awkwardly in the living room while Bill made use of the bathroom. Warren never talked about his family, and Taylor wondered if he'd made a mistake, inviting Bill in, when he was little more than a guest himself.

Bill returned, still patting his hands dry on his jeans, and it occurred to Taylor there might not even be towels in the main bath. He and Warren each had their own bathrooms and rarely used the one in the hallway. Bill stared at him expectantly, and Taylor said the first thing that popped into his head.

"Do you want a beer or something?"

Bill raised his eyebrows. "Is there beer in the house? Warren doesn't usually drink it."

"There're a couple in the back of the fridge. They've been there since—" He stopped short. He'd been about to say, *since I moved in*, but luckily, Bill went ahead and answered.

"Sure. A beer would really hit the spot."

Taylor went to the kitchen and pulled one from its resting place on the back of the top shelf. It wasn't a twist top, so he dug out the bottle opener and popped the lid. He turned to find Bill watching him.

"Guess you know your way around Warren's kitchen pretty well."

"I guess." Taylor handed him the bottle, wishing now he'd simply told him Warren wasn't home and sent him on his way.

"So, are you..." Bill let the question hang.

"Am I what?" *Your nephew's current boy toy? Yes.* But that didn't seem like the right thing to say.

"Well, I don't mean to pry. Just that Warren hasn't had anybody around since Stuart left. 'Course maybe there's been some I didn't know about." He took a hesitant drink of his beer. "You're the new boyfriend, then?"

"*Boyfriend?*" Taylor never thought of himself that way. The word carried implications he wasn't comfortable with. He crossed his arms, feeling inexplicably exposed in Warren's ruthlessly clean kitchen. "I'm not sure."

"You're not sure? How can you not be sure?"

How could Taylor answer that? He didn't want to spill out the exact truth in case it caused trouble for Warren, but he didn't want to mislead Bill either. "We've only been seeing each other a little while now, that's all. It's a bit early to label it, if you know what I mean."

"So you can move in, but you can't label it?"

Taylor's cheeks began to burn. "What makes you think I've moved in?"

"Haven't you?"

"I stay the night sometimes." That seemed like a safe enough answer.

Bill ducked his head and took a step backward. "Look, I'm sorry. I didn't mean any of that the way it sounded." He drained half the bottle in one swig and set it on the counter.

"And how do you think it sounded?" Taylor asked.

"Like I was judging you for it."

"Weren't you?"

"The two of you live in a different world than the one I grew up in, that's all. But after all the shit Warren's had go wrong in his life, I can't blame him for wanting to have a bit of fun."

Taylor was desperate to ask questions. What shit? What went wrong in Warren's life? Taylor knew almost nothing of Warren's history, but he felt like asking Bill anything would be a betrayal of some kind, so he kept his questions to himself.

Bill eyed Taylor up and down. "Do you make him happy?"

Taylor smiled, thinking about the many ways that question could be interpreted. "I do my best."

"Well, good enough for me, I guess. He deserves a bit of happiness." He glanced around the house, as if expecting to find Warren hiding somewhere. "Can you give him a message for me?"

"Of course."

"Tell him Jeff's getting married in a few months. June fourteenth. He'll get an invitation in a month or two. But after that, Jeff's moving to Idaho with his wife. And Roger and Greg quit, so—"

"Wait." Taylor was never going to remember all those names. He pulled a notepad and pen out of the top drawer and began scribbling as fast as he could. "Jeff getting married. June fourteenth. Idaho. Roger and Craig—"

"Greg."

"Greg. Sorry. Roger and Greg quit." He looked up at Bill. "Is that all?"

"Well, no. The thing is, I could really use Warren back. I sort of hoped to retire in the next few years, but Harper and Sons is all out of sons now. I'd rather pass it to a nephew than have the whole thing go to waste, you know?"

Taylor swallowed, realizing he'd somehow landed himself right in the middle of a little family drama. "I'll tell him."

"Thanks."

Taylor followed him into the living room, where Bill stopped at the bookshelf, staring at one of the knickknacks for a second. Taylor was beginning to worry the man might hang around all evening, but Bill turned then and gave him a small wave. "Thanks again for the beer."

Taylor watched him climb back into the Harper and Sons van and drive away. He'd been anxious for him to leave, but now he wished he'd had the nerve to ask more questions. He found himself at the bookshelf, studying the item Bill had stopped to look at.

It was a small black ceramic vase, with a round, bulbous bottom like an onion and a top that narrowed to a skinny opening. Taylor hadn't paid it much mind in the week he'd been living with Warren, but now, he saw why Bill had stopped to stare.

It was broken, and yet...

It had been mended.

Taylor took it carefully from the shelf, studying it. The round bottom fit perfectly in his palm. Somebody had pieced the parts back together, but rather than using Super Glue and trying to hide the cracks, they'd used some type of metallic gold resin, allowing it to form thick, shiny bands, highlighting each mended seam.

It was beautiful, and in Warren's strangely bare house, it seemed significant. Rather than ruining the vase, the cracks had become the very thing that made it special, and Taylor found himself thinking about the scars on Warren's face. Taylor knew people shied away from Warren in the grocery store. They sometimes didn't make eye contact. Warren used those scars to his advantage when dealing with people like Ted, but sometimes, Taylor wanted only to smooth those scars away, to see what kind of man Warren might have been if he'd never had them.

Would he still bring home a whore and give him a place to live?

Maybe Warren was better with the scars after all.

The back door banged open, causing Taylor to jump.

"Warren? Is that you?"

The next instant, Warren strode into sight. "Who else would it be?" He eyed Taylor, who still held the vase in his hands. "What are you doing with that?"

"Nothing. I just— I hadn't noticed it before, the way the cracks are the pretty part. I've never seen anything like it."

"My friend Charlie gave it to me."

"You have so few things. Is it an antique or something?"

"It's just a vase."

"Oh." Taylor placed it carefully back on the shelf, wondering if Warren was being frank, or if he was deflecting. It was hard to tell with him. Taylor opted to let it go and focus on the obvious. "You're home early."

"Yeah, but only for a minute." Warren passed Taylor on his way to the coat closet. "Forecast says snow on the way, and I wasn't planning on standing outside in a blizzard when I left the house." He pulled out a coat, a hat, and a pair of mittens. "Snow means it'll be a slow night for the girls, though."

"So, you'll be home early?"

"Maybe."

"Did Ted leave the money like you told him?"

Warren grinned at him as he closed the closet. "He did indeed. Made those cheerleaders happy, I can tell you that. Now we just have to hope he keeps up the other end of the bargain and leaves them alone."

"How many other women do you think he's done that to?"

Warren rubbed the scar on his jaw. "Too many." He crossed the living room in four long steps and stopped short just inside the kitchen, staring at the countertop. "What's this?"

He picked up the pad Taylor had taken notes on, and Taylor's heart jumped into high gear. He rushed into the kitchen, reaching for the note. "Your uncle—"

But Warren pulled the notepad out of Taylor's reach, his brow wrinkling as he struggled to read it, and Taylor's heart sank.

"I was going to read it to you."

Warren turned his dark gaze on Taylor, and Taylor wished he could shrink away to nothing rather than face the next few minutes.

"Please don't say anything."

A few slow seconds ticked by with neither of them speaking, but finally, Warren handed him the note. Taylor looked down at it, trying to figure out how many mistakes he'd made. He'd been in a hurry, and even he could see that at least a few of the letters were backward.

"Jeff's getting married on June fourteenth. He said you'll get an invitation soon. And then he's moving to Idaho. And Roger and Craig—"

"Greg."

"Right." Bill had even corrected him, but Taylor's scribbled attempt to correct it left the name illegible. "He said they quit, and he could really use you back."

Taylor didn't look up, but he could feel Warren's eyes on him. He desperately wanted to hide the traitorous notepad behind his back. People always threw the word "dyslexic" at him. That was probably part of it, but he'd never been diagnosed.

Still, it wasn't like he couldn't read. He could. It was just that words seemed to move around on him. Things like menus were easy enough, and graphic novels, where the text was all different sizes and with plenty of pictures to help him keep his place. But big blocks of text, like the ones in Warren's spy novels, always gave him trouble. He never understood how people managed to make their eyes go to the right place when they reached the end of a line of text. For him, the rows seemed to move up and down on the page. He always felt he was chasing them with his eyes, trying to pin them into place only to have them shift again. After only a page or two, he was always left with aching eyes and a pounding headache.

But still—he could read just fine. "Dyslexia" was an annoying word, but "illiterate" was far worse. He wasn't that, and if Warren said that word to him—

"Okay," Warren said.

Taylor risked a glance up at him. "What do you mean, 'okay'?"

"I mean, okay, I get it. All Bill's sons are gone, and he wants me to go work for him again. And okay, I guess I have a damn wedding to go to in June, unless I can find a decent reason to ditch it."

Taylor swallowed, the tension that had built up in his shoulders and jaws slowly giving way to relief. "That's all?"

"I don't know. Is that all, or did he say more?"

He asked if I was your boyfriend. He said you deserved to be happy. But both of those things felt too personal. He'd known Warren exactly a week, but he struck Taylor as the kind of guy who didn't like being put on the spot.

Taylor glanced at his note. It was mostly legible, he thought. Still, he'd be happy when he could throw it away. He wondered what Warren would say if he knew how carefully Taylor had worked on the one-word note he'd left on his bedroom door that first night. The word "anytime" contained only seven letters, but Taylor had been very careful not to get any of them backward.

"No, that's all."

Warren stepped closer, still staring at Taylor as if trying to bring him into focus. He put his hand on Taylor's shoulder and bent to plant a kiss on his forehead. "You did good."

It was a weird thing to say, and yet it warmed Taylor from the inside. "I did?"

"So far as I can tell, you always do."

He turned to go, and Taylor found himself smiling. "Don't be afraid to wake me when you get home."

Warren laughed as he let himself out the back door. "Careful what you wish for, kid."

Chapter 6

The next few weeks rolled by without incident for Warren. March progressed with its usual crankiness, reminding Warren of his grandmother. She'd always cursed the third month for making promises of spring but never following through. *"The slowest month,"* she'd always said. *"We should take two weeks away from it and give them to October."*

The only good thing about March was that it always ended eventually. With April only a week away, Warren couldn't help but count the days as his grandmother had done, testing the breeze for a hint of summer.

In the meantime, odd jobs came and went. One man paid Warren to follow his boyfriend, who was in town all week but always disappeared on the weekends. Warren's client feared he was having an affair. Warren felt like an ass reporting three days later that although the boyfriend's job kept him in Denver from Monday through Friday, he had a wife and three children in Laramie who he went home to every weekend. Another woman paid Warren to break into her ex's house and steal back her jewelry. A prostitute paid him to make sure her former pimp kept his distance. Another woman paid him to help her and her three children, all under the age of four, move into a shelter while her husband was at work. She didn't have any money, but presented him with a pan of homemade tamales as payment.

None of it was new to him. He'd seen it all before.

Every morning, Warren woke up and glanced into Taylor's room, expecting to find it empty, but it never was. With each passing day, Warren found himself more confused as to why Taylor ended up on the streets so often. The kid was the perfect roommate. He cooked, he cleaned up after himself, and he was the most enthusiastic sexual partner Warren had ever had. What in the world was it that made other men kick him to the curb?

It puzzled Warren, but he wasn't naive enough to assume he knew the whole story. Still, he enjoyed having Taylor around. They were surprisingly compatible. Taylor never complained about Warren's strange hours. He never griped about having to stay quiet for half the day while Warren caught up on his sleep. And when they found themselves with spare time together that wasn't spent in bed, they watched movies. With an almost fifteen-year age difference between them, they often stumbled across titles only one of them had seen.

Taylor was particularly fond of romantic comedies. They weren't Warren's favorite—he was more of an action kind of guy—but he liked watching Taylor get all teary-eyed over what passed for true love on film. Taylor also had a stash of well-worn graphic novels he pulled out on occasion. He seemed embarrassed by them and usually slid them under the couch or behind the cushion the minute Warren came in the room, as if he expected to be chastised. Warren chose to let him think he hadn't noticed. He also chose not to bring up Taylor's dyslexia, if that was what it was. The issue of illiteracy wasn't as black and white as people liked to believe. Between "illiterate" and "normal" lay a thousand miles of gray. Wherever Taylor fell in that expanse, Warren figured it was none of his business. Besides, he liked having Taylor around, and bringing it up would only make him uncomfortable.

All in all, things were good, and that scared the hell out of Warren.

At some point, it had to change. Like Phil had said, things were always good, right up until they weren't. But as the days trickled by, Warren admitted to himself he didn't want Taylor to leave. Sometimes, after they'd had sex but before Warren moved to his own bed, he lay there, watching Taylor sleep. He found himself wondering when an "arrangement" became a relationship.

It wasn't a topic he was ready to bring up.

One night, he came home to find Taylor curled into the corner of the couch, reading one of his graphic novels. He was wrapped in a faux fur blanket Warren hadn't seen in ages.

"You're home early," Taylor said, quickly sliding the graphic novel under the couch cushion as if he'd been caught with some kind of twisted porn rather than a graphic rendition of a bestselling YA novel.

Warren bypassed the closet and went straight to the couch. He took the book out from under the cushion and put it on the coffee table. "You don't have to hide stuff from me."

Taylor's cheeks turned red as he eyed the book. "Some people make fun of me for it."

Warren shook his head as he backtracked to the coat closet. "You have my permission to kick those people in the 'nads. Even if 'those people' ends up meaning me." He was glad when Taylor laughed at that. "Where'd you get that blanket?" He assumed Stuart had taken it with him when he'd left.

"I found it in a box under my bed. I hope it's okay that I'm using it."

It had been Stuart's, but somehow, it suited Taylor better. "It's fine."

"Is it cold out there? You look like you're freezing."

Even late in the month, March was always a mixed bag in Colorado. Some nights, it was warm enough to sleep with the windows open, but not this night. It'd been bitterly cold out, threatening snow, and Warren happily shed his many layers into the coat closet. "It could be worse."

"Come over here and I'll warm you up."

Warren laughed and settled on the couch next to Taylor. He slid his hand into Taylor's little faux fur cocoon to find nothing but hot, smooth flesh.

Taylor grinned at him, letting the blanket fall aside. He was completely bare underneath the fur, and utterly irresistible. He was like some kind of mythological being—a male seductress with supernatural powers—and Warren was powerless against him. Magical enchantment seemed like the only explanation for what Taylor had done to him. He'd become insatiable. He couldn't go a single day without stripping Taylor bare and having him in one way or another. He'd never felt so young and so old at the same time, trying to keep up with somebody almost fifteen years his junior. Not since he and Stuart had first met had he felt so consumed by the simple thought of sex with one specific person.

Now, faced with such raw sensuality, he could do nothing but fall into Taylor's arms with a moan. He was desperate to be inside him. At least he wasn't the only one so driven. Taylor tore at Warren's clothes in his impatience. Warren ended up with his shirt unbuttoned but still on, his pants around his knees as he spread Taylor's legs and pushed inside.

A month they'd been together, and Warren loved the way Taylor moaned every time Warren penetrated him. He loved the way Taylor fit in his arms. He loved the way Taylor responded to him, whether Warren was gentle or rough. He didn't think it was feigned either. Taylor truly seemed to enjoy the sex as much as Warren, even if he only let himself climax half as often. Warren held Taylor close, kissing his neck, trying to push as deep as he could. He found himself looking into Taylor's golden eyes as they moved together, wondering if Taylor could tell how Warren's feelings were trying to get the better of him.

Jesus, could he really be falling for this boy?

He was suddenly desperate to kiss him. All the times they'd had sex, they'd hardly ever kissed. Taylor always turned Warren away, subtly distracting him from kissing by offering something else, but right then, having his way with Taylor on the couch on a ridiculous faux fur blanket that had once belonged to Warren's ex, he wanted more.

He brushed his lips over Taylor's, and Taylor put his hands against Warren's chest, pushing him away. They were still moving, still doing something halfway between making love and outright fucking, but Taylor's eyes suddenly held something that looked like alarm.

Warren slowed his thrusts. He slid one hand down to stroke Taylor's erection.

But with the other hand, he grabbed a handful of Taylor's hair and forced him into a kiss.

Taylor's groan was half arousal, half aggravation. Warren wondered for a moment if he should stop—if this was unfair of him, forcing this intimacy on Taylor—but the very next instant, Taylor made a soft sound of surrender. He put his arms around Warren's neck, parted his lips, and let Warren in.

It felt like some kind of breakthrough. Warren sank into the kiss. Taylor's throaty moans came faster as Warren kissed him harder, his thrusts becoming more urgent. He wanted to taste every inch of Taylor, but not enough to stop what was already happening. He found himself wanting to whisper in Taylor's ear, wanting to say things he hadn't said in years. Things he'd almost vowed never to say again. Mostly, though, he just wanted to hold on to this moment forever.

Still, no matter how Warren tried to keep his orgasms at bay, he always came first. Each time, he wondered how it could be this good. He wondered when Taylor would get tired of him and move on.

Taylor held him after his climax, staring into Warren's eyes. There seemed to be a question there, and Warren didn't know what to say. How the hell this perfect person had fallen so easily into his life was a mystery to him, and he was afraid to examine it too closely. All he knew was he didn't want this amazing little interlude in his boring, bleak life to end.

Taylor touched his soft fingertip to each of Warren's scars in turn—the bridge of his nose, the side of his jaw, and finally ending with the one on Warren's left eyebrow.

"Tell me how you got them." It was a soft whisper.

"In Afghanistan."

Taylor wrinkled his brow. He pointed to the bookshelf. "You have textbooks from the University of Wyoming."

"I know."

"So you went to college?"

"For two years."

"Was the war before or after that?"

Warren sighed, letting his waning erection slide free. Still, Taylor held him, watching him, silently pleading for some kind of answer. "My grandmother and my mom both died the summer after my sophomore year." There was more to it than that, but he didn't want to get into it. "It messed me up pretty good, I guess, because I didn't enroll the next fall. That was 2001. I enlisted on September thirteenth, two days after the Towers came down."

"How long were you there?"

"Four years."

"And the scars?"

"It was my third tour." And something he still dreamed about more than he would have liked. "These days, everybody knows what an IED is, but at the time, they were still kind of new. The Humvees we had may as well have been made of cardboard, for all the protection they gave us. We'd Frankenstein scrap metal onto them whenever we could. They called it 'hillbilly armor,' but it didn't do much good."

"You hit one?"

"My friend Terry was in the lead vehicle. Gray and I were right behind him in our own Humvee."

"So, Terry hit it?"

Warren nodded. "The blast blew out our windshield."

"The glass cut you?"

"Glass or debris or shrapnel. I don't know for sure. I don't remember anything except coming to sometime later with a broken nose and blood all over my face. Gray says I saved his life, but I don't remember any of it." He still couldn't get over how lopsided it was. He and Gray walked away with a few cuts and mild concussions. Meanwhile, their friend Terry and the nineteen-year-old boy riding with him had literally been blown to pieces. Every time Warren looked in the mirror, he was reminded how lucky he'd been.

And how selfish.

"I'm sorry," Taylor said.

"You were, what? Twelve years old when it happened?" He laughed. "I don't think you get any of the blame."

Taylor touched Warren's cheek. He seemed strangely hesitant, and Warren still felt there was a question Taylor wasn't sure how to ask.

"What is it?" Warren asked. "Are you upset that I kissed you?"

"No." Taylor shook his head, and to Warren's surprise, his eyes filled with tears. "Why would that upset me?"

"I don't know. Maybe for the same reason you're suddenly about to cry. Tell me what's wrong."

Taylor wiped at his eyes, but they only filled again. He took a deep breath. Finally, he said, so quietly Warren could barely hear him, "I don't usually…"

"Don't usually what?"

"Feel this way."

Warren kissed him again, caressing him, trying to encourage him without prying. "What way?"

"I don't want—" Taylor had to stop and force another deep breath. "I don't want to have to leave."

Warren found himself smiling. He wanted to take Taylor down the hall—to Warren's bed, which they never slept in—and fall asleep with him in his arms. "Then don't. It seems simple enough to me."

Tears spilled out of Taylor's eyes. "I need to tell you something, Warren. And I'm afraid once you know the truth, you'll hate me."

"I doubt that."

"You will. I know you will, and I won't even blame you." He touched Warren's cheek again, as if trying to ground himself. "The thing is, I lied to you. On that first day—"

"About when you were last tested?"

Taylor's breath caught. "You knew?"

"I suspected."

Taylor's brow wrinkled, his eyes moving back and forth as he debated what to say next. "It's not like I've never been tested. It's just that the last time was more like October or November. Most guys use protection, but it's never been something I insisted on."

"I figured."

"But, why?" Taylor sniffled, shaking his head. "If you knew, why bring me home at all? Why go bareback? Why would you risk that?"

"Because I was supposed to be in Terry's Humvee that day." It was something he'd resisted talking about when he'd first come home, but he knew now it was better to let it out than to keep it in. "I swapped with the driver of the second car right before we headed out because Terry was in a shit-ass mood. His girl had just sent him a Dear John, and I didn't want to listen to him bitch all the way across the goddamn desert. And so this greener-than-grass nineteen-year-old recruit sat shotgun with Terry instead. They died because of me."

Taylor put his hand against Warren's cheek. "You can't blame yourself for that. You had no way of knowing."

It was the same thing Gray told him over and over. Still, it didn't make it any easier to stomach what he'd done. Maybe if Warren had been riding shotgun like he was supposed to, he would have seen the IED before Terry hit it.

Then again, maybe not. Maybe the only difference would have been that Warren would have ended up in pieces and the new recruit would have lived with nothing to show but a few scars on his face.

Either way, every day since then felt like borrowed time. Sometimes the burden was just too heavy. On those days, there was no such thing as "too risky" for Warren. Facing a whole lifetime of nothing but bitter memories seemed like a fate worse than death. What was a little unprotected sex when he'd already lived more than a decade too long?

He looked into Taylor's tearful eyes. Should he try to explain?

Warren suspected Taylor knew how it felt not to care one way or another whether he lived or died. After all, Taylor had agreed to bareback without even asking Warren's HIV status. They'd both chosen to gamble with their lives.

Yes, it'd been stupid. Crazy, even. He knew it, but sometimes it just didn't matter. The minute Taylor left, Warren knew he'd do it again. He'd be as reckless as ever.

Still.

Warren used the backs of his fingers to dry Taylor's tears. "We can go to the clinic together, first thing in the morning. Then we'll both know for sure."

"Really? You don't hate me?"

"Not even close." When he'd first brought Taylor home, he'd thought of him as little more than a whore. Now, he was Warren's entire reason for wanting to live.

Falling for Taylor was probably the most reckless thing he'd ever done.

Chapter 7

Sometimes Taylor knew what triggered his dark moods. Other times, it was a mystery. Sometimes they came on like tidal waves, barreling him over. Other times, they crept in like the tide, until he was drowning without knowing why.

This time was somewhere in between.

It was a Tuesday, and Warren was gone for the day. Taylor didn't know where he was or what he was doing, other than that it was what counted as "work" for him. Taylor was restless, and his restlessness made him edgy.

Their visit to the clinic the week before had assured them both they were two of the luckiest people in Denver. How they'd both managed to be so careless for so long without either of them contracting anything was a wonder to Taylor. Warren shrugged the whole thing off as if it didn't matter. Taylor tried to play it cool, but once Warren wasn't looking, he'd locked himself in his room and bawled like a baby.

He'd been a bit of an emotional basket case ever since.

He knew Warren didn't understand. Even worse, he knew his sudden moodiness had Warren worried. But the truth was, Taylor was falling for Warren, and falling hard. He hadn't made that mistake in a long time. And sometimes, when Warren looked into his eyes, he wondered if Warren was falling for him too.

But why would he? Taylor was trash—a man who exchanged sex for a warm place to sleep. Men like Warren didn't fall in love with people like Taylor. And even if Warren was stupid enough to make that mistake, Taylor was bound to screw it up.

He always did.

And if he was going to screw it up, maybe it'd be better to do it sooner rather than later. Maybe it'd be better to have Warren send him packing before he fell too hard. A little pain now to avoid a whole lot more pain later.

It made sense, but the thought was like a cold nugget of ice in his heart.

He turned on the TV, hoping to stop his downward spiral before it got too bad. *Supernatural* was on, and Taylor almost changed the channel. He hated *Supernatural*. He hated watching those brothers, who sometimes bickered and argued but always came back to each other in the end. He hated it for reasons he was only partially willing to admit—because he missed his own brother, but the world told him he shouldn't. He wanted to change the channel, but something stopped him, and the rage began to brew.

He suddenly didn't want to be at Warren's.

He wanted to go away. He longed to go back to Leroy's, where men shoved him down and did things to him they later didn't like to admit. He wanted to go to a club and let the men line up just to have their turn with him.

Would Warren care? Would he even notice that Taylor was gone?

No, he tried to tell himself. *You don't want to leave.*

Deep down, he knew it was true. He liked it here. He had his own room and his own bath and nobody trying to enforce any stupid rules. He adored Warren, who sometimes used him hard, but in the way Taylor found utterly gratifying. Some nights, Warren came home late. Taylor would wake up being dragged to the edge of the mattress where Warren would take him with a few hard thrusts before staggering into his own room and falling into bed. He always apologized for it later, no matter how many times Taylor told him he didn't mind. Other nights, Warren was gentle and tender. Sometimes, he spent a wonderfully extended period of time focusing only on making Taylor come.

Whichever way it went, Taylor loved it. They fit each other well. Warren's quiet, almost brutal sexual drive suited Taylor, who loved having a bit of force used against him.

So why was he suddenly angry?

Because of those stupid brothers.

Because of his own stupid brother.

A familiar darkness roiled in his chest, turning what had seemed like a good thing into a bad one. Warren left him here while he went out. Warren didn't care. Warren never asked about Taylor's day. Where before Taylor had seen freedom, suddenly he saw iron bars on his lovely cage. What right did Warren have to leave him here like this?

It was childish. He knew it, so he tried to redirect the dark energy in his heart. He went to work in the kitchen, scrubbing the floor, trying to pour all his frustration into something useful, but Warren was scrupulously neat. The floor didn't need scrubbing. Neither did the toilets or the tubs or the dishes. Taylor had nothing to give. He was worthless. He had no purpose, other than to be fucked. He had no reason to live, other than that he didn't know how to die. If he had a razor blade, he would have grabbed it and cut a few clean, hot slashes across his thigh, but he knew there were none in the house.

And still those stupid brothers were on the TV with their smiles and their angsty laughter and their fucking *purpose*, always running around saving the world. Taylor wanted to grab a kitchen chair and smash the TV, but it wasn't glass. He didn't even know if a chair would hurt it. Plus, it was Warren's. Warren would be mad. And if Warren was mad…

If Warren was mad…

And then the darkness boiled over and raged and took on a new, raw edge.

Taylor hadn't ever seen Warren angry, but he could picture it. Warren was big and strong, and he'd spent four years overseas, a chip on his shoulder, and a gun in his hands. If

Warren was mad, he might slam Taylor down on the table like he had that first day. He might hit him, or whip him with one of the things from the closet. Maybe Warren would tie Taylor down and really hurt him this time, or hold Taylor's face into the mattress until he could no longer breathe.

A thousand possibilities, and each one filled Taylor with a euphoric sense of finality. He wanted Warren to be angry. He *needed* Warren to be angry. Because if Warren wasn't angry—if he wouldn't do what Taylor needed—Taylor would have no choice but to leave. He'd have no choice but to go back to what he'd done before. But he wanted it to be Warren, not some stranger. Whether Warren fucked him or beat him or both, at least Taylor would have a purpose and his rage would be gone.

He ripped Warren's TV off the wall and let it crash to the ground. He stomped on it until something cracked and broke. The thought of whatever punishment this might merit made his pulse race. He grew hard in the tight confines of his jeans. He hoped Warren would beat him for it. Then fuck him. Or beat him while he fucked him. That'd be good too. Just as long as Warren hurt him. Just as long as Warren did what needed to be done.

But it felt like Warren had been gone for ages. When would he be home?

Taylor almost sobbed in frustration. He was coming apart from the inside, the black rage turning the world upside down, each second feeling like a horrible, slow eternity. He pictured himself drowning in minutes, choking on time, so desperate for this to be over, he couldn't wait for it to start.

He wanted to be punished. He *needed* to be punished.

And finally, Warren walked through the door.

Taylor flew at him, grabbing him when he was only halfway into the kitchen, practically crying in his desperation.

"I need you to fuck me, Warren. I need it. Please, God, I need it. I really need you to tie me down and beat me and fuck me." He was reckless, babbling in his need, frantic for Warren to understand. "Now. It has to be now. It has to be hard and fast and mean—"

But Warren did everything slow. He was careful and purposeful. He laughed, taking Taylor's wrists in his strong hands. "Okay, kid. Hang on. Just let me—"

"No!" Taylor shoved him hard with both hands. "No! I'm tired of waiting. I need this. I need it. Don't you see?"

He was shaking, almost panicking in his need to explain, tears spilling out of his eyes. It had exactly the wrong effect. Warren tried to soothe him, tried to pull him into his arms, saying things like "calm down," trying to offer comfort when what Taylor needed was pain. And Taylor pushed and fought and cried and begged. Warren wasn't helping at all! And then—

"What happened to the TV?"

The TV.

What had happened to the TV?

How could Warren care what happened to his stupid fucking TV when Taylor was being ripped apart from the inside? Taylor shoved him hard, screaming, "Why don't you just fuck me?"

"Taylor—"

"Or hit me!" He shoved Warren again. And again. And again, screaming, "Hit me! Just hit me! That's all I need. If you won't fuck me, at least hit me!"

"Taylor, stop." Warren tried to grab his wrists to stop him from shoving. Taylor went crazy, jerking his hands free, desperate to make Warren see how easy this all could be.

"Just hit me!" He smacked Warren across the face as hard as he could.

The surprise in Warren's eyes turned to anger. The vein at his temple began to pulse as he tried to rein in his temper, his fists held in tight balls at his sides. Warren, who had killed men overseas. Warren, who was huge and strong and had a closet full of ways to inflict pain. Finally, he was going to act. Finally, he'd realize punishing Taylor was the only option. Taylor only needed to push him a bit more. He was so angry, delirious even, so full of blackness he couldn't see anything but the path in front of him—pushing Warren to his boiling point.

He flew at Warren again, slamming into him with both hands, shoving him back hard enough that he hit the wall. "Why won't you just hit me?"

Warren came off the wall like a bull at a red flag. "*Enough!*" He grabbed Taylor by the wrist, his grip far too strong for Taylor to break, and turned to drag Taylor down the hall.

Now that the moment of Taylor's deliverance was here, he could only fight against it. If he went quietly, Warren might think this was over. He might think his burst of anger was enough, but it wasn't.

It never could be.

And so Taylor fought and screamed and kicked as Warren dragged him down the hall. He didn't even know what he was saying anymore—he only knew that this was where they needed to go. This was how it had to be. He fought for all he was worth as Warren picked him up bodily and threw him onto the bed.

Yes! Now they were getting somewhere. It almost didn't matter what came next. Taylor sobbed with relief as Warren took one wrist and dragged it to the leather cuff. He barely fought as Warren forced him onto his stomach and secured his second wrist. Warren undid Taylor's jeans and yanked them off. Taylor's underwear came next. And then his shirt, which Warren ripped open to leave Taylor's back exposed.

"Jesus," Warren said. "I can't decide whether to fuck you or beat you silly."

"Yes," Taylor cried into the mattress, torn between rage and relief. "Yes. Please."

Finally, Warren was going to make things right.

Warren had no idea what had brought on Taylor's fit, and now that he had him tied down, he had no idea what to do with him. Yes, having him naked and bound to the bed was hot, and the idea of just giving the kid what he'd initially asked for wasn't out of the question, but something made him hesitate.

Seeing Taylor there on the bed crying just seemed wrong, but when he reached out a hand to touch him, Taylor jerked away, screaming.

"Don't touch me," he snarled. "Don't touch me! Not like that!"

He was practically feral, as if he'd regressed to something not quite human, and Warren cast about desperately for what to do. Things had been good between them, and now to come home and find his TV ruined, to find Taylor in some kind of rage, left Warren reeling.

Taylor was still screaming, spitting venom at Warren. "Why won't you just fuck me or beat me? You're pathetic! I hate you! You can't do anything right!"

Warren did the only thing he could think of. He opened the closet, and Taylor's screams subsided into a sob that somehow sounded…

Grateful?

"Yes. Please Warren. Please."

From hating him to begging him in a second flat. Warren wasn't sure if he was turned on or sickened as he selected a flog. It had a dozen twenty-inch leather tails, and before Warren could think better of it, he turned and brought it down hard across Taylor's back.

Taylor screamed when it hit, then went back to crying. But now instead of rage, Warren heard only relief. "Again. Warren, please."

And Warren obliged. He was careful not to hit too hard, because he wasn't sure how much Taylor could take. He kept his blows high across Taylor's back, ensuring the ends of the straps didn't wrap around Taylor's sides. He hadn't done this in years, and he suddenly doubted himself more than he ever had back then, but Taylor kept begging, so Warren kept going. He brought the flog down again and again until Taylor suddenly panted, "No. Wait. Wait."

Warren stopped, wondering if he'd gone too far, or exactly far enough. Taylor lay motionless on the bed. The only movement was the hitching of his chest as he panted, whether in pleasure or pain or both, Warren wasn't sure.

"Taylor?" Warren started to say, reaching for him.

"Oh, Jesus," Taylor moaned. It wasn't a sound that spoke of pain or fear or anger. It sounded like nothing but need and sexual desire. Taylor lifted his hips, spreading his knees on the mattress, offering himself up. His erect cock dangled toward the bed. Good Lord, he was so fucking tempting, Warren found himself gripping his own cock through his jeans, trying to talk it back down.

"If I fuck you now, will you be happy?"

Taylor's breath shuddered through him. "I don't know I don't know I don't know just please please please." And then he was crying again, pulling at his bonds, his rage starting to build a second time.

Warren brought the flog down again, although only half as hard as before. He hoped it was enough to keep Taylor calm while he undressed, his erection now at full mast as he contemplated Taylor's ass, still pointing into the air, waiting to be claimed.

Finally, he climbed onto the bed behind him, reaching for the lube. Taylor started whispering again, "Please, please, please."

Warren squirted lube on his fingers and used them to push into Taylor. The boy moaned low in his throat, and Warren picked up the flog again. He put his cock where his fingers had been, and he began to move. He alternated his thrusts with the flog, keeping his blows even and light, never finding a smooth rhythm that Taylor could predict—just fucking and hearing the smack of the leather against flesh until Taylor's back was red and welted. Taylor went wild, moaning as Warren fucked him, pulling at his bonds less and less, and finally, he lay still, quietly moaning. Warren lay the flog aside. He grabbed a handful of Taylor's hair and pulled his head back.

"I want you on your back now. I'm going to undo your hands, and you're going to turn over like a good boy without freaking out on me again. You got it?"

Taylor nodded, breathless. "Yes. Yes. Okay."

Warren pulled free and undid the bonds. Taylor did as he was told, stopping only to toss his ruined shirt aside before turning onto his back, stretching his arms out to be bound again. His face was stained with tears, his eyes red and swollen. The look he gave Warren after he was once again secured to the bed was something close to worship, and Warren stopped, taken aback.

"Let me suck you first. Please, Warren. Please."

What man could resist a plea like that? Warren straddled him and guided his cock between Taylor's lips. Taylor let out a deep, satisfied moan as Warren began to thrust. He did his best to keep from ramming too hard or too fast, but God, it was hard to keep control with Taylor. And now, having Taylor suck him, it was easy to believe they were back to normal. Taylor's enjoyment was strong and so genuine. His enthusiasm made it that much harder for Warren to keep his orgasm at bay. In the end, he only stopped because he was afraid he was going to come, and he needed a minute to let his arousal abate before they went at it again.

"Where are you going?" Taylor asked when Warren stood up. He sounded desperate and scared. "Don't leave me. Please."

Warren didn't answer. Instead, he found the two matching cuffs to the ones on Taylor's wrists. Taylor groaned in excitement as Warren took each ankle in turn and secured it to rings halfway up the posts at the foot of the bed, leaving Taylor spread-eagle with his legs in the air and nowhere to go. He was begging again by the time Warren climbed between his legs. Warren slid his fingers into Taylor, deep and hard. He leaned forward to meet Taylor's eyes.

"I could walk out of here and leave you like this all goddamn day. How would that be?"

Taylor shook his head, breathless as Warren's fingers moved in him. "No! No no no—"

"I won't hit you. You understand? You may be able to trick people like Harry Truman into blacking your eyes, but I won't."

He kept his fingers moving, fucking Taylor ruthlessly, and Taylor could only nod.

"Is this what I have to expect? Are you going to start breaking my things on a daily basis just to get a little attention?"

Taylor shook his head. "No."

"Is that what all this was about?"

"I don't know." Taylor was practically crying again. "I don't know. I can't explain it. It just happens. I don't know why, Warren. I just don't know."

"Are you satisfied yet?"

Another headshake. "No."

"Are we close?"

A tear trickled down his cheek. "Maybe."

"You want me to fuck you again?"

"Please. Oh God, yes, please."

And Warren did. It started out hard and rough, but the more he stared at Taylor's tear-streaked face, the more tender he began to feel until at last, he leaned down and brushed his mouth over Taylor's lips.

Taylor groaned, trying to turn away. Warren grabbed his chin, turning him back to kiss him again. Taylor was stuck, all four limbs immobilized, and finally, he opened up to Warren the way he'd done on the couch that day.

In that moment, everything changed. Warren wouldn't quite have classified it as "making love," but it was as close as they'd ever come. Warren kissed him deeply, slowing his thrusts, using one hand to caress Taylor's cock. Taylor began to cry again, and Warren pulled away, thinking he'd misunderstood.

"No," Taylor gasped, shaking his head. "Keep going."

Warren deepened his kiss, tasting tears, caressing Taylor as his thrusts once again became hard and deep. Taylor let out a low, guttural moan. It was a sound Warren had learned to listen for—a signal that Taylor was about to come. It came as a surprise to Warren, but not an unwelcome one. Usually Warren had to fight for all he was worth to keep from coming too soon. It was a relief to let go and let Taylor's orgasm lead the way. The strength of his climax left him reeling.

When he caught his breath, he found himself eye to eye with Taylor. It was as if he was seeing him for the first time—this beautiful, strange, vulnerable, volatile boy he'd let into his home. Taylor's eyes were wet again, his lips swollen. His breath came in small hiccups.

"I'm sorry."

"Shh," Warren said, kissing him again. He was still hard, still deep in Taylor. He thought the kid could use some room, but when he started to pull away, Taylor shook his head.

"Don't pull out yet," he whispered. "Please. Will you—Warren, please—"

"Will I what?"

"You're still in me. You can do it. Some men think they can't when they're erect, but you can. Please. I'm begging. Please, Warren. I'm sorry. I'm so sorry. If you'll do this for me, I'll do anything. Please—" Warren was utterly confused, and Taylor kept talking, his words tumbling over each other in his haste to explain. "I was with a guy once who'd do it. After he fucked me, before he went soft. He'd stay in me, and he'd pee, and it was so warm and wonderful and—"

"What? Is that even safe?"

"Warren, please."

"Why would you want that?" He'd never understood the appeal of mixing urine with sex.

"Because he was giving me this special thing, don't you see? Because it was part of him, and I got to hold it. Like he scoured me clean and emptied me and then filled me up, because only I was special enough for that. Don't you see? And God, it felt so fucking good I could hardly stand it and—

and—" He hiccupped again, the tears coming faster down his cheeks.

"And, what?" Warren asked, torn between horror and intrigue.

"I've never felt so loved."

"Jesus." Warren rested his forehead against Taylor's, so sad for him that he felt guilty for everything he'd done since he'd come home. How could he have tied Taylor down and beaten him and fucked him when what he really needed was love and a bit of understanding? Except of course Taylor hadn't wanted that. When Warren had tried to be tender, Taylor had turned vicious. He'd begged for Warren to hit him. He'd done everything he could think of, including breaking the TV, just to ensure Warren's anger. It nearly broke Warren's heart, thinking about it. "Whoever taught you that it's okay to let men beat you and abuse you, but not to let them comfort you, was wrong. Do you understand what I'm saying? It's okay to just let people help."

Taylor closed his eyes and turned away as if he'd been slapped. He thought Warren had rejected him, when he'd only been trying to explain.

"Look, it's a little late now, that's all." And it was. He'd gone completely limp as they talked. "I'm not saying never."

Taylor turned his way again, his eyes bright. "Really?"

Warren debated. Was this really something he was considering? Maybe. It made no sense to him, but if it meant that much to Taylor, he wouldn't completely rule it out.

But the moment had passed. Taylor looked happier, already reassured. Warren used the backs of his fingers to dry Taylor's cheeks. "Tell me you feel better."

"I do."

"Want to tell me what happened?"

Taylor shook his head. "I'm sorry. I can't explain it. I don't really even know how it happens. I just—"

"Is this going to happen again?"

"I wish I could say no."

"But?"

To his dismay, Taylor's eyes once again filled with tears. "It *always* happens again."

Taylor slept late the next day. Warren moved the broken TV out of the middle of the floor, wondering what exactly had brought on Taylor's episode. Warren had tried asking as he'd uncuffed Taylor the night before, but Taylor had been evasive, whether because he didn't know or because he didn't want to talk about it, Warren wasn't sure. The result was the same, either way—Warren was as clueless now as he'd been the night before when he'd come home to find Taylor in the middle of a screaming, raging fit.

Warren pondered it as he showered and started breakfast, and by the time Taylor wandered into the kitchen, still rubbing sleep from his eyes, Warren had the barest beginning of a plan.

"I thought you didn't know how to cook," Taylor said. His voice held none of his usual humor. It was flat and utterly lifeless.

Warren laughed. "It's not so much that I *can't* cook as that I'm usually too lazy. But scrambled eggs and bacon, I can handle." He dished some onto a plate and turned to set it on the kitchen table. "Here. Sit down and eat."

Taylor shook his head, unwilling to meet Warren's gaze. He wore a full set of flannel pajamas that were at least a size too big. It amused Warren since Taylor always slept nude. The pajamas were more loungewear for Taylor than sleepwear.

"What's wrong?" Warren asked.

Taylor put one hand over his eyes. "I'm sorry. God, Warren, I'm so, so sorry. I just—"

"Don't worry about it. You're forgiven."

"I feel terrible. Especially about the TV."

"It's fine. Now I have an excuse to get one of those new, fancy kinds."

"But—"

"I've already forgiven you. It's okay to just leave it at that."

Taylor nodded, still looking dejected. He chewed his lip for a second, then took a deep breath and said, "Do you want me to leave?"

"Leave?" Warren was halfway through dishing up his own breakfast, and he set it aside to turn and face Taylor again. "What do you mean?"

"After what I did, I'd understand if you wanted me to move out. Most guys—"

"Stop." It wasn't as if he didn't know about Taylor's past, but having it tossed at him so casually bothered him more than he liked to admit. "I don't want to hear about 'most guys,' okay? I'm not them. And the only thing I want you to do is quit beating yourself up over it. Then sit down and eat."

Taylor nodded, risking a glance up at him. "I'd understand, though, if you wanted me gone."

"I don't."

Taylor stared at him, eyes wide and chin beginning to tremble, as if the words were hard for him to make sense of. As if he couldn't quite believe Warren had said them.

"I want you here. Yesterday didn't change that." He crossed the kitchen. He wanted nothing more than to pull Taylor into his arms, but he had a feeling Taylor would reject any type of tenderness. He didn't protest, though, when Warren gently turned him around and lifted his pajama top. The flog hadn't broken the skin and most of the redness had subsided, but there were still a few lingering welts across Taylor's back. Warren carefully brushed one with his fingertip, wondering how much it still hurt, but Taylor didn't flinch.

"I have some cream we can try—"

"I'm fine," Taylor said. He turned to face Warren, and Warren was relieved to see he was almost smiling. It was a small, sad smile, full of shame and embarrassment and heartache, but it was there nonetheless. "I don't think anybody's ever handled it that well before. I know it probably made no sense to you, but it's like this horrible darkness fills me up, and the only way I know to beat it is pain, or sex, or both at once. And it can't just be sex either. It has to be rough and mean, and—" He shook his head and brushed at his eyes, trying to hide his tears from Warren. "I can't explain. But I don't think you could have done any better than you did."

Now it was Warren's turn to shake his head. "No. I could have done better by not letting it get that bad in the first place."

"It wasn't your fault."

"Wasn't it? Are you sure? Because the way I see it, I haven't been entirely fair with you. I mean, I leave you here for hours at a time. You have no phone, no car, no computer access. You have nothing but the TV." He gestured toward it, then found himself chuckling when he remembered it was lying broken in the corner. "You don't even have that at the moment."

"It wasn't your fault," Taylor said again.

"Well, whether it was or not, I feel like an ass. I never thought much about it, to be honest, but I realize now it was shitty of me. I thought maybe we'd make a couple of changes."

Taylor blinked at him, clearly confused, but at least he wasn't crying anymore. "What are you saying?"

"First of all, I set up an account for you on the computer in my office. Use it as much as you want. And second..." He turned and opened the top drawer on the end—the one that held all the random stuff that didn't have a better place to go—and pulled out a keychain with a single key on it. He held it up, and there was no mistaking the way Taylor's eyes lit up at the sight of it. "This is to the white car in the garage. Somebody gave it to me as payment for a job right before Christmas. It's just been sitting there since then. You may as well make use of it."

"Really?" Taylor's grin was the most infectious thing Warren had seen in ages. "You don't mind?"

"I wouldn't be offering if I did."

Taylor's squeal was worthy of any twelve-year-old girl, and he threw his arms around Warren's neck. "Thank you. I promise, you won't regret it!"

Warren wasn't worried. There was no way in the world he'd regret anything that made Taylor this happy.

Chapter 8

Two hours later, Taylor happily waved goodbye to Warren as he backed the white car out the garage door. The house felt depressingly still and quiet with him gone. It was a horrible reminder of how lonely he'd be when Taylor decided to leave him for good.

Warren turned away, determined not to think about it.

He found himself in the living room, studying the broken TV. Plugging it in proved it was now worthless. The screen still lit up, and sound came out, but the picture never appeared. It looked like a trip to Sears or Best Buy was inevitable. The smart move would be to research his options online first, but that sounded like a pain in the ass. Maybe he could just go check the prices first.

He was still debating his options when his phone rang an hour later. A glance at the screen told him it was Sugar calling, which surprised him. It was only Wednesday, after all. She usually only worked weekends.

"Hello?"

There was silence for just a moment, and then a voice that definitely wasn't Sugar's said, "Are you the man who helps my mom?"

Warren sank slowly into a kitchen chair. The voice clearly belonged to a child—old enough to speak clearly, but still prepubescent. He couldn't determine gender at all. "Is this your mom's phone?"

"Yes. She needs help."

"Where is she?"

"Here."

"At your house?"

"Yes. At school, they say to call the nine-one-one when somebody's hurt, but she told me if there was ever an emergency not to call the cops. She said to call you or Lisa, and Lisa didn't answer her phone."

"Your mom's hurt?"

"Yes." And for the first time, Warren heard tears in the young voice. "I think she's hurt real bad."

Warren's hands shook as he took the notepad and pen from the drawer. "Tell me your address."

Twenty minutes later, he pulled up outside a row of tiny apartments, not much different on the outside from the motel room Sugar worked out of on weekends. He pounded on the door hard enough to rattle the windows. The door cracked open, and a small face peered out at him. Pale skin, bright blue eyes, and an unruly shock of black hair. Definitely male, now that Warren could see him, and probably about nine years old. "Are you Warren?"

"I am."

The boy's chin trembled, but he tried hard to keep it hidden as he opened the door and let Warren in.

The inside of the apartment wasn't much better than the outside. It was a single room—two twin beds on one side, an ancient TV with a very not-flat screen on the other. In between them was a small kitchen table, currently holding an old, clunky laptop and a pile of textbooks. A glance at the titles told Warren somebody was studying to become a paralegal, and he doubted it was the nine-year-old. The back wall of the room held a kitchen of sorts—a small fridge, a sink, and a two-burner stove. A door in the corner must have led to the bathroom.

"Where is she?"

The boy pointed to the spot between the beds. His lip quivered harder. He seemed unwilling to get too close.

Warren went cold when he saw her. Whoever had beaten her had focused on her face. Blood covered it from her eyebrows to her chin. Swelling had already begun, twisting her familiar features into a gruesome mask. Warren knelt at her side to assess the damage. He didn't need to check for a pulse because he could hear her breathing, and he sent up a small prayer of thanks to whoever was listening. At least her attacker hadn't actually killed her.

"Sugar?" He brushed her hair aside, gently turning her face to get a better look. "Sugar, can you hear me?"

"Her name's Susan. Her friends call her Susie."

"Okay," Warren said, still studying the damage. He wasn't a medic, but he thought her nose was broken, and maybe her eye socket. Her eyelids fluttered as he examined her, but she didn't seem aware of what was going on. "Susie, it's Warren. Can you hear me?"

No response.

Warren turned to the boy. "What's your name?"

"Jack."

"Jack, how long ago did this happen?" It looked recent. The blood on her face was sticky but not dry.

"I called you right after he left." His voice cracked on the words. "Is she going to die?"

"Not today."

Sugar was only about five-four, and didn't weigh more than a hundred and ten pounds. Lifting her in his arms was as easy as picking up a doll. He had Jack open the passenger door of the car. Warren strapped her in, reclining the seat just a bit to keep her from slumping forward. He turned to Jack, debating. He could take the boy with him, but it was better if he didn't. Having Jack there might mean Child Protective Services getting involved. He wanted to keep this as anonymous as possible. "Does she let you stay home alone?"

Jack hesitated but nodded. Warren suspected he'd been warned not to divulge this fact to anybody. Being a latchkey kid had been normal when Warren was a kid, but these days, it was practically considered abandonment.

"Do you still have your mom's phone?" Warren asked.

"Inside."

"Good. I'll call you on that if I need to, but don't worry. She's going to be fine. In the meantime, keep trying to call the other friend you mentioned."

"Lisa?"

He wondered if "Lisa" was the woman he knew as Candy. "Yes." He didn't figure Jack needed supervision as much as some emotional support. At his age, he probably wanted nothing more than to be able to burst into tears and let the adults handle it. "Maybe she can come stay with you."

He waited until Jack was back inside with the door locked before climbing into the driver's seat and starting the car. Sugar—or Susie, he supposed—moaned.

"Hang on," he told her. "You're going to be fine."

"Warren," she choked. "Not a hospital."

"You need a doctor."

"They'll want me file a report."

"And you don't want to do that?"

She shook her head. "He's a cop. He'll send CPS. All he has to do is tell them about my night job, and I'll lose Jack."

Warren clenched his jaw, fighting back his first response, and his second. His tires squealed as he pulled into traffic, adrenaline making him drive too fast. He didn't agree with her reasoning, but it wasn't his decision to make. He wanted to take her to an actual ER, or at least to Urgent Care, but she trusted him to do right by her, and he would. Luckily, he had a backup plan.

"Was it the ex you told me about?" he finally asked. "Robby?"

"Yes." Her head lolled back against the headrest. "Not a hospital."

"Was your son home when this happened? Did he see it?"

"I told him to lock himself in the bathroom."

Warren gripped the steering wheel, fighting his rage, trying not to remember the times he'd been instructed to do the exact same thing. He could blame Robby, or blame Sugar, or blame the police department for putting somebody who was obviously dangerous in a position of authority. He could blame the system that forced a young woman like Sugar to work the streets just to put herself through school and make ends meet, but in the end, none of it would do him any good. Afghanistan had taught him that anger and hatred rarely resulted in justice. They only produced more anger and more hatred. Bloodlust was good fuel in the short term, but it didn't solve the actual problem.

Still, he had a feeling he'd be meeting Robby real soon.

He took advantage of a red light to make a call. Charlie picked up on the fourth ring.

"Warren! Haven't heard from you in a while. What's up?"

"You home? I have a bit of an emergency here."

"What kind of emergency?"

"Not illegal, but not fond of cops."

"No problem. I'll be waiting."

Traffic moved way too slow for his liking. It took nearly thirty minutes to get to Charlie's, by which point Sugar—Susie!—had lapsed into something bordering on unconsciousness. Warren fought the urge to panic. He cursed at every car he passed, and finally pulled up in front of a tiny, white, cottage-like house. Stained-glass ornaments decorated the windows, rainbow wind socks hung from the eaves, and lawn gnomes guarded the flower beds. It was the type of house that made Warren picture a bespectacled, gray-haired grandma who spent her time knitting doilies and baking chocolate chip cookies. Instead, it housed a tattooed, bearded, two-hundred-pound, Harley-riding, male registered nurse.

The knitting and the cookies, though? That part was spot-on.

"Je-sus," Charlie said, opening the door. He pronounced it the way a Spanish speaker would, which always sounded to Warren like *Hey, Zeus!* "What the hell happened here?"

Warren half dragged, half carried Susie inside. "A little run-in with one of DPD's finest."

"Shit. Take her to the exam room."

The "exam room" was a tiny spare bedroom, set up for exactly this kind of thing. Charlie worked part-time at an urgent care facility, although thanks to a sizable inheritance, he didn't need to work at all. But outside of motorcycles, tattoos, and arts and crafts, his real passion was simply helping people who needed it. He had a steady supply of indigent neighbors—many of them in the country illegally—who came to him for random and assorted medical emergencies.

He couldn't always help them, but when he could, they knew it came free, and no questions asked.

Warren left them to it. Charlie didn't need his help. Warren would only be in the way. He paced Charlie's living room instead. It was the exact opposite of Warren's house, decorated to the hilt with various crafts. Cross-stitched pillows, quilted throws, and crocheted doilies. Charlie tried just about every craft at least once.

Ten minutes later, Warren's phone rang. This time, it was Candy.

"Warren? Is she okay?"

"She'll be fine, but I sure don't think she'll be working this weekend."

"That's gonna hurt. She's barely making ends meet, after paying tuition."

"Are you with Jack?"

"Yes. He had a good cry, but he finally fell asleep watching TV."

"Good." He'd done the exact same thing quite a few times after one of his dad's rages. "She wouldn't let me take her to a hospital."

"Then where are you?"

"I have a friend."

"The cop?"

"No. Another one."

She made a quiet sound that might have been a laugh. "You seem to have an odd assortment of friends."

"I suppose I do."

"That son of a bitch is going to kill her one of these days." Candy's voice dropped. "Unless somebody does something about it."

Warren clenched his jaw, debating. "Only if she asks me to."

"Then get her to ask."

In the end, Sugar didn't need to say anything. It was thinking about Jack that did it.

Warren couldn't count the number of times he'd hidden in the bathroom or the pantry or his bedroom closet during one of his parents' fights. The screaming, he could handle. It was the *thumps* that chilled him to the core. It was those ominous *bumps* and *cracks* after the yelling stopped that made him huddle into the corner, his hands over his ears to block the sound.

In his early teens, he'd tried to defend her, only to take the beatings himself. But as he grew bigger, the beatings stopped. His parents still argued from time to time, but the violence waned. His father's drinking had become constant by that point, and Warren stupidly assumed the old man had mellowed with age, or that maybe his mother had learned to deflect the arguments before they became violent. After high school, he'd offered to stay in Casper with her, but she'd encouraged him to use the money her parents had set aside for him to attend the University of Wyoming.

Once he was there, it was easy to forget about home. Suddenly there was schoolwork, harder than Warren had expected. There was football. Warren wasn't a star, but his size alone had been enough to earn him a spot as an offensive lineman. And there were parties. He'd never been much into drugs or alcohol—not after seeing what it did to people—but parties meant sex, and Warren had found plenty of that. Male or female hadn't mattered much to him back then. All that mattered was "willing," and he'd had his share of partners. He stayed at school over the holidays, and spent his summers in

Denver, working for his uncle. Why go home? Why go back to that shitty little house, always reeking of stale beer and pot? Every phone call, his mother assured him she was fine. Everything was great. His dad was behaving.

It'd all been lies, of course. Later, after her death, he'd realized the beatings had only stopped in his late teens because Warren had grown so big. But once he was gone, the fights had resumed. The coroner reported finding multiple bruises on his mother's body. Warren could complain until he was blue in the face that he knew who'd given them to her, but it was all a matter of hearsay. Warren longed for justice, but even if his father had driven her to her death, he hadn't actually killed her. It felt like a matter of mere semantics in Warren's mind, but it was a distinction the law hinged on. No charges were ever filed because, technically, no laws had been broken.

Warren had never forgiven himself. For those two years of college, he'd thought about nothing but football, homework, and getting laid, and his mother had paid the price for his selfishness.

Three months later, when the Twin Towers fell, Warren had seen his chance for salvation.

Of course, that hadn't gone as planned either. But no matter what, it all went back to that same place—a little boy hiding while his mom took a beating.

Warren wasn't going to let another boy go down that road. Not if he could help it.

Candy picked up on the first ring, and Warren asked one simple question. "Where do I find him?"

She gave him a list, starting with Robby's address and what kind of car he drove, and ending with his favorite bars. Warren took careful notes. When Charlie emerged from his exam room, he took one look at Warren and shook his head.

"Don't do it, man. It won't do her any good now."

Warren jabbed a finger toward the exam room door. "Her kid had to hide in the bathroom and listen to that happen."

"It won't do him any good either."

"Maybe not, but it might keep it from happening again." He didn't want to argue about it. "Can she go home yet?"

"I'd like to keep her here another hour or two, just to be safe. Does she have anybody to stay with her tonight?"

"Her friend's there now with the boy. I'm sure she'll stay if she needs to."

"And there's nothing I can say to talk you out of this?"

"I suppose you could call Gray."

They both knew he wouldn't do that, because his little home clinic wasn't exactly legal either. Not that Gray didn't know. Of course he did, just like he knew about Warren's not-always-legal jobs. Just like Phil the uptight, rule-following hospital pharmacist knew Charlie handed out illegally acquired meds to his non-citizen clientele. But underneath it all, they were friends. Two of them on the wrong side of the law, two on the right. It was deciding which side was which where things got murky.

They had one simple agreement: don't cause trouble for each other.

Charlie shook his head and sighed. "I get it. I ain't saying it's right, but I get it. Just do me a favor?"

"What is it?"

"Don't get caught."

It took nearly three hours to find Robby, but find him Warren did, having a beer with a fellow cop at a hole-in-the-wall bar. The place was too busy for Warren's purposes, but the narrow, dirty streets of the neighborhood were just right. He circled the block until he found Robby's car. That gave him a chance to scope out the route Robby would have to take once he left the bar.

Warren kept certain essentials in his trunk at all times. Before leaving Charlie's, he'd pulled out a black windbreaker, a cheap stocking cap, and a pair of leather driving gloves. He bought them secondhand whenever he could, always paying cash, never buying a full set at the same time. If anybody searched his garage, they'd find a box full of items a lot like these.

But nothing *exactly* like them.

He donned the windbreaker and hat, and put the gloves in his jacket pockets until he needed them. He parked the car two blocks away. Then he walked back to the bar, found a quiet spot in the shadow of the building across the street, and waited.

The streets were quiet. The area was strictly low-end business. Little to no residential, and nothing to draw big crowds, especially on a Wednesday night. Only a few people wandered past, at least half of them homeless. None of them spared Warren a glance, except the women, who kept their eyes on him and moved to the far side of the sidewalk, their steps quickening as they hurried away.

Technically, it might have been spring, but only barely. The temperature dropped, but Warren barely noticed. By eight o'clock, the sun was behind the mountains, the downtown tangle of narrow one-way streets illuminated only by flickering street lamps and neon signs in bar windows. A few minutes later, Robby emerged. Warren quietly fell into step behind him, pulling the gloves into place as he went.

He had a spot on their route in mind, but he had to time it just right. His groin and armpits tingled as a flood of adrenaline hit his system. His heart pounded in his ears. Warren flexed his fingers in the gloves, speeding up his pace, wanting to be right behind Robby as he crossed the dark alley between two brick buildings.

They were almost there. Warren glanced around, making sure nobody was watching.

The coast was clear. There wasn't enough traffic in this area to attract prostitutes or addicts. The only person in sight was a homeless man, sleeping on a grate half a block away.

Just three more steps.

Two.

One.

Warren pounced, driving one fist into Robby's kidneys even as he used his other hand to push him into the alley. He shoved him into the shadow of a Dumpster, being careful not to let the man see his face.

"I'm a cop," Robby said.

"I know."

Warren slammed Robby's face into the brick building, using his full body weight to pin the man, careful to keep Robby's right arm twisted behind his back for leverage. Another blow to the kidneys and one to the gut. That was enough to take the fight out of him for a minute. Then Warren did the real damage.

He concentrated on Robby's face, because that was what the slimeball had done to Sugar. He was careful, though. He could have killed him. He could easily have bashed the man's head in or broken his jaw or left him a drooling mess for the rest of his days. But that'd be dangerous. That'd be enough to bring the full attention of the Denver Police Department down on him.

No. He couldn't let things get too out of control. He had to give Robby just enough of a beating that everybody who saw him knew he'd had his ass kicked—just enough that all his friends knew he'd crossed the wrong man—but not enough that Rob's cop buddies would want to pursue the attacker. Besides, Robby wouldn't want that either. If anybody dug too deep, they'd find his own sins not far under the surface.

So Warren was ruthless, but he was also careful. Robby had to be able to pass it off as a mugging or a random bar fight. Something that wasn't worth investigating, even as he swallowed the shame of being on the losing side of a brawl.

Finally, when Robby's knees gave out and Warren had to hold him up, he stopped. He grabbed a handful of the man's hair and leaned close to speak into his ear.

"You touch her again, I'll make this little incident feel like a goddamned birthday party."

He let Robby fall and left the alley at a fast walk, headed for his car. The gloves went down a storm drain. The hat and jacket went to two different homeless men along his route. The whole thing had taken less than five minutes. His hands shook as he unlocked his car. His pants strained around an erection that wouldn't wane. He hated it. Certain battle situations had always had that effect on him.

It was done. He vowed to himself, as he started the car and turned toward home, that whatever happened, he wouldn't take his rage out on Taylor.

Chapter 9

Taylor felt good that day as he shopped. Warren had given him five hundred dollars several weeks earlier for helping set up Ted, and Taylor happily spent a healthy chunk of it. First, he stopped at a bookstore, where he splurged on a stack of new graphic novels. The ones he owned had been read and reread dozens of times. Some of his hosts over the years had mocked him for not reading "real" books, but Warren wasn't that type of man. Taylor no longer bothered trying to hide his hobby from Warren, and having new stories to dig into would help pass the time when Warren worked.

Next, he hit the mall. Most of his clothes were hand-me-downs, picked up from other men, usually left behind by former lovers, like the clothes still tucked into Stuart's drawers. Taylor bought jeans, a couple of shirts, and a pair of shoes. He finished his shopping spree off with a thick, fuzzy, powder-pink robe. He found it in the women's section, but so what? It made him feel cozy and decadent all at once, and it fit perfectly on his slender frame.

By the time he got home, he felt one-hundred-percent better. Finding the house empty was a bit of a disappointment, but wasn't necessarily a surprise. A note on the countertop said only, "Had to go out. —W."

Another of Warren's odd jobs, then. Taylor had quit asking about them. He'd tried, after the incident with Ted, but Warren always said the same thing. *"The less you know, the better."*

Whether that was to protect Taylor himself, or whether it was insurance for a time down the road when he thought Taylor might use it against him was hard to say. Either way, it wasn't worth pushing.

In the living room, Taylor came face-to-face with the broken TV. His heart sank, and he mentally kicked himself for being such a selfish ass. He shouldn't have spent his money on himself. He should have used it replacing Warren's TV. He gnawed his lip for a minute wondering if he should take everything back. Was that what Warren would want him to do?

He had no idea. He couldn't quite figure out the way the man thought.

Taylor spent a long time contemplating the vase on Warren's bookshelf, wondering what kind of man found beauty in something broken. What kind of man volunteered for more days like the one Taylor had put him through yesterday?

Taylor's newfound happiness faded a bit as doubt began to take hold.

Warren had no idea what he was in for. He hadn't yet seen one of Taylor's darkest days. When that happened, he'd kick Taylor to the curb, just like every other man had ever done. Taylor could count on one hand those who'd stuck with him after his first episode. Not a single one had remained through a second.

Taylor wanted to stay. He wanted to believe he'd never have to leave. Warren made him happy in a way nobody else ever had. The only thing he could do was try to return the favor and hope Warren wouldn't send him packing the next time the blackness came.

But that brought him full circle to the broken TV. He shouldn't have spent all his money on himself after breaking something that belonged to Warren.

After tossing it around a bit, Taylor decided he'd keep the robe. He went through the graphic novels, sorting a few into a "keep" pile and the majority into "return." The remainder of the day's purchases went back in the bags with the receipts, and he moved everything to the kitchen so he wouldn't be tempted to backslide. He'd talk to Warren. He'd confess his selfishness and volunteer to make up for it by returning most of what he'd bought and turning the money over to Warren. His heart lightened a bit at the thought. Whether Warren agreed to the plan or not, at least Taylor would have done his best.

After dinner, he stripped bare and donned only his new pink robe, wanting to surprise Warren. When Warren's car pulled into the driveway an hour later, Taylor set aside the new book he'd been reading and went to meet Warren in the kitchen.

He knew right away something was wrong.

Taylor had learned to interpret Warren's many scowls. There was the one where his eyebrows came down and his lips thinned, which spoke more of judgment, like when he saw somebody being mistreated. There was the one that was more a twisting of Warren's lips, and a narrowing of his eyes, which meant he was trying to decide just how much to say or which words to use. It was a scowl that spoke more of frustration with himself than with anything external. There was a third variety—the rarest one—that was almost a snarl, his eyes flashing and teeth bared, which meant he was truly angry or frustrated. Taylor had only seen that the previous day when he'd hit Warren.

But the look on Warren's face now was something Taylor had never seen before. His eyes were dark and cold, his jaw tight. His whole body spoke of barely contained energy and anger. His shoulders were tense, his hands balled into tight fists at his sides. There was a savageness about him that felt almost feral. Taylor instinctively took a step back.

"What's wrong?"

"What the hell are you wearing?"

"A robe I bought." Taylor suddenly felt foolish for it, although Warren had never made him feel that way before. "I can get rid of it. I just liked the way it felt—"

Warren growled and grabbed Taylor's arms, pushing him back against the kitchen counter so hard, it left Taylor breathless. With one hand, he grabbed a handful of Taylor's hair and yanked his head back. With the other, he found the opening to Taylor's robe and slid his hand inside. His growl became something ferocious when he found Taylor had nothing on underneath. "God, don't get rid of it."

Taylor breathed a sigh of relief as understanding dawned. Whatever had set Warren off—whatever had brought on this rage or anger or frustration—had also stoked his sexual appetite. He wasn't angry at Taylor. He was simply desperate to slake his lust.

Taylor had no problems with that.

Warren held him tight, kissing his neck, one hand sliding down between Taylor's cheeks. His fingers were cold and almost brutal as he probed there, the thick stubble on his jaw abrasive where it scraped Taylor's chin, his erection hard against Taylor's belly. Taylor relaxed with a moan, his body already responding the way it always did to Warren's aggression. He loved when Warren got like this.

"Jesus," Warren choked, suddenly trying to back away. "I told myself I wouldn't do this."

"Why? What's wrong?"

"I shouldn't—"

"Why not?"

"It's not right. I might hurt you. I'm sorry."

"Hush." Taylor pulled him close again and began undoing his pants. He wasn't sure why Warren was hesitant when they obviously both wanted the same thing. He looked up into Warren's eyes. "Remember our first time, here in the kitchen?"

Warren's eyes flashed. His voice when he answered was throaty and hoarse. "Yes."

"Remember how rough you were with me?"

Warren's cheeks flushed red. "Yes."

"You know now I don't usually come so easy. But I did that day. Know why?"

"Because you'd been riding your wave all day."

"No. Because of how rough you were. I love when you're like that." He slid his hand into Warren's pants to caress his erection, then stood on his toes to brush his lips over Warren's mouth. "Be as rough with me as you want."

"I don't want to hurt you."

Taylor moaned at the thought. "I like the way you hurt me." He took Warren's hand and guided it to his erection, wanting him to realize how turned on he was. He whimpered as Warren's strong fingers wrapped around his length. "I love the way you fuck me when you're really desperate to come." He kissed Warren, not having to feign his own impatience. "I'll beg if you want. I'll do anything. I want it, Warren. I want you to use me."

Warren groaned in defeat, but thankfully, he quit fighting whatever had him in its clutches. He ripped Taylor's robe open and pulled him close, attacking Taylor's neck as Taylor fought to push Warren's pants down over his hips. As soon as they were out of the way, Warren grabbed a handful of Taylor's hair and yanked, forcing Taylor to his knees.

It was like their first day, and yet, emotionally, so different. Back then, Taylor had been turned on as he always was by the simple taboo of sucking a guy he didn't even know. He'd been intrigued by Warren's ferocity and his strength, then pushed to a sudden and surprising orgasm by Warren's borderline violence at the end.

This time, Taylor was as aroused as he'd been that day, but there was more to it. Yes, Warren was rough and demanding and driven just as before. Those things still turned Taylor on. But what he liked best was simply that it was Warren. The feel of Warren's hardened flesh sliding between his lips was perfect and familiar. Taylor knew Warren's touch, and the way he tasted. He knew precisely what Warren liked and what he didn't. He knew exactly how much to resist Warren, and when to give in. Being with Warren felt natural and right. There was nobody in the world Taylor would rather give pleasure to. There was nothing in the universe he wouldn't have allowed Warren to do. And when Warren dragged him to his feet a minute later to bend him over the kitchen table, Taylor came as fast and hard as he had that first day, losing control the minute Warren penetrated him.

Warren needed only a few more thrusts, and then he collapsed on top of Taylor, panting. He stroked Taylor's hair and kissed the back of his head. "I'm sorry. Jesus, Taylor, I'm so sorry."

"Wh—what?" Taylor asked, still breathing hard. "Why?"

"I didn't mean to do that." He sounded like he was close to tears, and Taylor struggled to push Warren off his back so he could stand up and face him. He couldn't understand Warren's guilt when the proof of Taylor's pleasure was all over the kitchen floor between their feet.

Warren quickly pulled his pants into place and sank into a kitchen chair. He put his head in his hands, and Taylor decided the mess on the floor could wait. He tied his robe closed again, then slid the other chair close enough that he could put his hand on Warren's shoulder. "Where were you tonight, before you came home?" Because wherever Warren had been had brought this on. Of that, Taylor was certain.

Warren shook his head without looking up. "It's better if you—"

"Don't know. Right. You always say that." He sighed in frustration. "Why do you want to shut me out? Because you don't trust me?"

"That's not it."

"Because you think I can't handle it?"

"No." Warren still sounded aggravated and a bit ashamed, but he at least sat up and faced Taylor. "To protect you. So you won't have to lie if somebody asks you questions."

Taylor sat back and crossed his arms. "You mean the police."

Warren's wince was barely perceptible. "Yes."

"So what you do is illegal?"

"Not always."

"But it was tonight."

Warren's only answer was to lower his eyes.

Taylor scooted closer, ducking his head a bit to intercept Warren's gaze. "I don't care about deniability. And I'm not asking for a rundown of every job you've taken. I'm just asking where you went tonight."

"Sugar needed help."

"Did one of her customers cause trouble?"

Warren ran his hands through his hair. This time, his scowl was familiar to Taylor. It was the twisting of his lips that meant he was struggling with himself, trying to decide just how much to say.

Finally, he dropped his hands into his lap, and it was as if his defenses went with them. "It wasn't a customer. It was her ex." He grimaced. "He beat the shit out of her while her son hid in the bathroom."

"And what did you do?"

"I returned the favor."

Taylor's eyes automatically went to Warren's fists. There were no cuts or bruises there to indicate he'd been in a fight, but it seemed he had. And then he'd come home, seething with anger and frustration. He'd fucked Taylor hard but immediately felt the need to apologize.

The violence had trigged it.

"So, it's like bloodlust."

Warren turned away, his cheeks flushing with shame.

Taylor put his hand on Warren's knee. "It's biology, Warren. It's nothing to be ashamed of. It's just..." He searched for the word. "Primal."

Warren clenched his jaw. "Exactly. Primal. *Animal.* That means it's something humans should have beaten by now."

Taylor almost laughed. "Warren, I broke your TV yesterday because of a fictional show about demon hunters. I'm not exactly in a position to lecture you on impulse control."

He'd hoped it would lighten the mood, but Warren didn't smile. He looked half-afraid. He swallowed hard before saying the next part. "It happened over there too."

"In Afghanistan, you mean?"

"Yeah. Always scared the piss out of me. Like I might not be able to control it."

"But you did." He hoped.

Warren's head jerked in a quick nod. "Doesn't mean I didn't jack off the first chance I got, but I never hurt anybody." Warren eyed him. "Except maybe tonight."

"Did you hear me say no?" He didn't wait for Warren to answer. "I wanted you to do it. It's never been more than I could handle, and tonight was no different. I love when you're rough like that."

"Not sure that makes it right."

Taylor pushed him back in the chair and straddled his lap. He leaned close, forcing Warren to see him. "I don't care what causes it. I don't care how violent or primal it is. I like being the person who can give you what you need. Just like yesterday, you gave me what I needed."

Warren rested his big hands on Taylor's hips. "I don't want to hurt you."

"I like when you hurt me. You hurt me in exactly the right ways." Taylor gently touched Warren's scars, trying to smooth them away. Trying to urge Warren's lips into a smile. "It's one of the reasons we're so perfect together."

"Yeah?"

"Of course."

Warren shook his head. "I don't know how I got so lucky."

Taylor thought his heart might burst. Warren rarely expressed emotion. His simple statement felt enormous. Taylor wanted to return the favor. He longed to say something sweet. Something wonderful. Something that made Warren understand that Taylor was the one who'd somehow gotten lucky.

But before he could say anything, Warren tipped his head toward the pile of bags in the corner. "What's all that?"

So they were moving from battlefield horrors to emotional confessions, and back into the utterly mundane in the blink of an eye. Knowing Warren as he did, it wasn't a surprise. "Stuff I bought myself today."

Warren fingered the collar of Taylor's pink robe. "Anything else like this?"

There was a lightness to his voice that almost made the question a joke, and Taylor laughed. "Not really, no. It's all kind of boring." He thought again about the TV, and his guilt came back, even stronger than before. He'd promised himself he'd talk to Warren, and so he did. He told him all about the shopping spree, and his realization that he'd bought the wrong things, and his promise to himself that he'd return most of it. He vowed to give Warren every penny he got back.

Warren only laughed and kissed him. "Keep your books, Tay. I don't give a damn about the TV."

Taylor was up the next morning long before Warren. Warren had only been home for a little over an hour the night before. Then he'd had to turn around and leave for "work," protecting his Wednesday-night client. Taylor wasn't sure what time he came home. Whenever it was, Warren had chosen to let Taylor sleep.

Taylor wandered around the quiet house, suddenly unsure of his place in Warren's home. They'd just weathered two violent and stormy days—the first at Taylor's behest, the second at Warren's—and yet they'd shared some new level of intimacy. Taylor had gone to sleep thinking that for the first time in his life, he was exactly where he wanted to be.

They never slept in the same bed. Even when Warren came to Taylor's room, he always returned to his own room after sex. It hadn't bothered Taylor before, but waking up alone after what had passed between them hurt. It seemed to underscore the fact that this wasn't a relationship. It was an arrangement, plain and simple. Taylor was basically a lodger who paid rent in a nontraditional way. He suddenly hated it in a way he never had before. He desperately wanted to sneak into Warren's room and climb into bed with him, not because he wanted sex, but because he wanted to reclaim that feeling of closeness they'd shared over the last two days.

The problem was, he had no idea if that was allowed. Warren had taken him into the shower in the master bathroom on their first morning together, but other than that, Taylor had never been in Warren's bedroom, and certainly not in his bed. He'd glanced in from time to time, just enough to know it was the one room in the house that wasn't scrupulously neat, but beyond that, he'd never gone in, not even to snoop. He stood outside Warren's bedroom door, listening to him snore, wondering whether it was okay for him to enter or not. He was still debating when somebody knocked.

Taylor frowned, turning toward the sound. It seemed to be coming from the back door. That was the door Warren always used, but it seemed odd for anybody to knock on it. Besides, it was a bit early in the day for solicitors or drop-in visitors.

Taylor pulled his robe tighter around himself, making sure everything was covered before opening the door a few inches and peeking out.

It was a cop. He looked familiar, but Taylor couldn't think why. All he could think about was Warren's confession to beating somebody up the night before. "Can I help you?"

The cop blinked at him, taking a step back. "Who the hell are you?"

"None of your business. Why? Who the hell are you?"

The cop eyed him up and down, a smile tugging at the corner of his lips. Not bad-looking at all, and still oddly familiar. Maybe Taylor had once serviced him at Leroy's? "Is Warren home?"

"He's sleeping."

"I need you to wake him up."

"No."

The cop's eyebrows went up. "Really?"

"Really."

"Then how about you let me in, and I'll wake him up myself?"

"Do you have a warrant?"

If the guy's eyebrows climbed any higher up his head, they'd reach his hairline. "What are you, a lawyer?"

"I'm not letting you in without one."

The cop shook his head, chuckling, seeming torn between annoyance and amusement. He crossed his arms, squared his stance, and gave Taylor a killer smile. It transformed his face completely, and suddenly, Taylor knew exactly why he looked familiar—he was in two of the photos hidden in Warren's desk drawer. The guy who'd been in Afghanistan and the BDSM club.

Warren's friend.

"Look, kid," he said. "I don't know who you are or what you're afraid of, but I'm coming in there, one way or another. So you want to do this the easy way and go get Warren for me, or you want to try the hard way?"

Taylor sighed and went to get Warren.

"Warren, wake up. There's a cop here to see you."

Warren groaned into his pillow. He'd been dreaming about the desert, so waking up wasn't unwelcome, but God knew there were better ways to do it. He sat up, ran his hands through his hair, and checked the clock on the bedside table. Almost a full night's sleep, at any rate.

"Warren?" Taylor crept closer, his voice dropping to a whisper. Warren noticed he'd closed the bedroom door behind him too, as if barricading them in against the cop waiting in the living room. "Is it about yesterday?"

"I won't know until I talk to him." Warren stood up and started searching the floor for his pants. It seemed best not to greet the cop in his underwear.

Taylor wrung his hands, glancing toward the door. "I think he knows you."

"What makes you say that?"

"He came to the back door. He's—" His cheeks turned red, but he faced Warren as he said it. "He's the guy in the pictures in your desk drawer."

Warren stopped halfway through buttoning his jeans. "You went through my desk drawers?"

"Yes, and—"

"You said you were honest. That very first day, in my car—"

"I said I never steal from my hosts, and that was true. I never said I didn't snoop."

Warren almost laughed. He should've known Taylor would look around. It might have bothered him back when they first met, but at this point, he didn't care. Besides, Taylor looked scared to death.

"It's Gray," Warren said, finishing his pants and reaching for a shirt.

"What's gray?"

"I mean, that's his name. The cop." He eyed Taylor in his powder-pink robe. He didn't have to ask to know he was naked as sin underneath. "Is that how you answered the door?"

Taylor glanced down at himself. "Yeah. Why?"

"Nothing." But Warren had to laugh. He could only imagine the questions Gray would have for him now.

"Warren—"

"Don't worry." He gripped Taylor's arms and pulled him close to kiss him on the forehead. "We have nothing to worry about from Gray."

He hoped it was true.

Taylor followed him to the living room, where Gray stood, looking at the broken TV on the floor.

Gray was nearly Warren's height, but built like a welterweight boxer, with lean, hard muscles and a waistline that hadn't grown an inch in all the years Warren had known him. They'd met in Afghanistan. Gray was two years younger than Warren. He'd enlisted right after high school, and combat had somehow chiseled him down and made him hard without making him bitter. He'd adjusted to civilian life easier than any vet Warren knew. Maybe it was the uniform, which he wore today.

That told Warren this wasn't a casual visit.

"What happened here?" Gray asked, pointing to the TV.

"Mechanical trouble." Then, to Taylor, "You mind making some coffee? Gray takes his black."

Taylor had looked terrified in the bedroom, but not now. He looked as calm and collected as always. Warren made a mental note never to play poker with him. "Sure."

Gray pointed at Taylor's retreating back and raised an eyebrow at Warren. "Who's the twink?"

Even though he'd expected the question, Warren found he wasn't sure how to answer. "Boyfriend" felt wrong, as did "roommate." He could have said something glib like, *He's nobody*, but it would have been untrue, and would likely hurt Taylor's feelings to boot. After all, there was only a half wall between the living room and the kitchen. Taylor could hear every word they said. Warren opted for the simplest answer he could give. "That's Taylor."

Gray raised both eyebrows this time, waiting for more of an explanation, but Warren decided not to give him one. It was kind of fun making Gray work for what he wanted.

Warren gestured toward the couch instead. "Have a seat."

Gray did, although he perched on the edge of the couch, his elbows on his knees. He waited until Warren was seated too before asking, "You know a guy named Robert Jenson?"

Wow. That was fast. Warren hoped his poker face was as good as Taylor's. "I don't think so. Why?"

"Where were you yesterday?"

"What's this about?"

"Answer the question."

"No. *You* answer the question."

Gray lowered his head and pinched the bridge of his nose. "I don't want to be doing this, Warren."

"Then don't."

"It's not that simple."

"Lay it out for me, then. What've you got?"

Gray squinted at him as if sizing him up. Warren had often wondered if his parents had known his eyes would match his name, or if it'd been a happy coincidence. "A fellow officer got rolled last night, downtown. Somebody did a number on him."

"Bummer."

"He looks like he got run over by a train."

"Extra bummer."

"For some reason, he doesn't want anybody following up, but the chief wants somebody running it down anyway. And he picked me because he seems to think I have connections in the neighborhood."

"Sounds like a no-win to me."

"Warren, stop fucking with me."

"Stop being an asshole."

For a moment, they just stared at each other. A few other times over the years, their jobs had put them at odds like this. It was never comfortable, but so far, their friendship had always survived. Warren hoped it would this time too.

Taylor arrived carrying two cups of coffee, which he set down in front of them, on opposite sides of the coffee table. He caught Warren's eye, and Warren winked at him, wanting to somehow apologize for forcing him into the role of butler for the morning.

"So I'm chasing this bullshit down, whether I like it or not," Gray said as Taylor retreated back to the kitchen. "First thing, I went and found Rob's girlfriend, thinking she might know something. Want to guess what I found?"

"Not really."

"Pretty young girl looking like she got hit by the same train."

"Triple bummer."

Gray ignored that. "So then I think maybe they were together when it happened, but her son tells me no, some 'mean man' did this to his mom yesterday morning. And Rob didn't get his beating until that night."

"Sounds like justice to me."

"Want to guess what she does for a living?"

"Hm." Warren scratched his head and pretended to consider as Gray sipped his coffee. "Waitress?"

"Try prostitute. Not that she'd tell me that, of course. But she has a record."

"So find her pimp."

"We both know it wasn't her pimp."

"I don't know anything except what you've told me."

"Is that the way we're going to play this?"

Warren only stared at him.

"Fine." Gray set the coffee cup down. "In addition to one asshole of a boyfriend, this girl has a real nosy neighbor. And that nosy neighbor tells me that yesterday, around midday, a great big guy with scars on his face showed up. He put Susan in his car—a 4Runner, by the way—and drove her somewhere. The neighbor assumes to the hospital, since Susan looked like she was dead. Those were her exact words. 'Looked like she was dead.' But then, several hours later, some *other* big guy brings her home, all bandaged up. Neighbor said the second guy had a beard and a bunch of tattoos."

"So, this girl got beaten up in her house?"

"Her apartment, yeah."

"And did this nosy neighbor consider calling the cops when it all went down? Somebody this concerned with what's going on next door, you telling me she didn't hear anything?"

Gray shook his head, his fingers straying to his badge. "We're not exactly popular in that neighborhood."

"Wonder why that is?"

"Fuck you, Warren. You know I'm doing my best here."

Warren made an effort to rein in his condescension. Gray was one of the good ones. Warren knew that. "So, you have a girl who got beaten up by her boyfriend, and a boyfriend who got hit by a train. I don't see how I fit in."

Gray threw his hands up in frustration. "Christ, Warren! This is serious. It was obviously you and Charlie. If I half-ass this, the chief will know, but if I do it the right way, it ends in a bad way for two of my best friends."

"You're overreacting. There are probably plenty of guys in Denver with scars on their faces. 4Runners are a dime a dozen in Colorado. And a guy with tattoos and a beard? Hell, that's at least half the men in town under the age of fifty. Besides, you know eyewitness accounts aren't as reliable as we like to think. Prosecutors hate relying on them these days."

"Can you at least tell me where you were?"

Warren opened his mouth, wondering how much to lie and how much to keep deflecting. But before he could answer, Taylor spoke.

"He was here with me."

Gray's eyes swiveled Taylor's way.

Warren desperately wanted to rewind time and take back the last few seconds. He didn't want to put Taylor in the middle of this mess, but there was no changing it now.

"He was here with you when?" Gray asked.

"Pretty much all afternoon."

"Define 'pretty much.'"

Taylor took a few steps closer, coming to a stop behind Warren's chair. "I went shopping around noon and didn't get back until about five. I guess he could have gone out while I was away. But he was here when I got home, and he didn't leave again until just after ten."

That was good. It was mostly the truth, and although it didn't cover Warren for the time he'd been with Candy, it did cover him for the hours when Robby'd been attacked.

Gray squinted at Taylor. "What were you doing?"

Taylor gave him the wickedest grin Warren had ever seen on his face. "You want all the dirty details, or a full demonstration?"

Gray's lips twitched, but he didn't quite smile. His gaze returned to Warren. "So you were here from at least five until almost ten?"

"Yeah. Why? When did this happen?"

Gray pursed his lips, considering. It was hard to say whether he believed it or not. The thing was, he didn't necessarily have to believe it. He just needed to be able to officially cross Warren off his list.

"So, what happens to this cop?" Warren asked. "Sounds like he beat up his girlfriend. Is anything going to happen there?"

Gray dropped his eyes, shaking his head. He took another sip of coffee. "She refuses to press charges or to even confirm it was him."

"So, the abuser gets off scot-free, and you're busy chasing the justice train."

"Getting the shit beaten out of him in an alley isn't justice. Justice would be him kicked off the squad and facing charges."

"If one won't happen, seems like the other's the next best thing."

Gray shrugged. "Maybe. But that isn't my call to make."

"What about Charlie?"

Gray grinned at him. "Says he was at a rock and mineral show up at the Larimer County Fairgrounds all day."

"You believe him?"

"I can't prove he's lying." He shook his head, looking frustrated, but he sat back in his seat. "Christ, you guys are way more trouble than you're worth."

Warren laughed, relieved that the danger had passed. Gray wasn't stupid. He'd put two and two together and come up with four, but Charlie, Warren, and Taylor had given him enough that he could legitimately say his friends couldn't have been involved. And in the end, Warren was pretty sure that was all Gray wanted anyway.

Warren finally picked up his own coffee and took a drink. Taylor retreated again to the kitchen, and Gray watched him go. Now that he wasn't being a cop, he was once again the Gray Warren knew—the one who appreciated a good-looking young man as much as Warren. They'd always had similar taste in men.

Except for Stuart. Gray had never liked Stuart.

Warren watched him size Taylor up, obviously wondering exactly how he'd ended up answering Warren's door.

"You guys gonna spell this out for me," Gray finally asked Warren, his voice low, "or make me play twenty questions?"

Warren grinned at him over his coffee cup. "I don't know. I kind of like watching you flounder around."

"Looks like more than a one-night thing."

"He's been here six weeks or so, I guess."

Gray raised an eyebrow. "He lives here?"

"I do," Taylor said from the kitchen, proving their conversation was anything but private. "In the spare bedroom."

Gray grinned at Warren. "He means your old playroom." His appreciative gaze went back to Taylor. "You've seen the closet, then. You into that?"

Taylor smiled at him, practically batting his eyes at Gray. "I'm into anything."

Gray laughed. "Good answer."

It was funny, watching Taylor flirt with him. Warren knew how Gray thought. He knew right at that moment, Gray was imagining having Taylor tied to his own bed. He was wondering exactly what it was like having Taylor at the other end of his crop.

"Goddamn, Warren," Gray said, not bothering to lower his voice. "You are one lucky son of a bitch."

"You have no idea."

Chapter 10

Twenty minutes later, Gray finally left, leaving Warren and Taylor in awkward silence.

"You didn't have to do that," Warren said, sinking back into the armchair in his living room. "I never expected you to lie for me."

"I know." Taylor stood at the window, watching Gray pull away. "I didn't want you getting in trouble."

He still wore that damnably enticing robe. Something about the color accentuated the golden glow of his skin. Warren had a hard enough time resisting him to begin with. He was either going to have to ban the robe or buy Taylor a hundred more just like it.

"Do you think he believed me?" Taylor asked, letting the curtains fall back into place.

"I don't think it matters."

Taylor climbed onto Warren's lap, straddling his thighs. He put his hands on Warren's chest. "Were you lovers?"

"Who? Me and Gray, you mean?"

"Yes."

"Not the way you mean."

"That means you were."

Warren shifted uncomfortably, thinking back to a couple of hurried hand jobs in the desert. "It's hard to explain that war to people who weren't there. Everybody assumes it's like *Platoon* or *Full Metal Jacket*, but the Middle East isn't Vietnam.

We weren't slogging through some damn jungle, dodging snipers and mines. Afghanistan was more like occasional bursts of the scariest shit imaginable, punctuated by weeks and weeks of absolute boredom."

Taylor didn't answer, and Warren could tell he didn't understand.

Okay. Time to stop talking in circles and just be honest. Had he and Gray been lovers? "Yeah, we got each other off a couple of times, but only in Afghanistan. And even then, it was more a way to alleviate the boredom than anything. He's not my type, and I'm not his." He ran the backs of his fingers down Taylor's cheeks. "You, on the other hand, are *exactly* his type."

Taylor laughed and kissed him. "Good thing I'm not into cops."

"Can I ask you a question now?"

"Of course."

Warren slid the buttery-soft robe up Taylor's smooth thigh and touched the neat rows of scars there. "Tell me about these."

Taylor jumped off his lap so fast, Warren halfway expected him to fall. He wrapped his robe tighter around his body and moved away from Warren's chair to sink into the corner of the couch, his arms crossed and his gaze focused on the curtained front window.

"You won't tell me?"

Taylor shook his head. "I don't want to talk about that."

"Why not?"

"Because people never understand. Whenever I tell them, they start talking about counseling and abuse and all the ways they think they can fix me."

Warren did his best to keep his face impassive. Taylor would never talk to him if he thought there'd be judgment involved. "You don't like when they talk about trying to help?"

"I don't need help. Not like that, at any rate." Taylor scowled, his arms still crossed protectively over his chest.

"They don't understand. You can't just erase scars like that. They'll always be there."

Warren resisted the urge to touch the scars on his face. "You don't have to tell me. I know all about scars."

Taylor sighed, dropping his gaze. "I didn't mean it like that. I didn't mean the *actual* scars themselves so much."

"Then what?"

"People like that don't know what it's like to be broken. They want to make me like them. Like I can be normal. Like I was never broken to begin with. And it won't work that way. Some things go too deep, you know?"

"You're right. And you know I understand it as well as you do. So why don't you want to tell me?"

Taylor picked at a cuticle, considering. "We're good together, right?"

"We are. What does that have to do with it?"

Taylor's chin trembled a bit, reminding Warren of Sugar's son, but he seemed determined not to cry. "Because once you know, you won't want me anymore. All you'll ever see is somebody who's broken. You'll never see me the way you do now."

Warren considered. His living room felt warm and quiet and safe to him, but Taylor looked like he was ready to bolt.

Warren finally stood. He went to the bookshelf and took down the vase. He set it in front of Taylor on the coffee table, turning the patched side to face Taylor, then resumed his seat. "Broken once doesn't mean broken now." And he doubted anything could change the way he felt.

Taylor stared at the vase for a while, his jaw clenching and unclenching. Eventually, he sighed. "You first."

"Me first? What do you mean?"

"You tell me something first. Something true. Something other people don't understand."

Warren had to think about it for a bit. He could have gone with something simple—his violent father or his beaten mother. He could have talked about the war, or how hard it was to adjust to civilian life again once he was home. But

Taylor already knew those things. Maybe not the details, but he knew enough.

But the only other thing Warren had didn't feel like enough.

"Well?" Taylor prodded, impatient.

Warren leaned forward in the chair, resting his elbows on his knees. "I don't know if this truth will count for much."

Taylor's long lashes dipped at that. When he looked up again, some of the anger was gone from his eyes. "Try me."

"You asked when we first met how I knew Phil."

"You were in some sex thing together, right? Gray too. Like, some BDSM club?"

Warren nodded. "That's how it started, yeah. Me and Phil, and Gray, and our friend Charlie. Not any of us together, I mean. We all had other partners, at the time. The four of us were the Doms in our little clique."

"So?" The look on Taylor's face didn't quite mirror the petulance in his voice.

"The thing about BDSM is, it's a mixed bag, you know? There are the hardliners—the ones who look at it as a lifestyle. And then there's the *Fifty Shades* crowd—all these middle-aged couples just trying to put a bit of spice back in their sex life. And there's everything in between, right?"

Taylor nodded. "Right."

"But it's just like being part of the LGBT 'community.'" He made quotation marks with his fingers around the word. "They give a lot of lip service to 'diversity' and open-mindedness—and most of them follow through—but there's always this little, loudmouthed subset telling you how to behave and what to say. It starts out 'all for one, and one for all,' but by the end, somebody's drawing lines in the sand, telling you to choose a side. You can't be gay or bi or trans if you don't vote a certain way, act a certain way, follow some ridiculous set of rules. They all want you to be a round little peg in a round fucking hole. They want you to pick a box and a label so they know just where to put you, rather than accepting that we're all separate, unique people, and that our stories are all valid, no matter whether we fit in the box or not." He stopped, feeling himself headed into one of the rants that only Phil and Gray or Charlie would have understood. The confusion on Taylor's face was the response he was accustomed to. He took one more stab at it. "There's always that pissed-off minority who think their 'rules' outweigh your right to live your life."

Taylor waited, his expression unreadable.

"I guess it got to us all in different ways."

Taylor gave him a minute, but Warren had run out of steam. He had no idea where to go from where he'd ended up.

"So?" Taylor prompted at last. "Keep going. Somehow, this box you're talking about messed things up?"

"For Gray, well, he's kind of a rebel, you know? He fights against everything. You tell him the sky is blue, he'll want to know your source. You tell him something's been decided by the majority, he'll run down a checklist of why it's wrong. You tell him a gay Dom is supposed to act a certain way, and he'll turn around and push to go the other direction. You know what I mean?"

Taylor shook his head slowly. "No. But I don't really know Gray, so I don't care. What about you and Phil?"

"For Phil, I think it came down to respect. Nobody could take him seriously. I mean, you've seen him. He looks like a Boy Scout. He looks like Alex P. Keaton, for fuck's sake."

"Who?"

"Never mind." Warren ran his hand through his hair, wondering if it was wrong to share Phil's past with Taylor. He was supposed to be talking about himself, but where to begin? "When Stuart and I met, we were just two guys who were a bit unconventional in the bedroom. We loved each other. It was that simple. And it was good, you know? We were happy. I thought we'd be together forever."

"So what went wrong?"

"Somehow the sex became more important than the relationship."

"What do you mean?"

Warren shook his head, remembering. It was harder to talk about than he'd anticipated. "We started exploring the lifestyle, going deeper into that whole world. I thought it was just for fun, but I should've known better. Stuart never did things halfway. It was like somebody was selling heaven, and he bought the whole fucking burrito. By the end, all he cared about was the lifestyle. He wanted to be locked in a cage for hours at a time, to wear a chastity belt until I took it off. He wanted to make me the 'owner' of his orgasms or some crazy thing."

"You think that's wrong?"

"No, not wrong. It works for some people."

"But not for you, I take it."

"It just wasn't what I pictured for us. Whether or not we loved each other became irrelevant. Our entire relationship became about the 'rules,' and whether I was setting them right, or following them right, or allowing the right things." He thought back to the fights with Stuart and the pressure to live a certain way. "He had this fairy tale in his head where he got to live in a perpetual state of sexual bliss and I took care of everything else."

"And you couldn't give him that?"

"I tried. I really did. But I failed. Every day, I measured myself against some ridiculous ideal, and every single day, I came up short. And so, he left me."

"For somebody else?"

"Yes."

"Somebody in the lifestyle?"

"Yes."

A few seconds ticked by in silence.

"How does this relate to Phil and Gray and Charlie?"

"Their partners may have had different reasons, but the result was the same. The lifestyle felt like some kind of test, and we all scored big fat zeroes."

"And that's why you call yourselves the Heretic Doms Club."

Warren blinked over at him in surprise. "Did Phil tell you that?"

"I saw it once, snooping through his email."

Warren shook his head. He'd have to tell Phil to put a basic password protection on his computer if he was going to take men home with him. "Of course you did."

"Why heretics? Just because you didn't like the rules?"

Warren chuckled, remembering. "Initially, we called ourselves the Failed Doms, but then Gray's ex said something about him being a heretic because he's always arguing against what other people accept to be true, and he just embraced it. He sort of convinced us we hadn't failed. We'd just chosen to buck the rules. At the time, it gave us a bit of hope, I guess. It made us feel like rebels instead of losers, so we went with it." He held out his hands. "That's it. That's all I have. Only you can decide if that's a good enough truth."

Taylor steepled his fingers, debating. "Stuart's the man in the picture in your desk drawer?"

It was stupid to be surprised by the question. Taylor'd already admitted to snooping. Of course he'd seen the photo Warren kept hidden away. "Yes."

"Did you love him?"

"With all my heart."

"How long ago did he leave?"

"Five years now."

"Do you still love him?"

"No." Warren shook his head. "Sometimes I think I hate him, but I tell myself there's no point. It just wasn't meant to be."

Taylor pursed his lips, debating. Finally, he nodded. "Okay. That was a valid confession."

Warren sat back in his seat, waiting. It took Taylor a while to decide to talk, though. It was clearly something he had to work up to. Finally, he sighed. "If you say the words 'counseling' or 'therapy,' I'll be out the door before you've finished your sentence."

Warren nodded. "Fair enough."

Taylor chewed his lip a bit more. He took a pillow from the couch and hugged it to his chest. "I had a brother once."

It was a simple statement with heavy implications.

Once.

Not now.

But that wasn't all of it. Not even close. Warren knew that instinctively.

"He was two years older than me. His name was James. Everybody else in the family called him Jim or Jimmy." He smiled sadly. "He'll always be James to me, though."

Warren waited some more while Taylor wrestled with his demons.

"The thing is…"

And here it came. Warren braced himself, wanting to keep his poker face intact, no matter what Taylor divulged.

"We did things brothers aren't supposed to do." Taylor stopped, watching Warren, waiting for the judgment that statement probably normally elicited.

Warren only nodded. "Okay."

"At night sometimes, he'd come to my room. He'd come to my bed."

Warren nodded again. "Okay."

Taylor blew out his cheeks, gripping the pillow between his hands. "Sometimes he'd just touch me, or make me touch him." He twisted the pillow, his eyes on the ceiling, his cheeks slowly turning crimson. "But when he was mad, he'd do more."

"More?" Warren said, trying to urge him on without passing judgment. "You mean he'd hit you?"

Taylor nodded. "Sometimes, yes. But then, he'd…he'd penetrate me."

"Penetrate" was an interesting choice of words, especially for Taylor, who used the word "fucked" like it was going out of style.

Warren debated the next question. "With his fingers, or…?"

"Both," Taylor said, the words seeming to come easier now. "But I liked it best when he did it right."

Warren nodded, fighting to keep his face stony and blank. He made sure his voice was flat and impassive when he said, "You liked it when he had sex with you?"

Taylor smiled at him, his eyes suddenly brimming with tears. "I loved him."

Warren nodded, willing his heart to stay like stone. "Of course you did. He was your brother."

Taylor nodded, leaning forward, the pillow still clutched to his stomach. "See, nobody understands that! They say things like 'abused' and 'molested.' But it wasn't like that! James loved me."

"I'm sure he did."

Taylor chewed his lip again, and Warren decided to give him another push.

"You said 'when he got mad.' That's mostly when he did it the way you liked?"

Taylor nodded, his eyes begging for a level of understanding that Warren wasn't sure he could give. "Nobody else ever noticed me. Nobody cared. James was the jock, and the quarterback, and the star. And I was just the screwup accidental baby who couldn't even manage to pull C's in math or English. And the kids at school picked on me, but James understood me."

"He did?"

"Yes. He saw me when nobody else did."

"But you keep saying he'd make you do these things, like you weren't willing."

"At first, I wasn't. Later, I liked being with him, but he didn't like me to say yes too fast. He liked it when I said no."

Warren nodded, hoping Taylor couldn't see how that answer chilled him to his core. "So you'd resist, just to make him happy."

"Yes. And sometimes, I'd make him mad on purpose."

"So that he'd come to your room?"

Taylor nodded. "Exactly."

"And did it work?"

Taylor closed his eyes. "Yes." It was a whisper. Like some kind of prayer. "Sometimes he'd hit me first, but then he'd get behind me and make love to me. And sometimes he'd make me get on my knees and suck him. And then once…"

Warren waited, his stomach in knots.

"Once, he hadn't come to see me in a while. So I went into his room, and I broke three or four of his newest CDs. And that night, he dragged me out of my room by my hair, out into the empty property behind our house. Two of his friends were waiting."

Warren tried not to flinch, knowing what was coming.

"They passed me around for a while. Hitting me. Making me suck them. They made me do all kinds of things, I guess."

Warren forced himself to nod. "Okay."

"And up until that point, it was the most amazing orgasm of my life."

Nod. Keep nodding. Don't betray anything. "I see."

"And then James took me home and put me to bed. He tucked me in and told me he loved me. And he made me a promise."

"What did he promise?" Warren had a feeling it was something he wouldn't like.

"That he'd always be there. That he'd always take care of me like he had that night."

Warren's head spun with the wrongness of it. He kept his voice calm and reasonable, not letting Taylor hear any of his incredulousness or his skepticism. "And that was something you wanted?"

Taylor nodded, his eyes closed, a single tear rolling down his cheek. "More than anything."

"So?" Warren hoped his voice sounded gentle. "What happened?"

"He went away to college. And sometimes he had girlfriends, but that was okay, because I was still in high school. But eventually, I'd go to college too. And once that happened, there wouldn't be girlfriends. There'd just be me and James, and we'd be together the way he promised.

"But then, my senior year, he came home for Thanksgiving. He didn't have a girlfriend anymore, and I knew it was because he could never love them the way he loved me. But he wasn't spending any time with me. He went out every night alone." He swallowed and wiped tears from his face. "And I missed him. So I went into his room with the scissors. I cut holes in his high school letter jacket. I left it on his bed so he'd see it the minute he came home. And then I went back to my room, and I waited." He took a deep shuddering breath. Then another.

"Did he come?" Warren asked.

"No. I lay there all night. One minute I was scared, and the next minute I was anxious, you know? And ready, because I loved him, and I'd always be ready for him. I just wanted us to be together like before. But morning came and he hadn't come home at all." He wiped his face again. "And then the police knocked on the door." He finally met Warren's eyes. "He'd been drinking."

"He died that night?"

Taylor nodded. He took a few more deep breaths, trying to steady himself, although his eyes refused to stay dry. "There's a place on the reservoir where people would commit suicide by running into the cliff at the bottom of the road. They said that's what he'd done, but I knew it wasn't on purpose." He wiped his cheeks again, sniffling. "He was coming home to me. I know it. He would never have broken his promise to me."

"And that's why you cut yourself?"

Taylor nodded. "Sometimes it was the only way to stop thinking about him. It was easier to feel that pain than the real pain, you know?"

"What happened to James wasn't your fault," Warren said.

Taylor nodded. "I know. But I loved him. And I think about him every day. I think, if he'd only lived, I wouldn't be this way. I wouldn't be broken and fucked up, because he'd be taking care of me."

Warren forced himself to nod. "Maybe." Maybe not. Either way, it sure explained a few things. "Was James the one who, you know, did the other thing?" He didn't want to use the words "peed" or "urinated."

Taylor shook his head, wiping his eyes. "No. I wish he'd thought of that, but he didn't. That was somebody else. Somebody I was with for a while."

"When?"

"I don't know. When I was twenty or so. I thought he'd take care of me forever, like James promised to do, but he didn't. He was nobody. He'd be just another guy I fucked a few times if it hadn't been for that."

"You still miss James, then?"

"Every day. Don't you miss Stuart?"

So odd to have Taylor put them in the same sentence, as if their experiences were the same.

Or maybe it was silly of Warren to think they weren't.

"No," he said. "Hardly ever, these days."

Taylor nodded, his eyes on the vase. He reached forward and picked it up, cradling it gently. "Do you think somebody can be mended without being fixed? Do you think scars in a person can be beautiful the way they are in this vase?"

"I think you're worrying too much about semantics. The only thing you can really do is keep putting one foot in front the other."

Taylor nodded again, but he didn't really seem to have heard. He carefully set the vase back on the table.

"It's okay that you loved him," Warren said, because what else could he say? "It's okay that you miss him."

Taylor blinked at him, tears spilling down his cheeks. "Really?"

"Of course."

Taylor covered his face, his breath catching in his chest.

"Taylor?"

"You're the only person who's ever told me that."

And that, Warren thought, was wrong. Because as fucked up as things had been, James had somehow been Taylor's anchor.

Warren reached across the gap to touch him, hoping to hold him, but Taylor pushed his hand away, choosing instead to turn away and cry into the arm of the couch.

Even now, Taylor didn't know how to let somebody comfort him.

Chapter 11

Taylor acted gun-shy around him the rest of the day, and Warren did his best not to treat him any different. It was hard, but probably not for the reasons Taylor thought. He assumed Warren would somehow see him as tainted or flawed. In truth, the only thing Taylor's confession did was make Warren even more determined to protect him from anything down the road.

If only Taylor would let him.

Warren checked on Sugar that afternoon, picking up some takeout soup on the way. He had a feeling solid food would be out of the question for the next few days. But if he expected gratitude, it wasn't forthcoming.

"You shouldn't have done it," Sugar told him in the doorway. She looked awful. Her face was swollen and bruised. She was hardly recognizable as the pretty young girl Warren knew. "You had no business hurting Robby."

"I thought he could use a taste of his own medicine."

"Robby isn't a bad guy. He just—"

"Take the soup," Warren said, shoving the container into her hand. He didn't want to hear her make excuses for her abusive ex. He'd heard them all before from his mother.

He was getting into his car when Jack caught him. "Hey, mister?"

Warren turned in the open door of his car, one hand on the roof. "Yeah?"

Jack looked older today. Maybe it was only because he didn't look scared, like the last time Warren had seen him. "I'm glad you did it."

"I didn't do anything."

"He'll come back, though." He didn't just look older. He looked *old*. His eyes were like those of children he'd seen in Afghanistan—the ones forced into armies when they should have been playing with marbles. "You should've killed him."

Warren couldn't help thinking Jack was right. Men like Robby had nothing to offer the world but bruises and pain, but killing him would have meant a real investigation. It would have meant forcing Gray to look a lot deeper than a rocks and mineral show and a live-in boyfriend's shoddy alibi. Warren didn't worry much about things like prison, but he wouldn't want to cause trouble for Gray or Charlie.

Warren had never felt so old. He wanted nothing more than to go home and climb between the sheets with Taylor. Unfortunately, he had several hours of work between him and that simple goal.

Thursday night meant working with Taffy, who serviced her clients in cars. Warren always stood in the shadows, in a place where he could easily see what was happening. It was awkward, trying to watch without totally *watching*. He didn't need to see her sucking the guys off or watch them come. He just needed to make sure nobody got rough. The problem was, Taffy was edgy. Warren halfway wondered if she was a friend of Sugar's and had been told of his bad behavior. It wasn't until the end of the night that it all became clear.

"I don't think I'll need you after tonight." She'd just handed him his payment for the evening. She at least had the decency to meet his gaze while she fired him. "I appreciate you helping me all this time."

"You leaving the business?" Warren asked.

She shrugged. She wore a glittery tube top with a cropped fur jacket. The latter kept sliding off her shoulder. "I been working Fridays on my own. Haven't had any trouble in a while, you know? It's mostly regulars now, and they know how to behave. Truth is, my kid's hockey lessons are killing me. All the equipment and the travel? I need to cut costs. That's all."

Warren didn't like it, not because it meant losing his income but because he knew she was gambling with her life. Then again, it wasn't his business. She'd paid him all these years to keep her safe. Now she needed the money more than she needed protection.

At least he'd have his Thursday nights free from now on.

"Let me know if you change your mind."

She was only doing what she thought she had to do, but Warren still hated it. He felt like he was being punished for Robby, even though he'd only been trying to help.

Maybe he was too old for this gig. After Afghanistan, working as a bodyguard had been an easy option. It kept him awake and aware and gave his anger a purpose. These days, the anger was hard to find. All he felt now was tired.

He found Taylor fresh out of the shower, standing naked in his bedroom, rubbing a towel over his wet hair. He had his back to Warren, and for a moment, Warren simply stood there, watching him. Taylor seemed to grow more beautiful by the day, but Warren was intelligent enough to realize it wasn't Taylor changing at all. Warren's feelings for him were getting the best of him. The boy who'd come into his life as a whore now seemed to represent everything good and pure in Warren's world. Sometimes he almost believed he could soak up some of Taylor's brightness and youth and warmth just by touching him. But since Taylor's confession about James that morning, he'd kept Warren at arm's length.

"Hey," Warren said. "I'm home."

"Oh." Taylor turned to face him. Even now, he didn't seem completely comfortable with Warren. "I didn't hear you come in." He clutched the towel to his chest, reaching down with one hand to ensure it covered his nakedness. It was unlike him, hiding his body. Warren thought it had more to do with the scars on his thighs than his nudity. "Something must have happened," Taylor said. "You're scowling more than usual."

"Taffy fired me."

"You didn't beat up her boyfriend too, did you?"

Taylor was trying to get him to smile, but it was the last thing Warren felt like doing. "I think it was more a financial decision than a personal one."

"I see."

They fell silent. Warren hated the sudden awkwardness between them. He wanted nothing more than to rip Taylor's towel away. To tell him that scars or not, he was still gorgeous. More importantly, he wanted to make him understand that nothing had changed between them. Only twenty-four hours ago, Taylor would have been flaunting his nudity, not hiding it.

"You don't have to be afraid of me," Warren said.

Taylor's cheeks flushed, but with it came a hesitant smile. He let the towel fall to his waist. "I know." And yet he still looked half-terrified. "Can I ask you a question?"

"Sure."

Taylor went to the closet, opened it, and pointed to a wooden contraption tucked inside. "What's this?"

Warren had a feeling his scowl deepened, but it was hard to be sure. "A spanking horse."

Taylor only blinked at him, clearly unsatisfied with the answer.

"It opens up. It's an A-frame, you know?" Warren used his hands to trace the shape and size of it in the air. "Like a carpentry horse, but it has pads so you can lie on it, on your stomach."

"To be spanked?"

"Or fucked, yeah."

Taylor laughed. After the strange tension of their conversation, it was good to hear. "You don't sound very excited by the idea."

"Stuart wanted it." The idea of strapping Taylor down on the wooden horse was enough to stir his blood, but it'd never been his favorite toy. He could think of at least a dozen things he'd rather do with Taylor than spank him. He eyed Taylor up and down, considering.

Taylor smiled at him, although he still didn't drop his towel. "Are you going to take me to bed, or stand here gabbing all night?"

Compared to his usual invitations, this one felt lukewarm. "I'd pick the former, for sure. But only if it's what you want."

"Of course it is."

"Are you sure?"

Taylor's smile faltered. "Anytime you want. Isn't that the deal?"

Warren felt like he'd been kicked in the gut. "That's not the same as you wanting it, is it?" He turned toward the sanctuary of his own room. "Good night, Tay."

"Warren, wait." Taylor caught him by his wrist in the hallway, the towel still clutched in his other hand. "I didn't mean that the way it sounded."

"How else could you mean it?"

Taylor's lip quivered. "I only meant..." He sighed and looked down at the floor. "I don't know what I meant. I just hate that things are suddenly weird between us. I should never have told you about my brother."

Warren put his hand over Taylor's where it lay on his wrist. "Is that why you think things are suddenly off? Because you told me about James?"

Taylor looked up at him with his golden eyes. "Isn't it?"

No, not in Warren's mind. As far as he was concerned, things were different because Taylor was suddenly acting like he was afraid of Warren. But he wasn't sure how to say that.

"You don't want to touch me now," Taylor whispered.

"Oh, honey." Warren shook his head. "That's so far from the truth, I can't even tell you how wrong you are."

Taylor's lips twitched toward a smile. "Really?"

"Really."

"Then prove it."

He let Warren kiss him and touch him and guide him toward the bed. And yet still, he seemed strangely hesitant. None of his responses struck Warren as truly genuine. Maybe Warren was being too gentle. Taylor seemed to like it best when Warren was a bit rough, so Warren gripped Taylor's wrists, holding his hands down against the mattress while he kissed him. That earned him enough of a response that he thought maybe he was on the right track.

The wrist cuffs were still attached to the posts at the head of the bed from the last time they'd used them. Taylor didn't say a word as Warren strapped the first wrist in place, although he still held the towel over his naked groin. Taylor whimpered a bit as Warren buckled his second wrist in place, and Warren paused. It didn't sound like arousal or anticipation. It sounded like true fear.

He searched Taylor's face. "We don't have to do this. You can always say no."

Taylor shook his head. "I never say no."

Not exactly the response he was hoping for, but Warren finished buckling the cuff and stepped back to appreciate what he had. Taylor lay sprawled on the bed, his arms stretched up and out to the sides, the towel draped between his legs. Jesus, he was gorgeous. There were half a dozen things Warren wanted to do to him.

But still, something seemed off. Taylor was shaking, his eyes on the ceiling.

Warren climbed onto the bed, between Taylor's legs. He pulled the towel aside, and Taylor made that same soft, whimpering sound. Warren was a bit surprised Taylor wasn't erect. Usually just being tied down was enough to turn him on. Warren ran his hand gently up Taylor's leg. Taylor closed his eyes, wincing, as if he'd rather be anywhere than where he was.

"Talk to me, Tay," Warren said. "Tell me what's wrong. If you need to be untied—"

"No. No, it's not that."

"Then what is it?"

Taylor shook his head. "I don't know."

Warren moved so he was crouching over him, looking down into his face. He traced his finger slowly down Taylor's chest, but the nearer he got to Taylor's groin, the more Taylor tried to twist away. Warren stopped his caress. He did his best not to be hurt by Taylor's rejection.

"Taylor? Honey, look at me."

"I can't."

"You're afraid of me. Why now?"

"I'm not. I swear, I'm not." And yet he began tugging at the bonds, trying to pull free.

"Taylor—"

But when Warren tried to touch him again, Taylor almost sobbed. He wiggled away from Warren as fast as he could, as if he could take shelter against the headboard, even with his hands still tied. He was almost panicking in his struggle.

"It's okay," Warren said, trying to calm him down as he rushed to undo the cuffs. It was quicker to unhook the cuff from the O-ring in the bed frame than to unbuckle the part around Taylor's wrists. "You're fine. I'm not going to hurt you. Hang on. Just hang on."

Once both wrists were free, Taylor grabbed the blanket from the foot of the bed and pulled it to him, clutching it to his chest, the leather cuffs still strapped around his wrists. He took a deep, shuddering breath. The freedom seemed to have solved the problem, though.

That, Warren realized, or the blanket.

Warren reached out for Taylor's wrist, giving him plenty of time to object or pull away. But Taylor let him take one hand, then the other, and undo the leather cuffs.

"I don't know what happened," Taylor finally said, once both cuffs were off. He shook his head. "I don't know why—"

"You're afraid of me."

"No! Warren, you keep saying that, but that's not it."

"Then what? And don't just say you don't know. I want you to think about what made you freak out just now." He put his hand against Taylor's cheek and was pleased when Taylor leaned into his touch. "Maybe it isn't me exactly, but something about that situation had you scared to death."

Taylor's eyes moved back and forth as he thought about it, remembering what had happened. "I guess…"

"What?"

"It sounds stupid."

"Say it anyway."

"I'm not sure that I've ever felt that naked." He laughed, although it wasn't exactly a joyful sound. "I know that sounds ridiculous, after everything we've done. After all the other times you've tied me down. But it never felt like that." He looked down at where he still held the blanket tight against his naked body. "I just felt so naked. That's the only way I can put it." He shook his head. "Like, I said, it's stupid."

But Warren understood, even if Taylor didn't. It wasn't about being naked. It was about being vulnerable. Sure, he'd let Warren tie him up multiple times since they'd met. But now, having confessed his deepest, darkest secret to Warren, Taylor had lost his surety. He'd lost the cocky playfulness that usually stayed with him through the sex. He'd opened himself up in a way he wasn't entirely comfortable with, and now he didn't know how to go back to where they'd been before.

Warren debated. He wasn't good at giving up control. But Taylor had shown Warren his greatest weakness. It seemed only fair that Warren do the same.

"Hold out your hands."

"Why?"

Warren did his best to give him a reassuring smile. "Trust me. Please."

Taylor let the blanket fall to his lap. He held out his hands, palms up. Warren made himself lay the cuffs in them.

Taylor stared at them, clearly not understanding. Warren held his own wrists out to be bound, although it was one of the hardest things he'd ever done.

Taylor looked up at him, his eyes wide. "Do you mean it?"

Already, Warren's heart was pounding—not from arousal or excitement, but from something akin to panic. "I do." It scared the hell out of him, but that was sort of the point.

Taylor contemplated the cuffs in his hands, and Warren's proffered wrists, and the bed. Finally, he took a deep breath and said, "Will you get undressed?"

There was no note of command in his voice. It was more a plea than anything. Despite his unease, Warren almost laughed. "I will."

"Then, maybe sit up here." Taylor patted the head of the bed. "With your back against the headboard?"

It was a request more than an order, but Warren obliged. Taylor kept the blanket wrapped around him and moved off the bed to make room for Warren. Warren took Taylor's place, naked on the bed, his heart pounding. He held his arms out so Taylor could cuff each arm to one of the posts. He had to force himself to breathe deep. To stay calm. It took serious effort not to pull against his bonds. Some deep, primitive part of him wanted desperately to fight for freedom.

Taylor finally dropped the blanket and settled naked across Warren's lap, his hands on Warren's chest. At any other time, Warren would have been pleased, but it was all he could do to keep from straining against the cuffs.

Taylor kissed him. Not pushing at all, but parting his lips to let Warren in, the way he normally did when he was the one tied down. Warren tried to focus on how soft Taylor's lips were. On how sweet he tasted. On how gentle his touch was. But all he could think about was how utterly helpless he was, chained to the bed.

Taylor pulled back a bit, his brow wrinkling. He put his hand on Warren's cheek. "You don't like this?"

Warren tried to steady himself. He'd offered this for a reason. Backing out now would be an asshole move. "I like tying people down, but I've never understood how anybody could like being on this side of it."

Taylor's eyes went wide. "Really?"

"Really."

"You've never—"

"No." He had to take a deep breath. To remind himself that Taylor wasn't a threat. That ancient, animal part of his brain wasn't convinced.

Taylor studied him for a moment—taking in Warren's eyes, and his arms, which were taut and tense despite Warren's efforts to relax. Finally, understanding dawned. "You're afraid?" He seemed stunned by the idea. "You're actually afraid of me?"

"Not afraid," Warren said. "Vulnerable." Never mind that they both caused the same kind of panic. "That's why you panicked, right? You felt vulnerable."

Taylor sat back. "I guess so." He eyed the cuffs. "I should untie you."

"No. Don't do that."

"But you aren't enjoying it."

"Maybe not yet." And that was the gamble he was willing to make. "That doesn't mean I won't."

Taylor touched Warren's face the way he often did, gently caressing each of Warren's scars in turn. "Why are you doing this?"

"To make us even."

For a moment, Warren thought he didn't understand. But the very next instant, Taylor smiled, even as his eyes filled with tears. He took Warren's face between his smooth, soft palms. He brushed his lips lightly over Warren's. "Are you sure?" he asked, his breath shaky.

No. "Yes."

Taylor wiped his eyes, his smile growing. Whatever walls he'd built after telling Warren about James, Warren could almost see them crumbling. He could practically feel Taylor's usual flirtatious attitude seeping back in, bit by bit. Taylor slid one hand down to caress Warren's groin. "You're not vulnerable, Warren. Not ever. You're the strongest man I've ever met." He kissed Warren's neck as he talked, his right hand softly stroking Warren's cock into alertness. "You could pull out of those cuffs, if you really wanted to." Warren resisted the urge to try, focusing instead on Taylor's gentle ministrations. "But you don't need to. You don't need to be strong right this moment. All you need to do is lie there and let me make you feel good."

He started by moving down and taking Warren deep into his throat. Warren tilted his head back, closed his eyes, and did his best to let go.

It was harder than it should have been. Even with Taylor sucking him, it was difficult to quiet that part of his brain that wanted to be free. Taylor moved up to straddle Warren's lap again. He sank slowly onto Warren's cock, kissing him as he went, only letting Warren in by gradual degrees. Warren was desperate to push deeper, to grab Taylor and fuck him like mad, but he stayed perfectly still, letting Taylor work his way there. Even once Taylor was all the way down, Warren's cock as deep as it could go given their position, Taylor kept things slow, shifting his hips forward and back, rocking just a bit. He wrapped his arms around Warren's neck and tilted his head back, making soft little moaning sounds as he moved. Warren groaned in frustration, wanting to do more than just sit there. It felt good—of course it did!—but he wanted more. He wanted to plunge his tongue into Taylor's sweet mouth. He wanted to suck on his neck hard enough to leave marks. He wanted to thrust hard and fast until he came. Instead, he focused on the quiet sounds Taylor made as his movements shifted, his hips moving in slow circles.

"Oh God, Warren."

Watching Taylor made it easier to forget his bonds. He was still desperate to touch Taylor, or to kiss him, but if this was all he could have for the moment, he'd take it. Taylor was still sweet and sexy as hell. The slow rotation was teasingly delicious, especially as the circles became faster. Taylor's breathing sped up as his hips gained momentum.

"Oh God," he breathed again. "Yes. Yes, yes, yes!"

Faster and faster, the gyrations became more frantic and urgent until Taylor's forward motion was slamming Warren back against the headboard and Warren finally lost himself to it. He still wanted freedom. He still wanted more. But this wasn't about him. It was about Taylor, and Taylor's arousal was amazing to see. The look on his face and the sounds he made as their movements became more pronounced were worth letting himself be tied up.

"Oh God!"

Taylor sounded practically desperate now as he rocked wildly in Warren's lap. "More," he panted, suddenly clawing at the cuff holding Warren's right hand. "More! Jesus, more, Warren, more—"

Whether the cuff came undone or whether Warren simply broke the damn thing, he didn't know and didn't care. His hand came free, and Taylor guided it to his cock. He made a wonderfully satisfied sound deep in his throat as Warren began to stroke.

"Yes!"

Taylor leaned backward on his hands, his eyes closed, his back arching as he rocked his hips harder. Warren stroked him, matching his movements to the thrust of Taylor's hips, fighting to keep his own orgasm at bay just a moment longer. He had a feeling that was all it would take.

He wasn't wrong.

"Oohhhhh, *God!*"

Warren groaned with relief as he finally let go. It wasn't often they came at the same time, but it was damned nice when they did. After all his anxiety about being tied up, Warren didn't regret it one bit.

Once he'd caught his breath, Taylor leaned close again, his forehead against Warren's. "All this, just so we'd be even?"

"Only seemed fair."

Taylor smiled. "I think that's the nicest thing anybody's ever done for me."

Warren fought the urge to pull at the one remaining cuff. "You're welcome, I guess? Anything to make you feel better."

"I do." Taylor's smile was wickedly teasing. And best of all, it was *him*. It was familiar. It was as if he'd suddenly found his way home. "But I think I prefer when we do things the other way."

"I'm sure glad to hear it."

Warren's next few days were mundane but busy. Warmer weather meant more work for the various women he played bodyguard to. Sugar took the weekend off, but it only meant Candy was twice as busy. Between the long work hours and sleep, he barely saw Taylor at all. He hated it. After the intimacy of their confessions, he wanted to spend every minute by Taylor's side.

But of course, there was still work to be done and bills to be paid.

Gray called on Saturday afternoon to report his short-lived investigation into Robby's attack had been nixed. With no solid leads and a victim who seemed to have no interest in finding his assailant, the chief of police had decided it wasn't worth the man hours. Warren was relieved to find out he was in the clear, but quick on the heels of that came a call from Charlie.

"I need a favor."

Warren was in his car, on his way to the motel where he'd cover Candy all night. He wanted to say no. Charlie's favors were rarely simple, but Charlie had taken care of Sugar, then lied to Gray to cover Warren's ass. Warren figured he owed Charlie at least once over, if not twice. "Name it."

"Starting tomorrow, I'm babysitting a kid coming off heroin. I could use a wingman."

"Shit."

"Don't get too excited. I know it'll be a party, but—"

"You're talking at least a week."

"I know. It's a big one."

"Cold turkey?"

"Yep."

"With or without meds?"

"Only OTC."

That meant no methadone or buprenorphine. It was far from ideal, but Warren had to assume the user had a reason for turning down a medicated rehab in a cushy facility. "A friend of yours or what?"

"Not really a friend. He came by my clinic a couple of months ago, drug seeking. I wouldn't give him anything, of course, but he was already at that point of wanting to get clean. You know how it is."

Warren nodded in the privacy of his car. Even after deciding they wanted to quit using, it usually took addicts a while to make the commitment.

"Anyway," Charlie went on, "I told him once he was ready, I'd do everything I could to help. Two days ago, he knocked on my door, said he wanted to get clean. So, what do you say? Feel like helping out?"

No, but whether he liked it or not, he owed Charlie. "Tell me where and when."

Sunday afternoon, Warren arrived at the address he'd been given—a run-down building in a low-rent neighborhood. He climbed the exterior steps to the second-floor apartment. Based on the smell when Charlie let him in, the detox had already begun. The kitchen was full of dirty dishes, but they weren't the source of the odor. The reek of vomit and feces coming from the bedroom was almost enough to make Warren's eyes water.

"He's in the tub right now," Charlie told Warren. "Come on in."

Warren followed him through the narrow living room to the bathroom, where their patient sat rocking in the bathtub. He could have been anywhere from early twenties to late forties. It was hard to tell. He was stick thin, with stringy black hair.

"This is Riley," Charlie said. "Riley, this is my friend Warren. He'll be helping us out." Then, to Warren, "He had the chills, so we put him in a warm bath."

Riley rocked faster in the tub, his arms wrapped around his knees. "I can't do this, man. I can't do this. I can't do this—"

"Why no methadone?" Warren asked. Technically, it was prescription only, but he had a feeling Charlie could have tracked some down.

"No way, man," Riley said, still rocking in the tub. "I've seen what happens with that shit. Trade one addiction for another. It ain't no solution, man." His damp black hair swung wildly around his hair as he shook his head. "It ain't no solution."

"Okay," Warren said. "Fair enough." There was no "right" way to come off heroin. Regardless of the method, most addicts relapsed within a year. And Riley was right—methadone worked for some, but for others, the resulting dependency was just as hard to kick as the heroin had been. "How old are you?"

"Twenty-seven."

"How long you been using?"

"Five years, off and on."

"Relatively small doses," Charlie said. "That's in his favor."

That was better than the alternative, certainly. "This your first time quitting?" Warren asked Riley.

"Second."

Each subsequent attempt was supposed to be worse than the one before, but Riley had youth on his side. The fact he'd only been using for five years was also a bonus, albeit a small one.

"I gotta get out, man. I gotta get out."

"Are you feeling sick again?" Charlie asked.

"No. Just gotta move. Gotta move. Gotta move."

Restless legs were a common symptom of withdrawal. Riley paced the apartment for twenty straight minutes before succumbing to the next bout of vomiting and diarrhea. Charlie tended to him while Warren cleaned the kitchen and made some food. Rice, chicken broth, saltine crackers, and Gatorade.

Riley wouldn't have much of an appetite, but Warren would do his best to get a few bites into him when he could.

At eight, Charlie called it a night, with a promise to be back by six the next morning. He left behind Valerian root, melatonin, and chamomile tea, designed to help Riley sleep; an anti-diarrheic, for obvious reasons; an antihistamine, which some addicts claimed helped with the restless legs; and finally Phenergan—the one prescription medicine Charlie had with him—to help with the nausea. He also left a pile of what he claimed were Riley's favorite feel-good movies, acquired before the detox had begun, in hopes of helping alleviate the depression that always accompanied heroin withdrawal. The problem was, there was no TV or DVD player. Riley had undoubtedly hocked them at some point in order to buy drugs.

Riley managed to sleep in twenty-minute increments. The vomiting and diarrhea continued. The antihistamine did nothing to alleviate his nervous energy. He paced and paced until the chills because too much to bear, and then he was back in the tub. The apartment's tiny hot water heater couldn't keep up with the many baths Riley needed, at which point they tried using a pile of blankets. That proved to be a mistake, because it meant Riley couldn't get to the toilet fast enough when the diarrhea hit again. Warren snatched fragmented naps when he could, but they didn't add up to much. By the time Charlie arrived the next morning, Warren was exhausted.

"How's he doing?" Charlie asked.

"He's sleeping again a bit. He isn't drinking enough fluids. You might see if you can push that."

"Did you have to restrain him?"

"Not yet. The desire to quit is still a bit more than the hunger." It wouldn't be for long, though. At some point, things could get ugly. "I'll bring Jell-O when I come back tonight." It was easy on the stomach and offered a bit of fluid to boot. "Not much anxiety yet, but I have a feeling the depression's going to get bad. You checked the bathroom, right? No razor blades? Nothing he could try to OD on?"

Suicide attempts during withdrawal weren't out of the ordinary.

"I'll go through it again. Make sure I didn't miss anything."

"All right. I'm taking a load of laundry home to wash, since he doesn't have a machine. I'll be back in time for dinner."

"Thanks, man. The good news is, we only have a week to go."

"Your idea of good news is about a mile off the mark."

Back at home, Warren shoved Riley's vomit-and-feces-soaked laundry into the machine, started the cycle with prewash and extra rinse, and headed for bed. Taylor met him in the hallway wearing only his pink robe and a tired smile. He put his arms out as if to embrace Warren, but Warren held up his hands and backed away.

"I spent the last twelve hours cleaning up shit and puke. Trust me. You don't want to touch me until I've showered."

Taylor took a step back, covering his nose with the sleeve of his robe, as if he could suddenly smell what Warren had been dealing with at Riley's. He spoke around his hand. "I hate when you're gone all night."

"Me too. Do me a favor and put that laundry in the dryer when it's done?"

"Of course."

"Do we have any Jell-O?"

"I think so. Want me to make some?"

"If you would." Warren's weariness made it hard to think. It felt like the day he'd first brought Taylor home, when Warren had been so tired, he could barely stay on his feet. "I need to shower, then I'm going to bed." And the only reason bed wasn't happening first was because he'd rarely felt so disgusting. "Do me one more favor?"

"Don't wake you unless the world is ending?"

"Exactly."

He slept hard and woke several hours later to Taylor climbing into bed with him and snuggling close in his pink robe.

"The world isn't ending," Taylor whispered. "I thought I could sneak in without waking you."

Warren pulled him close and held him tight. The fluffy robe made it feel like cuddling a life-sized stuffed animal. "I don't mind." He'd slept long enough, and it felt good to simply lie there, holding Taylor. "I'm sorry I ordered you around like a servant. That was rude."

Taylor shifted, tilting his head back to look up at Warren. "You didn't order me to do anything. You asked me for a couple of little favors. It's no big deal."

Warren's gruffness had never boded well for his relationships. It confounded him that Taylor forgave him so easily. At some point, he knew Taylor would get tired of dealing with him.

"You have to go back tonight?" Taylor asked.

"Yep."

"For how long?"

"All night."

"No. I mean, how long will this job last?"

It wasn't much of a job, considering he wasn't getting paid, but that was neither here nor there. "At least a week, although I'll have to talk to Charlie about switching up hours on Wednesday and over the weekend so I can still help my regulars." At least his Thursday night would be clear now that Taffy had terminated his service.

"You'll hardly be home at all."

It wasn't quite an accusation, but Warren heard a note of bitterness in Taylor's voice. "I owe Charlie."

They lay there for a few more minutes, but somehow, the peacefulness of the moment was gone. Maybe it was knowing Taylor resented him for leaving. Maybe it was simply because Warren was already thinking about what the next few days would be like—exhausting and gross.

"Do you think people like us could ever have a normal life?" Taylor asked, his voice quiet.

"You don't think this is normal?"

"I just mean, like a regular job, where you'd leave in the morning and be home by dinner and get to sleep at night."

Warren let go of him and rolled onto his back to stare up at his bedroom ceiling. "I tried that, when I first came home. It didn't work."

"Why not?"

"It's hard to explain." Although he'd tried often enough over the years, and he'd talked with Gray about it. "Living over there, it's like every second is spent on a knife's edge, like you're half a second away from jumping into battle. Even the downtimes, when you're bored out of your skull, you're still wound up tight, waiting for the shit to hit the fan. You spend every second knowing your whole fucking world could be blown to hell at any moment. It's like a constant overdose of adrenaline. You're wired all the time." He shook his head, knowing he hadn't really captured the root of the problem. "It's a high that never goes away."

"Until you come home."

"Exactly."

"You worked for your uncle?"

"I tried, but I couldn't handle it. I'd be standing in somebody's perfect little house, listening to them gripe about how their outlets are loose and the computer won't stay plugged in, and all I wanted to do was smash their heads in. I wanted to cram their faces into the TV screen and tell them to pay attention to the fucking world. The government's been funding wars all over the world for decades. Kids in Third World countries die because we gave bombs and guns to the other side, and here the American civilians are not even bothering to pay attention. Just buying Starbucks and worrying about who made the playoffs."

Taylor sat up, pulling his robe tighter around him. "You hate all of us then, just a little bit."

"No." Maybe at some point he had, but not now. "That was a long time ago."

Since coming home, he'd realized most people only bothered being outraged when they felt personally inconvenienced. They picked out cars and lawnmowers and nail polish, ignoring decades full of death and horror unleashed on the world by their own government. They blindly believed it'd all work out for the best, never understanding that when it came to war, "the best" for one side always meant the worst for the other.

People died either way.

Warren had enlisted after his mother's death, hoping for a healthy outlet for his anger. Instead, Afghanistan transformed his rage into something fierce and impetuous. Something he could barely control. It'd nearly destroyed everything good left in his heart. But after coming home, there was no healthy way to keep feeding that beast. For better or worse, that knife's edge from Afghanistan had begun to dull. Warren could be outraged all he wanted, but all it did was drain his days of happiness. It didn't change anything, for anybody, anywhere. It was a hard pill to swallow, but it was true. The complacency of everyday life—the very thing that had nearly driven him mad when he'd first come home—held a certain amount of appeal for him now.

He reached out and took Taylor's hand. "As for us having a normal life, I'm not saying it's impossible, but I can't make any promises. Is that what you need? Some kind of guarantee?"

Taylor bit his lip and slowly shook his head. "No. It was just a question."

Maybe someday Warren would have an answer.

Chapter 12

Over the next few days, Taylor barely saw Warren. Between his regular "clients" and helping Charlie take care of Riley, he was only home long enough to shower and sleep. And so on Thursday, Taylor made his request.

"Take me with you."

Warren was in the laundry room, his back to Taylor as he pulled Riley's clean laundry out of the dryer. "You don't want to come, Tay. It's a mess."

"I don't care if it's a mess. I'd rather be with you than here alone."

"It isn't a party. It's—"

"I know what it is. But I can help, can't I?"

"What the hell makes you think you can help?"

Taylor fell back a step. Warren might as well have slapped him. He wanted to believe it was only Warren's weariness and frustration talking, but maybe this was truly how he saw Taylor. "Do you really think I'm that worthless?"

"Christ." Warren dropped the laundry and turned to drag Taylor into his arms. He kissed the top of Taylor's head. "I didn't mean it that way."

Taylor stood stiff in his embrace. "How else could you have meant it?"

Warren let him go and turned back to the laundry, although he was a bit rougher with the blankets and pillowcases than he needed to be. "It's just that this whole thing's pointless. Charlie and I can hold the kid's hand for a few more days, but the chances of him staying clean for more than a month are almost nil." He slammed the dryer door shut and turned to face Taylor again. "It's a shit storm. And that's a more literal description than you might realize."

Taylor stood strong, almost daring Warren to challenge him again. "I can help." Granted, he wasn't exactly sure how yet, but he'd know once they got there. If nothing else, he could watch Riley once in a while so Warren could get a bit of sleep. "Please, Warren. At least let me try."

Warren's scowl lapsed into something that was almost a smile. This time when he reached out to pull Taylor into his arms, Taylor went willingly. "Truth is, I wouldn't mind the company."

Taylor craned his neck back to look up at Warren's face. "Does that mean I can come?"

"It does. But don't say I didn't warn you."

The smell hit Taylor before he even stepped foot in Riley's apartment. Vomit and shit and a sickly, sour smell he couldn't quite identify. He resisted the urge to cover his nose, or to comment on it. He didn't want to do anything that might make Warren regret allowing him to tag along.

Warren went straight to the kitchen and began working on the dishes. Taylor found himself face-to-chest with a bearded, tattooed giant. He wasn't quite as tall as Warren, but he was every bit as wide and twice as hairy. Taylor recognized him from the photo in Warren's desk drawer—Charlie, the final member of the Heretic Doms Club.

"Well, well, well," Charlie said, eyeing Taylor up and down. "What have we here?"

"This is Taylor. He's helping me out tonight."

Charlie's eyes went back and forth between them. Taylor knew he wanted to ask questions, just as Gray had done. "I'm sort of his roommate," Taylor said, trying to nip the awkwardness in the bud.

Charlie grinned over at Warren. "Roommate, huh? No wonder you've been slightly less grumpy than usual."

Warren's only response was to scowl into his dishwater, but it was the type of scowl that spoke more of mild embarrassment than actual annoyance or anger. "Where's Riley?"

"Sleeping. He's been out more than an hour. I imagine he'll wake soon."

"How's he been?"

"Nausea's better. He ate a sandwich for lunch and kept it down."

"That's good."

"Yeah, but the depression's kicking in." Charlie pointed toward the corner of the tiny living room. "Brought my TV and DVD player so you could make use of those movies, if he's up for it. Might help keep his mind off it."

Charlie collected another basket of stinking laundry. The fact that they needed to do a load every twelve hours said a lot about what Taylor had to expect for the coming evening. Charlie nodded toward a backpack on the couch. "Grab that for me and help me out."

Taylor did so, following Charlie out the door. Charlie could easily have put the backpack on rather than having Taylor carry it for him. It was clearly nothing more than a ploy to get Taylor alone.

Charlie glanced over his shoulder at Taylor as they started down the stairs of the grungy apartment building. "Gray told me Warren had a new squeeze."

Taylor wondered whether he should be offended by the term. Then again, he didn't really have a better way of putting it. He was still reluctant to use the word "boyfriend." He stared at Charlie's broad back as they emerged into the parking lot. "Is that all he said?

"He said you were adorable and tough as nails, and that he'd be happy to take you off Warren's hands once you got tired of Warren being such a grump all the time."

Now, that *did* offend him. "So, what? I'm just some whore you can all pass from one to the next?" Although admittedly, that was exactly what he'd been these last few years.

Charlie laughed and stopped to drop his basket of laundry next to an old Cadillac. "Don't let Gray get to you. He's harmless. Not his fault he and Warren have the exact same taste in men." No electric fob for the Caddy. He used the key to open the driver's door, then reached in to unlock the back door by hand.

"Anyway, Warren isn't really grumpy," Taylor said, deciding to focus on the part of Charlie's statement that mattered. "He's just...just..."

"Trying to carry the weight of the world."

Taylor frowned. "Yeah. Kind of seems like he is."

Charlie loaded the basket of laundry into the backseat, then turned to take the backpack from Taylor. "So tell me, Taylor. How're you gonna help ease that burden?"

It wasn't a challenge. It seemed to be a genuine question. "Well, first of all, I'm not going anywhere like Gray thinks, whether Warren's grumpy or not. Not unless he decides to kick me out."

Charlie nodded and tossed his backpack across the Caddy's front seat. "That's a start."

"Is there something else I should be doing?"

"You tell me."

Taylor eyed him, thinking about the first time he'd heard Charlie's name from Warren. "You're the one who gave him the vase."

"The kintsugi?"

"Uh, I don't know. The one mended with gold."

"Yeah, that was me."

"Why? What does it mean?"

"What'd Warren say when you asked him?"

"He said it's just a vase."

Charlie laughed. "Figures." He leaned against the Caddy, squinting into the sun. "It's a Japanese thing. They think when an item's broken, it doesn't make it useless. It just adds interest.

Becomes part of the item's history. And its history is what makes it beautiful."

Taylor smiled, thinking of Warren's scars. He knew there was more to the vase than Warren had said. "It's perfect."

"I thought it suited Warren." Charlie turned to climb into his car, but Taylor stopped him.

"Wait. You asked how I'd ease his burden. Is there something else I should be doing?"

Charlie smiled at him. "Just make him happy. I don't know many folks who deserve to be happy as much as Warren does."

Taylor climbed the steps back to Riley's apartment, thinking about Charlie's words. *Trying to carry the weight of the world.* No matter what he'd said to Charlie, Taylor knew he didn't ease that burden at all. If anything, he probably made it worse.

"Charlie give you the third degree?" Warren asked as Taylor entered the apartment.

"Not really." And yet his admonishment to make Warren happy felt like the toughest challenge Taylor had ever faced. He wasn't sure he knew how. The only thing he could do was keep doing what he'd been doing since they'd met—keeping up on his part of the housework, and being there if and when Warren wanted him.

It seemed like a pathetic offering.

Taylor wandered around the tiny apartment for a few minutes. He'd begged Warren to bring him, but now he didn't know what to do with himself. Warren had almost finished the few dirty dishes. Besides, given Warren's size, there wasn't enough room for both of them in the tiny kitchen anyway. Taylor opened the apartment's only window, hoping a bit of fresh air would help with the smell.

Twenty minutes later, just as Taylor was starting to wish he'd brought one of his graphic novels with him to read, Riley groaned from the bedroom.

"Charlie?" he called.

ONE MAN'S TRASH

Taylor followed Warren into the bedroom. The smell knocked him back a step. Could it really be that much worse now than it was before?

"Charlie, I think I shit myself."

"Charlie's gone home," Warren said. "I'm here now."

The only answer was a sob.

"It's all right," Warren said, pulling the blankets aside. "Everything's gonna be fine. Don't go to pieces on me."

"I can't," Riley sobbed. "I can't do it. I need a fix, man. I really need a fix."

"No, you don't. You're doing great. Why don't you get out of bed? We'll get you cleaned up, and I'll change the sheets." He turned to Taylor. "Can you get the shower going?"

"Of course." Taylor was glad to be given a bit of direction.

He'd just gotten the hot water warmed up and the shower running when Riley appeared at the bathroom door, wearing nothing but his soiled boxers. He was pasty white and stick thin. Taylor could have counted his ribs, if he'd been so inclined. Stringy, dark hair hung in lank clumps around Riley's face. He didn't seem to notice Taylor at all. He just stood there, shaking, his arms gripped across his chest.

"Come on," Taylor said. "I'll help you."

He managed to get the boxers off Riley and Riley into the tub. Luckily, it wasn't a claw-foot tub like at Warren's. It was a regular bathtub, and Riley was able to lean against the wall for support. Taylor rinsed out the dirty boxers in the sink as well as he could. It was gross, no two ways about it, but he was determined to do what needed to be done. He'd told Warren he could help. He couldn't back down when things got messy.

When he glanced into the tub a few minutes later, Riley hadn't moved. He stood huddled against the wall, sobbing. Taylor eyed the shower nozzle, considering. It was the kind that could be taken off the wall and hand held.

"I can help, if you want."

Riley continued to cry.

163

Taylor stripped off his shoes and socks, rolled up his jeans, and climbed into the shower behind Riley. He managed to squeeze past Riley and retrieve the showerhead from the wall mount without getting completely soaked.

"I can't believe this is happening," Riley choked. "I can't believe I'm a fucking adult, and I'm shitting myself like a baby. I can't believe I'm in the shower with another man, all because I have to be hosed off like some kind of invalid."

"It's okay," Taylor said. "Everybody needs help sometimes."

Riley's sobs abated a bit as Taylor worked, using the shower to spray Riley clean. Taylor had bathed with more men than he could count over the years, but never like this. Never in a way that was so utterly unerotic. The shower left him feeling more dirty than clean.

It wasn't until the water was off and Taylor wrapped a towel around Riley's thin shoulders that Riley asked, "Who are you, anyway?"

"I'm Taylor. I'm a friend of Warren's. Come on. Let's get you dressed."

The night passed slowly. Sometimes Riley paced. Sometimes he slept, but rarely for more than twenty minutes at a time. He managed to eat without vomiting, but the trips to the bathroom continued. One minute he was shivering, his teeth chattering, and the next he was burning up, throwing off his blankets as fast as he could.

"I can't do this," he said over and over again. "I can't do this."

"You can," Taylor said, guiding him to the couch again. "I think you can."

Warren was kind but stoic. He was practical, but he wasn't exactly the nursing type. He dealt with concrete things like soiled linens or the simple need for sustenance, but he wasn't the type to give pep talks or to coddle Riley. In the end, Taylor realized the best way he could help was simply by being sympathetic to Riley and distracting him from his misery.

They watched one of the movies, albeit in twenty-minute increments. Riley paced in between visits to the bathroom, but he also managed to eat some soup and crackers. Around midnight, Taylor got him settled on the couch, wrapped in a blanket. Taylor took out the first movie and replaced it with the second. By the time he turned away from the DVD player, Riley had nodded off in his corner of the couch, and Warren was doing the same in the room's only armchair.

At least he wasn't snoring yet.

Taylor watched him for a minute. Even sleeping, he looked like he was worrying about something. Taylor touched his shoulder. "Hey. Wake up."

Warren immediately jerked upright, as if expecting to have to jump into action. "What?"

"Is the bed clean right now?"

"Yeah. Fresh sheets. Why?"

"Go sleep for a bit."

Warren glanced toward Riley, then back to Taylor. "Are you sure?"

"Yeah. I'm wide awake, really. And it's probably better to just let Riley sleep where he is, rather than waking him up."

Warren's gaze drifted toward Riley again. His shoulders fell a fraction of an inch. "Okay. Yeah. I could use a nap. But if he gets wild—"

"He won't."

"We had to tie him down last night."

"Well, if it gets that bad, I can just yell. It's not like the other side of the apartment is out of shouting range."

Warren almost smiled. "I guess not." He put his hand on the back of Taylor's neck and pulled him closer. "You're not worthless. I never thought that to begin with, but you've been great tonight."

The praise warmed him. Maybe it was silly, but knowing he was actually helping Warren a bit made him feel good. "Go sleep for a while. We'll be fine."

Taylor settled in Warren's place after he'd gone. He hit Play on the movie but kept the volume off so as not to disturb Riley. It was something with Jack Black and Amanda Peet. Taylor'd never seen it, and without the volume, he had no idea what was happening. It was only another thirty minutes, though, before Riley woke with a start, throwing off his blankets to run for the bathroom.

Taylor gave him a few minutes alone before knocking quietly on the bathroom door. "You okay?"

"I need another pair of shorts."

"Okay. Hang on."

Warren's snores filled the bedroom as Taylor snuck in to dig a pair of clean boxers out of the basket of laundry he and Warren had brought with them. Riley was still in the bathroom, and Taylor could hear the shower running. He cracked the door to peek inside. "You need help?"

"No. I got it. Thanks."

Taylor breathed a sigh of relief. He hadn't been looking forward to another shower scene.

Riley emerged ten minutes later, shivering and wet-headed, wearing only his boxers. He let Taylor guide him back to the couch, but he began to cry again as Taylor wrapped the blankets around him.

"I can't do it," he cried. "Jesus, I don't know why I ever thought I could do this."

Taylor put his arm around him. "Here. Lie down. Try not to think about it."

Riley did as he was told and lay down on the couch, his head on Taylor's thigh. But he continued to sob. "I can't do it. I can't."

Taylor stroked his hair and made soft hushing sounds. He thanked whatever angels had been watching over him all these years that he'd never sought out drugs. In many ways, Riley's withdrawal reminded Taylor of his black days. He knew what it was like to be eaten from the inside by an insatiable need nobody else understood. But in Taylor's case, alcohol and weed didn't help. In hindsight, it seemed like some kind of miracle he'd never tried anything worse.

"I can't do it. I can't," Riley cried. "All I can think about is how bad I want a fix."

Taylor stroked Riley's damp hair. "Maybe you should think about the reason you decided to quit. I'm sure you knew it would be hard, but something made you think it'd be worth it."

Riley's sobs quieted a bit. He seemed to be thinking about the question.

"What was it?" Taylor prodded gently.

"I guess because I wasn't me anymore."

"What do you mean?"

Riley took a few deep, hiccupping breaths. "I mean, my girl left me, and I barely noticed. My best friends couldn't stand to be with me. I blamed them at first, but then one of them told me how I never laugh anymore. I never have fun. I don't want to go to a movie or hang out. All I want is to get high. I just *need*. That's all I do." He sniffled. "From the time I get up until the time I go to bed, the only thing I think about is how to get my next fix. I don't work. I don't have friends. I don't have sex. I don't even jerk off anymore. I'm just a heroin depository, you know?"

Taylor continued to stroke Riley's hair. "I kind of get that." For years, his life had been just as Riley described—every waking moment spent thinking about where he'd get what he needed. In his case, not a drug, but a customer. He'd always worried about how he'd earn his next meal. Every day was a question of where he'd go to find somebody who was willing to pay for a few minutes of his time.

"I tried to kill myself."

The frank confession made Taylor freeze, his hand on Riley's temple. "Recently?"

"No. It was a while ago. I'd stolen some of my mom's jewelry to sell. Then I sold my car. It was a junker, but it was the last thing I had left. I started trying to figure out how I could break into my parents' house so I could steal something else. And it just hit me, you know, how far I'd fallen, ready to rip off my own family for more drugs. I sat in my bedroom, and I thought about how I just wanted to die."

Taylor could relate to that. Granted, he'd never actually tried to kill himself, but he'd certainly put himself in plenty of dangerous situations. He'd tempted fate more often than he liked to admit. "What happened?"

"The next day, instead of buying more smack, I used some of the money from selling my car to buy a gun. I mean, I don't know shit about guns, but I knew this guy down the street sold them. He sells everything, you know. That's what he always says. 'Whatever you're lookin' for, I got.' So I went to him. I didn't even know what to ask for, besides just saying a handgun. He gave me one for a hundred fifty dollars." He was quiet for a minute, remembering, and Taylor waited. "The thing is, I waited too long. If I'd had that gun the night before, I think I could have done it. But by the time I bought it and came home, all I could think about was how bad I wanted to get high. I wanted to kill myself, but I wanted the dope more."

Taylor waited, and when Riley didn't say anything else, Taylor prodded him. "So, what happened? Do you still have the gun?" He hoped not.

"No. I took it back to him. Asked him to return my money. He said no, but he'd buy it off me. He gave me thirty dollars. Even though I'd bought it from him that day for one-fifty, he only gave me thirty to buy it back." He sniffled and wiped his nose. "But it was enough for a couple hits of H, so I took it. I came back here and shot up and forgot all about how much I'd wanted to die."

"I'm glad you didn't go through with it." Taylor resumed stroking Riley's hair, thinking. "As bad as things seem, I think there's always a better option."

"Maybe." It sounded like a platitude. Riley wasn't convinced. "Things got worse after that, though."

"How?"

"I ran out of money. Had nothing left to hock. Nobody'd lend me anything. My family won't even let me in the door because I've stolen from them too many times. The only reason I still have a place to live is because my uncle owns the building and he quit charging me rent ages ago. But I still needed my dope. And so, this chick told me about a dealer who'd give me the drugs in exchange for…other things."

Taylor's heart went cold, but he kept his hand moving on Riley's hair. He kept his voice soft. "Sex?"

"He sort of pimps on the side, you know? Gets the girls hooked on the dope, then leases them out to johns." Riley's chest hitched. "I only had to give blow jobs, at first. God, I can't believe I'm telling you this."

"I've given plenty of blow jobs for less, believe me."

Riley twisted his head around to look up at him. "Are you fucking with me?"

"No. I'm serious. I've been a whore." More recently than he wanted to admit too.

Riley turned away again. "I'm not gay."

Okay. Admittedly, Taylor hadn't considered that. Did that make it worse? It was hard to say. Taylor had actually enjoyed his job more often than not, but there had certainly been clients along the way who disgusted him. "You said, just blow jobs, *at first*."

"The fourth time," Riley whispered, "the man he pimped me out to didn't want a blow job. He made me do more."

"He raped you."

"No. I told him he could." He shook his head, wiping at the tears that were coming faster again. "It hurt so much, though. I had no idea it'd be that bad. I tried to fight him. I couldn't help it. I just wanted it to stop hurting. So he hit me really hard—hard enough I couldn't even see for a minute—and he finished."

"That's rape," Taylor said. "I don't care if you gave consent at the beginning. That's still rape."

"It doesn't matter, though, because I got the drugs." His head was still in Taylor's lap, but his body seemed to curl in on itself. "I got my dope, and I was happy about it, man. I came home and shot that shit up, and fuck, it was good." He groaned, a sound of such mixed pleasure and pain that Taylor wondered if he was aroused, thinking about it.

About the rush of the heroin. Not what it had cost him.

"But that made you decide to quit," Taylor said, wanting to keep Riley focused. "You can say the rush from the heroin was good, but something about it made you change your mind."

Riley nodded. "I woke up the next morning, and my first thought was that I'd go back. Can you believe that? With as much as it hurt, I was going to go back. But then I went to the bathroom." He shook his head, remembering. "I'd been bleeding. I freaked when I saw all that blood dried in my shorts and on my ass. And then when I had to, you know, go to the bathroom for real, I just about passed out, it hurt so fucking bad."

Taylor continued stroking his hair. He remembered that pain. Granted, it'd been a long time since anybody had hurt him that way. He knew now how to relax and let things happen. But he still remembered how it felt.

"You don't want to go back to that," Taylor said. "I know you don't. *You* know you don't. You may feel like crap right now, but getting clean has to be better than letting somebody use you like that."

And yet, how many times in his life had Taylor let men use him in exactly the same way? He'd done it in exchange for money or food or a place to sleep rather than heroin, but was that really any better?

Taylor wasn't sure.

Riley cried for another minute or two, but he seemed to have found his willpower again. He didn't say anything more about wanting a fix. The tears eventually subsided. Taylor thought Riley might have drifted off to sleep, but suddenly, Riley spoke again.

"Were you really a whore?"

Taylor nodded, even though Riley couldn't really see it, the way he was lying. "I was."

"What happened?"

"I met Warren."

Riley's eyes shifted toward the bedroom door. "That guy always seems pissed off. I mean, I know he's helping me, and I should be grateful. But I can't help feeling like he'd just as soon walk away."

Taylor put his hand on Riley's thin shoulder, wondering how to explain the complexities of Warren.

"Warren's a good man. He seems surly, but it's only because he carries the weight of the world."

"Wake up, sleepyhead."

Warren stirred and opened his eyes. He experienced a second of sheer confusion as to where he was. Not his own bed. Not Taylor's bed either. Warren sat straight up, alarms sounding in his brain.

"Don't panic, buddy. The war was a long time ago."

Warren shook his head, trying to shake the cobwebs loose. In his dreams, he'd been back in the desert. Now, he was in Riley's bed, with Charlie standing next to it. The clock read 6:15. It'd been before one when Taylor had sent Warren to bed. There was no way Riley had slept through the night.

Then again, Charlie didn't seem worried. "They're both sound asleep on the couch," he said before Warren could ask. "It's kind of adorable."

Warren followed his friend into the living room. Taylor slumped awkwardly in the corner of the couch, Riley's head on his thigh. They didn't exactly look peaceful, but it was a damn sight closer than Warren might have expected, given the circumstances.

Taylor woke easily when Warren squeezed his shoulder. "How long's he been out?" Warren asked.

Taylor yawned and rubbed his eyes. "Since about two. What time is it now?"

"Almost six thirty," Charlie answered, keeping his voice low so as not to wake Riley. "A solid four hours of sleep for him, then. That's a good sign. Means we might be over the hump."

It was worth hoping for, at any rate.

Over the next few days, it appeared Charlie was right. Riley's diet and sleep patterns began to approach normal. The nausea and diarrhea came to a stop. He began greeting them with something like hope in his eyes rather than anguish.

Still, the sheer futility of their endeavor left Warren frustrated. He'd known a lot of junkies over the years, and he'd never once known one who managed to stay clean.

Even worse, in Warren's mind, was the sudden unwavering friendship that sprang up between Riley and Taylor. Through the last half of their week-long vigil, Taylor accompanied Warren every time he went to Riley's. Taylor sat up all night with Riley, talking to him, encouraging him, bonding with him. Even after Warren and Charlie's week of babysitting was over, Taylor continued going to Riley's.

"We did our job," Warren told him. "You don't owe him any more than that."

"But I hate being home alone, waiting for you," Taylor replied. "This way, Riley and I can keep each other company."

Warren resisted the urge to protest. It wasn't fair to dislike Riley just because of his past addiction. Instead, Warren did his best to be supportive. He bought Taylor a cell phone so he could call if he needed help. He also bought one for Riley—albeit the cheapest pay-as-you-go model he could find—so Riley could reach Taylor when the cravings got too bad. Warren told himself it was good that Riley and Taylor had found each other.

He couldn't quite make himself believe it. He had nightmares of finding Taylor with a needle in his arm.

Another week rolled by. Warren conceded that he was never going to do the proper research on TVs. Who the hell had time for shit like that? But he was tired of not having one at home. He bought one at a pawn shop, figuring if Taylor destroyed it again, at least he wouldn't be out too much money.

Taylor sat quietly on the couch as Warren installed the new wall mount that Friday afternoon. "Charlie took his TV back from Riley's place. He left the movies but didn't leave anything to watch them on. Did I tell you that?"

Warren squirmed mentally. Any mention of Riley tended to set him on edge. "Well, it was Charlie's TV. Did you think he'd leave it there forever?"

"No." Warren's back was to Taylor. He had nothing to go on but tone, but Taylor sounded defensive. "The thing is, now Riley doesn't have anything to keep his mind off the cravings."

Warren finished tightening the last screw. "That's Riley's problem."

That earned him a big fat helping of silence.

Warren sighed and turned to face Taylor. "You want me to buy him a TV? Is that what you're saying? Because if so, the answer's no."

Taylor's cheeks colored. "This one wasn't much. You said so yourself. And it wouldn't even have to be this big. Just a cheap one from the pawn shop—"

"Forget it."

Taylor's lips thinned into an angry line. "You won't even consider it?"

"I did consider it. The answer's still no."

Taylor stood up, his eyes hard and his face red. Not counting the day he'd broken Warren's TV, it was the only sign of anger Warren had ever seen in him. "Maybe I'll use my own money to buy him one, then."

Warren shrugged. "It's your money. I won't tell you how to spend it." He lifted the new TV to the wall mount. "Come hold this for me so I can screw them together."

Taylor moved to help without protest, but Warren could still feel the dissatisfaction coming off him. "You won't tell me how to spend it, but you still think I shouldn't."

"I think you'd be wasting your money."

"He's my friend, and it would help him. How would that be a waste?"

Warren concentrated on getting the screws through the wall mount and into the corresponding holes on the back of the TV. He had visions of Taylor throwing the thing on the ground and stomping on it again if Warren answered before it was secure.

"Warren?" Taylor finally prodded.

"You can let go now. It won't fall."

Taylor took a few steps back and crossed his arms. "Tell me why I shouldn't use my own money to help Riley."

Warren sighed and turned away from the TV to face him. "Because he'll just hock the damn thing for a fix. Maybe not today. Maybe not this week. But at some point down the road, it'll go from being something you gave him to something he can trade for heroin."

Taylor gritted his teeth, his jaw clenching and unclenching. "You don't have much faith in us, do you?"

Us? Since when had Taylor and Riley become an "us"? "I have plenty of faith in you," Warren said.

"But not him?"

Warren didn't answer.

"You don't get it, do you?" Taylor asked. "We're the same. That's why we're friends. That's why it works."

"You're not the same."

"We are."

"You're strong, Taylor. That's why you've made it this far without sticking a needle in your arm or a gun in your mouth. But him?" Warren shook his head. "He doesn't have what you have."

"You want him to fail."

"No, I don't. Of course I don't want him to fail. But the truth is, I'm pretty damn sure he will."

For a moment, Taylor only stood there, staring daggers at him. Warren waited for the next round to begin, but it never did. Instead, Taylor turned and left the house, grabbing the keys to the white car off the counter as he went.

Fine. Warren understood as well as anyone the need for space.

Chapter 13

Taylor had never been angry at Warren before.

Of course, there'd been his episode when he'd broken Warren's TV and told Warren he hated him, but Taylor didn't count that. He hadn't truly been mad at Warren that day. He'd been deep in the clutches of his blackness. Just as Riley's addiction might have driven him to extremes, Taylor's dark days caused him to do and say things he didn't really mean.

But this? This was different. This was proof positive that Warren didn't understand him and never would. He claimed to appreciate the outliers—the people who strayed from the norm—yet he refused to see that Riley might be one of them. How the hell could Warren claim to know what Riley would or wouldn't do down the road? How could he stand there and tell Taylor that he and Riley were different when Taylor knew in his heart they were the same?

And so Taylor resolved to follow his heart.

He drove straight to the nearest pawn shop. He didn't care what Warren thought. Having a friend was something new and special for him. He'd spent years going from host to host, job to job, occasionally meeting people along the way, but always losing touch with them before long. For the first time ever, Taylor felt truly connected to somebody without sex being involved. They spent hours talking about their past, comparing Riley's addiction to Taylor's years as a rent boy. Riley didn't judge him. He didn't think less of Taylor for being gay or for having been a whore all those years. They understood each other in a way nobody else ever could.

Maybe that was what it boiled down to—Taylor understood how badly Riley needed a TV. He appreciated how difficult it was for Riley to keep his mind off heroin. And if giving his friend what he needed most meant Taylor had to use his trust fund, then so be it. He hadn't touched it in nearly two years. In those twenty-three months, he'd suffered through hunger, he'd slept on park benches in the winter, and he'd gone home with men who disgusted him, all to keep from having to use that money.

But now, Riley's needs trumped all.

Inside the pawn shop, Taylor quickly made his choices—the cheapest flat-screen they had, plus a DVD player. He added some used DVDs to the pile, wanting Riley to have more than the couple of movies Charlie had left for him.

"Anything else?" the guy at the register asked.

"No. This is it." Taylor's fingers shook as he took the debit card from his wallet. He could almost feel the weight of his father's judgment. He could taste the bitterness of his mother's indifference. He handed the card over, his stomach roiling as the man ran it.

"You look familiar," the man said as he handed Taylor's Visa back. "Have we met?"

Taylor tore his eyes away from the card in his hand to study the man. Late thirties. Kind of cute, despite a receding hairline. A bit of a beer belly, but otherwise not in terrible shape. The name tag on his chest read "Scott." The name meant nothing to Taylor, but the braided rainbow bracelet around the man's wrist gave him his first clue.

Shit.

Taylor looked again at the man's face. It wasn't exactly familiar to him. Then again, he'd serviced a lot of men over the years. "I don't think so," he said, lowering his gaze as he tucked his card back into his wallet.

Scott's face split into a broad grin. "Yeah! I recognize you now. You're BJ, right?" He lowered his voice and leaned closer.

"From Leroy's?" The credit card machine spit out a slip of paper. Taylor stared pointedly at it, but Scott didn't take the hint. "Oh yeah," Scott said, his voice taking on a distinct note of suggestion. "I definitely remember you."

Taylor forced himself to meet the man's gaze. "I don't work there anymore."

"Oh. All right. It's cool."

Scott ripped the slip off the machine and handed it to Taylor to sign. He'd run into men from his past like this before, but it'd never upset him this much. His bile rose, and he concentrated on not vomiting as he scrawled his signature across the line. All this awkwardness would be worth it when he saw the look on Riley's face.

Scott smiled as he took the slip of paper back. "I'll help you carry this to your car."

Taylor wanted to object, but there was no way he could get the TV, the DVD player, and the DVDs in one trip. Besides, Scott had already hefted the TV onto his hip. "Thanks."

He felt Scott's gaze like a prickle between his shoulder blades all the way to his car. They were silent as they loaded the items into the backseat. Scott didn't seem ready to say goodbye, though. He leaned against the car, crossed his arms, and said, "You don't have to be embarrassed. Giving blow jobs for money is nothing to be ashamed of."

"I didn't say I was ashamed. I just said I don't work there anymore."

"Okay. I get it." Scott moved a bit closer. "You want to go out sometime?"

"I can't."

Scott's smile fell a bit. "What, you don't go out with guys like me unless we pay?"

"That's not what I meant."

Scott looked down at the pavement between them. Taylor wanted nothing more than to climb into the comfort of Warren's car and drive away, but he waited.

"I will, you know," Scott said, his voice low.

"You will what?"

Scott looked up at him, his cheeks red. "Pay, if that's what you want."

"I didn't mean—"

"Just come in the back room with me. Ten minutes. That's all I need."

Taylor's mouth fell open, but he had no idea what to say. In all his years as a hustler, he'd never rejected a chance to make a few dollars. The thing was, he'd never been in quite the position he was in now. "I'm kind of seeing someone."

"Does that matter?"

Good question. After all, it wasn't as if Taylor was married. He and Warren had an arrangement, plain and simple—sex in exchange for food and board. At no point had Warren specified monogamy. At no point had Taylor promised it either. Taylor could follow Scott inside, make a few dollars, and Warren would never even know.

And yet, something held him back.

He adored Warren. The last thing he wanted to do was risk what they had. Then again, if Warren kicked him out, it wouldn't hurt to have Scott on the line.

Taylor forced himself to smile at Scott. Their chests touched as Taylor moved into Scott's personal space. He wrapped one arm around the man's neck and trailed the other hand down his chest, stopping just short of his groin. "If my situation changes, you'll be the first to know. I promise."

It made Scott happy. Unfortunately, it made Taylor feel like garbage. His excitement about presenting Riley with his gifts felt lost to him. He tried to tell himself he hadn't cheated on Warren. He'd only given himself a little insurance in case Warren disposed of him sooner rather than later.

And Warren would. They always did.

He parked in front of Riley's building and carried the TV up the stairs. He propped it on his hip in order to knock. He was surprised when the door was answered not by Riley but by a middle-aged woman in a neat, dark blue pantsuit.

"Can I help you?" she asked.

"Uh—"

"Mom, that's Taylor," Riley said from behind her. "I told you about him, remember? Let him in."

Taylor eyed her, wishing he'd timed his visit better. Riley had told Taylor a bit about his family. The stories hadn't exactly painted them in a positive light.

Taylor stepped past her into the house, smiling self-consciously at Riley. "Look what I brought for you. There's a DVD player and some discs in the car, if you want to go grab them."

Riley's smile was so big and grateful, Taylor almost forgot what he'd gone through in order to earn it. "You're the best, man. Thanks."

But by sending Riley to get the remaining items out of the car, Taylor had doomed himself to a minute alone with Riley's mother.

"What kind of friend are you, anyway?" his mother asked once Riley was gone.

Taylor set the TV carefully in the corner of the room. "What do you mean?"

"Are you a junkie too?" She didn't wait for an answer. She grabbed his wrist and pulled his arm toward her to inspect. Her fingertips brushed lightly up his forearm. "No scars. How do you know Riley?"

Taylor pulled away from her grip, scowling. He wanted to tell her he had plenty of scars, even if they weren't the kind she meant. "I'm not an addict. I helped Riley get clean."

Her rigid posture relaxed a bit. "Well, I appreciate that." She eyed the TV, tapping a fingertip against her lips. "You shouldn't have bought him anything. He'll just sell it for drugs. It's what he always does."

"Maybe he won't this time."

She pursed her lips and dropped her gaze. Her shoulders fell a bit, and Taylor realized that what he'd thought was anger and animosity was really just overwhelming weariness. When she looked at him again, she looked ten years older. "I hope you're right."

She left soon afterward, and Riley went to work in the corner, happily plugging in the new devices and connecting the DVD player to the TV. "Thank you. I mean it. You have no idea how much this means to me."

But Taylor did know. That was why he'd done it. He understood how hard Riley was fighting to change. "Your mom's visiting now?" he asked, hoping he wasn't overstepping his bounds.

"Now that I'm clean, she brings me groceries. She won't give me cash, of course. She assumes I'll use it for heroin. But the food helps." He pushed in a DVD and moved to the couch. He eyed Taylor, his smile fading a bit. "What's wrong? Did she say something rude to you?"

"She said I shouldn't have bought them for you. That you'd only sell them to buy drugs." What was left of Riley's smile disappeared, and Taylor regretted saying it. It felt like just another shadow across what was supposed to have been a great afternoon.

"Whatever." Riley's shrug wasn't as casual as he probably hoped. "Is that all that's wrong?"

"No." Because the biggest part of Taylor's sadness had nothing to do with Riley's mom and everything to do with Taylor. "The guy at the pawn shop recognized me from Leroy's. He offered to pay me for sex."

"Did you do it?"

"No, but I didn't exactly tell him no, either." He chewed his lip nervously, but when he looked up, he found no judgment in Riley's eyes. "I sort of set him up as my next mark. It was like, that habit of always making sure I have somebody on the line just kicked in. I didn't put out because I wasn't sure how Warren would feel about it. But I felt like I couldn't burn that bridge either."

Riley nodded. "It makes sense. You've always had to worry about where your next meal would come from. Just like I always worried about where I'd get my next fix." He glanced at the TV. The movie's menu filled the screen. "My mom was right. In the past, I sold everything that wasn't nailed down."

He shrugged, looking dejected. "Maybe I'll do it again. I want to say I won't, but some days, getting a fix is the only thing I can think about."

Taylor remembered the feel of Riley's mom's fingers on his arm. He eyed the telltale marks on the backs of Riley's hands and the inside crook of his elbow. He knew from the times he'd helped Riley in the shower that he had marks on his thighs too. Riley caught the direction of his stare and put his hands over the track marks on his left forearm.

"I'm sorry," Taylor said. "You don't have to hide them from me."

"From everybody else, though."

"There's that saying—a scar is just proof that you're stronger than whatever tried to kill you."

Riley shook his head. "I don't feel stronger than the heroin. I keep waiting for the day I do, but so far, I just feel like I'm hiding from it."

Taylor chewed his lip again, debating. "I want to show you something." He stood and began undoing his pants.

"Uh, Taylor?" Riley asked, laughing nervously. "You know I'm not into guys, right?"

"It's not what you think." Taylor slid his jeans out of the way, turning so he wasn't necessarily showing off his package to Riley. Instead, he showed him the rows of scars on his right thigh.

Riley's lips tightened into a hard line. He reached out and ran a fingertip over the lines. "They don't look recent."

"Most of them aren't." Although he'd resorted to cutting a few times over the last couple of years.

"Both sides?"

"Yes."

"Why?"

"Probably for the same reasons you first stuck a needle in your arm."

"Why are you showing me this?"

"Your mom checked my arms for track marks," Taylor explained as he pulled his pants back into place. "I guess it bothered me that she assumed those were the only types of scars people can have."

"My mom's not a bad person. I've just let her down a lot."

"I figured." Taylor perched on the couch next to Riley. "I'd like to think we can prove her wrong, but sometimes I can't quite believe it myself, you know?" He thought about how easy it had been to lead Scott on. "Do you think we're just destined to keep doing the same thing over and over? Or do you think we can be something new?"

Riley's brow wrinkled as he considered the question. It was one of the things Taylor loved about Riley. He never brushed off Taylor's questions, even when they didn't necessarily make a lot of sense.

"I guess it depends on which thing we want more."

Taylor still hadn't come home when Warren left for his shift with Candy and Sugar, and that night when Warren snuck into the house at three thirty in the morning, he found Taylor's bedroom door closed to him for the first time ever.

Warren stood outside it for a moment, debating. It wasn't so much that he wanted sex as that he wanted to make things right between them. He tried the doorknob and found it unlocked.

Still, he hesitated.

If Taylor had gone so far as to lock the door, Warren would have retreated to his own room. Leaving the door closed but unlocked felt like an entirely different kind of statement.

Warren cracked the door open and peeked inside. Taylor's room was dark. Warren could just make out the dark shape of his form under the blankets.

"What do you want?" Taylor asked.

"I guess I wanted to know if you're still mad."

"Well, I am."

Warren nodded. "Okay. I'll leave you alone, then."

He turned to go, but Taylor said, "Wait."

"Yes?"

"Is that it? I tell you I'm still angry, and you just say okay?"

"I don't want to fight, Taylor. If you want me to go, I will."

Taylor was silent for a moment. "You can stay."

"Are you sure?"

"I thought I wanted to be left alone, but it just makes me feel worse, having you walk away."

Warren silently stripped down to his boxers and climbed into bed with Taylor. He put a questing hand on Taylor's hip. Taylor was naked, as always. It felt like an invitation, and Warren moved a bit closer to kiss Taylor's shoulder.

"I said you could stay. I didn't say you were forgiven."

"Okay." Warren kissed him again, playing his lips over the back of Taylor's neck. "Does that mean you want me to stop?"

"What happens if I say yes, I want you to stop?"

Warren stilled, pulling away a bit to put some distance between them. "Then I will."

A moment of silence. Then, his voice quieter, "What if I let you keep going?"

Warren ran his hand down Taylor's hip and forward, brushing his fingertips over the soft place where his pelvis met his thigh. "You tell me."

Taylor's breath caught in his throat, but he didn't protest. Warren took that as permission to continue. He moved closer again, kissing Taylor's neck, brushing his fingers slowly up Taylor's growing erection. He didn't push, but he put everything he had into simply persuading until Taylor gave a soft moan of surrender and rolled onto his back, spreading his legs to allow Warren better access to his groin. He met Warren's gaze in the near-darkness.

"This isn't fair. You're making it really hard to stay mad."

Warren chuckled and kissed Taylor's neck. "That was the idea."

"Wait." He put his hands on Warren's chest and pushed him away a bit. It stopped Warren from kissing him, but not from continuing his slow caresses under the cover. "I need to tell you something." He took a deep breath. "I bought Riley a TV."

"Okay."

"Okay? I feel like no matter what I say to you, that's your answer."

"It's your money. I won't tell you how to spend it."

Taylor sighed in aggravation. "That's not what I want to hear, Warren. I want you to admit that just maybe you're wrong this time. That maybe Riley will make it."

"Maybe he will," Warren said. "Maybe you're right, and I'm just too old and jaded. Either way, you did what you thought was right. You've been a friend to him when nobody else was. I think you deserve credit for that. More than I've been giving you, at any rate."

Taylor's breath caught. "Do you mean it?"

"I wouldn't have said it if I didn't."

Taylor pulled him close but stopped short of kissing him. "Thank you for that."

"You don't have to thank me. It's only the truth."

"You still think I shouldn't have bought the TV, though?"

"It's not what I would have done, but that doesn't make it wrong. Maybe it just proves you're a better person than me."

Taylor sighed and finally kissed him. "I'm not. Not really. I just couldn't stand to see him sad."

Warren wanted nothing more than to truly make love to him, but he held back. Taylor seemed strangely vulnerable, and Warren remembered the one time Taylor had ever told him no because he hadn't been able to bear their intimacy. Warren suspected they were near that point again. His suspicion was confirmed when he tried to kiss Taylor, only to have Taylor turn him away.

"Fuck me, Warren," Taylor whispered, turning to present his backside to Warren. "Fuck me hard."

Warren sighed, feeling defeated. Yes, he could try to make love to Taylor, but Taylor would shift things, reclaim his power by resisting Warren's tenderness. He'd find a way to turn their lovemaking into fucking. Not that there was anything wrong with plain old fucking, but it wasn't what Warren wanted tonight.

So instead of sex, Warren moved down. He used his hands and his mouth, sucking Taylor while teasing his prostate. He devoted every bit of his energy to making Taylor feel good, until Taylor finally shuddered his release, his fingers digging into the back of Warren's head.

For a minute, Warren simply lay there, his forehead against Taylor's stomach as Taylor's fingers moved through his hair. He felt torn in so many ways. His feelings for Taylor left him raw and vulnerable at every turn. Loving Stuart had never felt this difficult or treacherous, and yet there was no way to stop feeling what he felt. He'd fight for Taylor until he won, or until Taylor got tired of him and walked away.

Warren moved back up Taylor's body, careful not to put too much of his weight on him. This time when Warren kissed him, Taylor allowed it. Warren felt strangely reluctant to leave, but he was also exhausted. He brushed Taylor's hair aside in order to kiss him on the forehead. "Good night, kid."

"Wait." Taylor caught his hand. "Do you have to go?"

Warren stopped, one foot on the floor, one knee still on the bed. "No. It's just, I snore pretty bad." He touched the scar across the bridge of his nose. "Ever since this. It used to drive Stuart crazy. It's the whole reason he had his own room."

Taylor shook his head, tugging Warren back down. "I'm not him."

Warren laughed, thinking as he reclaimed his spot on the bed how horrified Stuart would have been by Taylor. Stuart, who in many ways was uptight and repressed and desperate for somebody to tell him it was okay to be however he wanted to be. He'd never been comfortable in his own skin. "Truer words were never spoken."

Taylor put his palm over Warren's heart. "Is that a bad thing? Do you wish I was more like Stuart?"

The question surprised him. "No. Not at all." He pulled Taylor closer. "I'm pretty fond of you just the way you are."

"Really?"

How in the world could Taylor still doubt Warren's feelings? Warren felt like he wore his heart on his sleeve. Then again, he'd never been great at expressing himself. "Really."

For a minute, they simply lay there. Warren had never tried to initiate any kind of postcoital cuddling with Taylor, mostly because he wasn't sure it would be appreciated. But now that Taylor seemed to want it, Warren didn't object. He held Taylor close, caressing his smooth, trim body, marveling that anybody so young and beautiful would want this kind of intimacy with him.

Taylor didn't relax against him, though, or return his touch. His neck and back remained tense under Warren's hands. He still seemed troubled, and Warren waited, wondering if he should prod Taylor more or leave him be.

In the end, it was a choice he didn't have to make. Taylor finally took a deep breath and said, "Can I ask you a stupid question?"

"Of course."

"You can be honest with me, no matter what. I won't freak out on you or anything, I promise."

What in the world could Taylor ask that would justify such a disclaimer? "What is it?"

Taylor nudged Warren onto his back and sat on top of him, straddling Warren's hips. He leaned close, his hands on Warren's chest. "Is this still just an agreement?"

Warren felt torn between laughter and tears, wondering if he was about to have his heart ripped in two. "Not to me it isn't. I haven't thought of you that way in ages."

"Even now? Even knowing how messed up I am?"

Warren ran his hand up the smooth flesh of Taylor's back. He wished they'd left the lights on so he could see Taylor's eyes better. "Knowing about James doesn't change the way I feel about you."

Taylor drew a breath, almost as if he'd been slapped. Then, in a small, frightened voice: "How do you feel about me?"

Jesus, talk about being put on the spot. But in some ways, it was a relief to finally have it out. He'd never been good at saying the word, but it was easy enough to explain. "Every morning, I open my eyes, and my very first thought is, 'What if he's gone?' It's like sheer panic. Like I can't even breathe until I get up and make sure you haven't snuck out in the middle of the night. And every time I leave the house for more than an hour or two, I think, 'This is it. He'll probably leave me now.' It drives me nuts, standing around outside cheap motel rooms, listening to people have sex, when the whole time, I'm wondering if I'll come home and find you gone." He sounded like an idiot saying it out loud, but it was all true. "I spend every minute we're together wondering when you'll decide to leave."

Taylor smiled. Warren couldn't see it, but he heard Taylor's soft exhale. Taylor lightly kissed the corner of Warren's mouth. "I don't plan on leaving."

The words should have made him feel better, but Warren couldn't quite believe him. Stuart had promised not leave too, for all the good that had done.

Taylor put his fingers against Warren's cheek. "If it isn't an agreement anymore, then what is it?"

"It's whatever you want it to be."

Taylor shook his head, and when Warren reached up to touch his face, he found tears on his cheeks. "I want to be as important to you as you are to me. But I'll screw it up. I'll ruin it. Not on purpose or anything, but it's what I do, whether I want to or not."

"How exactly do you ruin it? Do you mean more days like when you broke the TV? Or is there something I haven't seen yet?"

"No. Just more days like that. They always come back."

"And on a scale of one to ten, where one's a normal day, and ten's the worst day you've ever had, what was that?"

"A five, I guess." Taylor tilted his head, thinking. "Maybe a six."

Admittedly, Warren had sort of hoped he'd say that day had been a nine or a ten, because it would mean they'd already faced the worst. But Taylor's answer didn't change anything for him. "Then we'll handle it. If and when it happens again, we'll deal with it together. That's all."

"Oh my God." It was little more than a whisper. Taylor put his head into Warren's chest. Quietly crying, Warren realized, but trying to hide it. "How could you want me, Warren? Why would you ever want to tie yourself to somebody as messed up as me?"

The answer to that question was easy. "Because you make me happy. Because those moments when I peek into your room and realize you're still here, or when I come home and find you waiting on the couch—those are the brightest moments of my day. The brightest moments I've had in years, really."

"Oh my God," Taylor said again. He sat up a bit, meeting Warren's gaze in the darkness. His fingers were light on Warren's cheek. "I've never done this before. I don't know how to be in a relationship."

"It's no different from what we've already been doing."

Taylor shook his head. "I don't think you know what you're volunteering for."

Maybe not, but it didn't matter. He intended to keep Taylor around as long as he could. And now that he'd finally told Taylor the truth, he felt nothing but a calm, reassuring sense of joy. It seemed as if everything in his life would finally make sense, if he could only keep Taylor here, in his arms. He settled for kissing Taylor gently and holding him tight.

"I'm willing to risk it if you are."

Chapter 14

Another week went by, blustering April finally giving way to the golden warmth of May. Between sacrificing his odd jobs to babysitting Riley and losing both Sugar and Taffy, money began nagging at Warren's mind. He wasn't broke. Not quite. But when Sugar finally returned to work the following weekend, Warren breathed a sigh of relief.

The relief was short-lived, though. It was immediately apparent that Sugar and Candy were no longer on speaking terms.

"She went back to him," Candy told him later that night. She was between clients, and she leaned against the wall next to him, smoking a cigarette. Sugar's hearty moans echoed from the room she occupied.

"Robby?" Warren asked, wanting to make sure he understood.

"Yeah." Candy flicked ash at the ground. "She actually felt sorry for the son of a bitch." She took a drag and blew smoke at the sky. "Can you believe that shit? He nearly kills her, and she goes back to him, all because we tried to put a stop to it." She eyed him sideways, the cigarette still smoldering between her fingers. "I guess that's what really pisses me off. You and I tried to help, and all we did was make things worse."

That explained why Sugar had barely bothered to greet him when he'd arrived to begin his shift. "She planning to fire me?" Because that was the last thing he needed. Sugar and Candy were his primary source of income.

Candy shook her head. "No. She may be pissed, but she isn't stupid."

He watched her drop her cigarette and grind it out with the toe of her bright pump. "Well, I guess that's one bit of good news." But he had a feeling it was only a matter of time before the other shoe dropped. Either Robby would hit her again and she'd leave him, or she'd stay with Robby and decide Warren's protection wasn't worth the loss of wages.

It made him angry and frustrated. By the time he pulled into his driveway at four a.m., he was ready to hit somebody. That wasn't an option, but Taylor provided a better outlet anyway.

Warren woke him roughly, pulling the sheets aside. Taylor stirred, turning over to face him. He was slim and perfect and beautiful. Just looking at him was enough to rouse Warren's darkest urges. Something close to a growl escaped his throat.

Taylor grinned at him and spread his legs, his cock already stiffening against his flat stomach. "Do your worst, baby. You know I won't break."

Warren flipped him onto his stomach. He cuffed Taylor's wrists, then his ankles, so Taylor lay splayed across the bed, completely captive to whatever Warren chose to do. Taylor whimpered in anticipation as Warren undressed and took the flog from the closet.

It felt good to hit something. *Not too hard.* Warren repeated the mantra over and over as he brought the flog down. *Not too hard.* Keep the straps high across Taylor's back. Don't let the tips wrap around the side. It was less about putting his anger into the motion and more about changing the anger to lust, letting the blows amplify the arousal in both Taylor and himself. Taylor responded beautifully too, groaning and begging until Warren tossed the flog aside and climbed between Taylor's legs.

"Please please please," Taylor whispered. The bonds didn't stop him from gyrating his hips, working his cock against the sheets. "Please, Warren. Please please please."

Warren spread Taylor's cheeks and went to work there with his tongue. He licked and fucked with his mouth until his jaw couldn't take it anymore. Then he used his fingers, his thrusts hard and rough, and Taylor went wild. Warren could almost come just listening to Taylor's labored breathing and lusty pleas.

"Warren, please please please—"

"Not until you're ready to come too."

"I am! Jesus, Warren, I am!"

And finally, Warren fucked him for real, nearly screaming at how good it felt to finally slide his cock into Taylor's waiting ass. It was rough and raw, and Warren tucked his head into the crook of Taylor's neck and thrust again, as hard and deep as he could. Some primal part of him took over, telling him to stake his claim, to take Taylor as violently and forcefully as he could, and Warren obeyed. He felt like an animal, rutting out his lust, driven mad by Taylor's whimpers, reveling in the simple carnal pleasure of thrusting again and again.

He felt a thousand times better after he came. He could have fallen asleep in a heartbeat, but first, he needed to untie Taylor. Taylor's orgasm had left one hell of a wet spot in the middle of the bed, but neither of them felt inclined to deal with it right at that moment.

Taylor settled into his arms with a contented sigh. "Jesus, that was good."

Warren chuckled, so tired, he wasn't sure he could have made it to his own bed if he'd tried. He kissed the top of Taylor's head. "You're perfect. You know that, right?"

Taylor didn't answer. Or if he did, it was long after Warren had fallen asleep.

They both slept late the next day. They had only a few hours before Warren had to leave for work again. Taylor seemed oddly moody and withdrawn, but Warren let it go. It wasn't until Warren was getting dressed to leave for his night job that Taylor came and stood in his bedroom door.

"I forgot to tell you, your Uncle Bill called."

It wasn't quite the first thing Taylor had said to him all day, but it was close. Warren sat perched on the edge of his bed, one sock on and one sock still in his hand. "When?"

"Yesterday. He says he needs to talk to you."

"Shit."

"He wants you to meet him for lunch tomorrow. He said, 'No excuses.'"

It wasn't the way Warren would have chosen to spend his Sunday, but he couldn't avoid Uncle Bill forever.

Work that night consisted of more of the silent treatment from Sugar. It ended up being worth it, though. The girls were busier than ever, and by the time Warren returned home a little after four in the morning, his money worries seemed a bit less urgent.

He let Taylor sleep. It was almost dawn, and Warren didn't have the energy for sex anyway. Only a few hours of rest stood between him and his meeting with Bill. His uncle wasn't a bad guy, but that didn't stop Warren from wanting to hate him.

Just after noon on Sunday, Warren strolled into the diner his uncle had chosen, hoping he looked more at ease than he felt. Bill waved to him from a back booth, and Warren headed his way. He hadn't actually been face-to-face with his Uncle Bill in close to two years, and he was surprised at how much older the man looked.

"I figured you'd stand me up," Bill said as Warren took his seat.

"I said I'd be here, so I am." Warren took a menu from the little metal holder at the end of the table and made a point of studying it.

"You look good."

Warren doubted that was true. He'd barely slept the night before. He felt like hell. "Thanks."

The waitress stopped to take their order. She was young but with old eyes. Warren found himself wondering what her story was. Was she studying to be a paralegal, like Sugar? Was she doing work on the side as a prostitute? Did she have a boyfriend who got his kicks by beating her?

The things his job made him wonder about sometimes made him hate himself.

They ordered drinks, and the waitress said she'd give them "a few minutes with the menu."

Bill sat back in the booth and studied Warren. "So, was the guy who took my message Friday the same kid you had living at your place when I stopped by a while back?"

The thought of Taylor did funny things to Warren. He wanted to smile, just hearing his name. He wanted to stop loving him so much, so it'd hurt less when he left. "Yes."

"What's his name again?"

"Taylor."

"Taylor. Right." Bill paused while the waitress stopped to plunk down a giant Coke in front of Bill, and a cup of coffee for Warren. They placed their orders—a hamburger for Bill and a Denver omelet for Warren. Once she was gone again, the questions resumed. "He's a bit young for you, isn't he?"

Warren sighed and looked out the diner window. It was a gusty day. Fat, palatial clouds flew across the sky at a surreal pace, as if racing to reach Kansas. "I suppose."

"Does he make you happy?"

Jesus, he had no idea how to answer that question. Yes, Taylor made him happy. Happier than he'd been in years, certainly, but sometimes that happiness felt so fragile and fleeting, it was almost more than Warren could bear. "He's better than I deserve."

"I doubt that."

Warren finally met his uncle's gaze. He was surprised at the gentleness he found there.

"Did he tell you about Jeff?"

"Yeah. Getting married in June, huh? Do you like the girl?"

Bill shrugged. "Seems fine, I guess."

Warren laughed. "So no, you don't like her?"

Bill granted him a smile. "I don't like that she's taking him to Idaho."

So, they'd finally come to the real reason Bill wanted to meet. "Roger and Greg quit?"

"Roger's selling used cars, of all things. Greg's a manager at Home Depot."

"He'd choose that over electrical work?"

Bill shrugged and looked away. "It comes with benefits. I can't compete with that."

Their food arrived, and for a few minutes, they ate in silence. But the real point of contention was unavoidable.

"I could really use you back, Warren."

"It didn't work last time we tried."

Bill nodded as he dragged a fry through his ketchup. "True. But that was ages ago. You've been home a long time now."

He was right, of course. Warren remembered the night a few weeks before, when Taylor had asked if men like them could ever have normal jobs and normal lives. He thought about how it would feel, working a simple nine-to-five. Even given some emergency calls on evenings and weekends, it'd be light years better than the hours he worked now. He'd have to renew his license. The huge gap in his work history might complicate things, but it wouldn't be impossible.

The only thing left was his personal aversion to the idea of working for Bill.

Every man on the maternal side of his family was an electrician. His mother had worked as their office manager. That was how she'd met Warren's father, who was a journeyman at the time. Warren had been raised on wires and circuits, watts and amps. But he'd also been raised on anger and abuse, alcohol and addiction.

"You left her there," Warren said, his eyes on his half-eaten omelet. "You knew what he was doing, and you never even tried to get her out of there."

For a moment, Bill was silent. Warren forced himself to look up. To meet his uncle's eyes.

"Is that really what you think?" Bill asked. "You think we didn't offer to come and get her at least twice a year? You think our mother didn't beg her to leave him?" Bill leaned closer and lowered his voice. "I drove up to Casper myself on three different occasions and tangled with him, trying to get her free. And every time, she told me to leave."

Warren reeled, sitting back in his seat, the coffee and eggs he'd eaten threatening to come back up. "But, why?" All these years, he'd laid equal amounts of blame on his mother's family and on himself. To hear now, all these years later, that the blame was his alone was almost more than he could take. "Why would she stay with him?"

"Warren." Bill's voice was gentle. He reached across the table and put his gnarled, calloused hand over Warren's. "I would have done anything to save her. But you of all people should know, you can't help a person who won't help themselves."

Even after the lunch was over, Warren had a hard time wrapping his head around Bill's statements. For years, he'd wondered why nobody had tried to help his mother. Now, he found himself thinking back, remembering surprise visits from Bill or his grandparents. Remembering the times his grandmother had taken him out for ice cream so his grandfather could stay and talk to his mom. He remembered tearful, whispered arguments, all of the adults suddenly quieting and breaking into false smiles when he'd entered the room.

"Damn it!" Warren slammed the heel of his hand against the steering wheel. How could he have been so blind and so stupid?

The answer was easy—because he'd wanted somebody to share the blame. He hadn't wanted to believe it all fell on him.

You can't help a person who won't help themselves.

His mother had never smoked, rarely drank, and—as far as Warren knew—had never done any of the many drugs his father kept around the house. And yet, she'd stayed. She'd endured the beatings and the drunken fights and the fear of having the police knock on the door. Why?

Because she loved him.

It was mind-boggling to consider. Warren had hated his father for as long as he could remember. Although he'd understood in some superficial way that his mother must have loved his father, it had never quite occurred to him just how strong that love must have been. He thought about the way he'd once loved Stuart. The way he now loved Taylor. The sheer hopelessness he felt when faced with the power of that feeling. Yes, love made people do inexplicable things. For Warren, it was hard to imagine letting somebody beat him like that. He couldn't quite fathom a love that transcended that kind of abuse. He thought of Sugar, and her steely eyed insistence that Robby wasn't a bad guy.

The truth was, Robby *was* a bad guy, just as Warren's dad had been. But Sugar apparently loved him anyway. Maybe Bill was right. There was no helping a person who was unwilling to help themselves.

The house was empty when Warren arrived, which meant Taylor was visiting Riley. Warren bit back a scowl at the thought. He'd promised Taylor he'd be more open-minded about Riley, but in Warren's book, addicts were all the same. Like his mother, they were unwilling to do what needed to be done. It was only a matter of time before Riley broke Taylor's heart.

He couldn't stand sitting around the house, so he headed for the gym. He'd been slacking on his exercise routine since meeting Taylor, and it was time he got back into the groove. No matter how great the sex, it couldn't make up for lost cardio, and the waistline of his favorite jeans was beginning to cut into his sides a bit more than he liked. He ran two miles around the gym's elevated track, then spent another hour on weights. By the time he hit the shower, he felt better. Exhausted, but better.

There was no going back. No helping his mother at this late date. That brought him full circle to the real purpose of his lunch with Bill: Did he want to give up his wayward lifestyle and go back to being an electrician?

Common sense said yes. Get off these streets, away from the criminal elements, and settle into something simple. But some part of him revolted at the thought.

He was still debating whether or not to tell Taylor about the conversation when he walked into his house and ran face-first into the whirlwind.

"Warren!" Taylor flew at him the minute he stepped inside. His hair was a mess, his eyes wild, both cheeks raked with red lines from clawing at his own face. He clutched at Warren like a life raft in a flood. "I need you to hit me. I need it. Right now. Please. Just tie me down and hit me—"

"Honey," Warren said, catching Taylor's wrists in his hands. "Calm down. If you want me to tie you down, I will. But not until you've settled down—"

"No!" Taylor jerked away from him, going from begging to livid in a second flat. "You promised you'd take care of me! You promised you'd fix me when I had my bad days!"

"And I will. Or, I'll try." Although at that moment, it was the last thing he wanted to do. He tried again to reach for Taylor. "Honey, please—"

"No! Fuck you! I knew you were lying! I knew you couldn't handle it. I hate you—"

"What happened, Taylor? What's going on?"

"What's going on is that it's back! Don't you understand?" He slammed both hands into Warren's chest, knocking him back a step. "Just hit me! That's all you have to do is hit me!"

"No."

"Then fuck me!" He clutched at Warren again. "Then fuck me. Please. Please, Warren."

He put his forehead against Warren's chest, a sob racking his slender body, but when Warren tried to put his arms around him—tried to comfort him—Taylor screamed and hit him again. It was just like the day Taylor had broken his TV. He was angry and vicious and practically seething in his ferocity.

The difference was that this time, Warren felt nothing but pity.

He thought about what he'd done that day—how he'd dragged Taylor to the bedroom, tied him down, and beaten him with the flog. He thought about how ruthlessly he'd fucked the poor boy. And yes, it had worked. They'd somehow vanquished Taylor's demons, but the thought of going through it again made Warren's bile rise.

"Do something!" Taylor yelled, slamming him in the chest again. "Goddamn it, why won't you do something?"

Warren had to be rough. He hated it, but that was the only thing Taylor understood when he got like this, so Warren grabbed his arms. He pulled him down the hall to the bedroom, even though Taylor fought him every step of the way. He got the first wrist cuff on, but when he reached for the second one, Taylor smacked him hard across the face. It was a good hit, and it knocked Warren back a bit.

"Damn it, Taylor, stop!" Warren yelled. "Do you want this or not?"

Taylor fell back, panting. "Yes. Yes. I'm sorry."

He still resisted a bit when Warren grabbed his other hand, almost like he couldn't help it. He had tears in his eyes, and Warren stopped, still gripping Taylor's wrist tight so he couldn't hit him again.

"Taylor, please."

He wasn't even sure what he was asking for, except that he wanted more than anything to be tender with Taylor when he got like this, rather than rough.

He might as well have tried to pet a rabid dog. Taylor screamed and tried to pull away. The cuff held him in place, but he fought with the only thing he had left—his legs and feet. One foot landed squarely in Warren's solar plexus. It knocked the wind out of him and threw him back, off the bed. His head snapped against the dresser, hard enough to blacken his vision for half a second.

"Jesus, Taylor. Knock it off!" Warren stood, touching the sore spot on his scalp. He took one tentative step toward the bed, still hoping to calm Taylor down.

Taylor backed away as far as he could with one wrist still bound. "No! Don't touch me! Not like that! This isn't what I need!"

"You don't know what you need! All you know is what's worked in the past, but it isn't healthy. It isn't—"

"Fuck you! You're a coward and a pussy and a big, fat, lazy piece of shit, and I hate you! I can't believe I ever let you touch me!"

Warren fell back a step, reeling. Part of him wanted to believe this was only Taylor's way of trying to infuriate him—an attempt to bait him into violence—but part of him couldn't help but wonder if this was what Taylor really thought of him. Maybe everything before this had been nothing but pretty lies, just so Warren would keep paying the bills.

Warren's doubts were worse than the kick to the gut he'd received. He felt as if his entire world had suddenly been turned on its head. "Taylor. Honey, please—"

"I hate you!" Taylor raged on. "Fuck you! Just cut me loose and let me go. Let me go!" He grabbed the only thing in reach—the bottle of lube—and threw it at Warren's head. It went wide, and he screamed as if somebody had personally ruined his revenge. "I hate you! Get away from me! Just get away!"

And Warren did the only thing he could think to do—he obeyed. He turned and walked out of the room with Taylor's vitriol still ringing in his ears. He grabbed his keys and slammed through the back door, practically ripping it off the hinges in his anger. He hadn't been so hurt or angry in years. His blood pounded in his ears. He couldn't stop his hands from shaking. Jesus, no wonder the kid had been able to push poor, sad Harry Truman into punching him. No wonder Phil had cut him loose rather than dealing with it. Warren's tires screeched across the asphalt as he backed out of the driveway and slammed the car into gear.

He had no idea where he was going.

He made it a block before he pulled over. He sat there with his forehead against the steering wheel, breathing deep, trying to figure out what the hell he was supposed to do. Logic said to just do what he'd done last time—tie Taylor down and flog him until he subsided—but the thought turned his stomach. He wasn't even sure it would work. This time was worse, and Warren simply didn't have it in him.

He sat back in the seat, floundering for a solution. He pulled out his phone, found Phil's number, and hit Call.

"Hello?"

Just hearing Phil's calm, reasonable voice was reassuring. "Tell me I'm an idiot."

"You're an idiot."

Warren almost laughed. Leave it to Phil to do exactly what he'd asked. "Thanks a lot, friend."

"Is this about TJ? Taylor. Whatever his name is?"

Warren sighed. Outside his window, people were going about their normal days, buying groceries, heading to Starbucks, and here Warren sat, afraid to go home because a boy who barely weighed a hundred and thirty pounds soaking wet had called him a pussy. "Yes," he said.

"Warren?"

"What?"

"You're not an idiot. You're probably the most compassionate man I know. If you're this upset, it's only because you think there's something in him worth saving. Otherwise you'd have done what every other man in his life has done and walked away."

"You really think so?"

"I do." A second of silence. "Then again, your theory was decent too. Maybe you really are just a fool."

"Could be a bit of both."

"Yet another possibility."

Warren smiled. "You busy? I could use a drink."

"You always forget I don't drink."

"Shit." It was a stupid thing for him to forget too. They'd both grown up with addicts. It was part of what bound them together. "Sorry."

"It's okay. You should call Gray. If I know him, he's just itching to argue with somebody about something. He'll be happy to tell you all the ways you're an idiot."

Warren chuckled, shaking his head. "I'm sure he will."

Twenty minutes later, he arrived at Gray's dive bar of choice. It was something of a cop hangout, although definitely on the sleazy side. Warren tried not to be self-conscious as he crossed to the bar and took the stool next to Gray, who had clearly just finished a shift, because he was still in uniform.

"What're you drinking?" Gray asked.

"Whatever."

Gray had a bowl of peanuts in front of him, and a pint glass holding something that looked more like foamy tar than beer. He eyed Warren up and down, then said to the bartender, "Get him a 90 Shilling."

"You know I don't like beer."

Gray grinned and popped a peanut into his mouth. "This way, it goes down slow and I don't have to worry about letting you drive home."

"Wow, what are friends for?" But he drained half the pint as soon as it landed on the bar in front of him.

"What's eating you? Is it that kid you've got chained up in your old playroom?"

Warren ducked his head, thinking how Gray didn't know how right he was—Warren had left Taylor still shackled to the bed. With his other hand free, it wouldn't take long for him to let himself loose, though. "I don't know what to do with him."

Gray just watched him, and before Warren knew it, the whole thing was spilling out—how mean and angry and vicious Taylor got, and the way he literally begged to be beaten. Warren didn't tell Gray about James, or about how sad and vulnerable he really thought Taylor was. That was a bit more than he was likely to share with anybody over a single beer in a crappy bar, but he gave him the gist of it.

"So tell me," he finally said. "How come a guy with a closet full of gear can't just whip his ass the way he wants?"

"Because it won't work." Gray had barely touched his beer, but his bowl of peanuts was almost gone. "What he's looking for isn't about pain or sex or even about being dominated. It's about humiliation, and you can't do that."

"Why not?"

Gray laughed—a loud guffaw that made the few other patrons turn their way. "What, are you serious?"

Warren tried not to be annoyed. "Yeah, I'm serious."

Gray's mirth subsided a bit. "Because you like him. I mean, more than that. You *value* him, and that's the opposite of what he's looking for. You see buried treasure when what he wants right now is to be somebody's trash."

Warren found himself nodding. "Okay. Yeah. That makes sense."

"Want to know what I think you should do?"

"Sure."

"Rent him out. Let somebody else do the hard part. Then you take care of him when it's all said and done."

Warren's first instinct was horror, but only for a second. Gray's suggestion actually made a certain amount of sense. Taylor didn't want tenderness, and Warren no longer knew how to touch him without at least part of what he felt coming through. Why not let somebody else provide the outlet Taylor needed?

Could it really be that easy?

"Rent him out to who? I can't just let any asshole off Craigslist touch him."

Gray's face fell in a mask of mock hurt. "Are you serious? You got three guys on speed dial able to take care of this without you having to worry one bit." He laughed and took a drink of his beer. "Actually, Charlie has friends in town for some leather thing, so there you go. Problem solved."

There was a chance it could work. But could he convince Taylor to calm down long enough to listen to his plan? He didn't want to just spring it on him, even though he suspected Taylor would be one-hundred percent onboard. He was about to ask Gray to follow him home and help him out when his phone rang.

Leroy's.

Warren's heart sank, and he slowly lifted the phone to his face. "Yeah?"

"Warren? You care what happens to this kid, or did you kick him loose?"

"I care." So much it hurt.

"Then you need to get down here."

"Is it the glory hole?"

"It's worse. And it ain't pretty."

"I'll be right there." He ended the call and turned to Gray. "You mind giving me a hand?"

Gray pulled out his wallet and dropped a twenty on the bar. "Lead the way."

Chapter 15

They took separate cars, but arrived at Leroy's door within seconds of each other. The shop shared a back alley with a gay bar that was as much a meat market as anything, and it was in this alley that Warren and Gray found Taylor on his knees in the middle of a circle.

Warren stopped short at the sight, torn between rage and grief. Taylor already had a bruise forming around his left eye, although there was no way of knowing who had given it to him. Two of the men were currently taking turns in Taylor's mouth while a third held him by the hair, directing him. Three more stood with their pants open and ready, some of them slowly stroking as they watched. Warren wanted to kill every man standing there waiting his turn, and yet the only thing he'd get from Taylor for his effort would be more rage.

"This is taking too long," one of the spectators said. "Why don't we just fuck him too? Then it'll go twice as fast."

And the worst part was the way Taylor nodded and began to unbuttoning his pants.

"Jesus," Gray said under his breath.

There was a lump in Warren's throat. "Yeah."

"Well, you could just let this play out and—"

"No." He wished he had his fake badge or his blackjack with him, but his fists would have to do. He eyed Gray's uniform. "You can stay out of this, if you want." It wouldn't do much good for a cop to get caught in a scene like this.

"Fuck that," Gray said, giving him the same grin he'd often had as they headed into sketchy situations while in the army together. "Let's do this."

Warren almost wanted a brawl. He wanted to be able to take out his rage on somebody other than Taylor. But in the end, Taylor was the only person who fought him at all.

"Fuck you!" Taylor screamed as Warren hauled him back through Leroy's to his car. "I hate you! Why couldn't you just leave me be? Why couldn't you just let me get what I need?" The knees of his jeans were filthy, the collar of his T-shirt soaked with semen. All Warren wanted to do was hold Taylor and tell him he was fine, that he didn't need to keep doing these things. Whatever had pushed him to this point, there had to be a better way to deal with it.

He didn't try, though. He knew Taylor wasn't in any kind of place to accept tenderness or understand logic.

Warren shoved him into the passenger seat of the 4Runner and turned to Gray. "Give me forty-five minutes to get it set up."

Gray gave him one wicked smile. "I'll call the boys."

Warren climbed into the passenger seat, quickly wiping the tears out of his eyes before Taylor saw them, wondering if he was doing the right thing. The thought of what was to come made him sick, but far less so than what he'd just seen.

He just had to hope Gray's idea worked.

It'd only taken Taylor a few minutes to get free of the cuff once Warren had left. A small voice in the back of his mind told him to wait. He had a good thing here. He liked Warren. A lot. And Warren cared about him, more than anybody.

More than anybody, except maybe James.

But the thought of James did bad, terrible things to him. And Warren had left him. After his promise last time that he'd handle Taylor's bad days, he'd walked out the door without a backward glance.

And then there was just blackness again, filling Taylor's chest and his mind, making him rage. To hell with this! He wasn't going to sit here waiting for Warren to come back! He wasn't going to give Warren another chance to try to calm him down, to tell him that everything would be okay. It *wouldn't* be okay. He didn't want Warren's love or his pity. He just wanted to stop feeling the way he felt right now. And he knew from experience there were only a few ways that happened.

First option: he could cut himself. Not just once, because that wouldn't be enough, but over and over until the pain blocked out everything else. Until the loss of blood lured him into sleep. But he couldn't find a razor blade at Warren's. He found only kitchen knives, and none of them very sharp.

Second option: he could go downtown and do what he'd done in the past. There was always somebody willing to abuse a young, pretty face.

He went straight to Leroy's, and when he found a couple of men waiting in line for whoever was in the glory hole, he told them to forget it, all they had to do was follow him outside. And when another group of men who were smoking behind the dance club saw what was up, it hadn't taken them long to join the circle. Taylor was glad. He was happy there in the alley with the gravel digging painfully into his knees. He'd liked the way they pulled his hair as they fought over who got to go next. And when one suggested they fuck him too, he felt nothing but relief. He was ready. He was hard and excited as they began pulling down his pants—

And then Warren was there, with his cop friend, scaring them all away, dragging Taylor back to his car.

He threw Taylor inside, and Taylor subsided into angry, bitter tears. He'd only barely begun to beat the darkness, and now Warren was letting it all come pouring back in.

It was always worse the second time.

He could leave. He could jump out of the car and run, but the sane part of his brain told him no, this was better. Warren would take care of him.

"I'll handcuff you if I have to," Warren said, his voice like stone. "But one way or another, I'm taking you home."

"Will you help me?" Taylor asked, tears streaming down his cheeks. "Can you help me like before?"

Warren's jaw clenched, but he nodded. "I have a plan."

The relief was overwhelming. He'd have a weapon against the blackness. Warren would tie him down. Warren would use the flog. Warren would fix everything.

But once they were home, Taylor's rage kicked in again. He knew instinctively it wasn't going to work. Warren was being too nice. He was too tender. Every time he looked at Taylor, Taylor saw pity there. It was the last thing he wanted, and so he went into fight mode again as Warren dragged him down the hall.

"Let me go!"

"No!"

"I hate you!"

"Fine. Hate me if you want. I'm not sure I care anymore."

That hurt, far more than Taylor expected. A sob tore from his chest. Warren would abandon him for sure after this. The thought felt like a knife in his chest, but there was no backing out now. He couldn't worry about the repercussions. The only thing he could do was fight the blackness, so Taylor put every ounce of his pain into striking Warren with his one free hand. "You're not helping me!" Warren still had one arm in his vise grip, but Taylor shoved him as hard as he could with the other. "You're not letting me find what I need!"

Warren grabbed him by both arms and slammed him against the wall—not hard enough to truly hurt, but enough to take Taylor's breath away. Just enough to send a rush of euphoria through Taylor—a glimmering bit of hope that Warren understood. God yes, let Warren beat him against the wall. Let Warren force him down onto the bed. He just needed pain or sex, or both at once.

"I will," Warren said. "But you're a fucking mess. You think I'm going to let my friends see you like this?"

Friends? That was enough to give Taylor pause.

What friends?

Warren took advantage of the momentary reprieve. He dragged Taylor into his bedroom and shoved him roughly into the bathroom.

"Get undressed. Then get yourself clean. And I mean everywhere." Warren stepped closer, his eyes pinning Taylor in place, one thick, hard finger in Taylor's face. "*Everywhere.* Do you understand what I mean by that?"

Taylor nodded, his heart pounding. "I understand."

"You wait here until I come and get you. If you start screaming and fighting again, I'll just chain you to the towel bar and leave you all damn night. If you want to fix this, you'll do what I say. You hear me?"

Taylor's pulse pounded, something in the back of his mind telling him yes, this was it. "I hear."

"Good. And don't bother putting your clothes back on."

He left, and Taylor did what he was told. His hands shook as he undressed and cleaned himself inside and out. His heart pounded. That horrible, dark mass in his chest was still there, still choking him, clouding his vision, still making him want to find a razor and make a row of clean, hot slices across his thigh. The pain would be wonderful. It would make everything better.

But no.

Maybe Warren understood. Maybe Warren would get it right.

He hardly dared hope.

He heard Warren digging in Taylor's closet, rifling through all those things they barely used. He heard furniture being moved. His curiosity was a small, insignificant thing next to the black mass that filled his body, but it gave him a focus point.

What was Warren doing?

Finally, the door opened. Warren's face was an unreadable mask, his eyes steely.

"Go into the dining room."

Taylor did, reveling in the humiliation of his nakedness, of the bruise around his eye and the abrasions on his knees. His shame felt like a beacon, and he embraced it.

Taylor stopped when he reached the kitchen, his breath coming quicker, his cock beginning to rise. The kitchen table had been shoved to the side. In its place was the spanking horse, ready for him.

"One more thing," Warren said.

He slowly and methodically strapped Taylor into a leather chastity belt. Three buckles in the front held Taylor's cock pinned against his belly, the bare tip pointing upward. A strap below wrapped around his scrotum, keeping his testes pulled down and away from his body. He'd be able to get hard, but it'd be uncomfortable. He'd be able to come, but not easily.

The tunnel vision came then, blocking out the edges of the blackness. Taylor's blood roared in his ears, and he panted, more impatient now than ever. Next to the horse was a small table. On the table lay a huge black dildo, a crop, a small suede flogger, a box of condoms, and a bottle of lube.

"You're going to use condoms?"

"I won't be the one fucking you."

Taylor moaned, his cock already fighting against the bonds holding it. He closed his eyes, almost overwhelmed by relief.

Warren understood after all.

"Get on the table."

Taylor did. A vinyl cushion on top allowed him to lie comfortably on his stomach. Padded rests on the sides held his knees and elbows, so he was effectively crouched on all fours while still being at the right height for a man to stand behind him. His groin and ass hung over the edge, leaving him naked and exposed in the best possible way. A face cradle kept his head from hanging to the floor, but left plenty of space for men to come at him from the front.

Warren buckled straps around Taylor's wrists and forearms, around his calves, and finally, one around his waist, leaving Taylor utterly trapped, unable to move anything but his head and neck.

"I could strap your head down too," Warren said, as if reading Taylor's mind, "but I think you'll be able to suck guys off better if I leave it free."

Taylor nodded and tried to calm his breathing. He tried to force his erection to wane, even if it was only for a moment. He was torn between fear and longing, shame and relief. Yes, this could work. This could solve everything.

And then the doorbell rang.

He whimpered without meaning to, whether out of terror or arousal, he didn't know. He waited, trembling, as Warren went slowly to the door. He heard voices, but was too lost in his anxious need to make sense of their words.

Oh Jesus, oh Jesus, oh Jesus.

It went on and on, a sacrilegious mantra in his head as he wondered how far this would go. That black horror in his chest roiled and raged, but soon enough, it'd be wrestled back into its cage.

Oh God, please let this be enough.

Suddenly, Warren knelt in front of him, meeting his eyes.

"The safe word is Froot Loops. Got it?"

Safe word? Who was he kidding? Taylor shook his head. "I don't need it."

"You have one anyway. The minute you say it, this stops."

Taylor shook his head again. "I hate Froot Loops." *And I hate safe words, and right at this moment, I hate you.*

Warren sighed and stood. He took a single step back. And then he said to the men in the room, "Have at him, boys."

Warren stood in the living room, watching. He had a clear view of everything.

Charlie had come in full-on Dom gear, clad in leather from head to toe. He was the first. He knelt behind Taylor and spread his cheeks wide. He leaned forward and tongued Taylor's rim, and Taylor moaned. Gray, still in his cop uniform, undid his pants and slid his hand inside, but made no move yet to engage. The man who'd come with Charlie picked up the flog and tested it across Taylor's back.

Warren held perfectly still, determined not to flinch. Determined not to turn away. Phil stood next to him looking like a straight-laced accountant in khaki pants, loafers, and a button-down shirt covered by a sports coat. "What's going on with you, Warren? First the phone call, and now this?"

Warren shook his head, watching. There was no doubt Taylor liked what was being done to him. He panted and moaned and bucked against his bonds. When Charlie finally stood and pushed into Taylor's ass, Taylor cried out—not in pain or fear or anger, but with lusty gratification. Gray moved forward and presented his erection to Taylor's waiting mouth, and Taylor took it all like a parched man begging for water.

"Jesus," Phil said, under his breath. "I forgot how damn hot he is."

"Don't hold back on my account."

Phil laughed. "I won't, believe me. But I kind of like waiting my turn." He turned and eyed Warren up and down. "I mean it. What's with you?"

"What do you mean?"

"Don't play dumb with me." He gestured toward the dining room, where Charlie was still fucking Taylor. Charlie's friend and Gray swapped off in front, although it was clear Gray wasn't done. He was just biding his time. "You hate this shit. You hate orgies. You hate group sex and the whole humiliation thing. So why now?"

Warren thought about the best way to answer that. "Something Gray said." That only got him a raised eyebrow, so he went on. "You remember when you first told me about Taylor, and I asked if you wanted me to rough him up, and you said, 'He'd probably like that'?"

Phil nodded. "I do."

He didn't say anything else, and Warren finally looked away from what was being done to Taylor, just long enough to grin over at his friend. "Well. You tell me. What made you say that?"

"Just, him. I mean, you've seen those scars on his thighs."

"I have. But I know you didn't kick him out because of a few scars."

"Not scars exactly, but something about them. About him, and the way he was in bed. There was always this undercurrent I wasn't comfortable with. Not masochism, because it wasn't about pain, but…" He waved his hand in circles, searching for a word, but never found it. He sighed. "I don't know what it is."

"And that's why it ended?"

"Is that what he told you?"

"About why you'd broken things off? No. He said you were one of the nice ones, but he was high maintenance."

"Not the phrase I would have used, but yes. It was this. He was always pushing. He begged me once to hit him. Not like spanking or flogging, but something more. Something that felt less like sex and more like abuse." He shook his head. "Learning obedience wasn't going to give him what he needed, and frankly, I wasn't invested enough to try to figure out what would." He was silent for a moment, watching. "Do you think this will help?"

"I have no idea, to tell you the truth. I only know something sets him off, and he gets angry and vicious and desperate for *something*. It's like, this dark corner where I can't reach him. And he craves this thing I can't quite give. The more I care about him, the less I can help." He faced the spanking table again and didn't let himself look away, even though he wanted to. He was torn between arousal and grief, watching the men take turns with the boy he'd somehow grown to love. "Gray suggested this."

"It was a good idea."

Charlie came hard, his grunts interrupting Phil's words. He finished quickly and moved aside to let Gray take his place.

Phil shifted, seemingly uncomfortable, although Warren knew it wouldn't last. "That sounded selfish," Phil said. "Yeah, it's a good idea because I'm going to get my turn too. But honestly, I think it's a good idea because it just might work."

That gave Warren hope. "You really think so?"

Phil shrugged. "One way to find out, right? Charlie has two more friends on the way, and four more he can call after that, if you need him to."

Warren nodded, his heart clenching. *Jesus, let these first six be enough.*

Next to him, Phil shifted on his feet. He put a hand over his groin, as if trying to hide his erection.

Warren found himself smiling. "Go ahead. I wouldn't have invited you if I didn't want you touching him."

"You sure?"

"I am. But listen. Can you stay until the end? I want to have a bath ready for him, but I don't want to leave him alone."

"You don't trust these guys?"

"That isn't the point."

"Okay. No problem." Phil took a step forward but stopped to look back. "Last chance to tell me to zip up and go home."

Warren laughed. Of all the men there, Phil was the one he was least worried about. Phil liked control, but he wasn't into pain. "Go. Do whatever you want to do."

And I'll just have to hope it's enough.

For Taylor, everything outside Warren's house ceased to exist. He never knew which man was behind him or which in front or even how many there were. He never knew who held the flogger or who held the crop. There was only the glorious pain and the pleasure as one man took him, and then another. One man fucked his ass, the other fucked his face. One man beat him, another pulled his hair. And with each thrust, each slap, each swallow of cum, the blackness in his chest receded. The anger and the rage began to fade away.

They fucked him and used him and fucked him some more, and Taylor reveled in every minute of it. He loved the constant friction as they took their turns. He loved the sounds they made and the smell of their lust. One reached under the table to tease the protruding tip of Taylor's cock until Taylor almost sobbed from the exquisite torture of it.

"Not yet, little boy," the man said, his voice deep but not without humor. "You best rein it in, son. We plan to be here all night."

And then he fucked Taylor some more.

Through it all, Warren stood in the living room and watched, his arms crossed and his face unreadable. At one point, he talked quietly with Phil, until Phil laughed and came to take his turn at Taylor's mouth.

And still it went on.

Taylor drifted, lost in the sea of both pleasure and pain. Some of the men were gentle, some were rough. Some used the dildo or their fingers instead of their cock. One teased his prostate ruthlessly until one of the others told him he was going to ruin their fun. They left his ass alone for a while after that, concentrating instead on his mouth, and on laying the crop across his back.

Taylor's erection waned, but his arousal didn't. He was breathless and a bit sore and almost euphorically happy.

"Fuck me," he finally managed to pant. "Jesus, somebody fuck me."

The men laughed, and Taylor moaned when one finally obliged. Blood rushed into his cock, making it strain painfully against the buckles on the chastity belt. His balls ached. He was almost to that wonderful point where the shame and guilt and horror he'd felt earlier were gone.

But not quite.

Whoever was behind him finished, grunting as he came.

"Move out of the way," another said. "I've waited all this time."

Taylor's breath hitched in a sob.

"Are you the last?" Warren asked.

"He is," Phil said.

No, Taylor wanted to cry. *Not yet.*

Warren knelt in front of the table, meeting Taylor's eyes. "Do you have what you need?"

"No." Taylor knew he was crying, but he didn't bother fighting it. "No, don't let them stop."

Warren's expression was unreadable, but he nodded and stood. "Go ahead," he said to the man behind Taylor. And then, to somebody else, "Call your friends."

And it started again.

The man behind him alternated his thrusts with feathery touches on Taylor's cock. Every once in a while, he pulled out and bent to use his tongue on Taylor's rim. By the time the second group arrived, Taylor was so close to climaxing, he could hardly stand it. A naked cock appeared at his face, and Taylor gratefully opened his mouth, anxious for something to focus on. Sucking cocks made him feel dirty and cheap in the way he craved most. They made it easier for him to keep his orgasm at bay by taking his mind off the sheer pleasure of being fucked. He sucked for all he was worth, trying to concentrate on giving good head rather than on how desperately he needed to come.

He was almost there now—almost at that place where the blackness was gone. Almost at the place where he was so low, there was no place to look but up.

"I can't even see the welts anymore," one of the new arrivals said. And in the next moment, Taylor felt the splay of the flogger across his back. He cried out around the cock in his mouth. The one in his ass disappeared and was replaced by blunt, probing fingers, and Taylor sank deeper into this perfect union of heaven and hell.

This group was rougher. The bit of tenderness Warren's friends had shown him was gone. These new men spanked him and whipped him and fucked him raw, and Taylor lost all sense of himself. He lay there with his face in the cradle, sobbing and begging, although he couldn't have said what it was he begged for.

"Please," he finally said.

A second later, Warren was there, kneeling to meet Taylor's eyes.

"Do you have what you need?"

Taylor opened his mouth—tried to say yes—and yet it stalled in his throat. "Almost."

This time, he saw Warren wince. He noticed the terrible sadness around his eyes as he said to the man behind Taylor, "Keep going."

And the man did.

And then another.

And then another, although Taylor was sure he'd been one of the first group—one who'd already come.

And finally, Taylor lay there in his restraints, sobbing uncontrollably, unable to move. Unable to feel. Unable to respond when another man presented his cock at Taylor's face. He lost time and light and balance. He was almost gone, rubbed raw and scoured clean, stretched thin as tissue paper, his memory of what had driven him here as insubstantial as smoke.

His balls ached with the need for release. That was the only thing left.

He was vaguely aware of the room emptying—of Warren showing them all out the door.

And then, there was only Warren.

Warren, who hadn't touched him all night.

"Please," Taylor said again.

"Hang on, Tay. We're almost there." The relief when Warren unbuckled the chastity belt was almost enough to make Taylor climax, but he held it. He waited for Warren to touch him. Finally it would be Warren fucking him. Finally, he'd get to come, and then he'd get to tumble into oblivion.

But first, Warren set a chair under Taylor's face, directly in his line of sight. On it, he placed the vase.

The cracked and mended vase.

He kept his hand on Taylor's back as he moved behind him. It seemed to take forever for Warren to undo his pants, but finally, he slid his hard cock inside. Taylor thought he'd scream from how good it felt, just knowing who was behind him this time. How could he have ever thought he hated Warren? How could he have ever wanted to leave?

"Do you see this thing?" Warren asked, just barely thrusting. "Do you see this thing that belongs to me?"

Taylor nodded.

"I can't hear you, Tay."

He focused on the vase. It took three tries to make his voice work. "I see it."

"It's mine," Warren said, his voice soft. "It belongs to me. Do you understand?"

"Yes." Although his mind was reeling at where this was going.

"It belongs to me and me alone. You don't get to decide what happens to my property. You don't get to take this thing that belongs to me down to the bar. You don't get to let other men touch it or use it or abuse it without my permission. Do you understand?"

Taylor nodded, finally understanding, his tears coming faster now. "Yes."

"You don't get to take this possession that I cherish and let other men put it in danger. Only I get to say who touches it and how. Only I get to say how and when it gets used. You got that?"

Taylor nodded a third time, tears streaming from his eyes. The need to come was so strong, he could barely hold it back, but he did.

For Warren, who somehow found a way to cherish him.

Warren, who was still inside of him, but no longer moving.

"You don't get to take something I value—something I hold dear—and risk its safety with those who don't see its beauty the way I do. Is that clear?"

"Yes," Taylor sobbed, this time with relief. "I understand."

"Good."

Warren reached under the table and took Taylor's aching cock in his hard, strong fingers. He pushed in as deep as he could go and tucked his head against the top of Taylor's spine, holding perfectly still. It was so quiet and strange, and Taylor wondered for a moment what he was supposed to do.

And then he felt it, the thing he craved most, at the same moment that Warren groaned with the strain of relieving himself with his cock still mostly erect. It was a hot, wonderful rush of fluid, and Taylor sobbed, barely noticing his own climax, barely noticing as Warren stroked him through it. All he felt was that beautiful heat, that glorious sensation of being pumped full of something new and dear and precious, and Taylor cried at the joy of it. He'd told Warren what this meant to him. He'd confessed his deepest cravings, and now Warren was giving him exactly what he needed. He'd let those other men scrub him clean, and now he filled Taylor with something sterile and pure. He was granting Taylor a new sense of purpose, and Taylor took it gratefully, unable to hold back his tears, so full of joy he wanted to die then and there rather than face whatever came next. He practically held his breath, and that sweet sensation went on and on and on and finally waned.

When it was done, Warren leaned gently over Taylor's back. He ran his fingers through Taylor's hair.

"Do we understand each other?" Warren asked, his voice a soft whisper in Taylor's ear.

Taylor could only nod and cry. "Yes," he tried to say, but it came out a sob. "I understand."

Warren kissed his jaw. "Good boy."

He was afraid he'd feel abandoned and empty once Warren pulled away, but he didn't. He still had that secret gift inside him, the knowledge that he might be cracked and flawed, but he could be mended too, because Warren trusted him. Somehow, Warren valued him.

His tears abated as Warren undid the bonds and then helped him stand. His legs felt like rubber, and Warren half carried him through Taylor's bedroom, into his little bathroom, where the claw-foot tub was already full of water.

"I had Phil run it for you," Warren said, "but it was a while ago. Hopefully it isn't too cold."

Taylor shook his head. "It won't be."

"Take as long as you need," Warren said. "I'm going to go clean up. And when you come out, I'll be waiting, okay?"

Taylor was glad to be left alone. There wasn't exactly anything dignified in what came next. He was glad Warren had made the others wear condoms, though. He'd never been glad of such a thing before, but he was now. It meant what Warren had given him wasn't sullied by what those men had done first.

He took his time on the toilet, letting everything relax. Most of what had gone in wouldn't come out until later, and he was glad. Warren didn't expect him to hold it forever. He was cracked and broken, after all. But for now, Taylor would keep most of what had been entrusted to him.

He brushed his teeth twice, then finally sank slowly into the bath. The water was chilly, and he curled into a ball in the end of the claw-foot tub, his forehead against the cold edge, and he drifted.

The sensation of being fucked for so long and by so many was still there, a quiet, rhythmic ache in his most intimate place. His throat burned from swallowing semen. But what flashed before his mind's eye wasn't those men or their cocks or their lust. It was the sadness in Warren's eyes, and that vase, sitting on the chair.

Cherished.

Valued.

Mine.

Taylor's shame drove him to these dark places. It stoked the craving for things others thought demeaning and base. But when it was all said and done, he was left quiet and perfect and pure.

He felt that now.

Nothing could touch him. He'd been pushed to the bottom, and then Warren had given him a hand up. He only needed to stay here, in the safety of this bathroom. This tub.

This water, which was now frigid, but he didn't care. He could die here and never have to feel anything else, ever again.

"Taylor?" Warren asked, knocking lightly at the door. "Are you okay?"

Taylor couldn't answer. He was barely conscious. He seemed to watch from someplace outside his body as Warren came in. He noted the alarm on Warren's face.

"You're freezing, Taylor. Why are you still in the tub?"

Because I'm perfect, right now, for this moment only, Taylor thought, but couldn't speak.

"Come on. Get up."

Warren pulled the plug on the tub and helped Taylor stand. He toweled him dry while Taylor stood shivering.

"Are you hungry?"

Taylor managed to shake his head no. He didn't want to eat.

Taylor followed him obediently into the bedroom. Warren undressed first, before guiding Taylor into bed, under the covers. Taylor's teeth were chattering when Warren finally pulled Taylor into his arms.

The warmth came as a shock. Warren's hands felt like hot irons on Taylor's back. He was so big and strong, like some kind of furnace, and Taylor huddled against him, still trembling, feeling tears once again pricking at the back of his tired, sandblasted eyes. He felt wrung out and exhausted, but he never wanted to leave this moment, being warmed by Warren. "I'm sorry," he said as the tears came again. "I'm sorry. I'm so, so sorry."

"Shh, honey. It's all over."

"I don't hate you, Warren. I don't. I could never hate you."

"It's okay."

"I'm sorry. Oh God, Warren—"

"Hush now," Warren said, his voice gentle. "We need to talk for a minute. Can you do that?"

Taylor took a deep breath, and then another, trying to calm his crying. "Yes."

"Good. Did you understand what I told you there at the end?"

Taylor nodded.

"Tell me."

"I belong to you," Taylor said, his voice hoarse and shaky. "You'll decide who touches me and who uses me. And when I need to be punished again, you'll take care of it. You'll make sure the punishment is done right."

Warren's breathing was tight and tense. Taylor didn't understand that, but he understood the soothing hand moving up and down his back. "And what else?"

"You cherish me. I'm broken and flawed and messed up, but you still value me enough to make me yours. You love me just enough to give me part of you to hold. And I will. I'll make it part of me. I won't let you down."

Warren's cheeks were damp, and his breath hitched in his chest, but he kissed Taylor's forehead. "Good. Good boy."

"Warren?"

"Yes?"

"Did I make you proud?"

Warren's arms tightened around him. "Yes, my sweet Tay. You made me proud."

Taylor didn't think he'd ever be able to stop crying, but at least he'd be in this warm safe place when it happened. He clung to Warren like a life raft in a stormy sea. Warren would keep him safe, no matter what. Warren would take care of him, in a way nobody else ever had. "Thank you."

"Shh." Warren rubbed his back and kissed his hair. "Sleep now, honey. It's been a long day."

Taylor couldn't have disobeyed that order, even if he'd wanted to.

Warren lay there thinking, long after Taylor had finally fallen asleep.

He'd learned long ago that it was valuable to have people repeat things back, because what they heard wasn't always what was said. Taylor's recollection of what Warren had told him was a perfect example.

"And when I need to be punished again, you'll take care of it. You'll make sure the punishment is done right."

Warren had never used the word "punished." But that was what Taylor had heard.

Warren hadn't used the word "love" either, but Taylor had heard it anyway.

Warren sighed and buried his nose in Taylor's hair, happy just to hold him while he slept.

Whether he'd ever managed to use the word or not, it was true. He loved Taylor, but he couldn't go through many days like the one they'd just had. Seeing Taylor on his knees in that alley had nearly sent Warren over the edge. It'd felt like Afghanistan all over again. He'd wanted to kill every man there.

Since then, his emotions had been up and down and all over. He'd been aroused and angry and embarrassed, for both Taylor and himself. He'd almost choked on his own doubt as he'd watched the men take turns. Only the support of Phil and Gray had kept him on track. His uncertainty and constant questioning of his own agenda were part of why he'd never been good at the "lifestyle."

It was why he'd never been good enough for Stuart.

As the other men had used Taylor in just about every possible way, Warren had stood to the side, drinking water. He'd held it all evening, never once going to the bathroom. He knew how the night had to end, all because when Taylor had first asked Warren to do it, he'd said, *"I've never felt so loved."*

Warren had never urinated in a man before, and certainly not as part of sex. It'd taken a ridiculous amount of concentration to push it through despite his erection, to overcome the thought of coming first and peeing later. It'd been strange and arousing and disturbing all at once. But whatever it was, Taylor had responded beautifully. Warren knew he'd do it a thousand times over before he let Taylor go back downtown to work the glory hole, or to be abused in the alley behind the bar. If that was what it took to bring Taylor back from his episodes, Warren would oblige.

But would it be enough next time, or the time after that, or the time after that? The downward spiral of Taylor's episodes worried him. There was nothing wrong with liking pain or restraint. There was nothing wrong with wanting to be fucked or used by any number of men. There wasn't even anything wrong with wanting to be humiliated, if it was done right. But what Taylor sought didn't feel like any of those things. What Taylor craved felt dark and wrong.

Something that felt less like sex and more like abuse, Phil had said, and he was right.

Warren feared that each time Taylor asked for this treatment, he'd become a bit more immune. Each time, they'd have to go one step further. At some point, no amount of pain and humiliation would be enough. At some point, he feared Taylor would take a razor blade to his wrists instead of his thigh.

If they didn't find a healthier way to handle Taylor's emotional issues, it could get ugly. Warren wasn't sure if he could handle it.

But if he didn't, who would?

He settled closer to Taylor, trying to quiet his mind. It was almost four a.m.

There was no telling what the next morning would bring. It was possible the whole night had been for nothing and tomorrow, they'd be right back where they started.

Warren had no idea what he'd do then.

Chapter 16

Taylor woke to the smell of bacon. Hunger made his stomach rumble.

A glance at the clock told him it was eleven o'clock. Why had he slept so late? He usually woke between eight and nine. And Warren never cooked for him. He'd done that only once, the morning after Taylor's episode. But yesterday—

Yesterday.

Oh no.

The memory hit him hard, the depth of it taking his breath away, curling him into a ball under the sheet. He remembered his horrible black rage, and the alley, and the spanking horse, and the endless round of men fucking him.

And finally Warren. He remembered the look on Warren's face at the beginning of the night, when Taylor had called him a fat, lazy piece of shit.

Warren, who had done the one thing Taylor somehow equated with love.

Warren, who had used words like "valued" and "cherished."

Taylor climbed slowly from the bed, wincing. The men hadn't been as rough as they could have been, but he was still sore. At that moment, he wished they'd fucked him less and beaten him more. He deserved it.

He took a long time in the bathroom, although his stomach ached for food. Eventually, he heard a soft knock on the bedroom door.

"Taylor?" Warren called. "I know you're up. You must be hungry. Come out and eat."

"I'm coming," Taylor called.

He looked at his reflection, studying the dark bruise around his left eye. He remembered Warren holding him tight as he'd fallen asleep. He'd felt so at peace, but now, the thought of walking out the door and seeing Warren made him break out in a cold sweat.

He'd become an expert through the years at driving men away. He didn't know how to face one who chose to stay.

He dressed slowly and went down the hall, his stomach twisting with hunger and nerves. Warren had already eaten and was rinsing off his plate. Another sat on the table—scrambled eggs, bacon, a piece of buttered toast, and a glass of orange juice. As Taylor stood watching, Warren placed a cup of hot coffee next to it.

"Sit," he said gently.

Taylor couldn't even look at him. "I'm sorry."

"I'm the one who should be sorry, Taylor. I said after your last episode that I'd handle your bad days, but when the time came to prove it, I failed you."

"No." Taylor choked on the word, fighting tears. "Warren—"

"It doesn't matter. You're forgiven. And hopefully you can forgive me."

"You didn't do anything wrong."

"I didn't do much right either. I think the best thing we can do is accept that we both handled it poorly, and promise each other we'll do better next time. Agreed?"

Taylor's head spun. No, he couldn't agree to that. He didn't think Warren deserved a single ounce of the blame. Not after everything Taylor had done. Not after the things he'd said.

"Sit down and eat," Warren said, his voice gentle.

But that was too simple. "No. I kicked you. And I slapped you. I said horrible things. Things I didn't mean."

"You're forgiven."

Taylor shook his head. "I don't deserve that."

Warren moved closer. He reached out to put his hand on Taylor's cheek, and Taylor jerked away. "Don't."

Warren made a low sound in his throat—something like a growl—something that spoke more of frustration than anger. "If I were to punch you right now, you'd take it without complaint, wouldn't you?"

Taylor nodded, almost hoping it would happen. He'd welcome the punishment. "Yes. I'd deserve it."

"And yet when I try to show you any amount of affection, you pull away."

Taylor blinked, shaking his head, trying to force it all to make sense. He was trying to make things right, and somehow, he was only making it worse. "I don't want you to be mad at me." And it was the truth. "I was terrible to you."

Warren sighed. He reached out again, this time to take Taylor's hand, and Taylor let him.

"Do you remember last night?" Warren asked. "The end of the night, after everyone had gone home?"

Taylor nodded. "Yes." It came out a whisper.

"You remember what happened right before I untied you?"

"I do." And the memory of that warm, wonderful gift filled him with light and happiness. "I remember."

"Tell me what it meant. Tell me what you remember most."

One word came instantly to mind. "Cherished. You said 'cherished.'"

This time he didn't pull away when Warren put his hand against his cheek. He didn't resist when Warren tilted his head back so he had to meet Warren's eyes. "There's nothing wrong with being cherished, is there?"

Taylor's eyes filled with tears again. He was so tired of crying! "Yes. There is something wrong with it, because I don't deserve it."

"You don't decide that, Taylor. I do." He put one giant hand on each side of Taylor's face, his touch firm but gentle. "Think of the vase. You don't get to tell me how I feel about it, do you?"

Such a simple question, and yet the answer surprised him. "No."

"I decide the value of what belongs to me. Me. Not you."

"But—"

"I say which of my possessions is precious and beautiful and important. Not you. Do you understand?"

It was like some kind of optical illusion—clearly one thing, until he looked at it another way. Taylor nodded, feeling as if the world were shifting beneath his feet. "I think maybe I do."

"You don't get to tell me which things I cherish and which I don't."

"I guess not."

"So, are you mine, or aren't you?"

"Yes." He put his whole heart into that single word, and it filled him with a radiant kind of peace. "Yes, if you really think you want me."

"Oh, honey." Warren's smile was gentle. "I wouldn't still be here if I didn't."

And then Warren kissed him. It was deep and slow and tender, like a question, and Taylor wrapped his arms around Warren's neck and did his best to say yes. *Yes, I belong to you. Yes, you can have me.* He felt nothing but hope and relief and love, and Taylor lost himself in the sweetness of it. He'd spent years being scared, but now there was no need. He could put his whole life in Warren's strong, capable hands.

Warren would take care of him, no matter what. Things hadn't gone quite right, but Warren vowed to do better next time, and Taylor believed him. Warren wasn't the type to make promises lightly.

Warren wouldn't abandon him just because he had a bad day.

Warren would be strong for him.

When the kiss finally ended, Taylor found he was smiling. Warren brushed his thumb over Taylor's lips, looking pleased.

"So on a scale of one to ten, what was yesterday?"

Taylor might have laughed if the memory didn't hurt. "A solid eleven."

"Okay, then. That means we've been through the worst, right?"

"Hopefully."

"I'm sorry. Whether you're ready to admit it or not, I screwed up yesterday, but it won't happen again. I won't leave you next time, no matter what you do, I promise."

"I believe you."

Warren nodded toward the table. "Now sit down and eat, okay?"

Taylor couldn't believe how hungry he was once he started eating. He felt significantly better after breakfast, although he still wasn't entirely sure how he was supposed to act around Warren now. When he was done eating, Warren handed him a jacket and said, "Come on. We're going out."

Taylor followed him obediently to the car. It wasn't until he was in the passenger seat and they were rolling down the road, sunlight strobing through the tree branches in blinding flashes against the windshield, that he asked, "Where are we going?"

"First, to the grocery store." Warren dug into his pocket and held a familiar key ring out to Taylor. "Then we'll stop by Leroy's and you can bring the car back."

Those words made Taylor remember why the car was downtown. He remembered the gravel of the alley digging into his knees, and the horrible grief on Warren's face. He looked at the floor, the words *I'm sorry* on the tip of his tongue, but Warren said quietly, "Don't apologize again. It's done, and you're still forgiven, just like you were forty minutes ago."

Taylor nodded. He wiped his eyes. The left one was tender in a way that had become familiar to him over the years. He dropped the sun visor to check his reflection in the mirror. "I wish this bruise wasn't so noticeable."

"Don't worry. Everybody will just assume I beat you."

It was said casually, and Taylor almost laughed. "I suppose." But how unfair would that be, to let people think that, when Warren was the one who kept trying to save him?

They reached the store and climbed out of the car. It was a gorgeous, promising day, the sky clear and shockingly blue. It was the kind of day that hinted at picnics and hot dogs and sailing Frisbees snatched from the air by ecstatic mutts. Taylor felt almost like himself again as he followed Warren past the rows of parked cars to the front of the store. But he stopped short before going inside.

Potted roses stood like sentinels along the entire brick front of the store.

They weren't in bloom yet, but they were green, their leaves trembling in the breeze as if fighting to protect the gentle little treasures they hid. The buds were tiny, tightly held secrets, too small and new to reveal what color the roses would be when they bloomed. They held so much promise—so much *potential*—and Taylor stood there in awe, thinking about the dead rose bushes in Warren's back yard.

"What is it?" Warren asked, turning on his heel to look back.

Taylor touched one tiny, delicate bud. He almost expected it to wither and die at his touch, but it didn't. It was indifferent, and beautiful. "Can we buy roses?"

Warren's brow wrinkled, and Taylor realized this probably hurt. This probably reminded Warren of the man in the picture he kept hidden in his desk drawer. It undoubtedly made him think about Stuart, who he'd once loved. But Warren said only, "Do you know anything about growing roses?"

Taylor's heart sank. "No." It had never even occurred to him that there might be more involved than just putting them in the ground.

Warren took two slow steps back to him. "I'm sure you could learn."

"How?" He felt stupid for even asking.

Warren pulled a tag from the rose planter in front of them and handed it to Taylor. "You can start with the instructions on the back."

Taylor turned it over and tried to read it, but it was the worst kind of print—tiny and dense, with no breaks in the paragraphs or images to help him break up the text. The bit of dirt still clinging to the tag didn't help. He wondered if he'd have to confess that he couldn't read it.

Warren sensed his hesitation and took it from him to read out loud. "Plant in full sun in soil amended with compost. When first transplanted, keep soil moist. Once established, water regularly. Fertilize in early spring and again in early summer, but no later than three to four weeks before first frost. Prune bushes in late winter to approximately two and a half to three feet in height. Remove spent blooms as needed."

"What does 'amended with compost' mean?"

"Mixed with."

"Why don't they just say that?"

Warren almost smiled. "Good question."

"It all sounds easy enough, right? I can do all that."

"I don't see why not, if it's something that appeals to you." Warren fingered one tiny bud. "Roses don't usually bloom until June in Colorado, but these were obviously grown in a greenhouse somewhere. As long as it stays warm out, they'll probably bloom in a week or two. We'll have to watch the weather. Be careful of late frosts."

"That doesn't sound too hard."

"Nope. Hell, there's probably an app for it." Warren glanced up and down the rows. "How about four, to start with? Does that sound good?"

"Really?"

"Sure. There are still tools in the shed, but we'll need to buy the compost. And maybe some Miracle-Gro. Stuart always said that stuff was like magic."

He glanced at Taylor as if trying to judge whether the mention of his old lover bothered him, but Taylor didn't have room in his heart for jealousy, especially not for a man who Warren had told him he no longer missed.

Warren was buying him roses.

He threw his arms around Warren's neck, laughing. He didn't know why he was suddenly desperate to try to grow flowers in the cold, hard dirt, but whatever his reasons, Warren was willing to help him.

And that meant more than he could say.

"Thank you."

Warren hugged him back and kissed the side of his head. "You're welcome."

Back at home, Warren took Taylor into the shed in the far corner of the yard. In addition to the lawnmower and weed whacker, there were shovels and clippers of all sizes. There were hoes, saws, a chainsaw, and some kind of big machine the size of a snowblower that Taylor didn't recognize. Warren handed Taylor a pair of heavy gloves.

"You'll want these."

Dirt caked the palm side, and Taylor pulled them on, surprised at their stiffness. Bits of dirt trapped inside for years tickled his fingertips. The gloves still smelled like leather, despite the layer of grit covering them. Taylor smiled, clenching and unclenching his fists to loosen them up. He didn't care that they'd once been Stuart's. He felt fiercely possessive of them.

"Nobody's worked that soil in years," Warren said. "I don't water enough, and it gets almost full sun back there."

"What does that mean?"

"Means it'll be like digging concrete at first."

Taylor's heart sank a bit. He hadn't thought about that. He eyed the shovels, wondering if he'd even be strong enough to do it.

"I'll let you get started while I put the groceries away," Warren said. "Once we get the old bush out of there, we'll rototill the whole area. Mix in the compost and soil we bought. It'll be easy enough to work with after that."

Taylor took the shovel and went to work. Warren was right. Even standing on the shovel with all his weight, he couldn't get it to sink in more than an inch or two. By the time Warren emerged to help him, he'd barely made a dent. Even working together, it took longer than he expected to get the old, dead rosebush out of the ground. It felt good, though. Taylor felt triumphant when the last sign of Stuart was gone, and he didn't think he was the only one who was glad to see it go. Warren smiled at the gaping hole in the earth next to the back porch.

"I should have ripped that out ages ago."

"Now there'll be a new one there instead of just an empty place."

"Where will you put the others?"

Taylor had already thought about it. "All along this wall, just like at the store." It didn't look like the grass in that area was all that healthy to begin with. "Unless you have a better idea."

"I'm no gardener. Do whatever you want to do."

Warren dragged the big, unidentified machine out of the shed and showed Taylor how to operate it. The curvy blades in front churned up the dirt like a plow, chopping the hard clumps into workable dirt, stirring in the compost and soil they'd bought at the store. The first pass over the hard earth was difficult, but after that, it was just a matter of moving the heavy machine forward.

"I can do the rest," Taylor told Warren, feeling strangely possessive of the project as a whole. He was glad Warren had helped him. He never would have been able to break through the sun-hardened soil on his own. He would have given up in frustration before ever getting started. But now Warren had laid the groundwork, so to speak, and Taylor longed for something he could point to and call his own. He put his hand on Warren's arm. "Thank you."

"Let me know if you need anything," Warren said.

"I will."

And after that, there was just Taylor and a strange, newfound joy he'd never even thought to look for. Dirt caked the knees of his jeans and the toes of his shoes. The gloves became soft and pliant on his hands. Half an inch below the sun-warmed surface, the soil was cool and fragrant and fresh. Birds chirped in the trees, and insects buzzed in his ears. Occasionally, he noticed the sound of cars driving by, or neighbors doing their own yard work. But for the most part, there was only Taylor, and the simple beauty of Warren's backyard. Once the holes were ready, he freed the rose bushes from their cheap plastic pots and settled them in the earth.

When all four plants were in the ground, Taylor stood back, admiring his work. He was unaccustomed to physical labor. His shoulders, arms, and hands ached. The skin on the back of his neck felt hot and tight. He'd have to head back to the store for some aloe. Even then, he knew it'd peel. His four rose bushes seemed small against the backdrop of Warren's house. They seemed like nothing.

In his heart, though, they were already blooming. And they weren't alone.

He imagined all the other things he could add to the flat, boring space behind Warren's house. More flowers, for sure. But he also pictured a birdbath, and feeders, and maybe one of those pretty, reflective balls. He wondered about butterflies and hummingbirds. Were there certain flowers they flocked to, or would any flower work?

He stopped, mentally chiding himself. Why get carried away? Why imagine something so grand this soon? The roses might be dead by morning. Bird seed sprouted into weeds, and Warren might not want a cheesy birdbath or one of those stupid balls in his yard. Taylor might end up with nothing to show but a sunburned neck for the one and only day of real work he'd ever done.

He couldn't believe it, though. Doubt refused to take root. Warren would grant him anything he asked for, within reason. And at that moment, Taylor knew he wanted to spend the next day with his hands in the dirt. And the one after that, and the one after that too. He pictured the days lined up one after the other like a series of pretty paintings—spring blooming into summer, summer giving way to fall, fall turning into winter— and himself, standing in Warren's yard, like a strong, solid thread sewn through each and every one of them, connecting the current him—the version of Taylor who still had a bruise on his eye and scars on his thighs and a throat that burned from swallowing semen—to some future Taylor who was somehow made whole. Some future Taylor who let only Warren touch him unless Warren wanted it otherwise. A Taylor who wasn't afraid of coming face-to-face with his past.

It nearly took Taylor's breath away.

For the first time since losing James, he knew exactly where he'd wake up in the morning, not just the next day, but for a whole series of days, and he was glad. For the first time, he didn't wonder how much longer he had before his host sent him packing. And for the first time in more years than he wanted to count, Taylor actually cared whether he woke up each and every morning down the road. So many times in the past, he'd wanted to give up. He'd let men fuck him bareback any time they asked, almost hoping something would go wrong. He'd never truly been suicidal because he was too scared to follow through. Suicide would only have proven to his father what a screwup Taylor truly was. But in some dark, secret part of his heart, he'd wanted to die. He'd hoped the end would come soon, whether at the hands of a violent man who got carried away, or as the result of unprotected sex. He'd longed for it, because living had simply become too hard.

But now, standing in Warren's backyard, seeing the future laid out before him like one of those scenic charity calendars that showed up in the mail, Taylor wanted to see it. He *wanted* to wake up each morning in Warren's house, if not in his bed. He wanted to see what the future would bring. For the first time in forever, Taylor liked his life. He almost even liked himself. And Warren had given him that.

He went through the back door, his head spinning. He found Warren in the kitchen, squinting at the directions on a box of frozen lasagna.

"Either I'm getting old, or everything's printed smaller these days." He glanced over at Taylor, stopping short at the sight of the dirty leather gloves still covering Taylor's hands. "Everything okay?"

Taylor had no words. He crossed the room and threw his arms around Warren's neck, although he had to strain to his tippy-toes to do it. A lump lodged in his throat. His chest felt tight, his heart so huge and full and fragile, he almost couldn't breathe, and all he could do was kiss the part of Warren's stubbly jaw he could reach. "Thank you."

Warren's big, strong hand moved slowly up his spine. "You're welcome, I guess?" There was laughter in his voice. "What exactly are you thanking me for?"

He didn't understand. Of course he didn't. How could he? How could he possibly know how much he'd done?

Taylor pulled back to meet Warren's eyes, although even on his toes, he had to strain his neck to do it. The scars on Warren's face made him look older than he was, and meaner than he was. He always looked as if he was ready to fight everybody's battles for them, and yet he took it all without complaint, just like he'd taken in a broken whore and given him the world.

I love you.

Taylor wanted desperately to say it, but he couldn't. He'd only ever said those words to James, and to say them now felt treasonous—not because he'd be betraying James, but because it'd belittle what Warren meant to him. Because Warren deserved something bigger and better than what he'd given James. Taylor had loved James because it was the only thing he could do. It was the only way he could make peace with everything James had done to him. Loving James had been built into him, sewn into his DNA, whether he wanted it or not. Anything James demanded, Taylor gave willingly with all his heart, because it was the only option he had.

Warren couldn't have been more different. Warren never demanded anything Taylor wasn't willing to give. He gave and gave and gave some more, and Taylor wished he had something to give back. He wished saying "I love you" could be enough, but it couldn't. Not after the way his brother had twisted and cheapened those words. And so Taylor would do the only thing he could think to do—he'd grow roses, and lilies, and daisies, and whatever else he could find. He'd hang up birdhouses and bird feeders. He'd plant flowers that attracted butterflies. He'd fill Warren's corner of the world with as much light and color and life as he could manage. He'd turn Warren's sterile, sparse house into a home.

It was the only thing he had to give.

Warren stared at him, his brow wrinkled in amused concern. He brushed the backs of his fingers down Taylor's cheek. "Everything all right, Tay?"

"It's perfect," Taylor said, pulling him into a kiss. "My life has never been this perfect."

Chapter 17

It wasn't so much the ringing phone that woke Taylor. It was Warren sitting straight up in bed, saying, "What the fuck is that?" His tension was almost palpable. He often came instantly awake like this, as if he expected to have to jump into battle.

The phone rang again, and Taylor grabbed it off his bedside table. The only person besides Warren who had the number was Riley. "Hello?"

"Taylor?" Riley sounded strung out in a way he hadn't since their first week as friends. "Jesus, Taylor, it's bad."

"I'll be there in ten minutes."

Taylor hung up the phone, jumped out of bed, and began pulling on clothes.

"What is it?" Warren asked, rubbing sleep out of his eyes.

"Riley's in trouble. I have to go." He turned to face Warren in the darkness. "Are you mad?"

"No. I think he's lucky to have you."

Despite Warren's tacit approval, Taylor still worried as he left the house. After his day in the garden and the wonderful understanding he thought he'd found with Warren, Warren hadn't wanted to have sex. Taylor had offered, more than once, but each time, Warren had gently turned him down. It was as if he couldn't bear to touch Taylor now that he'd seen his friends make use of him. And yet when Taylor asked if that was why, Warren had told him no, that he simply wasn't in the mood. And when Taylor asked Warren to sleep in his bed with him, Warren had readily agreed. He'd held Taylor tight until he'd fallen asleep.

Still, it bothered Taylor. He couldn't help but think he'd ruined everything.

Ten minutes later, Taylor found Riley pacing his apartment. The nausea and diarrhea had long since passed, but the restlessness remained. "I'm sorry," Riley said, pulling at his hair. "God, I'm sorry."

"It's fine."

"I hadn't heard from you in a couple of days. I thought maybe you were mad at me or something. That I'd done something wrong."

"No. Of course not." He mentally kicked himself for not checking in with Riley. "I had a relapse, I guess you could say."

Riley stopped his pacing, all his attention suddenly on Taylor. Riley had a way of looking at him that made him feel like he was the most important person in the world. "You did?"

Taylor swallowed his shame and told Riley the whole thing. It was embarrassing, but it gave Riley something to focus on. He eventually stopped pacing as Taylor explained how the simplest bit of praise from Warren had triggered some ancient memory. How a simple nap next to Riley had made things worse. How he'd gone to Leroy's and betrayed Warren in the worst possible way. And finally, how he'd spent the next day exploring the unexpected joy of digging holes in the ground.

"You have to see my roses," he said. Riley's restlessness and cravings had finally passed, and they now lay side by side on Riley's bed. "I'm going back later today for more plants. Warren gave me money. He said I could. And once it's in bloom, you'll have to see it. I'll bring you flowers every day."

The only answer was the slow, even sound of Riley's breathing. Taylor turned to face him, studying his face in his sleep. He'd gained a tiny bit of weight since quitting, and his color was better. His dark hair had new luster and seemed thicker now that it was clean. They'd slept next to each other a few times, and Taylor was stunned each time at how simple and innocent and wonderful it felt. Riley never expected sex, and Taylor knew he never would. They could lie next to each other as friends.

As brothers.

It was part of what had set him off two days earlier, realizing that this was how brothers were supposed to feel together. That everything he'd had with James had been wrong in some way.

He pushed the memory from his mind. He didn't want to think about it again, for fear he'd find himself back in his dark place.

Instead, he held Riley's hand. He thought about his garden until he drifted off to sleep.

Taylor called Warren first thing in the morning to let him know everything was okay. If Warren was annoyed that Taylor hadn't come home, he kept it to himself.

Riley's mom had apparently continued bringing him food. Taylor dug eggs and bacon out of the fridge and made them breakfast, which they ate together at Riley's tiny kitchen table.

"I'm sorry I woke you up in the middle of the night."

"It's fine. That's what I'm here for."

Riley took their plates to the sink and spoke with his back to Taylor. "I need to do something. It's easier when you're here, but once you're gone, all I think about is getting high."

"I could loan you some of my graphic novels."

Riley shook his head. "I can't sit still long enough to read."

"Maybe you should get a job."

Riley turned to stare at him, and Taylor felt his cheeks warm. He couldn't believe the words had come out of his mouth. He'd had them thrown at him enough of the years. How many people had asked why he didn't get a "real job" rather than working as a whore? It was a question Taylor hated.

But Riley's stunned look gave way to a hesitant smile. "That's not a bad idea, actually."

"Really?"

Riley shrugged. "Probably be good to get out of the house sometimes, right?"

Taylor couldn't believe Riley was going for this. "I suppose so."

"Yeah." Riley nodded, pushing his hair off his face as his smile broadened. "It'd be nice to have my own money again too. To not have to rely on my parents for groceries. I mean, Jesus. Am I an adult or not?"

Taylor squirmed in his seat, hating the questions Riley's sudden certainty raised in his mind. "Sure."

"Where, though? I don't have a car. It'd have to be someplace within walking distance."

"Let's go see what we can find."

It was barely nine o'clock, but Taylor could tell they were in for a gorgeous May day. The temperature was already over sixty. Not a single cloud dotted the bright Colorado sky. The afternoon would be warm and breezy, with temperatures in the high seventies. Taylor couldn't help but think what a perfect day it would be for digging more holes in the ground.

But first, he'd do what he could to help Riley.

Taylor assumed they'd take his car, but Riley stopped on the sidewalk, peering up the street. A darkness seemed to pass over his face. "Not that way," he said, his voice quiet. "There's lots of gas stations and liquor stores I could apply at." He shook his head. "But I know where to score if I go that direction."

"Okay. Then we'll go the other way."

Taylor didn't know the neighborhood well at all, but he followed Riley down the street. At first, he was skeptical. The area seemed so run-down and forgotten. But the weather was good, and Riley seemed happier than he had since Taylor met him, so Taylor simply followed along.

They turned a corner, went another block, and found themselves at an intersection that seemed to bridge two worlds. Across the street lay a shopping complex, anchored on one end by a huge home improvement store and on the other end by a similarly large grocery store. In between sat the usual assortment of shoe and clothing stores, post offices masquerading as drycleaners, and several restaurants. Beyond the entire monstrosity, Taylor could just make out the edge of a neighborhood of small, single-family homes.

"There has to be something here," Riley said, smiling.

Taylor couldn't quite understand his excitement, but he wasn't going to say anything to ruin Riley's good mood.

Inside the grocery store, they found three job application kiosks, side by side in the corner of the busy building.

"What about you?" Riley asked, taking a seat at one of them. "You could use a job too, right?"

Taylor frowned, considering. A small income of his own would be nice. After all, it hardly seemed fair to expect Warren to support him forever. And more than anything, he wanted flowers—lilies and mums and daisies and orchids. Flowers cost money, and he didn't want to be asking Warren for cash. It made him feel cheap. Sure, bagging groceries wasn't exactly the job of his dreams, but the years spent on his knees hadn't exactly qualified him for any kind of real career.

"Come on," Riley said, smiling at him. "We could come into work together. Sounds like fun, right?"

And in the end, Taylor went through the application process, not because he wanted the job, but because the one friend he had in the entire world asked him to.

Over the next few days, Taylor seemed to blossom like one of the roses he tended so carefully in the backyard.

Warren gave him a couple hundred dollars, just wanting to keep that smile on his face, and Taylor went back and forth to the nursery, coming home with more and more plants. He spent several hours each day in the yard, planning and planting. He was happier than Warren had ever seen him.

Warren also purchased a couple of waterproof mattress pads for Taylor's bed. Taylor had nearly cried from happiness when he saw them. For himself, Warren didn't think he'd ever be comfortable enough with the act to make urine a regular part of their sex lives, but he didn't want to rule it out entirely. Not knowing how much it meant to Taylor.

All things considered, Warren should have felt better, but some part of him couldn't stop worrying. Yes, things were good now, but something about Taylor's episode and the orgy still bothered Warren. Something nagged at him, like an itch between his shoulder blades he couldn't quite reach, telling him he was missing the forest for the trees. He was relishing Taylor's sudden happiness when he should have been building bulwarks against the next bad day. Warren was relieved on Sunday when Gray called him just after noon.

"How about I pick you up and we go shoot some pool?"

Warren sucked at pool, but whatever. A few hours with one of his buddies sounded like exactly what he needed.

Twenty minutes later, Gray knocked on the back door. It wasn't until Taylor was about to open it that Warren realized how awkward it might be, having the two of them face-to-face. They'd only met twice before, and the latter of those had been with Taylor strapped to the spanking table, begging to be fucked from both ends at once.

Taylor's cheeks turned a bit red when he saw who stood outside. He stepped aside to let Gray in, although he kept his eyes on the floor. Warren wondered if he'd try to pretend he didn't know Gray had been one of the men involved.

Gray wasn't one to allow such delusions.

"Hey, sweetie." Gray pulled Taylor close and kissed his temple. "Not going to ask me if I have a warrant this time?"

Taylor laughed a bit, seemingly torn between amusement and embarrassment. "I'll just assume you don't."

Gray kept him there, one hand on Taylor's cheek. He brushed his thumb over Taylor's lips and shook his head.

"Goddamn, you are the juiciest peach on the tree, aren't you? I've never been so jealous of Warren in my life."

Warren crossed his arms, scowling, wondering whether there was any point in stepping in. Gray was a lot like Taylor. He was highly sexual, with few restraints, and he was the best-looking man Warren had ever met, with a muscular, chiseled body few people could resist. But he was also Warren's friend. He was a flirt, but he wasn't cruel. He wouldn't really try to take Taylor away from Warren.

Still, Warren couldn't help but think that given the choice between himself and Gray, the smart money would be on Gray every day of the week.

Taylor bit his lip, stepping back, away from Gray's touch. "You wouldn't be jealous if you knew what a pain in the neck I am." The look he sent Warren's way was heavy with apology, although whether he was apologizing for himself or Gray was hard to say.

Gray laughed. "Good thing you found Warren first, then. He has more patience than Buddha."

Seeing the way Gray was still eyeing Taylor, Warren was feeling rather un-Buddha-like. He sort of wanted to slam his best friend's face into the wall.

"We going or what?" he asked.

Gray grinned at him, and Warren had the uncomfortable feeling Gray could read his mind. "I'm waiting on you, old man."

Warren wondered if it was rude not to even invite Taylor along, but in truth, he wanted time alone with Gray to help him hash out whatever it was he had caught in his craw. Besides, Taylor looked happy enough as he followed them into the backyard, Stuart's old gardening gloves already on his hands. He stopped Warren with a touch on his arm.

"How do you feel about a birdbath?"

Warren smiled and kissed him on the forehead. "I draw the line at yard gnomes."

Taylor's smile was brighter than the sun in the Colorado sky. "Okay."

The temp sat just north of seventy, but inside Gray's car was like an oven thanks to the unwavering sun. Gray gave Warren a weighted look as he turned the key in the ignition. "You're 'drawing the line,' huh? We both know all that kid has to do is bat his eyes at you, and you'll suddenly have more lawn gnomes than Charlie."

Warren laughed, conceding the fact. "Let's hope it doesn't come to that."

Traffic was light as they headed away from downtown. The air was thick with the smell of flowering trees. It was almost a shame to go inside on such a gorgeous day, but they did anyway. It wasn't until Warren and Gray were standing around a pool table inside a dark bar that Gray asked the obvious question.

"What's eating you, anyway? You have one of those looks."

Warren didn't bother denying it. Taylor joked about Warren's many scowls, and he was sure he was wearing one now. "Can't stop thinking about the other night."

"That makes two of us." Gray shook his head as he got ready to break the triangular bundle of balls at the end of the table. "I meant what I said back there, man. We've known each other a lot of years, and I've never wanted to snatch something out of your hands the way I do when I see him." The crack of the cue ball as it sent the rest scattering across the green felt seemed thunderous in the quiet bar. Not many patrons on a Sunday afternoon when there was no football on TV. "That kid has the sweetest—"

"Shut up, will you?"

Gray laughed and sank the twelve. "I got stripes."

"Yeah, I saw."

Gray walked slowly around the table, eyeing his options. "What are you worried about anyway? He's not going anywhere. That boy thinks you hung the moon."

Warren shifted on his feet, uncomfortable with the words.

"Don't believe me?" Gray asked.

"Not really."

"He lied to me without batting an eye so you'd have an alibi for Robby's ass-whooping. I know you didn't ask him to do it either."

There was no safe way to answer that. Warren kept his eyes on the game, not wanting to give anything away.

Luckily, Gray didn't seem to expect a response. He resumed his slow survey of the table. "For what it's worth, I meant the other thing I said to him too. It's good he has you and not me. If I'd walked into that alley and seen my partner in that circle?" He shook his head again. "I would have come unglued."

"It was close, believe me."

"What was that all about, anyway?"

"I wish I knew. It's like I told you that night. He just gets wild."

"Well, whatever the reason, it had to feel like a kick in the balls. You handled it well."

"Not sure I did."

"The spanking horse, you mean?" Gray missed the fifteen and stood back to let Warren take his turn. "You sorry you did it?"

"Maybe. I don't know." Warren took his own circle of the table, although he was so busy thinking about Taylor, he was having a hard time focusing on which balls were his. "It's not that I regret it. You were right. I couldn't give him what he wanted. But something about the whole thing is eating at me."

"Well, it was all because of these weird fits he has, right? The question is, did it work?"

"It did." Warren kept his attention on lining up his stick, the cue ball, the red three, and the corner pocket. "I just can't help but feel like…" His shot was solid, but his aim was off. The three bounced off the edge of the pocket and back out into the center of the table.

"Like what?" Gray prodded.

Warren sighed and met his friend's gaze across the expanse of green felt. "Like it was wrong."

"Oh, for fuck's sake. Don't tell me you've turned into one of those prudes who thinks everybody in the lifestyle just needs to be fixed. Like only broken people like getting tied up once in a while."

"No." Although it was interesting that he'd used Taylor's own word—broken. "That's not what I meant."

"Good, because it's bullshit." Gray methodically sank the ten, then the thirteen, before missing his third shot. "Everybody there consented. That's all that matters."

"Most of the time, yes. And on any normal night, whatever we do in the bedroom, I know it's fine. He likes things rough—"

"Jesus, don't tease me."

"And there's nothing wrong with that, normally. But I'm telling you, that night was different." The night Taylor had broken his TV had been different too. Just on a smaller scale. "There's something off about what we did."

"Why? What the fuck's 'off' about it?"

"I don't know! That's what I'm trying to tell you. I can't figure that part out, and it's driving me crazy."

Gray waited, watching as Warren missed another shot. Warren would have liked to blame his bad aim on Gray's weighted scrutiny, but pool just wasn't his game.

"Is Taylor upset about it?" Gray asked.

"No." Warren considered it as Gray leaned over the table. "It's like, we gave him what he wanted. What he thought he needed. But it wasn't really the *right* thing, you know? Yeah, it took care of the problem. But it still bothers me." Gray's shot was perfect. The eleven ball fell smoothly into the side pocket. Warren scowled in frustration, shaking his head. "I can't explain it."

He waited for Gray to argue, but Gray simply stood there staring at him, both hands wrapped around his pool stick. "Huh."

"What does that mean?"

"Nothing." Gray scratched his jaw, then bent to take his next shot. "It's just, those words you used. What he *wanted*.

What he thought he *needed*. You know what those words sound like to me?"

"No."

"Addiction."

Warren rolled his eyes. "Oh, come on. You're telling me he's a sex addict? No way." Sure, Taylor was highly sexual. Yes, he'd spent years trading sex and blow jobs for a place to stay. He'd told Warren how much he liked being on his knees. But an addict? That didn't quite fit.

Gray sank another stripe. Only the nine and the eight ball stood between him and victory. "I don't mean he's addicted to the sex, necessarily."

"Then what?"

"Think about it. In a lot of cases—not all, probably, but a lot—the addiction's a symptom. Or, a result, I guess. It's the Band-Aid. Can't handle stress? Have another drink. Mommy issues? Have some coke. Daddy issues? A couple of Vicodin will make it all go away." He banked the nine off the rail, straight into the side pocket. "Maybe for Taylor, it's the same."

Warren nodded as the pieces fell into place. He remembered the scars on Taylor's thighs, and Taylor's explanation of how it had started. *"It was easier to feel that pain than the real pain."* "He used to cut himself, until he learned he could use sex as an outlet instead." Taylor had confessed it their first night together. Warren mentally kicked himself for not seeing the connection sooner.

"There it is, then. And you're probably right to be worried. He's replaced one type of self-harm with another. If he'd asked for the gang bang simply 'cause it sounded like fun, it'd be different. But he wasn't looking for fun. He specifically wanted it to be an act of self-destruction." He circled the table, trying to find a clear line to the eight. Most of Warren's balls were still on the green, blocking his way. "It's a fine line, man. A murky area, for sure. But it all points to the same thing."

"He's running from something."

"Sounds that way. You know what it is?"

Warren considered Taylor's confession about his brother. "Maybe."

"Well, that's your first step. Somebody once told me it isn't enough to slay your demons. You gotta dissect those bastards. Cut open their bellies and see what they've been feeding on. *Then* you'll know the real problem."

Great. All he had to do was dissect Taylor's demons. That sounded like about as much fun as dancing with a nest of hornets. But would it solve the problem?

Warren thought about it as Gray proceeded to kick his ass at pool three more times. It made sense. It wasn't the sex that was wrong, or the bondage, or the fact they'd pulled a train on him. The problem was, they'd only aided Taylor in running from the real issue. He'd begged for a metaphorical hit of heroin, and rather than talking him down, they'd given it to him.

So what was Taylor running from?

He had a feeling it all led back to James.

He arrived back at home just before five. He found Taylor at the kitchen sink scrubbing dirt from beneath his nails. Soil from the garden still clung to his knees and tennis shoes. The time in the sun had done him good, adding a healthy pink glow to his cheeks and golden highlights to his dark blond hair.

"I'm just about to start dinner," Taylor said over his shoulder.

Warren sat down at the table, debating his approach. "Don't worry about it."

"Aren't you hungry?"

Warren shrugged. "Maybe we'll go out?"

Taylor turned to him, his eyes wide with delight. "Really?"

Going out for dinner never failed to cheer Taylor up. "Really. But first, come talk to me for a minute."

Taylor's excitement wilted a bit. He shut off the water and eyed Warren over his shoulder, his dripping hands hanging over the edge of the sink. "What is it? Did I do something wrong?"

"No. I just want to talk to you."

Taylor's skepticism was obvious, but he dried his hands on the dishtowel, then slowly crossed the kitchen to sink into the chair next to Warren. Warren reached out and took his hand, hoping to reassure him.

"I want to talk about your bad days."

Taylor blinked, pulling back, as if he'd been slapped. "No! Why now, Warren? I'm doing good right now. I don't want to risk it."

Warren kept hold of Taylor's hand, his thumb rubbing slow circles over Taylor's slender fingers. "I just think I'll have a better chance next time if I know what I'm up against."

Taylor shook his head, turning his head to the side to stare out the window over the sink.

"Please," Warren begged. "I just need to understand what's going on in your head when it happens."

"I don't know if I can explain."

"Try."

Taylor sighed. "I told you. It's like a blackness."

"Okay." He waited, hoping for more.

Taylor gnawed his bottom lip, but he seemed to be debating rather than stalling, so Warren gave him time. A second later, Taylor stood up, pulling his hand from Warren's grip in the process. He went to the corner drawer and came back with the notepad and a pencil.

"It's like my regular life is still water." He drew a line across the top of the paper. "And mostly, I just drift around, and it's okay. But sometimes, there's this storm inside the water." He drew a cone, the circle at the top just below the surface of the water. The point ended half an inch above the bottom of the page. He began coloring in the bottom point of the cone, pushing so hard on the pencil, Warren was surprised it didn't tear through the paper. "Like a whirlpool, I guess. It's thick and dark, and it pulls me in." He continued coloring, shading the cone with the pencil. Toward the top, the gray faded away, but the bottom point was black as night. "More like tar. It sucks me in and weighs me down until I can't breathe."

Warren nodded, studying the simple drawing. "Okay." It reminded him of something Charlie had once shown him as he'd tried to explain how to achieve serenity—some kind of "cone of enlightenment." Warren hadn't paid much attention. It was all too New Age and woo-woo for him. But it'd looked a lot like the cone in Taylor's drawing. And now, years later, Warren remembered very clearly what the darkest, bottommost point of that cone represented.

Shame.

"So tell me how the sex or the pain helps. Does it keep you from falling in?"

Taylor shook his head. "No. It's like it pushes me out the bottom." He drew a quick line down, through the cone, out the pointed tip to the edge of the page. "Instead of staying in there, drowning, I get pushed underneath the storm, where it can't reach me." He set down his pencil, but his eyes remained on the paper. "I can't even lift my head because it might sideswipe me and I'll have to start over. But if I can stay here…" He touched the bottom edge of the page. "If I can stay really flat and still underneath it, I can wait it out. And eventually, it goes away."

"All right. That's good," Warren said, wanting to encourage him. "I think I get it. The question is, what do we do about it?"

Taylor's cheeks turned red. His mouth hardened into a thin line. "I already know what to do about it. So do you."

Warren shook his head. "I don't think that's a solution. I think that's your way of running from the real issue." He could see Taylor's resistance to that statement in the stiffness of his shoulders and the tightness of his jaw. Warren pushed on, trying to explain. "Look, I've felt the blackness too. I'm not saying it's exactly the same thing, but after my mom died, I felt something like this." He touched the black cone on the page. "I was pissed at everything. Pissed at my dad because he was the one who drove her to it. Pissed at the cops 'cause there was nothing they could do. Pissed at my uncle for not trying harder to save her. But most of all, I was pissed at myself because I went off to college like some jackass and left her there, alone with my father." He stopped, trying to steady himself. He'd given Taylor a brief version in the past, but it had been years since he'd talked candidly about his guilt over his mother's death.

"Your mom." Taylor's voice was quiet. "You said he drove her to it. Are you saying—"

"Her mom had just died a couple of weeks before. I guess she just didn't want to keep going after that. She locked herself in the garage with the car running."

"Oh no, Warren. I'm sorry."

Me too. But there was nothing to be done about it. At the time, he'd been twenty years old and utterly lost. "And then, less than two months later on a regular old Tuesday morning, two airplanes crashed into the World Trade Center. I watched that footage on TV, just like every other American. I watched those towers collapse. And suddenly, all that blackness had a purpose."

Taylor's expression was hard to read, but at least he was listening. "That's why you enlisted?"

Warren nodded. "I thought if I killed enough al-Qaeda, I'd beat it. But you know what? It didn't do a goddamned thing. Maybe it helped me keep my mind off it for a few minutes at a time. But after four years of death and war, that blackness was no better than before. If anything, it was worse."

"Is it still there?"

Warren shook his head. "No. Or if it is, it's small now, and it's manageable. But it took time. Even after I got home, it took a while to figure out how to beat it."

"So, how did you do it?"

"With my friends. And my job. And Stuart."

Taylor slumped a bit. "You're trying to tell me it's all about love or some stupid shit like that."

251

"Maybe that was part of it, yeah. But the main thing was, I was able to work through it. I had people I could talk to about it. Gray was in that war with me. He knew how hard it was to come back to a regular nine-to-five. I met Charlie next. He helped me see all the people who had it worse than me, and all the ways I could help. Then I met Stuart. He gave me a reason to wake up each morning. And finally, I met Phil. He grew up with an addict too, which I guess gave us a kind of bond most people don't understand. There are certain things Phil understands in ways none of the others can. Somehow, it all came together. The odd jobs and the lifestyle and the four of us." He shook his head, chuckling. "It may sound stupid, but keeping a couple of call girls safe does a lot more to beat the blackness than killing al-Qaeda ever did."

Taylor sat unmoving, staring at him. He looked so young and lost. "What does that mean for me? I can't do what you do."

Warren almost laughed, thinking about it—Taylor being the guard instead of the person being guarded. Either way, he'd be in danger, and Warren wouldn't allow that. "No, I suppose not."

"What, then? You say we have to beat this some new way, but you still haven't told me how."

"That's because I'm not sure myself." *"It isn't enough to slay your demons. You gotta dissect those bastards. Cut open their bellies and see what they've been feeding on."* "Tell me this. When the blackness comes, what causes it to form?"

Taylor turned away, scooting back in his chair a bit. "I don't know."

Warren thought he was lying. He moved a bit closer and gently took Taylor's hand again. "How about the day you broke my TV? What started it that day?"

Taylor shook his head, trying to pull his hand away. "I don't want to talk about this, Warren. I don't—"

"Think," Warren said, refusing to let Taylor go. He didn't hold Taylor's hand tight enough to hurt him, but he wasn't going to let him run either. "Think back to that afternoon. Tell me how it began."

Taylor went still and closed his eyes. His chin trembled a bit, but no tears appeared.

"*Supernatural.*"

It was little more than a whisper, and Warren sat back, confused. "Supernatural? What does that mean? Like, a ghost or something?"

Taylor's eyes flew open, and he laughed. After being so serious, it was good to see him smiling, even if it was at Warren's stupidity. "No. I mean, the TV show, *Supernatural*. Haven't you seen it?"

"No."

"Oh. Well. It's about these two brothers." His smile fell a bit but didn't disappear. Warren thought that was a good sign. "They hunt demons and ghosts. Stuff like that."

"I see." Warren was pretty sure the first part was what really mattered: two brothers. "And what about the other day?"

"The night before, you came home, and we had sex."

That happened a lot. There had to be more to it than that. "And?" Warren prodded.

"You told me I was perfect."

Warren remembered the moment. "That was bad?"

"It's something James used to say."

Warren winced, wishing he'd known that. He never would have said it. "I'm sorry."

Taylor shook his head. "No. That was okay. The way he said it was different. Sort of sarcastic. I don't think he meant it the way you did. But then, I went to Riley's that day."

His tone was hesitant, and Warren knew it was because he feared being criticized for his friendship with Riley. Warren did his best to keep any judgment out of his voice. "And what happened?"

"We fell asleep in his bed together." He seemed to search Warren's eyes. "It wasn't sexual, I swear. It's never been that way between us."

"I believe you."

"But the thing is, I was lying there next to him, thinking how much I love being that close to him. How I've shared beds with a lot of men, but it's never been like it is with him. It's never felt so innocent. And that's why I love it."

"Because it's innocent?"

"Because it feels like the way brothers would be." He bit his lip and wiped the tears that leaked from his eyes. "The way brothers *should* be, I mean."

"So, do you think the blackness is always about James, then?"

"I don't know."

"Can you think of any time the blackness came that it wasn't attached to James?"

"I don't know, all right?" Taylor jumped to his feet, pulling his hand out of Warren's grasp. He crossed the kitchen to stand at the sink, staring out the window. Warren felt sure he was checking on his rose bushes. He took a deep, unsteady breath. "Can we please stop talking about this now?"

Warren felt they'd only scratched the surface, but he also knew pushing for too much, too soon was bound to backfire. "Okay."

Taylor's shoulders fell, and he stared down into the sink.

"I'm sorry," Warren said. "I'm only trying to help."

"I know. But these last few days have been good."

"They have."

"Sometimes I think it's like that big eye thing on the tower in those *Lord of the Rings* movies, turning to look for me. When I'm happy, I'm hidden. But once I think about the blackness, it's like sending up a flare, and it finds me."

It sounded about right. Warren had often thought of depression in much the same way. He hated it, though. He wished Taylor's demons were something tangible. Something he could beat into submission with his fists. Instead, he could only wait and hope for the best.

"You hungry?" he asked, figuring he'd put Taylor on the spot enough for one night.

Taylor wiped his eyes before turning to face Warren, his smile small but grateful. "Starving, actually."

"Still want to go out to eat?"

"Yes." Taylor's smile grew. He glanced down at his dirty jeans. "I just need a minute to change."

"That's fine."

"Where are we going?"

"I'll take you wherever you want to go."

Chapter 18

Warren took Taylor to a steak house, then laughed when Taylor ordered his steak chicken-fried anyway. Things felt easy and natural between them in a way they hadn't in days, and Taylor felt some horrible unease in his chest begin to loosen.

They'd had sex only once since Taylor's episode, and even that hadn't quite been right. Taylor couldn't explain what about it felt wrong, except that Warren seemed to be holding himself back, as if he didn't really want the sex but was only acting out a role. The rage and the passion that Taylor loved so much about their sex life had been absent. Taylor lay awake long after Warren drifted into sleep, wondering if he'd ruined everything. Maybe after watching his friends take turns with him, Warren could no longer stand to touch Taylor? And yet, Warren purchased waterproof mattress pads for Taylor's bed. Whenever Warren looked at him, Taylor saw the same gentle reassurance he'd come to expect from him. When Warren kissed him, he felt as if he were being claimed.

But it never went beyond that.

Tonight would be different. Taylor didn't know if it was simply a matter of time having passed or the couple of drinks they shared over dinner, but he knew tonight, they'd break through that barrier. They'd find each other again between the sheets. When Warren looked at him across the table after paying the check, Taylor's entire body reacted, every inch of him suddenly feeling alert and alive. Warren was the sun, and

Taylor was one of the little flowers in the garden that only opened when it felt the warm rays.

Tonight, he'd finally belong to Warren again.

On the drive home, Taylor reached across the gap between the seats. He slid his hand between Warren's legs and found Warren already fully erect. Warren's breath hissed between his teeth as Taylor rubbed his length through the denim.

But Warren's iron grip on his wrist stilled him. "Wait."

Taylor sat on his hands, his heart pounding, stunned by the rejection. Back at home, his knees shook as he climbed from the car and entered the house with Warren at his heels. The kitchen was dark, only a square of moonlight spilling through the lone window to splatter across the floor. Taylor stood in its center, shaking and frightened, and turned to face Warren.

"Why don't you want me anymore?"

Warren's face was lost in shadow. "Is that what you think?"

Taylor could only nod. He stood perfectly still as Warren stepped into the light with him. Warren's hand against his cheek made him shiver. The way he brushed his thumb over Taylor's lips gave Taylor hope. "I've never stopped wanting you. You don't need to worry about that."

"Then tell me what's wrong. Tell me why nothing has been the same since that night."

Warren tilted his head, thinking. "Maybe because what I want most from you right now is something you've never been willing to give."

Taylor shook his head, holding on to Warren as hard as he could. He'd never denied Warren anything. He'd let Warren tie him up and flog him. He'd let Warren fuck him bareback. He'd let himself be taken in the dead of night without a word said between them, the entire act as quick and impersonal as a bank transaction. True, Taylor had loved every minute of those things. He'd never resented Warren for any of them. But now, to hear that it hadn't been enough hurt more than he could say.

But it intrigued him too. His blood roared in his ears. He wasn't sure if he was upset or aroused.

What could Warren possibly want that Taylor hadn't already given consent for a hundred times over?

"Then do it," Taylor whispered. "Take it, whatever it is. Make me do it. I'll never say no to you. You know that." He was so anxious to feel Warren truly touch him again. He would have done anything.

Warren pulled him close, one hand on the small of Taylor's back, the other gripping a handful of Taylor's hair. "It's not something I can take. It's something you have to give."

Taylor nodded, breathless, unsure what it was, but it didn't matter. "I will. I promise, I will."

Warren kissed him then, yanking on Taylor's hair, demanding entrance to Taylor's mouth, and Taylor gave it. He made himself soft in Warren's arms, as pliant as he knew how to be. Warren made a sound like a growl and lifted Taylor onto the countertop. One hand slid under Taylor's shirt to pinch his nipple, and Taylor moaned. God, it felt good to have Warren desire him again. He wanted nothing more than to be dragged into the bedroom, to be fucked the way only Warren fucked him. He felt like an empty vessel, just waiting to be filled.

"Please," Warren whispered as he kissed Taylor's neck. "Please don't tell me no tonight."

"I won't. I swear I won't."

Warren lifted him off the counter and Taylor wrapped his legs around Warren's waist. He let himself be carried like a child down the hall to the bedroom. Warren spent a long time undressing them both, kissing Taylor as he went. Taylor still didn't fully understand what it was Warren wanted or what it was Taylor was supposed to give. Warren was aggressive but tender. Demanding and yet gentle, and Taylor gave up trying to figure it out. He simply let himself be led. He let Warren lay him down on the bed and cuff his wrists to the headboard. His ankles went into the cuffs next, midway up the posts, holding his legs in the air.

Warren climbed between Taylor's legs, his cock hard and beaded with moisture. He put lubricant on his fingers and leaned over Taylor, forcing Taylor to meet his eyes as he used those fingers to make Taylor ready. His touch was gentler than usual, and Taylor moaned, loving the way it felt.

"Fuck me," Taylor whispered, pulling against the wrist cuffs. "Fuck me now, please."

Warren shook his head, taking his hand away. "Not tonight."

"Warren, please. Tell me what you want me to do."

"I want you to stop being afraid of what this means."

"I don't understand."

"I know."

"Then what—"

Warren leaned over him again, his eyes only inches away from Taylor's. "Look at me," he said quietly. "Don't talk. Don't think. Just look at me, and let this happen. Can you do that?"

Taylor nodded because he didn't know what else to do. He was scared and ashamed and yet so desperate for Warren's touch and approval, he would have done anything. He lay there, utterly helpless, forcing himself to face Warren's unwavering gaze as Warren began to touch him.

It took his breath away. Warren's big, rough hands moved slowly over his body, exploring Taylor's thighs and stomach and arms. He caressed Taylor's hips, carefully skirting his groin. Warren's fingers sought and teased new points of torture—the dip above Taylor's hipbone, and the crook of his armpit, which brought a hint of fear, childhood memories of being held down and tickled—and yet Warren's touch was gentle, his eyes locked on Taylor's.

"Trust me."

"I do," Taylor told him. "You know I do."

Warren didn't reply, but he caressed those ticklish spots until Taylor had no choice but to stop fighting him and relax. He settled into it, feeling Warren's gaze on him as he surrendered to the strange discomfort it brought.

"Good," Warren said, his voice soft. He slid his hand across Taylor's chest, brushing Taylor's nipple with his thumb, sending a delicious shiver toward Taylor's groin. "Good," he said again, rewarding Taylor with another caress of his nipple, this time on the opposite side. "Just breathe. That's all you need to do."

Warren's hands moved down. He spent ages brushing his fingertips over the sensitive place where Taylor's leg met his pelvis, until Taylor thought he'd lose his mind. Those thick fingers moved agonizingly close to his aching balls and his erect cock, but never gave him the satisfaction of direct contact. He found himself panting in impatience, but he kept his eyes on Warren's.

"Please," Taylor begged.

Warren smiled and kissed him, using one strong hand on Taylor's neck to hold him in place. He nudged his tongue into Taylor's mouth, his kiss somehow soft yet demanding at the same time. It felt like a test, and Taylor wanted to pass, so he relaxed everything. He opened his mouth and let Warren have his way. He whimpered shamelessly as Warren deepened the kiss, plunging his tongue in deep, crushing Taylor's lips beneath his.

Ravished.

The word sprang into Taylor's head as Warren's kiss grew more urgent, the grip on the base of Taylor's neck tightening like a vise.

He was being ravished, like one of those women on the covers of the books his mother used to read. His usual defenses had been stripped away. Warren could do anything to him, and Taylor had no way to stop it. It was at once the most horrifying and the most gratifying thing he'd ever experienced. He never wanted it to stop, and yet he was afraid to go on. He was glad he was tied to the bed, pinned in place by the weight of Warren's body. Some part of him wanted to cry and flee in terror, but the base part of his mind, the part rooted in pleasure, wanted nothing more than to let this go on forever, to remain a victim to whatever Warren had planned.

Warren broke the kiss, breathless, his eyes locked on Taylor's. His hands were moving again, the fingers of his right hand brushing pointedly over that almost painful spot in Taylor's armpit, as if daring Taylor to flinch. "Can you handle this?" Warren asked, his eyes dark and intense, his voice hoarse and thick. "Can you really let it happen this time?"

Taylor wanted to say that he'd never denied Warren anything, but then he remembered the day he'd had to be untied. It had felt like this—horrifying, even as he found himself wanting to beg for more. The vulnerability, not just of being bound and helpless, but of letting Warren look into his eyes, had been more than he could bear. The intimacy of Warren's hands and his lips moving over Taylor's body had felt like the worst kind of violation. He'd let men do horrible things to him over the years, but letting Warren truly make love to him scared him in ways he couldn't explain.

That, he realized suddenly, was what Warren wanted. Whether Taylor liked admitting it or not, it was the one thing Taylor had always denied him. Anytime Warren had tried to be too tender, Taylor turned it away by talking dirty, by begging for roughness instead. He'd wanted to believe fucking was somehow the same thing as making love. He'd told himself making Warren come was all that mattered.

It wasn't. Warren didn't want to fuck him. Warren wanted what happened tonight to be an act of true intimacy, but the difference between those things had never felt so horrifying.

But God, he couldn't back out now.

"Please," Taylor whispered, unsure what he was even asking for.

Warren groaned and kissed him again. He rolled Taylor's nipple between his thumb and forefinger, making Taylor gasp in mixed pleasure and pain. Warren pushed between Taylor's legs, his cock nudging insistently against Taylor's rim. Taylor whimpered again, overwhelmed by how anxious he was to feel Warren inside of him. He moved his hips as much as the bonds allowed, seeking the angle that would allow Warren entrance. He was taut and breathless with impatience, but unable to do anything about it. He wanted to beg, but it felt wrong. He knew asking to be fucked now would ruin everything. All he could do was wait.

At last, the tip of Warren's cock slid into place, as perfect as a key in a lock, and Taylor shuddered, whispering, "*Yes.*"

Warren didn't push any deeper, just slid the head of his erection in and out, in and out, until Taylor was as soft and pliant as water, whimpering and gasping beneath him. Warren's hands never stopped moving, often brushing that almost painful spot in Taylor's armpit. Taylor shivered again, another whimper escaping his throat. For some indeterminable amount of time, there was only that—Warren's hands and his hard, demanding kisses and the careful and incomplete union of their bodies, just barely moving—and Taylor felt tears well up in his eyes.

At last, Warren pushed gently past that second barrier. Something akin to a sob hitched in Taylor's chest. His heart pounded, but he wanted more. He was used to men shoving their way in, deep and hard, but this was something different—a slow, gentle progression of flesh inside him, a whisper in his ear, a careful deepening of everything at once. It was an agonizingly gradual build until finally, Warren was as deep as he could be. They stayed like that for a minute, locked together, straining to push closer. Taylor had never felt as complete as he did at that moment. The sudden surety that this was how they were meant to be took his breath away. And yet still, the desire to fight—to beg for Warren to simply fuck him like usual—was almost overwhelming.

He wouldn't do it. He'd made a promise to Warren, and he intended to keep it.

"Yes," he said again, still forcing himself to meet Warren's eyes. "Yes, a thousand times. Please."

Warren began to thrust, his movements slow and steady. The pressure on that ticklish spot under Taylor's arm and Warren's eyes boring into his made him want to cry, but the slow, deliberate movement of Warren's cock and the sweetness of his kisses only made him want more. He wanted to pull at his bonds—to break free before letting Warren any closer than he already was—and yet why, when nothing had ever felt so good?

"Are you with me, Taylor?" Warren asked.

Taylor gasped, trying to force words when all he wanted to do was whimper. "I'm scared."

"Of me?"

"Yes." He shook his head. "*No.*" Tears once again filled his eyes. "What's happening to me?"

"Oh, honey," Warren whispered. "All the times you've let men fuck you, but you've never learned about this." Warren pushed in again, and Taylor had the unnerving feeling that his entire being had been opened up. The pleasure of Warren's cock moving over his prostate, sliding in and out of his body, was a brilliant spark of electricity. It jolted through his body, meeting those points where Warren's fingers brushed and tickled. And all that energy seemed to blaze to life when Taylor looked into Warren's eyes. He was burning away from the inside, all because of the way Warren looked at him.

Vulnerable.

Exposed.

Ravished.

It was unnerving but perfect. It was a pleasure that went beyond physical. It was like having Warren touch the most delicate, hidden parts of Taylor's soul, only to rip them open and lay them bare. It felt like something that should result in shame—something that should be hidden away from the light—and yet it felt so pure. Warren sought out Taylor's fears and pinned them down and forced Taylor to face and accept his scrutiny.

"This is what it's all about," Warren said, his forehead almost touching Taylor's, his hips still moving. "This is what men have written poetry about since the dawn of time. This is what we kill and die for." Another thrust, and Taylor moaned. The pleasure of it all felt too big to be contained in his fragile, trapped body. He worried he'd fly apart and never be able to reclaim anything this grand again. "Wars have been fought and empires toppled," Warren said, thrusting again, "all for this."

"For sex?" Taylor gasped, still confused.

"Hell, no." His fingers tightened again on the back of Taylor's neck. "For love. Jesus, Taylor. Don't you know how much I love you?"

Taylor almost broke. The only thing that kept him from bursting into tears was the simple euphoric pleasure of their coupling and the irrational worry that this was all a dream, that his orgasm would wake him and somehow ruin everything.

Warren loved him.

Another thrust, another kiss, the words whispered in his ear. "I love you, Taylor. I love you so much."

Taylor shivered and closed his eyes, reeling at the change those words sparked in him.

Warren loved him, and that simple fact made his entire world shift on its axis. It was as if Taylor'd been clinging to the shore in a raging flood, and he finally had the courage to let go. He threw himself into the deepest, roughest part of the raging rapids and found himself in hands that were warm and swift and sure. This current would carry him exactly where he wanted to go.

How could he have fought this so hard and for so long? Allowing himself to be vulnerable with Warren meant learning he was safe. Being exposed only meant learning he was understood. There was no reason to hide or pretend or push Warren away. The meeting of their bodies and their minds was beyond anything he'd ever felt. The almost-pain where Warren's fingers moved became only another shiver of delight. Taylor felt more at ease than he ever had as Warren kissed him again, gasping against Taylor's lips.

"God, I can't believe how much I love you," Warren whispered.

I love you too.

But he refused to say it. Instead, he put every ounce of what he felt into giving back, into responding to Warren's touch. He opened himself up to Warren as he never had before, doing his best to tell Warren how he felt using only his body and his eyes and his quiet moans. He didn't fight to keep his orgasm at bay but let Warren's passion carry him over the edge. It was the most perfect thing he could have imagined, having Warren's lips on his, Warren's hand stroking him as he came, Warren's throaty voice in his ear as they found that release together. Not a climactic ending, but a simple, shared transition that left them both breathless.

Warren loved him.

And yet the entire thing left Taylor feeling inadequate. Warren had given him the greatest gift he could, and Taylor had nothing to offer in return.

"I can't say it," he said, meeting Warren's eyes. "Not because I don't feel it, but because it's the wrong word."

Warren frowned, confused, and Taylor rushed on, desperate for Warren to understand. "James ruined that word. What I feel for you is so much more. What you and I have is bigger and better, don't you see? Because it's not secret or wrong or twisted." He shook his head, his eyes once again filling with tears. "I don't have a word big enough, Warren. Not for you."

Warren's frown fell away, leaving behind nothing but a naked vulnerability that Taylor knew Warren didn't often let people see.

"I don't even need for you to love me," Warren said, his voice choked with emotion. "I just need you to stay. I think losing you now would kill me."

"Oh, Warren." Taylor wished his arms were free, only so he could put them around Warren's neck. He had to settle for what they already had—their foreheads and noses meeting, their bodies still locked intimately together. "I'm yours in every way. Don't you know that? There's nothing in the world that could make me leave."

Chapter 19

A week later, Taylor discovered one of his roses had blossomed in the quiet, clear light of the mid-May morning. It was yellow with pink tinges around the edge of each delicate petal, and Taylor thought it was the most beautiful thing he'd ever seen.

The buds had been there when he'd planted the bush in the backyard, so he couldn't take full credit, but it made him happy nonetheless. He debated for a while whether to clip it and take it inside or let it grow, but after eyeing the many other buds only a day or two from bloom, he opted to take it in.

He carried it as carefully as a gem but stopped dead in the kitchen. Now what? There was only one vase in the entire house—the one on the bookshelf that had somehow come to symbolize his own fractured, flawed existence. Taylor examined it, wondering if he should use it. It might not be watertight. Even if it was, there was a chance the water would dissolve the golden resin holding the vase together.

He couldn't have that.

He made a quick trip to the store, where he bought a single carnation, just to get the little plastic vial on the end of the stem. Back at home, he settled it carefully into the neck of the vase. It fit perfectly, hidden from view, allowing him to keep the rose stem in water without risking the vase.

He put the whole thing back on the shelf and stood back, smiling at the sight.

It was a good start, but what he envisioned for their home was so much more. He wanted flowers everywhere.

Vases would be easy. He could find those at yard sales for a few cents apiece. But flowers cost quite a bit more. He'd already spent the two hundred dollars Warren had given him. He debated asking for more, but immediately rejected the idea. How could he ask for money without making it sound like he wanted payment for services rendered? Besides, he had no idea what Warren's finances were like. Warren could have been filthy rich or borderline penniless, for all Taylor knew.

That left one obvious option: Taylor's trust fund. For years, he'd only used it in absolute emergencies. But he'd already used his account to buy Riley a TV, and the world hadn't ended. Maybe his dad no longer cared where he was or what he did. Besides, it was his money. Using a bit of it to buy flowers only seemed fair.

Ironically, he received the phone call that might have changed his mind only a few hours after spending sixty dollars at the nearest nursery.

"Taylor Reynolds?"

"Yes, this is Taylor." Only Riley and Warren ever called him. He couldn't figure out who else would even have the number.

"My name's Sam Wilson. I'm the shift manager at Lowe's. You filled out an application recently?"

Taylor's heart began to beat a bit too fast. He'd forgotten all about applying for jobs with Riley. "Oh. Yeah. Hi."

"We have some seasonal spots available in our garden center. The position would be part-time. Technically, it'd only be for the summer, although depending on how things go and how many employees we lose over the next few months, there's a chance you could stay on after that. Is that something you'd be interested in?"

The garden center! Could it really be that perfect? "Yeah. I mean, yes. Of course."

"Can you come in for an interview tomorrow morning?"

"Absolutely."

Taylor was dying to share his news with someone. Granted, he didn't actually have the job yet, but Sam had made it sound like the interview was little more than a formality. But who could he tell? Warren had already left for the afternoon and wouldn't be home until the wee hours of the morning. That left Riley.

He wondered, as he drove to Riley's house, if Sam had him called him too.

He found Riley pacing his apartment. The curtains were drawn, the windows shut tight despite the nice day. Dirty dishes littered the coffee table. Riley usually seemed happy to see Taylor, but this time, he gave Taylor a scowl that would have been more at home on Warren's face. "I feel like I hardly see you these days."

"Oh." Taylor's happiness wilted a bit in his chest. It was true he'd been spending more free time in his garden rather than with Riley. Still, it wasn't as if they'd lost touch completely. He still checked in on a daily basis, albeit sometimes by phone rather than in person.

He began gathering the dirty dishes. It wasn't like Riley to be so sloppy. "Have the cravings been bad?"

"I don't know." Riley's frustration was easy to hear. "They're not getting worse, but they aren't exactly getting better either."

"I'm sorry. I should have been here."

Riley sighed, deflating like a balloon, all the anger going out of him at once. "It isn't your fault. I don't blame you for not wanting to sit here listening to me whine. Jesus. I'm being a fucking baby, aren't I?"

Taylor smiled. "Not really."

"Here. You don't need to do that." He helped Taylor gather the last of the dishes and followed him into the kitchen.

Taylor cleared out the sink and began filling it with water. "I'll wash if you dry." The kitchen was awfully small to work side by side, but they could make it work.

"I mean it, Taylor. You don't need to clean up after me."

"I know. I don't mind." He shut off the water and started on the first glass.

Riley took his place next to him, a dishtowel in one hand. Their shoulders touched, and Riley leaned into him, nudging him a bit. "Thanks for helping."

"Sure." He thought over the last few days as he washed. After all the time he'd spent with Riley before the spanking horse, it probably did feel like he'd suddenly abandoned him. "I'm sorry I've been a bit MIA. I guess I've just been excited about the flowers." Riley didn't answer, so Taylor kept talking. "The first rose bloomed today. You should see it. Hopefully in a week or two, I can bring you some."

Riley chuckled as he rinsed the first of the clean dishes. "I don't need flowers." But the way he said it implied there was something else on his mind.

"Okay. What do you need, then?"

Riley turned away, his cheeks burning red. "Forget I said anything."

"No. Really. Tell me what you need. You know I'll help if I can."

Riley gave him an embarrassed grin. "Truthfully? I'd kill for a blow job right now."

Taylor instinctively stepped away from Riley. He felt himself shrink a bit. "Oh."

"The heroin cuts down on testosterone production, so I didn't miss it before. But now that I'm clean, it's like I'm in overdrive or something." He finished drying the glass in his hand and placed it in the cupboard. "It's driving me crazy. I don't think I've jacked off so much in years." He began drying the next glass. "I could really use the real thing, know what I mean?"

Taylor felt his cheeks flush. He hoped more than anything that he was misunderstanding Riley's point. He had a hard time forcing the question he needed to ask past his lips. "Are you asking me for a blow job?"

"What?" Riley's head whipped his way. The astonishment in his eyes seemed genuine. "No! Of course not." He laughed, and it was like a balm on the wound Taylor hadn't realized he still had. "Taylor, come on. Even if I was into guys, I'd never ask you to do that. After all the talks we've had about my addiction and your days as a whore? No way. Asking you for that would be like you asking me to hold your heroin stash, know what I mean?"

Taylor laughed too, although it was more a matter of embarrassment than amusement. "Yeah. Sorry." Knowing Riley wasn't asking for that kind of favor was a huge relief. The complete lack of sexual tension between them was part of why Taylor valued his friendship so much. He resumed his spot next to Riley at the sink and started on the plates. "I'm glad that wasn't what you meant."

Riley only smiled and nudged his shoulder again, playfully trying to push Taylor off-balance. It was another thing he did that made Taylor think of how brothers were supposed to behave.

"Hey, I got a call today from Lowe's. I have an interview tomorrow."

Riley's smile faded a bit as he took the wet plate from Taylor. "Really? That's great."

"Did they call you too?"

Riley shook his head, all his attention seemingly on drying. "No. Guess nobody wants an addict for an employee."

"Come on. How would they know? I assume you didn't put it on the application or anything."

"Of course not."

"Then, it could still happen, right? He said they need seasonal help for the garden center. The guy I talked to today seemed really nice. If I have a chance, I'll put in a good word for you, I promise."

"You'd really do that for me?"

"Of course."

By the end of the visit, any awkwardness between them seemed long forgotten. Still, as Taylor drove himself home several hours later, he couldn't help but think that Riley seemed more on edge than ever.

Warren should have been happy.

In many ways, he was. He'd never been comfortable using the L-word, and yet after breaking down and confessing the depths of his feelings for Taylor, he felt better. Not only that, he thought Taylor did too. He was still strangely uncomfortable when confronted with tenderness, but he at least recognized his own resistance. And it wasn't as if they had to leave the kinkier aspects of their sex life behind. There was no reason the two things couldn't meld into one glorious act, and meld they did. Over the next few nights, their lovemaking took on a new level of passion. It sometimes felt as if they were trying to claw their way into each other's skin, sharing some new, bold understanding.

Everything should have been perfect, but over the next few days, several incidents kept Warren from feeling completely at ease.

The first was the arrival of his cousin Jeff's wedding invitation. Warren had managed to forget his recent conversation with his uncle, but the invitation brought it all back. Should he try to go back to being an electrician? On one hand, he worried the monotony of it would drive him crazy. On the other hand, he was tired. Tired of the hookers and the borderline-illegal jobs and the long, sleepless nights. He wondered what it would feel like to bring home a paycheck without having to rub elbows with Denver's least desirables.

It was something to think about.

Hot on the heels of that came a surprising announcement from Taylor.

"I got a job!"

Warren had barely managed to drag himself out of bed after a long night of guarding Sugar and Candy. Taylor had let him sleep in, as he always did, but it was clear he'd been practically bursting with his desire to share his news.

Warren stood at the kitchen counter and poured coffee into his cup. He sort of wished Taylor was still naked except for his fluffy pink robe, but Taylor had already showered and dressed for the day. "When did this happen?"

"They called yesterday afternoon. I had an interview this morning." He practically bounced on his toes as he explained. "And I got the job!"

"Where at?"

"Lowe's. Technically, it's seasonal for the garden department, but if it works out, I could end up staying on into the fall." Taylor made a little clapping motion. His smile was as big as Warren had ever seen it. "Isn't that perfect? I'll be outside most of the day, and it'll give me a chance to learn more about flowers. There's even an employee discount."

Warren sipped his coffee, considering. It surprised him, but it wasn't unwelcome. "I didn't realize you were looking."

"Well, I wasn't really, but I tagged along with Riley when he applied."

"Riley's getting a job?" That surprised him even more than Taylor suddenly wanting one.

"He said he needed something to keep him busy. To get him out of the house. We applied at King Soopers together, and then at Lowe's." Taylor chewed his lip. "They haven't called him yet, but the guy who hired me seemed really nice. I thought I'd ask him to consider hiring Riley too."

Warren drank his coffee and resisted the urge to argue. He didn't think it would be worth Taylor sticking his neck out. Chances of Riley holding down a job through the summer were slim, especially since he'd likely blow his very first paycheck on drugs, but Warren knew better than to voice that thought. In Riley's defense, he'd already stayed clean longer than Warren expected. Warren knew a lot of the credit for that went to Taylor.

So instead of arguing, he simply smiled and said, "It's worth a shot."

The final incident came two days later, a few hours after Taylor had left for his first day of training at Lowe's. It started with the doorbell.

Warren debated not answering. Of his friends, only Gray would show up without calling first, but Gray would have come to the back door, not the front. There was at least a seventy percent chance it was a solicitor. But there was also a chance it was Bill, trying to squeeze an answer out of Warren, or something as innocent as a neighbor delivering a piece of mail that had landed in the wrong box. Or hell, maybe it'd be Girl Scouts and he could snag a box of Thin Mints.

But there were no Girl Scouts on his doorstep. Instead, he found a man who looked to be in his early fifties, with thinning hair and dark circles shadowing his pale brown eyes. He wore dark slacks and a dress shirt unbuttoned at the collar. He was a good four inches shorter than Warren, and upon getting a good look at Warren's face, he fell back a step.

"Can I help you?" Warren asked.

"Uh, I hope so." The man ran a shaking hand through his hair and attempted to smile. "I'm looking for Taylor Reynolds."

"What's this about?"

"I need to speak with him."

"He's not here right now."

"But he does live here, right? Can you tell me what time he'll be home?"

Warren scowled. "Why should I tell you anything?"

"Well." He gave an uncomfortable shrug and stuffed his hands into his pants pockets. "Because I'm his father."

Now it was Warren's turn to fall back a step. Taylor never talked about his parents or about his life at all prior to being a whore. Warren understood not wanting to dredge up the past, and so he'd let it lie. He'd never even bothered to ask if Taylor's family was local, or what his father did for a living, or if things had been good before James's death.

But now here was Taylor's father, wanting to see him.

"He'll be home in a couple of hours. You're welcome to come in and wait, if you like."

"Thanks."

They stepped inside, but no farther. It was a moment of sheer awkwardness, each of them clearly assessing the other, wondering how this conversation would go. Taylor and his dad shared the same lion-colored eyes and dark blond hair, but other than that, Warren saw little resemblance between them.

"I'm Warren." He held out his hand and was relieved when the man shook it.

"Dennis."

"Have a seat. You want some coffee or something?"

"Water would be good, I guess."

They settled into their seats a minute later, Dennis on the couch and Warren in the armchair. The coffee table between them felt as huge as the Grand Canyon.

"So." Dennis sat stiffly on the edge of the couch as if poised to flee. His eyes moved over Warren, then flicked away to take in the room in all its nondescript glory. "Taylor does live here, then?"

"He does."

Dennis's gaze returned to Warren. "Can I ask the nature of your relationship?"

Warren hesitated. He had no idea how much Taylor's parents knew about his personal life. Did they know he was gay? Did they care? Warren mentally chided himself for not asking more questions. "Does it matter?" he asked.

Dennis's shoulders slumped a bit, his eyes falling away. "I heard he's been…" He winced and pinched the bridge of his nose. "Hustling, I guess is the term."

"Where'd you hear that?"

Dennis leaned forward as if to pick up the glass of water, but stopped short. "You have to realize, we hadn't heard from him in three years. Back then, I had a private investigator track him down. He was living on the street. We talked on the phone. I told him he could come home, but he made it quite clear he wanted nothing to do with us." He shook his head.

"His mother said to forget him. He didn't want our help." He finally took a drink of the water, although Warren suspected it was only to buy himself some time. "We assumed he was using drugs."

"No. If he'd been using, he would've drained the account and come asking for more. The fact that he never touched the money should have told you he was clean."

Dennis blinked at him. "I never considered that." He set the glass carefully in its place on the coffee table. "Well. After this last stretch, two whole years without him touching the money, I assumed he was dead. I mean, I didn't want to believe it, but it seemed like the only explanation. And then a couple of weeks ago, there was suddenly activity on the account."

"A pawn shop." The TV and DVD player he'd bought for Riley.

"I can't even tell you how happy it made me, seeing that blip on his account. But I worried it wasn't really him. That somebody else had his card. I called Stan, the private investigator I'd used before. Stan found out from the man at the pawn shop that Taylor had been hustling, although he said Taylor had told him he was in a relationship now. He said he didn't know where Taylor lived, but he sent Stan to some place. I forget the name. It started with an L."

"Leroy's?"

"Yes. But the man there didn't want to help. Said he didn't know anything about anybody named Taylor, although Stan seemed to think he was lying."

Warren bit back a smile. Leroy knew exactly where to find Taylor, but he apparently hadn't wanted to share that information with a stranger. Warren would have to thank him next time he saw him.

"Then last week, there was another transaction. Sixty dollars at a nursery just down the street. It turned out they'd put him into their customer database. You know how everybody does that these days, so they can send you emails."

Warren nodded. The fact that Taylor would have given the information to the nursery surprised him but comforted him too. It meant Taylor had finally stopped giving everybody he met a fake name. He felt at home enough to give Warren's address as his own.

Dennis spread his hands. "So, that's my story. That's how I got this far." He sat back for the first time, his eyes on Warren. "Your turn now."

"Well, he isn't hustling anymore. I can tell you that much."

"So you're the relationship he was talking about?"

"I am."

"A bit old for him, aren't you?"

"And you're a bit late showing your paternal concern."

Dennis picked at a cuticle. "I suppose I am."

Warren sipped his lukewarm coffee, considering. Maybe that had been petty of him. Then again, having the age difference between them pointed out always made him cranky.

A second later, Dennis spoke again. "Has he told you about Jimmy?"

It took Warren half a second to realize "Jimmy" was also "James." Taylor had said everybody else called him Jim or Jimmy. "About him dying? Yes." And a whole lot more, but Warren didn't think it was his place to bring up the abuse.

"Taylor was never the same after that." He kept his eyes on the floor. "I guess none of us were."

"Taylor says he was a screwup. That only James ever noticed him. I think he assumes you only loved James."

Dennis pinched the bridge of his nose again. "That wasn't it."

"I think once James was gone, Taylor felt he could never live up to what his brother had been."

"No." Dennis shook his head, dropping his hand to face Warren head-on. "I'm telling you, that wasn't it."

"I didn't say it was. I only said I think that's how Taylor sees it."

"They were just so different. James was so…" He held up his hands. "So *big*, I guess you could say. He always wanted to be at the center of things. Even as babies, they were different. James was always screaming for attention. But Taylor?" He smiled, remembering, and in that moment, Warren knew the man wasn't lying. He'd loved Taylor once, no matter how he felt about him now. "He was always sweet and quiet. He never fussed. I remember once, Jimmy was sick. He had a fever. Couldn't keep anything down. Lisa and I were worried, of course. Fussing over him, the way you always do when they're sick. Taylor wasn't quite a year old at the time, and at some point, we realized it was almost bedtime, and we hadn't fed him since breakfast. He hadn't had lunch or dinner, and he was still sitting in his crib. His diaper was soaked through. He must have been starving. But he just sat there, waiting for us to remember him." He shook his head, smiling. "And I remember that night, holding him, looking into his eyes and thinking, 'This kid's got it all figured out.'"

Warren tried to imagine that. "He didn't, though."

"No. I suppose not. And once Jim died, Taylor was never the same. Like some light inside him went out. I've never quite understood it. They weren't close. Not like some brothers. They lived together, obviously, but Jimmy always had friends and sports and girlfriends and dances. And he got into so much trouble. We were always dealing with calls from the principal, or even the police."

"Taylor never mentioned that."

"I don't think he knew. We hoped he didn't. He always seemed to be in awe of Jim. It was like, I don't know, some kind of hero worship. We were afraid if he knew about Jim's bad behavior, he'd want to copy him."

Warren sat back in his seat, stunned. The hero-worship comment made sense to him, given what he knew. "I don't think he wanted to be like James. I think he just wanted James to notice him."

Dennis nodded, but Warren wasn't sure he'd really heard. "After Jim's suicide—"

"Was it definitely suicide?"

Dennis's brow wrinkled. "Of course."

"Taylor said it wasn't. He told me everybody thought that, but he didn't agree."

"I know. He's never accepted it. He's always wanted to believe it was an accident."

"Could it have been?"

"No. Jimmy left a note. He knew exactly what he was doing when he got in the car that night."

Warren ducked his head, suddenly feeling like a traitor for hearing things Taylor clearly didn't want to face.

"He'd had some trouble at college that year. A girl accused him of trying to rape her. There'd been cops, and the school was talking about suspending him—"

"Does Taylor know about this?"

Dennis shook his head emphatically. "No. We might have told him, if Jim had lived, but after his death, we didn't want Taylor's memory of him to be tainted. We wanted him to remember Jimmy as his brother, not some kind of criminal."

Warren reeled at the irony of them trying to hide James's predatory sexual nature from Taylor. He sat forward, his elbows on his knees. "So, you've never talked to Taylor about the exact nature of his relationship with James?"

Dennis blinked at him. "What do you mean?"

Warren had to tread carefully here. It wasn't his place to reveal too much. On the other hand, he knew Taylor and his father could never truly understand each other while the secret remained. "I think there was a great deal more to their relationship than you realize."

"Well, they were brothers—"

"Obviously."

"You don't understand." Dennis held up his hands to stop Warren's words. "I'm not explaining it right. Things fell apart when he died, but Jimmy wasn't the issue. The real problem was us—the way we handled his death. That's where it all went wrong."

"What do you mean?"

"We were heartbroken. It wasn't because we loved Jimmy more than Taylor. That was never it. But when you bury a child…" His eyes welled up with tears, and he hurriedly wiped them away. "I can't describe it. Unless it's happened to you, you can't comprehend how it changes you."

Warren tilted his head, conceding the point, but didn't answer.

"His mother. Well. I told you how Jim's death killed the light inside Taylor, but it killed more than that in Lisa. She sank pretty deep. She'd go days barely leaving her bed. I felt like I'd lost my son and my wife all at once. And I guess I got so tied up in trying to make her well, I forgot about Taylor. It was just like when he was a baby. He was quiet and calm through all of it. Stoic, no matter what. I remember thinking, 'He's handling it better than any of us.' I remember telling my brother how Taylor was a rock. He seemed so strong." He wiped his cheeks. He seemed more at ease now. As if he'd gotten through the worst. "I was wrong, of course. It wasn't until I found out he was suddenly failing all his classes that I realized how much he was hurting. He'd always struggled in school, but not like that. I tried to tell Lisa, but she just kept saying he was fine, that he'd bounce back."

"But he didn't."

"No. I tried talking to him, but it was like that sweet, gentle little boy I remembered was gone, and I had this wild animal in his place. He'd just scream at me to get away. To leave him alone. Then one day, I found blood on his sheets. I didn't know what to think. But just a day or two later, I caught him. In the bathroom."

Warren didn't need to ask to know what exactly Dennis had caught him doing. "He was cutting himself."

Dennis's head jerked in a semblance of a nod. "Yes. How did you know?"

"I've seen the scars."

"There was blood everywhere. He'd passed out there on the bathroom floor. I took him to the hospital. And after that, I tried to convince him to get counseling, but—"

"I know how he feels about that."

"It's because of me." He offered Warren a weak smile. "I'm a psychologist. I think Taylor looked at me and at Lisa and at how our entire family had fallen apart overnight, and he thought, 'What the hell do you know?'" He shrugged. "And he was right. I can sit there with my clients and spout psychological theory, but when it's my own family? Nothing seemed to fit. Nothing I did helped. Nothing I said to Taylor ever brought him back."

Warren leaned back in his seat and crossed his arms. "Is that what you want? To take him home? Because I can tell you right now, he won't want to go."

"I know that. He's not a child. But he's still my son. And he's the only thing I have left."

Chapter 20

Taylor's first day of training went well. He'd worried that his reading difficulties would be problematic, but there wasn't much reading involved in restocking rakes or ringing up sales. He mostly worked in the fenced-in, outside portion of the store. An overhead awning shaded part of it, but not all. Birds fluttered around between the towering rows of shelves, and squirrels dodged his steps. It was perfect. Taylor smiled all day, thinking about all the plants he'd be able to buy once his first paycheck came in.

He made good on his promise to Riley too by mentioning to Sam that he had a friend who could really use the work. Sam assured him he'd look for Riley's application and give him a call.

The drive home took him right past Riley's apartment. He still felt guilty about having partially abandoned Riley for the sake of his garden, so Taylor decided to stop by.

He found Riley lying on the couch. "Hey, man," Riley said, grinning at him. "You're here. What's up?"

There was something off about his speech. It was too slow, as if Riley were drunk, and Taylor froze in his steps, a horrible suspicion coalescing in his mind. "What's going on, Riley? Are you okay?"

Riley continued grinning at him from his place on the couch. "I'm great." He scratched at his arm. "Yeah. Really, really great."

The TV and DVD player were still in the corner, along with the pile of DVDs, which meant Riley wouldn't have had money for heroin, even if he'd wanted it. And yet watching him, the way he kept grinning while absentmindedly scratching, Taylor suspected something was up.

He crossed the room and perched on the edge of the couch, next to Riley's chest. Riley's pupils were tiny pinpricks, his eyes glassy. Taylor took Riley's left hand and turned it over, examining it.

There, on the thick vein on the back of Riley's wrist, was a brand new needle track.

Taylor's heart sank. "You're high."

Riley's smile faded a bit. "So what, man? Jesus. You know how hard it's been to stay clean."

"Exactly. I know how hard you've worked. Why would you throw it all away now?"

"I didn't."

"Are you telling me you're not high right now?"

"No. I mean, I am. But man. I wasn't looking for it, you know?"

"How'd you pay for it?"

"I didn't. That's what I'm saying. I didn't have any cash, but I went down the road, looking."

"Looking for drugs."

"No. For sex, man." He laughed, scratching at his stomach. "I've just been so horny, and I used to know some girls down there. I thought maybe I could talk one of them into a freebie."

"So where does the heroin come in?"

Riley's smile disappeared. "I couldn't find the girls, but I ran into my old dealer. And he spotted me a hit."

"Spotted you? You mean he gave it to you for free?"

"Yeah. I thought about flushing it all the way home. But once I got here?" The goofy grin came back, full-force. "I thought, why not? It wasn't much, you know. Just a little to stop the cravings. It's no big deal, man. Feels good to stop wanting it so much. Just take the edge off the withdrawal, that's all."

Could it really work that way? Taylor had assumed this meant a full-blown relapse, but maybe he was wrong. What the hell did he know about heroin? "No more, okay? I'll stop by tomorrow, and we'll make sure you stay clean."

"Whatever, man." Riley made a shooing motion with his hands. "You're totally fucking with my high."

Taylor's disappointment was like a shadow on his tail all the way home. He felt like Riley had failed him, but maybe it was he who'd failed Riley. And now Taylor would have Warren to face. He couldn't decide if he'd tell Warren about Riley's relapse or not.

He was still debating it when he walked into the living and found his father staring back at him. He and Warren both jumped to their feet when Taylor entered as if they'd been caught gossiping about him. Which, Taylor realized, might have been exactly the case. Taylor was shocked at how old his father looked. He'd talked to him three years earlier, but it'd been closer to five since they'd seen each other, and his father had aged considerably in that time. He was pale, and thinner than Taylor had ever seen him.

"Taylor." His dad stepped toward him as if to hug him. "I'm so glad to finally see you."

Taylor backed away, holding up his hands to ward off his father's advance. "What are you doing here?" He hated it. He felt like the most precious part of his life had suddenly turned ugly. The only safe place he'd ever known was suddenly hostile ground. He'd been near tears already, having seen Riley, and this only made it worse. He turned on Warren. "Did you call him? Did you tell him I was here?"

"Of course not, Tay." Warren was calm and reasonable as always. "How could I have? I didn't even know his name until today."

"Then how did he find me?"

It was his dad who answered. "You used your account—"

Of course. How could Taylor have been so stupid? "I won't make that mistake again." He pointed at the door. "You can go now."

His father exchanged a nervous glance with Warren. "I'd really like a chance to talk."

"Well, I don't want to talk to you, so it was a wasted trip."

"Taylor, please. Just give me a chance."

But Taylor didn't heed him. He turned on his heel and went down the hall to his bedroom. He closed the door and sat on his bed, his heart pounding and his cheeks burning. First Riley, and now this. How could his father come here? How could he try to interfere now, when Taylor finally had something good? Taylor wanted to go back in time. To have never used his account. He wanted to rewind to before, when everything had felt safe and right.

He waited, listening to the muffled sound of his father and Warren's voices, although he couldn't make out their words. Then Warren's slow, heavy tread echoed down the hallway. He knocked on Taylor's door.

"Go away."

Warren didn't obey. He opened the door just far enough to step inside before closing the door behind him.

"Did you make him leave?"

"No."

"Why not?"

"Because I think maybe you should talk to him."

"You want to get rid of me? Is that it? You're hoping he'll take me off your hands?"

Warren shook his head. He crouched in front of Taylor so he could look up into his eyes. "Taylor, you know I'd never do that. The last thing I want is for you to leave. I—" He stopped short, his cheeks flushing red. "You know how I feel about you."

"Then why?"

"Because I think he honestly wants to make peace."

"Why didn't my mother come?"

"Well." Warren's expression was guarded. "That's one of the things you need to talk to him about. It's not really my place to tell you."

Taylor swallowed the lump in his throat, suddenly feeling small and petty. He wished he could be like Warren, facing everything with such calm, quiet strength.

Warren stood up, holding his hand out to Taylor. "Come on. Maybe it won't be as bad as you think."

"You don't believe that, do you?"

Warren sighed. "Maybe not. But I think you should hear what he has to say."

Taylor nodded. He didn't want to agree. He wanted to rage and fight against it, but he'd never win. Not with Warren pitted against him too.

Taylor let himself be led like a child down the hallway to the living room, where his dad still stood. His eyes were red, a bit of dampness still on his cheeks, and Taylor stopped short at the sight. He'd seen his father cry before, but not since James's death, when his mother had locked herself in her room for days at a time, becoming as thin and insubstantial as a ghost.

"Where's Mom?"

"That's partly why I'm here. Can we sit down, please?"

Taylor sank slowly to his seat, a dark sense of foreboding filling his chest. Warren perched on the arm of the chair and put one big, heavy hand between Taylor's shoulder blades. It grounded him, but it scared him too. Warren seemed to expect him to fall apart any minute.

"I didn't know where you were," his dad said, resuming his seat on the couch. "Not until you made that purchase at the pawn shop. I thought maybe you'd died." He shook his head. "I wanted to find you the minute we found out, but I had no idea how to locate you."

"The minute you found out what? What happened?"

His dad sat with his elbows on his knees. He didn't look at Taylor. He kept his eyes on his hands, clasped together in front of him. "It was adenocarcinoma."

The word sank like a rock in the stillness of the room. "What is that?" Taylor asked. "Carcinoma? That's a kind of cancer, right?"

His dad nodded. "Non-small cell lung cancer. By the time they figured out what was wrong, it had spread to her brain. She only lived another six weeks."

Taylor leaned back an inch or two—just enough to feel the solidity of Warren's hand on his back. "Lung cancer? But, how? She didn't smoke."

"I know." His dad held out his hands but still refused to meet Taylor's eyes. "It happens sometimes. They say maybe radon exposure. Maybe something genetic. They don't really know."

Taylor looked down at the floor, trying to steady himself. Nothing seemed to fit in place. None of what he was hearing made sense. His dad didn't belong here, in Warren's house, and his mother, who'd always been so healthy, should have been safe from lung cancer. "When?"

"August of last year."

Taylor didn't know how he should feel. In many ways, his mother had been dead to him for years. She'd never been the same after James's death. She'd shut Taylor out of her heart and her life so completely, he'd told himself he might as well have been an orphan. But now, to know she was truly gone, that he'd never had a chance to make amends, left a horrible dark hole in his heart.

"You're all I have left, Taylor," his dad said.

It felt like a knife in his chest. A familiar bitterness bubbled up in his chest. "And you hate me for that, don't you? You wish it had been me that died and James who lived."

"No." His dad sounded as calm and reasonable as Warren so often did. "I wish I hadn't lost either one of you. But I promise, if things had been reversed, I would have grieved for you every bit as much as I grieved for him. Maybe more, if I'm being honest."

Taylor's surprise caused him to look up at his dad, to try to weigh the sincerity of that last bit. He'd never been good at understanding his father. His father must have seen the doubt in his eyes.

"You're my son, Taylor. I love you now as much as I ever did."

Taylor gulped, feeling like he was drowning. "What about Mom?"

"The last wish she had was to see you before she died."

Taylor covered his eyes, torn between shame and disbelief. He'd fostered so much anger over the years, but he suddenly wasn't sure his parents deserved any of it. As always, it was Taylor who seemed to have failed.

"I know nothing has been the same since Jimmy died," his dad continued. "I know how much his suicide hurt you."

"No, you don't." For a moment, the room was silent. Taylor's grief felt too big for tears. All he really wanted to do was curl into a ball and fall asleep. To just drift away and never have to come back. He felt like he could sleep forever. "You've never understood."

"Well, maybe not. But I want to try."

"Dennis," Warren said, his voice quiet. "Tell Taylor about James. About the allegations."

That got Taylor's attention. He looked up to find his father blinking in surprise at Warren.

"What are you talking about?" Taylor asked.

His dad shook his head. "I don't think that's a good idea. I don't see how it can help anything at this point."

"Trust me. It'll matter to Taylor."

Taylor had no idea what they were talking about, but the fact that Warren knew something he didn't intrigued him. Warren wouldn't have insisted if he didn't think it was important.

His father opened and closed his mouth a couple of times. Taylor thought he wanted to argue, but in the end, he sighed, his shoulders slumping in defeat. Taylor sat forward in his seat, waiting.

"That last year," his dad said, finally meeting Taylor's eyes. "When Jimmy was at college, a girl there accused him of trying to rape her."

Taylor felt as if his heart stopped beating. He put his hand over his chest, his mind boggling at this new revelation. It was like being on an old-fashioned, wooden-rail roller coaster, the entire world shaking. It felt like he had the worst hangover ever. The room spun crazily around him. He had to fight to keep from vomiting. "Is that why he…?" But no. James hadn't killed himself. Taylor couldn't make himself believe that. He certainly couldn't say it out loud. James would never have left him on purpose.

His dad cleared his throat, glancing again toward Warren, as if for support. "The lawyers said it probably wouldn't have stuck. Things like that are hard to prove anyway. It was a 'he said, she said' kind of thing. After Jimmy died, the case was dropped. There was no point in pursuing it any further."

"You never told me."

"We didn't want you to know."

"What if it had gone to trial?" Taylor asked, his shock turning to anger. "Would you have lied about it then too?"

His dad held up his hands in an awkward shrug. "I honestly don't know. We just hoped it wouldn't get that far. Your mom was sure he was innocent."

"Of course she was." Taylor practically spit the words at him. Maybe his father didn't deserve his bitterness, but he had nowhere else for it to go. "She always thought he was perfect."

"No. Not perfect. She just didn't think he was capable of rape."

"Well, he was." Taylor dug his fingers into the arms of the chair trying to stop the world's crazy spin. "Trust me, he was capable of it, no matter what you wanted to think."

Had he really said those words to his father? After all these years, he'd suddenly betrayed James in the worst possible way. For a moment, his dad simply stared at him, his mouth open. Surprise gave way to confusion. Confusion slowly coalesced into something Taylor couldn't bear to see.

Taylor shut his eyes tight, wishing he could rewind to that morning. When he'd left Lowe's, the sun was shining, birds singing. He'd still believed Riley was clean, and that his mother was alive. It was way too perfect a day for such awful revelations.

The room spun faster than ever. His stomach heaved.

"Taylor," his dad said quietly. "Jesus."

Taylor could tell by his father's voice that he was crying again. For Taylor, the simple relief of tears felt like something reserved only for others. The room continued to circle and tilt around him. The urge to vomit was stronger than ever.

"Are you telling me—"

"No." Taylor jumped to his feet, unsure if he could even make it to the bathroom before being sick. Even the kitchen sink seemed too far away. "I'm not telling you anything. I need for you to leave."

He made it farther than he expected—through the kitchen, out the back door, all the way to the farthest flower bed before he fell to his knees, retching so hard, his vision went black. He hadn't eaten since breakfast. The only thing that came up was pale, watery bile. He raked handfuls of rich, dark soil toward him and buried the evidence of his weakness, hiding it from sight.

Finally, he put his forehead on the ground and cried.

Warren stood there in his living room, not knowing what to do. Every instinct he had told him to go after Taylor. Unfortunately, Dennis seemed to have the same instinct, and Warren knew Taylor couldn't take any more of his father today.

"Don't," Warren said, grabbing Dennis's arm to stop him from following his son. "Let him go."

Dennis at least had the grace not to fight him. He relented easily. "He never told me," he said, turning to face Warren. "He never said anything."

"I don't think he's told many people, to be honest."

"But he adored Jimmy. He followed him around like a puppy. If Jim was— If he was—" He stumbled, unable to say the words. "Why didn't Taylor tell somebody Jim was hurting him?"

"Because Taylor loved him. James was the most important person in his life. Whatever happened between them, Taylor chose to believe that it was normal. Or, maybe not normal, but…" He struggled to find the right words. "Healthy, I guess. He chose to see it as a form of love."

"Jesus." Dennis sank to the couch with his head in his hands. "My own sons. In my own house. What kind of psychologist am I? How could I not see it?" He looked up at Warren, his expression something between defensiveness and grief. "That's what you want to know, right? How could I not have seen it?"

"I didn't say that. I've never had kids. What would I know?" Besides, he understood now how easy it was to be blind to things in one's own home. All the years he'd blamed his father for the abuse, and blamed his uncle for not helping, he'd never seen that it was his mother who chose to stay. He took a step to the side, straining to see out the back window. He could just make out Taylor crouched in the far corner of the yard. "Look, I don't mean to be rude, but I think he's right. I think it's time for you to leave."

"But—"

Warren held up his hands, stopping Dennis's words. "It's a lot for one day. That's all I'm saying."

Dennis swallowed and wiped his eyes. "Okay." He nodded. "I suppose it is."

"How far away do you live?"

"Fort Collins. An hour, assuming no wrecks on the interstate."

"Why don't you give me your number? I'll try to keep you in the loop, as much as he'll let me. I think, if you give him some time, he may come around."

It was only a guess. He had no way of knowing if Taylor would ever be ready to face his father.

A minute later, he showed Dennis out the front door. Finally, he could go to Taylor.

He found him on his knees in the dirt, muddy tracks down his cheeks marking where his tears had been. Warren crouched next to him, his joints popping as he did. "Are you okay?"

Taylor's head moved in a slow nod.

Warren put his hand on Taylor's shoulder. He tried to gently pull Taylor toward him, but Taylor sat still and stiff, resisting his touch.

"Talk to me, Taylor."

"I planted snapdragons here. Did you see them?"

Warren shook his head. "I don't think I did."

"They were so pretty." His voice broke on the words, but he kept talking. "Not quite pink and not quite orange. Some color in between I don't know the name for. They were the prettiest flowers I've ever seen."

"So what happened? Did they die?"

"The rabbits." A single tear rolled down his cheek, and Taylor brushed it away, leaving behind a smudge of dirt. "They ate them, all the way down to the dirt."

"I'm sorry."

"The lady at the nursery said you can buy poison for the rabbits, but I don't want to kill them. That just seems mean. So, I guess I just can't have snapdragons, right?"

It broke Warren's heart that even now, Taylor couldn't accept comfort. After everything they'd been through, Taylor still pushed him away. "Taylor. Honey. It's okay to cry. It's okay to be upset, or angry, or sad. It's okay if you want to scream or yell or rage or hit somebody—"

"They're just flowers," Taylor said, refusing to hear him. "They were pretty, but I guess that's why—" His breath caught, and it took him a second to go on. "That's why roses have thorns."

No matter how many years it'd been since the war, the dreams never stopped. At least once a month, Warren found himself back in the god-forsaken desert, driving a Humvee while Gray sat in the passenger seat, spouting a steady stream of decidedly un-PC humor.

And then the slow-motion explosion, the Humvee in front of them flying into the air.

In truth, Warren hadn't seen enough of it to form a true memory, but that didn't stop his subconscious from filling in the blanks, showing him fire and death, his friend Terry's dismembered arm hitting the windshield.

"Warren, wake up! I need your help."

Warren was on his feet before he was fully awake, his heart hammering, his hand reaching for a gun that wasn't at his hip. "What's wrong?"

"I need your help." Taylor held up his cell phone. "I signed up for this weather alert, and they're predicting a frost tonight."

Warren blinked, the last dozen years disappearing into the fog as he finally found his place in time again. "A frost?" He glanced toward the window, but the curtains were drawn. A frost in mid-May was on the late side of normal, but not exactly newsworthy. "Is that some kind of emergency?"

"I need to cover my roses, but I have no idea how to do that."

Warren blinked, thinking it was the most Taylor had said to him in two days. Ever since his dad's visit, Taylor had stumbled around in a daze. He went to work. He visited Riley. He worked the garden. But it was as if his body was on autopilot, the real Taylor lost somewhere in the void.

Warren had tried talking to him, but each time, Taylor said he was fine, that there was nothing to say. He'd rejected every ounce of tenderness Warren tried to give him. The one time they'd had sex, Taylor had seemed removed from the entire act, so distant Warren might as well not have bothered. Not that the sex mattered in and of itself. If Taylor wanted space,

Warren would give it. But he felt like Taylor was slipping away from him, vanishing before his eyes.

And yet now here he was, at twelve thirty at night, asking for Warren's help.

"Okay," Warren said. "Let me put on some pants."

Taylor bounced impatiently on the balls of his feet as Warren pulled on jeans and a T-shirt, then a pair of shoes, minus socks.

"What do we cover them with?" Taylor asked as he followed Warren into the living room.

"I'm pretty sure there's stuff in the shed." Warren pulled on his jacket, then tossed one to Taylor. "Let's go."

They found a pile of tarps and ratty old blankets on a back shelf of the shed, underneath the chainsaw. "These are what Stuart used." He grabbed the blankets off the shelf. "Grab rocks or anything heavy you can find to weight the edges down."

It took longer than he expected. Some of the plants were too small and fragile to have a blanket tossed over them. They found some old tomato cages in the shed and used them as support. Taylor didn't speak at all, only followed directions, an edge of panic making his movements jerky and unnatural. Thirty minutes later, they had most of Taylor's precious flowers covered.

"Will they be okay?" Taylor asked as he followed Warren back inside.

"I'm no expert, but I think so."

"I don't know what I'll do if they die." Taylor sounded small and frightened, and Warren turned to face him in the dim light of the living room. "I really don't." His voice cracked, and Warren realized Taylor was fighting tears. "They can't die. They can't. Oh God, they can't, they can't, they can't."

He covered his face with his hands, and Warren crept toward him. "Honey." He brushed his fingers lightly up Taylor's arm.

"I'm fine."

293

But he didn't pull away, and Warren moved closer. He held Taylor's thin shoulders. "It's okay to admit that you're upset. You know that, right? It's okay to just let go and be sad."

Taylor's head jerked to the right as if was trying to shake his head no, but ran out of steam. "They're just flowers."

Warren gripped his shoulders harder, shaking him just a bit so Taylor dropped his hands and met Warren's gaze. "This isn't just about plants, Taylor. I don't know if it's about your mom or your dad or both. The thing is, I *want* to know. I want you to tell me everything going on in that head of yours. No matter what you're thinking, no matter how it makes you feel, I want to be the person who helps you with it." Taylor continued staring at him, his chin trembling. "Let me help you, honey. Please."

Taylor shook his head again, tears filling his eyes. "I can't!"

"Why not?"

"Because I'm just so… I'm so…"

"So what?"

"I don't even know!" He threw up his hands. "Don't you see? I'm so stupid! I don't even know how I feel!" He put his face in his hands and burst into tears.

Even now that he was crying, Taylor couldn't simply allow himself to be held. But Warren was bigger and stronger, and when it came to comforting Taylor, he was tired of being told no. He wrapped Taylor in his arms and held him tight—held him as Taylor tried to fight. Held him as Taylor struggled and begged for Warren to let him go. Held him until Taylor finally surrendered, sobbing against Warren's chest. It felt like the most monumental victory he'd ever scored, finally being allowed to offer something useful. "It's about time," Warren mumbled, stroking Taylor's hair.

"Wh-what?"

"Nothing, honey. Cry as much as you want."

And cry Taylor did, great racking sobs that shook his entire body. It was more than grief. It was rage and frustration and vulnerability, all rolled into one, and Warren simply held him until the storm had passed.

Finally, he led Taylor to the couch, where Taylor huddled against Warren's chest, still hiccupping a bit as his tears subsided. "Now," Warren said, "talk to me. Tell me what all this is about."

And to his great relief, Taylor obeyed, pouring out a disjointed narrative punctuated by bursts of tears. His dad, who maybe loved him after all. His mom, who he'd never see again. His fear that they'd never deserved his hatred at all. His shame at finally revealing his secret about James to his father. The fact that he'd wanted desperately to cut himself, but couldn't find a razor and hadn't wanted Warren to make a fuss. And finally, the one thing Warren hadn't known about at all: the fact that Riley had relapsed.

"I'm sorry," Warren said, over and over again. "I'm sorry it has to hurt so much."

"He'd sold the movies, last time I was there." Between the tears and the talking, Taylor was hoarse and sniffly. "He hadn't sold the TV or DVD player yet, and I thought, 'I should take them so he can't sell those too.' But then he said I must not have much faith in him, so I left them." He sniffled again, dabbing his nose with a tissue. "You were right, Warren. If only I'd never bought the TV, my dad wouldn't have found me, and I wouldn't know about my mom."

"Do you honestly think that would be better?"

"Maybe. It'd be better for Riley. If I hadn't spent all my time in my garden, maybe he'd still be clean. If I'd been there more instead of being selfish—"

"No, honey. You didn't do anything wrong. If it weren't for you, he probably would have relapsed sooner. He made his choice."

"But why? After everything he went through to get clean!"

"He had to want it more than you did, and I'm not sure he did."

"Why would his dealer give him heroin for free like that?"

"Junkies are a steady source of income. His dealer had nothing to gain by helping him stay sober."

"I wish I could kill him for giving Riley drugs," Taylor said, his voice rising as anger burned through his grief. "It's probably good I don't know who he is, because I'd beg you to find him and kill him for what he did."

Warren smiled, although it broke his heart. "You know I'd do anything you asked. But even if that dealer suddenly disappeared forever, a junkie will always find a way."

"You told me. I'm so stupid. I should have listened."

"No. He's your friend. The fact that you're less jaded than me—that you truly wanted to help him—that's to your credit, Tay. It doesn't mean you're stupid. It means you care. Don't beat yourself up for it."

Taylor considered that for a moment. Finally, he sighed, settling more comfortably in Warren's arms. "Thank you."

"For what?"

"For always saying the right thing. And for letting me be a big, sloppy, sobbing mess."

"That's one of the things I'm here for." He was just glad Taylor had finally let him help. He kissed the top of Taylor's head. "Do you feel better?"

"I do. Exhausted but better. I kept thinking I was doing good, because I was keeping the blackness away, and I didn't have to cut myself to do it. But it felt like it took every ounce of my energy."

"Sometimes it's better not to fight it. It's better to just let yourself cry."

"But I hate crying! I feel like it's all I do these days. I'm like a spoiled little kid, always blubbering about something. I wish I was stronger. I wish I could just take it all in stride like you do."

"No, you don't." Warren rubbed his hand up and down Taylor's back. The thought of Taylor without his soft side was enough to break Warren's heart. "Crying doesn't mean you're weak. I just think you feel things deeper than most." In

Warren's mind, Taylor's tears only indicated how passionate he was. Warren almost envied him.

Just proof the grass was always greener.

Chapter 21

Taylor couldn't believe how much better he felt after sobbing his eyes out on the couch. Then again, the way Warren had made love to him after they'd returned to bed cheered him up as much as anything. He still felt like an emotional fool for crying so much, but Warren didn't seem to think any less of him for it. And after all the fuss he'd made, his roses had all survived the frost.

Friday night, Warren left for work as usual, and Taylor checked on Riley. This time, he found the DVD player gone and Riley in his bedroom, even more out of it than before.

"I guess Warren and your mom were right after all," Taylor said, unable to keep his disappointment in check. "It was only a matter of time before you sold it."

"I'll pay you back, I promise."

"Whatever. I suppose the TV's next."

"Taylor—"

"Forget it. Did Sam from Lowe's ever call about the job?"

Riley blinked at him in confusion. "I don't know. I only answer if it's you."

"Well, don't expect me to stick my neck out for you like that again." Taylor turned to leave.

"Taylor, wait."

Taylor stopped in the door, turning back to the dark room.

"I'm sorry. I fucked up, I know. But you're my friend, man. The only one I have left. I don't want you to be mad at me."

Taylor sighed, feeling like the biggest ass in the world. "I'm not mad." And he wasn't. Not really. He was disappointed, for sure. Frustrated. Maybe deep down, a little worried. He'd always believed he and Riley were the same. If Riley could relapse so easily, what did it mean for Taylor's chances down the road?

Then again, maybe Warren was right. Maybe they weren't the same at all. Sure, Taylor had his bad days, but at least once they passed, they were over. Gone, if not forgotten. He didn't wake up the next morning jonesing to do it all over again. He got to start fresh again each time.

Riley's addiction was far more complicated. It wasn't just a matter of waking up with a few bruises or a bad taste in his mouth after he fell off the wagon. He had to deal with withdrawal that was far worse, in many ways, than the addition itself.

Taylor perched on the edge of the bed and put his hand on Riley's shoulder. "I'll help you get clean again. I'll stay here twenty-four seven. I'll quit Lowe's if I have to. Whatever it takes to get through it."

"Sure," Riley said, scratching at his arm. "Sure thing, man. You're right. This is my last fix, then I'm clean. For good this time, I promise."

"Okay. It's a deal." He leaned over and kissed Riley's forehead. "I'll stop by tomorrow, okay?"

"Wait." Riley grabbed his hand before he could stand. "Will you stay with me awhile? I know Warren's working late tonight. Just lay with me, will you? Sleep here for a bit. I feel better when you're here."

Taylor considered. The truth was, he loved lying there with Riley, talking. Granted, he'd have preferred it if Riley weren't high, but what kind of friend would he be to run out on Riley now? "You bet."

Taylor got home around four in the morning, but slept only a few more hours. He had an idea. A crazy idea, maybe. One he suspected Warren would disapprove of, and yet Taylor was anxious to ask his opinion. He needed to know whether or not Warren would support him on it, but of course Warren slept late, having worked the night before.

Taylor also needed to see Riley. He'd promised to check on him, but he wanted to talk to Warren first, and so he waited, despite his impatience. He was sitting on the couch watching TV and eating a popsicle when somebody knocked on the back door around two.

Taylor smiled to himself. It had to be Gray. As far as Taylor was concerned, Warren was worth ten of his friend, but that didn't mean Taylor didn't enjoy flirting with him. It was fun seeing the way Gray looked at him. It felt good knowing somebody else saw value in him.

Taylor answered the door, popsicle in hand. He was surprised to find Gray in full uniform. Taylor grinned and batted his eyelashes. "Going to show me your warrant this time?"

Gray laughed, although his heart wasn't in it. "Honey, I'll show you anything you like. Just say the word." He put his hand on the back of Taylor's neck and pulled him into a kiss. It was short but warm and sensuous, the tip of his tongue tasting Taylor's lip. Not deep enough or long enough to be inappropriate, but it wasn't quite casual either. "Damn, you taste good, kid. You sure you aren't ready to move in with me?"

"I'm sure. I'm right where I want to be."

Gray shook his head, his eyes on Taylor's lips. "Just love to tease me, don't you?"

"Want me to stop?"

"Hell, no."

But despite Gray's flirtation, there was a darkness in his eyes that troubled Taylor. He stepped back, out of Gray's reach. "You need Warren?"

That hint of worry in Gray's eyes seemed to deepen. "I do."

"I'll go get him."

"Wait." Gray took hold of his arm, turning Taylor to face him. In the blink of an eye, his teasing humor was gone. He was as solemn as Taylor had ever seen him. "Listen to me, okay?"

"I'm listening."

"I need to give Warren some bad news. He might try to act all calm and in control while I'm here, but the minute I leave, he's going to try to do something stupid."

"What do you mean? What happened?"

"You'll find out when I tell him. But once I leave, I need you to do whatever it takes to keep him here."

Taylor gulped, his heart racing. What did Gray mean, exactly?

"Promise me," Gray said. "Promise me you won't let him leave."

Taylor shook his head. "I don't know if I can stop him, once he has his mind set."

"Trust me, kid. If anybody can do it, it's you."

Taylor wasn't sure if that was true or not, but he nodded. "I'll try."

"That's all I can ask." This time, the kiss landed on his forehead, short and casual. "Go wake him up for me."

Five minutes later, they gathered in the living room. It was just like the day Gray had come to question Warren about Robby's beating. Warren sat in the armchair, Gray on the couch. Taylor hovered behind Warren, wondering what was about to happen.

"I have something to tell you," Gray said to Warren. "But first, I want you to promise me you won't do anything stupid."

Warren seemed halfway amused by this pronouncement. "Okay. Sure."

"I mean it, Warren. I know you. I know how you think. But I need you to trust me. We've been friends a long time. All I'm asking is that you trust me."

Warren's eyebrows came together in puzzlement. "I do. You know that."

"Maybe in Afghanistan you did, but not when it comes to my job. Not when it comes to letting me do what I need to do."

"What do you mean? You're always the one I call when shit goes bad—"

"Warren." Gray held up his hand to cut Warren off. He shook his head as if words had somehow failed him. "Stop arguing with me, for fuck's sake. I'm trying to save your ass here."

The room became still, a sense of gravitas Taylor had never experienced before settling over them all. Gray was solemn and serious, and there was no choice but to respond in kind.

Warren sat forward in his seat, all amusement gone. "What happened?"

"You worked with Susan Branson last night?"

"Sugar? Yeah, I covered her."

"Until when?"

"About one."

"Did anything out of the ordinary happen?"

"Hard to say." Warren scratched at the stubble on his cheek, considering. "The fact that she left at one was a bit odd. She and Candy had clients lined up until three, but Sugar canceled hers. Said she had to go."

"You didn't hear from her after that?"

"No. Why?"

"Were any of her clients last night unusual? Any incidents?"

"No. Mostly regulars. Nobody who's ever caused a problem. *Why?*"

"What about Robby? Did you see him at all?"

"No. Now stop asking me questions, and tell me what happened."

Gray licked his lips nervously. "Promise me you won't go after him."

Warren jumped to his feet. "*What the fuck happened?*"

Gray stood too, as if expecting to have to head Warren off. Taylor moved closer, clasping his hands in front of him as if praying, fighting to keep them from shaking. He knew now what Gray had meant when he said not to let Warren leave.

"We found her an hour ago."

"Where?"

"In her house."

"Dead?"

Gray nodded.

"How?"

"Beaten."

Warren put his hands on his head, his chest seeming to swell as the anger hit him. "And her son?"

"He spent the night at a friend's house. He wasn't there. He didn't hear or see anything."

"Small comfort."

Gray ignored him and kept talking. "He couldn't get ahold of her after the sleepover to pick him up. The friend's mom finally drove him home, and that's when they found her. Child Protective Services has him now. They're trying to find next of kin."

"Damn it, Gray, I told you! You could have arrested him! I told you—"

"Warren, my hands were tied. She wouldn't press charges. There was nothing I could do."

"Bullshit!"

Gray ignored that outburst too. "I'll get him, Warren. I promise you. Do you understand me? He's number one on our list."

"What the hell good does that do? He's a cop! He'll get off again, just like before!"

"No, he won't. Murder's murder. There's no free pass." Gray's voice was strained, but he was keeping his cool much better than Warren was. Much better than Taylor would have if he'd been in Gray's place. "I'll find him, Warren. This is what I mean when I say I need you to trust me. I *will* find him. I promise you that."

Warren turned his back on Gray, his fists tight knots at his side. "Is that all?"

"Don't go after him, Warren. I mean it."

"You can go now."

"You'll only slow me down. Do you understand that? I can start looking for him right now, but not if I have to worry about you on top of it. Promise me."

"I'm not promising anything. Get out."

"Warren—"

"*Get out!*"

"Okay. I'm going." Gray grabbed Taylor by the arm as he passed. He dragged him into the kitchen and pinned Taylor there with his stormy eyes. "I meant what I said." He kept his voice low enough that Warren wouldn't hear them in the other room. "I'll get the bastard. Nothing good can happen if Warren finds him first."

Taylor's hands shook. So did his voice. "He won't listen to me."

"Then he'll end up in prison. Is that what you want?"

The thought made Taylor's blood run cold. "No! Of course not."

"Then keep him here."

The back door slammed behind him as he left. Warren stood at the front window and watched until Gray backed out of the driveway. He waited until Gray's car was out of sight.

"Warren," Taylor said, his voice sounding small after Warren and Gray's argument. "I think you should listen to him. I think—"

"Go to Riley's."

Warren had never told him to leave before. He'd certainly never encouraged him to spend extra time with Riley, especially since Riley's relapse. "No. I'm not going anywhere."

"Don't argue with me. Do as I say. Get the hell out of here." Warren turned and left him standing there in the

ONE MAN'S TRASH

kitchen. He went into his bedroom and closed the door. Taylor floundered, unsure what to do.

How in the world could he keep Warren from going after Robby?

Taylor went quickly down the hall. He knocked and got no answer. He tried the knob and breathed a sigh of relief when the door opened.

Warren was on the bed with a gun in his hand. It brought Taylor up short. Taylor knew Warren carried a gun sometimes, but this was the first time he'd actually seen it. It was like watching a movie, the way Warren worked the gun—letting the clip fall into his hand, checking it before slamming it back into place. He pulled the top of the pistol back, checking that there was a round in the chamber. Lots of sharp movements and loud clicks. Taylor suspected if he tried to hold that gun, it'd feel like it weighed a hundred pounds, but it looked tiny in Warren's big hands.

"Warren, stop. Please. You're scaring me."

"I mean it, Taylor. Go to Riley's."

"No. I won't." His voice shook as he said it.

"Then go in your room. Say you were napping. It's better if you don't know when I leave."

"You have to stay here. You have to do what Gray said."

"To hell with that."

"I won't cover for you again." It was a lie. A horrible, blatant lie. He would have done anything for Warren. But it was the only thing he could think to say that might change Warren's mind.

"Good. I never asked you to do it the first time, and I'm not asking you to do it now." Warren stood and yanked a dark jacket from a hanger in the closet.

"Gray will find him."

Warren zipped the jacket and turned to face him. "And he'll get what? A slap on the wrist?"

"I don't know, but—" Warren slipped the gun into place at the small of his back. He squared his shoulders, and Taylor did the only thing he could think to do—he put himself square in the middle of the doorway. "I won't let you leave."

Warren at least had the decency not to laugh. He was taller than Taylor by a good eight inches and probably outweighed him by more than fifty pounds. "Do you really think you can stop me?"

"No." But he heard Gray's voice in his head saying, *"If anybody can do it, it's you."* "Please," he said again. "Give Gray a chance. Let him handle it."

"I guarantee I can find Robby quicker than Gray."

"You told Gray you trusted him."

"I do. It's the system I don't trust."

"Warren—"

"Enough. I'm done talking." He grabbed Taylor's shoulders in his big hands and gently but firmly pushed him back, out of the way. "I'm leaving. What you tell the cops when they come is up to you."

He went down the hall and Taylor chased after him, pleading the whole way. "Wait. Please, Warren. Don't do this."

Warren ignored him and grabbed his keys off the counter. "Go to Riley's. The less you know, the better."

"No!"

Warren kissed him once on the forehead, the same place Gray had. "I love you."

Outside of that one night in the bedroom, it was the only time he'd ever said it. "Then stay. Please."

"I can't. I'm sorry." And with that, he was out the door.

Taylor hugged himself, shaking, wondering what to do. He could chase after Warren, but to what end? He could call Gray, and deal with Warren's wrath later.

His eyes landed on the vase.

Vases littered the house now, all filled with flowers, but that first one occupied a special place on their shelves. It always held his prettiest bloom. It meant something to them both.

Taylor grabbed it off the shelf. He let the rose fall to the floor as he chased Warren out the door. "Warren, wait!"

He caught him at the car, before Warren had a chance to unlock the door.

"Please." He grabbed Warren, shoving the vase into his hand. "Listen to me, please."

Warren looked at the vase, a familiar scowl twisting his features. "What's this for?"

Taylor had to take a couple of deep breaths before he could speak. He was amazed at himself that he hadn't started crying yet, but adrenaline made him breathless and shaky. He couldn't let that stop him, though. He had to make Warren understand.

"Do you see this thing?" he asked. "Do you see this thing that you value? This thing that belongs to you that nobody else could ever cherish? Do you see it?"

"Yeah, I see it. So what?"

"If you leave, it goes back to being trash. If you leave, nobody else will ever value it the way you do. Is that what you want?"

Warren's shoulders fell a bit, his scowl giving way to something more tender. "Taylor. Honey—"

"It's selfish of me, I know! I should have a better reason to keep you here. I should have a reason that isn't about me. But I don't. The only thing I have is this." He pointed to the vase in Warren's strong hands. "You're determined to do what you think is right, and I respect you for that, because you want justice for your friend. But all I can think is, what happens to me when Gray takes you to jail?" He shook his head, his heart aching at the thought. "I'll go back to being a whore."

"No—"

"What else could I do?"

"Taylor—"

"I can't go back to that. Not after this. Not after knowing what it's like to be loved. Warren, please." He buried his face in Warren's chest and wrapped his arms around Warren's waist, holding on to him as tight as he could. "Please stay with this thing you said you cherished. Please don't make me go back to being trash."

He felt Warren's anger and determination leave by small degrees—the muscles in his back slowly softening under Taylor's hands, his chest somehow shrinking as Taylor held him. A few seconds later, his lips touched the top of Taylor's head, and his hand slid up Taylor's back, holding him close.

"Somebody has to avenge Sugar," he said into Taylor's hair. "Robby needs to pay."

"You're right. But that's not your job."

"My job was to protect her."

"From her johns. You couldn't protect her from somebody she loved."

"I guess not."

It felt like a step in the right direction, but not a full-scale surrender. Taylor had no cards left to play. "Please, Warren. I don't know what else I can say."

Warren chuckled. "You wouldn't have to go back to being a whore. You know how Gray feels about you. He'd be happy to take you in."

It was said in jest, but Taylor didn't feel like laughing. He shook his head emphatically. "I'd never choose him over you." Selfish or not, Taylor was certain losing Warren would kill him. He tipped his head back to meet Warren's eyes. "Did you mean it when you said you loved me? Did you mean it when you used the word 'cherished'?"

"You know I did."

"Then prove it. Come back inside."

Warren sighed and bent to put his forehead against Taylor's. In that moment, Taylor knew the fight was over.

"Okay," Warren said at last, his voice low and gentle. "You win."

It didn't take Warren long to figure out Gray hadn't relied entirely on Taylor to keep him home. The next time he looked out his front window, he found Phil parked at the end of his driveway, reading a book in his car. Sometime around dusk, Phil left and Charlie arrived. Neither of them came to the door or tried to talk to him. They probably assumed he'd be too grumpy to tolerate.

At first, Warren resented it. How dare Gray involve everybody close to him? It felt like emotional blackmail, and he grumbled about it to Taylor as they sat watching TV.

"So you'd rather your best friends just sit back and watch while you run around like a vigilante and wind up in jail?" Taylor asked.

"It's none of their business."

Taylor looked like he was barely managing not to laugh. "Look, Warren. I hate to burst your bubble, but you're not Daredevil, you know? You're not Arrow."

Warren blinked at him. "What the hell are you talking about?"

"I'm just saying, this isn't a TV show where the vigilante gets away clean and becomes some kind of hero. In real life, guys like that go to jail. You won't be able to help anybody from prison."

Warren subsided after that, but he had to admit, Taylor had hit the proverbial nail on the head. Warren wanted to help people. That simple desire had driven him for years. And yet, he couldn't deny how tired he was. He also couldn't deny that it had begun to feel futile.

He looked over at Taylor happily sucking a popsicle. He thought about how happy it'd make Taylor if he gave up the side jobs and accepted Uncle Bill's job offer.

"Come on," Taylor said, half an hour later. He held his hand out to Warren. "Come to bed with me."

Warren followed him down the hall, but his mind was elsewhere. Even as Taylor undressed, Warren couldn't stop wondering how it would feel to leave it all behind.

He pulled the curtain aside and glanced outside. Charlie was still sitting in his car at the end of the driveway, drumming his fingers on the steering wheel as he sang along to some song Warren couldn't hear.

"I'll be back in a minute."

Taylor's eyes widened in alarm. "No! You're going after him, aren't you?"

"No. Just going to talk to Charlie a minute. I promise, I'll be right back."

Taylor looked skeptical, but he didn't protest. Warren stopped in the kitchen first to brew a cup of Earl Grey. He only had it in the house because of Charlie. He added a bit of milk, then carried the steaming mug out the front door wearing only his boxers and a T-shirt, wincing a bit as his bare feet found tiny stones on the driveway. Charlie grinned at him and leaned over to unlock the passenger door.

"Hey! Thanks for coming to keep me company."

He turned the stereo down as Warren slipped inside, but not before Warren caught the song. "You're Never Fully Dressed Without a Smile," from *Annie*. Charlie was a sucker for show tunes.

Charlie eyed the tea. "Is that for me?"

Warren passed him the mug. "Least I can do, I guess, since you're stuck out here because of me."

"Not coming out to convince me you're duty bound to go after that scumbag, are you?"

"Taylor talked me into leaving the justice to Gray."

"Good for him." Charlie sipped the tea and made a happy humming noise. "Honestly, I expected you to be way more pissed off about being babysat."

"Taylor talked me out of that too."

Charlie laughed, the tattoos on his big biceps shaking, although he managed not to spill the tea. "I think I like that kid."

"Yeah," Warren said. "Me too." He could practically feel Charlie's questioning stare after that confession, though, so he decided to get to the point. "My Uncle Bill wants me to come work for him full time. Take over the business in a couple of years, when he retires."

Charlie's eyebrows rose. "Is that something you're considering?"

"Maybe."

"Good for you, man."

"I guess." Warren stared out the windshield of the Caddy at his familiar, quiet street. It looked innocent. Wholesome. He'd always considered it little more than a pretty lie. And yet, behind those windows sat regular civilians, maybe having a beer after dinner, or tucking in their kids before watching *The Late Show*. Maybe it didn't have to be a lie at all. "It feels selfish."

"Selfish? How is being an electrician selfish?"

"I just mean, how does that help anybody?"

"Hey, when I needed my exam room rewired, having you on hand was plenty helpful, believe me. No way will I mess with that shit."

"Yeah, but it's not the same."

"Isn't it?"

Warren shook his head. "You know what happened when I worked for him after coming home. It didn't work out."

"Warren, that was more than ten years ago. Everything's different now."

"How so?"

Charlie set the mug on the dashboard and shifted in the seat to face Warren. "Look. You spent four years over there in that shithole. Then you came home and tried being a regular old Joe. But you were still wired for combat. On the outside, you were trying to be a civilian, but on the inside, you were waiting for a truck bomb to come rolling into the compound."

Warren nodded. "It drove me mad." Almost literally. He'd been homeless for a year because wondering where he was going to sleep every night or where he'd get dinner had almost been easier than *knowing* where he'd sleep or how he'd eat. But then his dad had died, and he'd bought the house and a computer—not the iMac back then, but an ancient piece-of-shit PC that was barely better than dial-up. He'd started running ads in the discreet places Charlie told him about, offering his services to people who had no place else to go.

He'd started building a life.

"Helping people helped me."

"I get it, Warren. I really do. But the thing is, you did your time. There's nothing wrong with deciding maybe you've had enough."

The steaming tea formed a circle of condensation on the windshield. Beyond that, the familiar streets of his neighborhood sat, quiet and still. Yes, it was peaceful enough here, but only a few miles away, hookers were being beaten. Drugs were being sold to minors. Minors were being sold to perverts. He shook his head, thinking about Charlie's in-home clinic. If anybody understood his need to help people, it was Charlie. "Do you think you could walk away?"

"Hell yes, I do. Maybe not yet, but I don't plan on doing this shit forever, man. One of these days, I'm buying myself a nice little house in the 'burbs, and I'll never look back."

Warren blinked at him, stunned. "Do you really think you could do that? You don't think you'd lie awake at night, wondering who needed your help?"

"Warren, somebody will always need something, but it isn't our job to save the world, you know? We both do what we can, but I don't think we owe it to anybody to do this shit forever. At some point, you have to accept that it doesn't even matter in the long run."

"But it *does* matter. It *has* to matter."

Charlie pulled at his beard, shaking his head. "You have any idea how many teen boys come to my house with knife wounds, and I patch them up only to find out they've been shot three days later? Or how many thirteen-year-old girls come to me for free birth control, and six months later, they're at my door asking where they can get an abortion? Last month, I helped this little old grandma from Mexico because she's not a citizen. She and her husband paid every cent they had to roast in the back of a fucking truck for days coming across the border. That was years ago, when her kids were just babies, and they spent all these years working their asses off to give those kids a better life. But then her *grandkids* start joining gangs instead, and three days after she came to me for help with a cold that was probably going to turn into pneumonia, one of her grandkids shot her dead, just so he could steal her TV. Stupid TV wasn't even a flat-screen. He probably sold it for all of five dollars, and for that, his grandma's gone."

"Jesus." Warren covered his eyes, wishing he hadn't heard any of that.

"Meanwhile, here you are, Warren. You protect a whore who turns around and goes right back to the man who ends up killing her. Not even a john, but her fucking boyfriend, man. You and I and Taylor busted our asses getting Riley clean, and now he's using more than ever. The fact is, no matter how much you and I stand in the ocean trying to turn back the tide with our little oars, it's never going to fucking happen. You have to see that."

"So, what? We just give up? Don't help anybody at all?"

"You've done your part, Warren. Between Afghanistan and the years you've been home, you've helped more people already than most folks help in their entire lives. All I'm saying is, there's no shame in deciding you've had enough." He turned to eye Warren's house. As they watched, the curtains in the master bedroom parted a bit. Warren couldn't see Taylor, but he knew he was there, peeking out. Charlie pointed toward the window. "That kid needs you as much as anyone you've come across. The difference is, he actually wants to be helped. And he wants to help you. There's nothing wrong with deciding that maybe taking care of each other is enough."

It was true that all Warren really wanted to do was keep Taylor safe. Helping all the whores in the world wouldn't be worth it if he lost Taylor in the bargain. "He'd love it if I quit," Warren said as the curtain fell back into place. "He'll never ask me to do it, but I know he wishes I was home with him at night." And God knew it would make his uncle happy too.

"Then do it, man. Choose happiness."

"It still feels selfish."

"To hell with that. You know what the first step to serenity is?"

Warren chuckled. Even after all these years, it cracked him up when the huge, tattooed biker boy started talking New Age spirituality. "No. I have no idea."

"It's loving yourself. Now, I don't quite think you're ready to do that. Not yet." He pointed a thick finger toward the bedroom window. "But you love Taylor, and he loves you. That just might get you two-thirds of the way there."

Chapter 22

Taylor had been on edge all day.

He'd woken up with what felt like a wonderful idea—an idea he was sure Warren would hate.

It wasn't that he *needed* Warren's approval. He didn't. But he wanted it nonetheless. He didn't want anything to cause trouble between them, and so he decided he'd talk to Warren before he did anything else. It might end in an argument, but he had to try.

But then Gray showed up with news of Sugar's death, and his afternoon turned into a whirlwind.

He'd promised Riley the night before that he'd check on him, but he didn't dare leave Warren. He managed to sneak in one phone call late in the afternoon. The conversation with Riley was brief but enough to confirm his fears—Riley was high again.

"I'll come see you tomorrow morning," Taylor told him. "I promise. And then we'll get you clean. I have an idea. Something that'll work, I know. Just promise me you'll try."

"Of course, man. Anything for you. You know that."

Taylor spent the next couple of hours sitting with Warren, ostensibly watching TV, but Taylor's mind was a million miles away. After waiting all day to talk to Warren, he suddenly had no idea how to broach the topic. He told himself he'd talk to Warren that night as they lay in bed together. Sometimes that was easier than having to face him in the light of the living room. But then Warren had gone outside to talk to Charlie.

Taylor parted the curtains and peeked out. He hoped Warren wasn't fighting with his friend, trying to talk Charlie into letting him leave. He couldn't quite see what was happening in the car, but everything seemed peaceful enough.

Taylor let the curtains fall shut and called Riley again, wanting to say good night. Riley didn't answer, and Taylor slumped onto the bed, feeling defeated. Riley was probably still high, or high again. Taylor had no idea how long heroin lasted. He only knew he wished Riley would answer. Taylor was itching to share his plan—to let Riley know it'd all be okay—but first, he needed to talk to Warren.

Taylor wrapped himself in his pink robe, climbed into Warren's bed, and waited. He felt like an intruder—like Goldilocks sleeping in Papa Bear's bed—but he loved it. The rest of the house felt more lived in, now that Taylor had his flowers strewn about, but Warren's room had a certain messiness Taylor found comforting. Dirty clothes overflowed from the hamper, jackets hung off the doorknobs, jeans deemed "clean enough for one more wear" filled the chair. Half a dozen ratty paperbacks littered the bedside table. Best of all, the pillowcases always smelled like Warren's shampoo.

Finally, Warren returned and got ready for bed. He climbed under the covers wearing only his boxers and pulled Taylor into his arms.

"Wearing your robe to bed?"

"I was cold without you."

Warren's big, strong hands moved over him. "I can't decide if I like you better with it off or on." He kissed Taylor's neck, and one hand snuck inside Taylor's robe to slide up his thigh. "I have something to tell you."

Taylor tried to focus on what he needed to say. He didn't want Warren to distract him with sex.

Not quite yet, at any rate.

"Oh yeah? What is it?"

"I've decided to take the job with my uncle."

"Wait. Really?" He pushed on Warren's broad chest, trying to put enough distance between them to see Warren's face. Warren was having none of it. Not that it would have done much good in the dark room anyway. "Are you serious?"

"I am." Warren spoke between ravaging kisses on Taylor's neck. "Charlie convinced me."

"Oh my God!" He hadn't even dared hope for this. It was selfish, he knew. He wanted Warren home with him at nights. He wanted them to be able to wake up next to each other every morning, like normal couples. But he also wanted Warren safe. Being an electrician meant fewer times when Gray knocked on the door in his uniform. It meant no more days like today, worrying that Warren would run off and do something that could land him in prison for a long, long time.

Taylor put his arms around Warren's neck, so happy he almost wanted to cry. "I think I love Charlie for talking you into it. I feel like I should go tell him."

"You should. Kiss him while you're at it. It'll make Gray jealous as hell."

Taylor laughed. Both Warren's hands had found their way inside his robe by this point, and he probably had at least one dark mark on his neck already. It was tempting to let himself be carried away by Warren's passion, but if he didn't talk to Warren now, he'd just have to do it tomorrow. It wasn't going to get any easier.

"Wait," he said, trying to catch Warren's wandering hands. "I have something I need to tell you too."

Warren continued kissing his neck, trying to rid Taylor of the robe. "What is it?"

"Warren, I mean it. Please."

Warren stopped, pulling back a bit, his hands finally ceasing their quest. "What's wrong?"

He was afraid. Taylor heard it in his voice. Just a few words from Taylor were enough to send big, strong Warren into a tailspin. It still amazed Taylor how Warren seemed to expect him to break things off at any moment. "Nothing's wrong, really." Taylor pulled his robe closed again so as not to distract Warren. He hoped what he was about to say didn't result in a sudden, unhappy end to their intimacy. "I made a decision. And I'm afraid it'll make you mad. But I hope not, Warren, because I'm going to need your help. I'd really like it if you could support me on this." He took a deep breath and made himself say the words. "I want you to help me check Riley into an inpatient rehab center."

Warren was silent for a moment. Then, his voice a low rumble in the dark room, "And how do you intend to pay for it?"

He knew, though. Taylor could tell Warren had already anticipated his answer. "I'm going to use my trust fund."

Warren groaned and rolled onto his back, away from Taylor.

"It won't take all of it," Taylor said, hoping it was true. Most of the websites had been frustratingly vague when it came to cost. "Only a few thousand dollars for one here in town, I think."

"Honey, it's your money. I can't tell you how to spend it. I just want you to realize that those programs? They don't work much better than what we've already tried."

"But sometimes they do."

"Sometimes," Warren admitted. "But Riley has to want it too. If it's just you pushing him into it, it'll never work. You'll be poorer, and he'll be no better off than he is now."

"I know. But I can talk him into it. I know I can. He's sold everything now. He probably sold the TV today, but whatever money he made from that and the DVD player must be almost gone." He hoped, at least. He didn't really have any idea how much Riley would have made from selling those things, or how much heroin the money would buy, or how long it would last. But he needed Warren's support on this, for reasons even he didn't entirely understand. "He wants to be clean. I know he does. And I want to help him, any way I can."

For a moment, Warren was still and quiet, and Taylor feared he'd made him angry. But then Warren made a soft sigh of defeat. He rolled toward Taylor again and pulled him close, letting their bodies line up against each other as they had before. "Okay."

"Really?"

"Really." Warren brushed his fingers over Taylor's cheek. "I don't know if it will work, but I know if it was you who needed help, I'd do anything in my power to get it for you. I know that's how you feel about Riley."

"Thank you." He put his arms around Warren's neck, his forehead against Warren's. "Do you think I'm naive?"

"Maybe. But that isn't always a bad thing. I'm glad you aren't jaded like me." He kissed Taylor's forehead. "I admire you for seeing the good in him. And frankly, him kicking the habit for good is more likely to happen if he has somebody like you on his side."

"So you'll help me? Even if it means talking to my father about the money?" Technically, the money belonged to Taylor, but his dad still might object.

"I'll help." Warren's hand moved back to Taylor's thigh. "But only if you let me take that robe off again."

They drove to Riley's together the next day. Taylor wasn't sure he'd ever been so happy. Warren was leaving behind his dangerous, illegal jobs, and soon, Riley would be clean. Taylor refused to let Warren's pessimism taint his mood.

It amazed him, looking back over the last few months. He thanked his lucky stars for the day he'd met Phil, and for the asshole who'd bashed up the wrong car and started the chain of events that led to Warren dragging Taylor out of Leroy's. How had he gone from a whore to somebody so in love with life, he sometimes felt like he couldn't even breathe?

"I know I can talk him into it," he told Warren for what felt like the hundredth time. "He told me yesterday he'd do whatever it took."

Warren simply nodded. Taylor was pretty sure the look of intense concentration on his face was his attempt not to scowl. "I'll let you talk to him alone. But if he agrees, I'll help you get him out of the house and checked into the facility before he changes his mind."

"Thank you, Warren."

Warren's not-quite-scowl deepened. It was almost enough to make Taylor laugh.

"You're helping me, but you're not exactly happy about it, are you?"

Warren's gaze slid his way for only a moment before returning to the road. "I just don't want him to break your heart."

Despite his pretense of surety, Taylor was scared to death. He and Warren had spent the morning researching online and making phone calls, figuring out where to take Riley. Most of them cost significantly more than Taylor had expected, but they'd finally found one that would work. Riley had promised Taylor over the phone he'd do whatever it took, but following through was something else entirely. Still, Riley didn't know what Taylor had planned. With professional help, Taylor was sure he and Riley could beat heroin together.

Taylor's heart pounded as Warren parked the car. He waffled between excitement and apprehension as he climbed the stairs to Riley's apartment.

He knocked but got no answer. He tried the knob but found it locked. Could Riley have gone out? His heart sank as he considered it. The only reason he would have gone out was for more heroin. Taylor hoped that wasn't the case.

He pulled out his phone and called Riley's number. A second later, a tinny rendition of "Für Elise" reached him from inside Riley's apartment. If he'd gone out, he'd left his phone at home.

Taylor hung up and knocked again. "Riley?" he called through the door. "Wake up. It's me."

Nothing.

Riley's living room had only one window. By leaning over the balcony railing, Taylor could just barely reach the edge of it and peer inside. He cupped his hand over his eyes and leaned against the glass, straining to see into the dimly lit living room. He could just make out the empty corner where the TV had been. The empty armchair, where Warren had once fallen asleep. The empty couch—

But no.

He squinted, leaning closer.

Only the very end of the couch was in view, but on that bit of couch was Riley's familiar knock-off Converse, his bare ankle barely visible.

He was home, at least. Very likely high, but home. That was a start.

Taylor went back to knocking, yelling louder this time. "Riley? It's Taylor. Open the door. Riley?"

Still no answer, and another peek through the window showed that Riley's foot hadn't moved.

Taylor went cold, a horrible thought sneaking its way into his brain.

"Riley!" He yelled loud enough that a neighbor opened their door and peeked out. He pounded on the door with all his strength. "Riley, wake up! Open the door. It's me. I have something to tell you."

But still there was no answer. His glance through the window showed the same view of Riley's foot, unmoving on the couch.

Taylor turned toward the parking lot, waving for Warren to come. Taylor fought to stay calm. To keep from panicking. Riley had passed out. That was all. It couldn't be anything more than that.

"What is it?" Warren asked, coming slowly up the stairs.

"I can see him." But despite his efforts to stay calm, he was beginning to panic. Even high, Riley should have heard him. "Look."

Warren leaned over the balcony. He was so big, Taylor worried the railing would break under his weight. It creaked once, but held, and Warren's greater height gave him a better view.

"That's not good," Warren said, his voice quiet.

"What?" Taylor's heart pounded so hard, he felt it all the way in his toes. It seemed to throb in his skull. "Warren?" he said, his voice small and shaking. "What's wrong?"

Warren's usual scowl changed to something that bordered on grief. He backed Taylor up a few steps, then pointed a thick finger in Taylor's face. "Stay here. You hear me? I want you to promise me you won't follow me in."

Taylor couldn't answer. He might have nodded, but he couldn't be sure. All he knew was that he desperately hoped that nothing was what it seemed.

Warren knocked the door open with a solid right kick and went in. Taylor stood rooted in his position. He waited for Riley to yell. To ask what the hell Warren was doing in his house. He waited for Warren to tell him everything was okay.

It might have only been a second. It might have been an hour. The next thing he knew, Warren was there, grabbing him by the arms, dragging him away from the apartment, toward the stairs, where Taylor could see sunlight and blue skies, even though they felt like the most traitorous things in the world.

"I have to see," Taylor said, choking on the words. "I have to talk to him. Warren, please."

"No." He'd never seen such compassion in Warren's eyes. "Honey, you were the last friend he had. He wouldn't want you to see him this way." He took out his phone and dialed a number. "It's better that you remember him the way he was."

"No! No, no, no."

Taylor's knees gave out. He landed heavily on the wooden boards of the stairs.

This was all his fault. He'd bought the TV and DVD player that had allowed Riley to buy drugs. He'd spent time in his garden that should have been spent with his friend. He'd taken a job at Lowe's just so he could buy flowers when he should have been helping Riley.

Why had it not occurred to him sooner to use his money for some kind of in-house detox program? Why hadn't he told Riley about his decision when they'd spoken, rather than waiting? Wasn't that what a real friend would have done? At that moment, Taylor would have given every penny in his trust fund just to have Riley back.

But Riley wouldn't be coming back. Not clean. Not using. Not at all.

"Oh my God." The grief bent him in half, a sob tearing from his throat.

Warren's hand landed on his back, warm and heavy. "Hang on, Tay. This is going to be rough."

Gray arrived, and then more police. They talked to Warren. Taylor was vaguely aware of Gray trying to ask him questions, but Taylor could barely hear him. He felt like he was drowning, like Gray was speaking to him from some distant shore, miles and miles away.

Eventually, Warren led him to the car. He turned toward home. They rode for a while in silence. It took Taylor most of the trip home to turn his thoughts into simple words.

"Did he overdose?"

"That's how it looks."

"There wasn't a gun, right?" Taylor asked, remembering Riley's confession. "It wasn't on purpose?"

"No gun. Whether or not it was on purpose?" He shrugged. "I didn't see a note. That's all I can say."

"It's my fault."

"No, it isn't."

But it was. There was no denying it. His first friend in years, and Taylor had failed him more ways than he could count. He thought about how it had felt to lie next to Riley in bed, just talking about their pasts. He'd never have that simple comfort again.

He'd never even shown Riley his flowers. He'd been so caught up in all his petty little dramas, he'd lost the only person besides Warren he cared about.

The only person besides Warren he'd ever truly loved.

The only real brother he'd ever have.

And just like that, the blackness grabbed him and dragged him under, fast and deep. The strength of it constricted his chest and darkened his vision. He choked, gasping at the force of it.

How could he have let things go so wrong?

"Taylor," Warren said. "Honey, it's better if you keep talking."

"No. What is there to say? It's my fault."

"It isn't."

"Both of my brothers are gone, because of me."

"No, honey. They made their choices. You did everything you could."

"I didn't!" Taylor put his face in his hands, pulling his hair, wanting to feel pain. "I didn't do enough. I ruined everything!"

The darkness roiled and raged. Taylor thought about razor blades. About how easy it would be to let some man who wasn't Warren beat him. He was vaguely aware of them arriving home. Of Warren parking the car, then coming around to Taylor's side.

"Taylor? Come inside, honey."

"No!" It was all wrong. All that niceness was the exact opposite of what Taylor needed. Warren reached in, trying to help him from the car, and Taylor slapped his hands away. "No!" He escaped from the car, dodging Warren's hands. "It's my fault! Why won't you just admit it?"

"Try to calm down, Taylor. Please. You're scaring me."

Taylor didn't care. He *couldn't* care. All he could feel was the blackness and the rage, and the surety that there was only one way to make it go away.

"I need you to hit me," Taylor said, choking on the words. He clutched at Warren's chest, his knees almost too weak to hold him up. "Please, just hit me, Warren. Please." The thought was a buoy, holding him up. Pure, physical pain would be easier than what he felt right now. He imagined Warren's big hand slamming across his face. He imagined how much pain Warren could cause him if he only tried. "Please, Warren. God, please! I'll feel better if you'll just hit me."

"I won't do that. You know I won't. Just come inside—"

"No!"

"Try to breathe—"

"Fuck you! I don't need to breathe! I don't want to talk. I don't want you to tell me it isn't my fault, because it is! I know it is. I killed him, and you need to do something!"

"Taylor—"

"You said you'd punish me when I needed it. You said—"

"I said I'd try to help you through these bad days, and I will—"

"You said you'd punish me!"

"I never said that." Warren's voice was calm and reasonable as always. "I said I'd help, and I will. But I won't hit you."

"Then you're not helping at all!" Taylor shoved him. From where he stood, hanging on to Warren's chest, it didn't have much force. It barely budged Warren, so Taylor did it again. He slammed into Warren hard, knocking him back a step. "Hit me!"

"No."

"Yes!" He shoved Warren again, knowing from his past episodes it'd work eventually. "Hit me!" He shoved Warren again, and again. "Hit me!" Each time, Warren took it with the same calm stoicism. "Why won't you just hit me?" Taylor raged.

"Because it won't help."

Taylor screamed, his rage and his blackness choking out the sun and the yard, demanding some kind of payment. "Yes it will! What do you know? You don't know anything! You're stupid and worthless and pathetic, and I hate you!"

"Well, I don't hate you. I don't now, and I never will, no matter how much you try to make it happen."

Taylor sagged, a sob building in his chest. Even this, he couldn't do right. "But I need you to hit me," he screamed. "I need you to punish me. I hate you! You promised me, and you lied, just like them. They said they'd stay, and they didn't. You said you'd help, but you won't! You're fat and worthless and I hate you!" He threw himself at Warren, his hands flying, swinging for Warren's face. "I hate you!"

Warren took the first slap, blocked the second, managed to trap Taylor's wrists in his big hands before the third one fell. "I don't believe you. And even if it's true, I still won't hit you."

"You promised!" Taylor cried, trying to kick Warren now that his hands were trapped. "You promised you'd punish me."

"Is that what you want? To be punished?"

"Yes." Wasn't that what he'd been saying since arriving home?

Warren let go of one wrist in order to point a finger in Taylor's face. "You wait right here."

He left Taylor in the backyard, the sun shining, the birds singing as if Taylor hadn't just killed his best friend. As if Riley hadn't abandoned him just like James. Warren went into the shed and came out a few seconds later with the chainsaw in his hands.

"What's that for?"

"You wanted to be punished." Warren pulled the chain. It took a couple of tries, but the engine finally roared to life before settling into a gentle hum, although the horrible rotating blade was motionless. "Take it."

He shoved it into Taylor's hands. It was heavy, and Taylor struggled to hold it. "This isn't helping, Warren. You said you'd punish me!"

"And I will." Warren stood behind him and helped him heft it. "You pull here, see?" The powerful grumble of the motor went loud then soft, loud then soft, as Warren demonstrated how the lever near the handle had to be held down to make the blade run. "That way if you drop it, it stops running. Do you see?"

"Yes!" But he was angry and confused and he had no idea why Warren was putting this huge, heavy thing in his hands. "I don't care!"

And then Warren turned him toward the house.

Toward his rose bushes, which were in full bloom, palm-sized red and white and yellow and pink blossoms glowing against the green of the leaves. Warren pushed him forward. "Cut them down."

Warren might as well have kicked him in the stomach. "What? No! I don't—"

Warren pushed him again, closer to the bushes. Bees buzzed around the blooms, oblivious to the drama playing out only a few feet away. "Cut them down."

The horror of it left him reeling. "I can't."

"You have to. Do it. This is your punishment. I won't let you stop until there's nothing left but twigs in the dirt. Now start cutting."

"No!"

Warren stepped up behind him again, wrapping his arms around Taylor to lift the horrible chainsaw. He pulled the lever, revving the rotating blade into life. "Cut. Them. Down."

Taylor pictured it—the churning blade slicing through the thickest part of his roses. The blooms falling to the ground. The bees fleeing the scene of the crime. His beautiful, precious roses, which had thorns to protect them from rabbits and deer, but nothing to protect them from Warren. Nothing but Taylor, his arms straining to hold the chainsaw. "I can't." He choked, pulling away. "I can't. Warren, please—"

Warren pushed him forward again. "Do it now!"

Taylor fell to the ground, feeling as if the heavy instrument in his hands were pulling him down, tugging him under the horrible surface of his grief. The blade was motionless, the chainsaw idling in his hands, but Taylor could still hear the horrible rumble of its motor in his head. "Please, Warren. Please don't make me."

In one quick movement, Warren yanked the chainsaw out of Taylor's hands. For one horrible, excruciating heartbeat, Taylor thought he was going to do it himself. He thought Warren was going to destroy the only life Taylor had ever managed to build. "No!" he cried, lunging toward him.

But Warren only turned the chainsaw off and tossed it aside. He knelt in front of Taylor and took Taylor's face between his big strong hands, forcing Taylor to meet his gaze. "Listen to me, Tay: *you are my roses.* Do you understand what I'm saying? And it kills me when you ask me to cut you down."

Taylor's head spun. Warren never intended to destroy his garden! It was such sweet relief. But hot on its heels came the weight of Warren's words. The pain in Warren's dark eyes as he tried to make Taylor understand. It was too much to take. Taylor pulled away, wanting to curl into a ball and disappear. He was about to start bawling again like some kind of spoiled child. No! He had to rage! He'd practically killed his best friend, and being punished was the only answer. That was the only way—

"You can hit me," Warren said, "and kick me, and say as many horrible things as you like, but I'm not leaving. Do you hear me? I don't care how many times you say you hate me. I won't leave you."

"But—"

"I'm *not* James."

That name drove the wind from Taylor's lungs. It made his head ache and his bile rise. He fought to keep from vomiting in the dirt. James, who had hurt him and loved him and twisted him and then abandoned him, despite every promise he'd ever made.

James, who he still loved, even though he didn't know why.

"He left me," Taylor cried, unable to stop his words. "He left me, just like Riley."

"I know."

"He knew what he was doing. He told me he'd never leave, but then he did. He left a note saying he couldn't handle it anymore. He apologized to my parents, but not me! He took the easy way out, and he left me here to live alone with everything he'd done!"

"I know, honey," Warren said, pulling him close, his big hand moving in soothing circles on Taylor's back as he cried. "I know."

"I wasn't good enough."

"That's not it. That's not why."

"I failed him, just like I failed Riley."

"You didn't fail anybody."

"James promised me!"

"I know."

"It isn't fair."

"It isn't. You're right. And it's okay to be sad or angry or proud or ashamed. It's okay to love him, or hate him, or both. There's no right or wrong to how you feel."

God, how he would have loved to be able to take one of those everyday words and apply it to his tangled emotions. How wonderful it would have been to spell out the horrible blackness in his heart in just a few simple letters. But he couldn't. All he could feel was the horror and the rage and the need to do something—to find some kind of release. That blackness was like a gaping wound in his chest, and he knew only one way to close it.

He grasped at Warren, desperate. "Please," he begged. "I need to do something. I can't— I can't—"

"You can't keep running from it, honey. At some point, you're going to have to feel it. You're going to have to face it."

"No. No! You said you'd help when I got like this. You said you'd help when I needed to be punished."

Warren's wince at that word was almost imperceptible. "What exactly do you want me to do?"

"The spanking horse. And your friends. And—"

"Is that really what you want?" Warren asked, and Taylor was amazed to see tears brimming in his eyes. "Because I can do that. If that's really what you want, we can go that route again. But I'm begging you, Taylor—please don't make me. Think about the roses and all the reasons you didn't want to cut them down." He shook his head, and a single tear rolled down his cheek. "What we did that day? I don't know if I can watch something like that again."

Taylor felt his world cracking in two. His chest ached. The need to find some kind of escape was strong and insistent. But he understood what Warren was trying to tell him. He thought about the weight of the chainsaw in his hands—his vision of destroying the thing he loved most in the world—and he knew he couldn't do that to Warren.

"Then what?" he asked, his voice cracking. He clutched his chest, wanting to claw the horrible darkness out of his heart, wanting to see it whither and dissipate in the light. "I can't keep feeling this. I can't keep this all here. I can't—"

Warren held Taylor's face again, the way he always did when he was trying to make him listen. "Please." His voice was thick with unshed tears. "Let me find somebody for you to talk to. Let me—"

"No!" Taylor pushed him away. "No. It always comes down to this. It always comes down to therapy, but you can't fix me!"

"You don't need to be fixed." Warren raised his voice just enough to override Taylor's protests. He reached out and took Taylor's hand. "It's like you said, back when you first told me about James. Some things can't be fixed. Some scars run too deep. You can't go back and undo them."

"Then why see a therapist if you know I'll always be ruined?"

"Not ruined," Warren said, shaking his head. "Just a little bit confused. You don't need to be fixed. But I think you need to make peace with how much your brother hurt you. Whether he meant to or not, whether he loved you or not—none of that matters now. You're the one left with all the grief and love, the anger and shame. All you can do is find the best way to live with it."

It sounded so reasonable coming from Warren. Taylor's instinct was to fight and deny—to say that talking to some moron would never help—but then he realized…

He already felt a tiny bit better.

It wasn't much, and if he dwelled on it too long, the darkness would be back. He still missed Riley, and he probably always would. But saying James's name out loud, hearing Warren talk about Taylor's darkest secrets here, in the bright, warm sunlight, with Taylor's roses in full, glorious bloom only a few feet away, Taylor realized that gaping, seething ache in his chest had abated just a bit.

"Honey," Warren said, his voice so gentle, it made Taylor start to cry again. "Please. You have to want the help."

Taylor doubled over, his forehead to the dirt, remembering a conversation he'd had with Riley before his relapse. Taylor had asked him, *"Do you think we're just destined to keep doing the same thing over and over? Or do you think we can be something new?"* And Riley's answer had been, *"I guess it depends on which thing we want more."* Riley hadn't wanted his sobriety enough to stick with it. The question was, what did Taylor want?

The answer was simple: he wanted to stay with Warren forever. He wanted to ease Warren's burden, not add to it. But the thought of going to therapy scared him more than he could say.

He sat up again, needing to see Warren's face. "I'd have to talk about all of it. I don't know if I can stand that. I'd have to tell them everything James did to me."

"I know, honey. But I won't send you to just any idiot, I promise. I'll find somebody good. Somebody who's dealt with stuff like this before, who won't judge you or pity you."

Taylor tried to picture it, just him and some faceless person in a cheerily nondescript room. "Will you go with me?"

"If that's what you want."

But what Warren was talking about would take time, and he didn't have that. "But what about now?" Because abated or not, the blackness was still there. "What about today?"

"Today?" Warren said. He looked over at Taylor's rose bushes. "I think you should focus on what you love. We'll go to the nursery and buy you more roses. I'll buy you every rose they have if you want. I'll help you dig the holes. Then you can pick the blooms you want to bring inside. You can fill every vase in the house. You can choose the best ones for Riley. Think about how much you loved him. Somebody should put roses on his grave."

It sounded good, but it wasn't enough to stop his tears. "What if that isn't enough?"

"Then I'll take you to bed. I'll tie you down. I'll use the flog. I'll give you anything you need to get through this. But I want what we do in bed together to lift you up, not cut you down."

Taylor thought about it as tears continued running down his cheeks. He thought about the warm sun on his back and the stiff leather gardening gloves on his hands and the feel of the soil beneath his feet. He thought about being on his knees in the safety of Warren's backyard rather than in some alley, about planting roses rather than asking men to beat him. He thought about what it meant to nurture something. To value it. To cherish it, even.

He loved his roses. And he loved Warren.

"Okay," he said, feeling the relief of that simple surrender. He would once again place his life in Warren's capable hands and trust that everything would be okay. "Let's do it."

He didn't know if it would work.

He didn't know if it would be enough.

But he knew it was worth a try.

Epilogue

The car was thick with the smell of roses.

Warren had grown used to the odor since May. Once upon a time, it'd inexplicably reminded him of his grandfather's Copenhagen. Now, roses would always remind him of Taylor.

"How're you doing?" Warren asked, glancing Taylor's way.

Taylor sat stiff in the passenger seat, his face unreadable. "I'm fine."

Warren checked the navigation app on his phone. He was glad he hadn't relied on Taylor to get him to the Fort Collins cemetery. Taylor had claimed to know the way, but the minute they'd left the interstate, heading west toward the sprawling university town, he'd gone silent.

"Talk to me, Tay. Turn toward it."

Taylor sighed, although it was more a sound of amusement than aggravation. "*Turn toward it. Turn toward it.* Jesus. I hate when you say that. I feel like you and Suzanne are in league against me."

Suzanne was his therapist. Warren had met her twice, but after that, Taylor had chosen to go alone. Riley's death had shaken him, bringing a lot of things to the surface that had more to do with James than anything, but the appointments seemed to be helping. They'd had only one bad day since Riley's death. Granted, it had been a horrible, dark day, full of tears and screaming. Warren had ended up chaining Taylor to the bed, enduring an onslaught of venom, pleading with Taylor until he finally subsided.

In the end, Taylor had let Warren hold him while he cried. It had felt like victory. Bloody and bittersweet, but victory nonetheless.

"Not in league *against* you, honey," Warren assured him. "In league *for* you, if anything."

"I know." Taylor snapped the rubber band around his wrist and leaned his forehead against the window.

"So?" Warren prodded. The crux of Taylor's therapy was to face the emotions that made the blackness rather than using pain or sex to avoid them. "Talk to me. How do you feel?"

"Mad. Scared. Confused." *Snap.* "I think I might throw up."

"Do I need to pull over?"

"No." *Snap.*

"Tell me if I do."

Snap. "I will."

Warren didn't like the rubber band. In his mind, it gave Taylor an approved way of hurting himself. Still, he couldn't deny that Taylor responded well to it. It gave him something to focus on when the feelings became too much.

And today of all days, it wasn't surprising that he was overwhelmed.

Dennis had been thrilled to hear that Taylor had agreed to counseling, and had immediately offered to pay. Accepting Dennis's money was a small blow to Warren's pride, but refusing it would have been foolish. Dennis wanted to help his son. And besides, Warren had a feeling the man could afford it more easily than Warren could. If accepting Dennis's offer meant a better therapist for Taylor, Warren would take it, his ego be damned.

But that wasn't what had brought them to the cemetery. Taylor hadn't actually spoken to his father since the day Dennis had come to the house, but Dennis had pleaded with Taylor via Warren to join him at the cemetery for the one-year anniversary of his mother's death. Warren knew Taylor would have agreed almost immediately if it hadn't been for one simple fact: James's grave lay right next to Lisa's.

"Thank you for taking the day off," Taylor said.

"Of course."

As if a day of running wires would have kept Warren from being at Taylor's side for this. There was nothing about being an electrician that couldn't wait until the next day. Overall, working for Uncle Bill was going better than expected. People talked to him about their kids and their dogs. They pondered whether or not it would rain that afternoon or whether the Rockies would make the playoffs.

Normal things.

Warren found comfort in the simplicity. He still took the occasional odd job, but only if it was on the right side of legal. He enjoyed knowing he'd be home every evening in time for dinner. He liked having his nights free to spend with the person he loved. Most of all, he relished falling asleep with Taylor in his arms, no longer having to question if he'd be gone when Warren woke.

Taylor made him happy. It was that simple. Charlie had once told him, *"Never let the sadness of your past or your fear of the future distract you from the joy of the present."*

At the time, Warren had rolled his eyes. Now, he understood. Wondering if or when Taylor would leave him did nothing but create heartache and stress, and so Warren had finally resolved to let go of his fears. Yes, it was a leap of faith, trusting that Taylor would stay, but trust was the only thing he could do.

It felt pretty damned good.

Life went on, just as Charlie had promised. Taffy still worked the streets, unprotected by her own choice. Gray found Robby and charged him with murder. Candy found somebody else to watch her motel room door. Last Warren knew, Jack had been shipped off to live with a pair of grandparents he'd never met. Meanwhile, Taylor filled Warren's house with flowers and color and light. He gave Warren a reason to wake up every single day. Maybe saving Taylor wasn't the same as saving the world, but Warren wouldn't have had it any other way.

Warren found the cemetery and parked, the silence in the car feeling more oppressive than the midday August heat. They were nearly fifteen minutes early. Dennis was nowhere in sight. Warren glanced into the backseat.

A whole bundle of white roses, which Taylor had carefully cut the thorns from, and one red outlier, thorns intact. Every few days, Taylor stopped at the Denver cemetery to put a yellow rose on Riley's grave, but he'd saved all the white for this.

"Why white?" Warren asked.

It took Taylor a minute to answer. "After James died, I used to imagine I was little again. I just wanted to climb into my mother's lap and have her hold me, you know? I wanted her to make it all better, like when I was a kid."

Warren nodded. "That's understandable." Unfortunately, Lisa hadn't been able to provide the comfort her son so desperately needed. "How does that tie in to the roses?"

Taylor shrugged, looking miserable, despite the fact that he'd gone to great efforts to look nice for the occasion. He'd even bought a sports coat that could easily have come straight out of Phil's preppy closet. "I'd just imagine myself in her lap, all wrapped up in her arms. And it was white. I just pictured softness and white." *Snap.* "God, I sound stupid."

"No, you don't." He nudged Taylor's knee. "Come on. Maybe it'll be easier if you have a minute alone before your dad shows up."

He helped Taylor gather up the flowers, and they trudged through the rows of markers, following Dennis's directions. Finally, they found it. Lisa Catherine (McKay) Reynolds and James Franklin Reynolds, side by side.

The white roses went onto Lisa's grave without comment. Taylor took a deep breath and faced the second headstone. "I didn't come when they buried him. My parents let me stay home."

Warren waited, not so much because he knew Taylor had more to say as because he had no idea how to respond.

Taylor sank to his knees and laid the single red rose in front of the stone. "I can turn toward James all day, but I still don't know what I feel." He shook his head. "Crooked. That's the only word I can find. I feel crooked."

Warren waited again, not wanting to disturb him.

"I still love him."

"I know."

"Jesus. What the hell's wrong with me that I could love him?"

"Would you feel better if you hated your own brother?"

Taylor considered for a moment. "I'm not sure."

"That's fine too."

Taylor laughed and climbed slowly to his feet. "No matter what I say, you say it's fine."

"Because it is."

Taylor laid his forehead against Warren's chest. "Thank you."

Warren simply stood there, being a rock, if that was what Taylor needed.

"He'll be here soon," Taylor said a minute later. He stood up straight, smoothed his hair, and straightened his jacket. "Do I look okay?"

"Yeah. A bit sweaty in that jacket, maybe, but I don't think he'll care."

Taylor gave him a shy smile. "Can I tell him?"

Two months earlier, at Warren's cousin's wedding, Taylor had hesitantly asked Warren if he thought he'd ever want to get married. "Just say the word," Warren had told him, feeling like his heart might burst. "You'll get no objection from me."

But Taylor had wanted to wait until he was on speaking terms again with his father, and Warren agreed. Since meeting Dennis in May, Warren had talked with him by phone and text quite a bit, and he'd grown fond of him. The man seemed to genuinely want to be part of Taylor's life. There was no doubt in Warren's mind that Dennis loved his son with all his heart, and that simple fact made Warren want to root for him. But it had to be Taylor's choice. No matter what, Taylor's happiness would always be Warren's first priority.

"Tell him if you like. It's your call."

"Would it be silly to have him give me away? Or is that only for women?"

"I think you can do whatever you want to do."

They stood there a moment longer, waiting for whatever the future would bring.

"There he is," Taylor said, his whole body going tense.

"Turn toward it."

"If you say that again, I'm going to hit you." But he reached out and took Warren's hand. "I'm scared. And don't even bother telling me it's fine." Taylor watched his father climb from the driver's seat. His grip on Warren's hand tightened. "I take it back. Tell me it's going to be fine."

"It will be."

"Warren?"

"Yes?"

"I'm never leaving."

It was Taylor's way of saying *I love you*, and it made Warren smile every time. Whatever the future had in store for them, they'd conquer it together.

"I know. And neither am I."

About the Author

Marie Sexton lives in Colorado. She's a fan of just about anything that involves muscular young men piling on top of each other. In particular, she loves the Denver Broncos and enjoys going to the games with her husband. Her imaginary friends often tag along. Marie has one daughter, two cats, and one dog, all of whom seem bent on destroying what remains of her sanity. She loves them anyway.

Website and Blog:
http://mariesexton.net/

Facebook:
http://www.facebook.com/MarieSexton.author/

Twitter:
https://twitter.com/MarieSexton

Email: msexton.author@gmail.com

Also by Marie Sexton

Promises
A to Z
The Letter Z
Strawberries for Dessert
Paris A to Z
Fear, Hope, and Bread Pudding
Between Sinners and Saints
Song of Oestend
Saviours of Oestend
Blind Space
Second Hand
Never a Hero
Family Man
Flowers for Him
One More Soldier
Cinder
Normal Enough
Roped In
Chapter 5 and the Axe-Wielding Maniac
Apartment 14 and the Devil Next Door
Lost Along the Way
Shotgun
Winter Oranges
Damned If You Do
Trailer Trash
Making Waves
The Well

Made in United States
Troutdale, OR
06/07/2024